UNREQUITED

ONE GIRL, THIRTEEN BOYFRIENDS, AND VODKA.

CHRISTY HERON

Unrequited is dedicated to my mom, Kathy,
even though she'll probably never be able to endure
what is written between this page, and the last.
I love you.

You are magnificent.

Unrequited
Page by Page

He ate my heart, then he ate my brain.

That boy is a monster.

— Lady Gaga

May 1, 2008

I blame Frank Sinatra.

Years ago I watched a movie about the Rat Pack starring Ray Liotta as Sinatra and a bunch of other guys starring as the rest of the Rat Pack. At one point, the pack attended a fancy dinner at a boozy Kennedy's house. The stupid-rich grande dame of the party, with her sexy, middle-aged drawl, explained the appeal of Sinatra to an intrigued redhead sitting across from her. Milky Chanel dress, too much makeup, a haze of smoke surrounding her, she commanded the gold-rimmed table while Redhead leaned in. Chanel elegantly growled a smoker's growl, her eyes never parting from Sinatra's:

"You want to fuck him; you want to mother him; you don't want to piss him off."

The dialogue she exhaled legitimized everything I felt for Jack. Her lyrical bluntness stoked my own personal bonfire, which I feared might never be extinguished, or feared would be. Chanel, with a snow-white cigarette filter a fingerbreadth from her mouth, stylishly sashayed around my head. Because of her pragmatic and subjective exclamation, I plotted. I pressed pause on the remote and grabbed a pencil.

A direct route to constant, uninhibited sex with Jack was the easy part. Next.

I created maps and studied instructions, malleting together an Ikea furniture friendship. From my studies, I honed my radar. Collecting information and relaying back anything I thought he would enjoy (and respond to) became my mission. Reconnoitered Intel went into specific files: songs, articles, photographs, movies, TV shows, sex preferences, family tree—anything to up the daily communiqué and constrict the gap between whatever kept us apart that particular week.

After I nailed together this rickety rapport, I attempted the rash, stupid, and intolerable quest: the nurturer role.

Soup, house calls, and sex when he was sick (he loved fucking when he had the flu). Pep talks when he was down: *You rock. It will work out. Hang in there. I'm here for you.* Compliments when he was up: *Amazing. Wonderful. Funny. You are great in bed. You are God.* I offered him me: every painted toenail, pound, blemish, and highlighted hair. I wanted to devote myself to him, and I did.

I thought this was love.

With love, a simultaneous hatred treaded a few steps behind. As I pursued Jack with an anorexic hunger, my stomach wrapped two sticks of dynamite with furies and duct tape. This contention held a determination I couldn't know as my finger grazed the lighter's thumbwheel.

A cliché was part of the problem.

"January, guys like the chase. They don't want to be pursued; they want to pursue you," my brother theorized between swigs of a Fat Tire.

While pulverizing beer and nachos, he admonished me and zoned out to an episode of *The Amazing Race* above our heads. I whined, drank Ketel One and soda, and didn't acknowledge the nachos. My brother looked like Brad Pitt—a taller, non-manicured, childless version.

I squinched my eyes at this detested, modern-American, you-must-follow-the-rules-enforced female mentality. A "no control over my own romantic (or sex) life and might not get what I want" philosophy set forth for the stupid and desperate. Set forth by whom? Who can I blame for this colossal waste of time and advice? Parents? Dumber than a dartboard girlfriends? Movies? Books? Shrinks on Nancy Grace and Dr. Phil? Me? DNA? The boys themselves?

The "January still doesn't get the fucking hint" conversation repeatedly played itself out with my brother (Childless Brad Pitt) or one of my suffering girlfriends. What followed was a duel between my vodka/soda/with three limes and my phone, wondering,

Would Short Fat Fuck be here tonight?

Whether at an afternoon barbecue, concert at the beach, or in a noisy, dark bar with friends (or on a date) eventually I'd sneak away to tipsily dial Jack's number and announce my desire, or love, depending on my blood alcohol level. On Friday or Saturday nights (*years'* worth of Friday or Saturday nights) his voice mail became my confessional.

Press 3 to delete.

My voice wasn't the only criminal.

In the last few years our texts became a symbiosis of violence and pornographic obsession that didn't want to be tamed.

On the Childless Brad Pitt/Nachos/Fat Tire day, I wasn't black-out drunk, so I texted Jack. As I walked outside "Owner," the owner of the Shack, flirted with a hand outstretched, tugging on one of my unbelted belt loops. A pageant smile plastered my face: fair skin, chin-acne free for that day at least, and blushed from Sunday afternoon cocktails. I lowered my head, kept walking, and started typing.

Me: I'm an idiot. Why do I leave my boyfriend in Pismo to come see you? And then you fucking bail as soon as I ask about what bar you're at. What is your problem? Am I that horrible you don't want to be seen with me in public? Instead of just being upfront, you just don't respond to my texts. Really classy. Am I too available for you? What the hell have I done to you to deserve to be treated like a piece of shit?

Jack: Sorry sweetie the lady showed up.

Me: Go fuck yourself.

I lit a cigarette.

Jack: Ur really being that mean.

Me: you treat me like a whore and a piece of shit. What do you expect? Do you care about my feelings even somewhat? I stupidly assumed that you had broken up...there's a lot more I'd like to tell u.

Jack: i am sorry. I thought u knew what was going on. I apologise.

Me: And the worst part is I'm dating a great guy and its getting serious and I leave him last nite bc I wanted to see u!! I'm a fucking idiot. Don't apologize. Its my fault. And how would I know "what's going on"? You don't tell me shit! Anyway, I gotta go.

Jack: Sorry. Have a good day.

I tossed the Parliament Light and walked back inside the Shack. I didn't know what to do with myself. Drink? Call the current boyfriend? Eat?

"What happened to B11?" (Current boyfriend = B11) Childless Brad Pitt ordered a sandwich and fries in the time I was gone.

"Exactly," I sighed and pulled out my stool. During a silent pause on the jukebox, my chair scraping the floor of the bar reminded me of where I was, and my previous 24 hours of mistakes.

I nodded at Too Tan, the bartender. After a few sucks on my straw, I set it down on my napkin and grabbed my Blackberry, again. I deleted his contact with fingertip-spraining gusto, smelled finality and rebirth, and couldn't feel any worse than I did at that moment.

Omg Omg Omg.

I hate him I hate him I hate him.

Short Fat Fuck. Short Fat Fuck. Short Fat Fuck.

A few years ago one of my oldest friends, St. Croix, nicknamed Jack "Short Fat Fuck." Most of the time I couldn't say Jack's name out loud, so Short Fat Fuck he would be for weeks and months and years, in whispers, laughs, slurs, screams, and tears. Jack. Short Fat Fuck. SFF. One and the same.

But that day, the "Sorry Sweetie, the lady showed up" day, he was *asshole asshole asshole*.

For the 500th time, the next few hours blurred into grays, whites, and lime greens, as I hunched on my saddle under *The Amazing Race*. It didn't matter if the B's (the boyfriends) trickled down around me like rain on an umbrella. Or if one, secure, agreeable, current boyfriend—B11—provided SFF substitutes for conversation, hands, and lips. Writing, days and nights, breathing—my whole world—crippled into melancholia and made no sense if I didn't have Jack.

When my brother asked if I was texting Jack, I told him I was asking Vanity Fair a question about a fundraiser we were organizing next week. I tippled as I lied, and gold-medaled at each. Only the black plastic container in front of me—with its cherry, lemon-and lime-slice, and straw compartments—knew how (*truly*) sad and wartorn I'd become in four years.

I rubbernecked, swilling the ice in my glass. "You ever notice this place looks like a high school cafeteria?" Childless Brad Pitt rotated a centimeter left and right and grunted.

Here was the Shack, but it was also Moondoggies or the Roost. Those were just three of the varied establishments (luxe weaving into divey) dotting the Central Coast, a section of California mapped with numerous towns as consequential and small as bits of dust. Pismo Beach was the best bit of dust: less agriculture and fewer blue collars, more resorts and polo shirts. The vibe, people, beach, pier, and six-foot-tall clam sculpture greeted me as I veered right off one of its two freeway exits. Eight thousand people lived along the 101's palisades—a beach town without beach weather. Colder than most. I'd rather be cold than hot.

Pismo's three bars lay a proud claim to the divey end of the spectrum. The Shack, Moondoggies, or the Roost's patrons and vast vineyards became my discipleship as I drank, cried, and experienced pure elation at all of them. Since getting slizzard in one of the three bars usually led me down a glazed pathway to Jack—and the possibility of the two of us entangled—the stools I sat on and the hops-drenched air I breathed were essential. We now *shared* these establishments—a factor out of his control—and, irrationally, in mine.

I silently demanded a recount from my brother while splashing vodka on my knee. Why do I have to wait around for Jack to call me, text me, want me? I would be the exception to the rule. *All* of the rules. My amorous mania shoulder-convinced me (an Eminem-like "rap, tap, tap" on my shoulder from behind) that I would, eventually, get what I wanted. I was smart, somewhat easy on the eyes, and good in bed (according to him and others) so why wouldn't he want me? Why the hell *couldn't* I pursue him?

So, I did. And here we are.

Jack. Short Fat Fuck. I wanted to die over him. I thought this was love. I loved him, and I needed to know, *now*, if he felt the same.

It's not Sinatra's fault.

I blame Ray Liotta.

May 7, 2008 / One week later

"I need to ask you something." My makeup smeared into the phone. I switched hands and lit a cigarette. Slouched on a step leading up to my house, I stared through the Parliament Lights box.

"Oh no." Jack giggled.

"No, no, it's not bad. I just—." *Lie.*

"Ok, Sweetie." His pitch consisted of the usual corrupted mix of high, soft, and kind. Unconsciously, I must have already known the answer so difficult to pull from his teeth. Did I want the pain of this? From the masochistic "talk." A final anti-Elysian twist, if I didn't hear it out loud, I would never, ever stop the repining wrapped around my entire existence, cauterizing me at the head. If I didn't ask, I would be alone in the end. Alone—with a "fuck buddy."

"Look, I just need to end this and move on. Or take it to another level, I mean, don't you feel anything for me?" I inhaled. "Don't you—"

Politely, unflinchingly, laughably and institutionalizingly, he cut me off: "I'm sorry, I just don't feel that way about you. And honestly, I never will. I just don't feel that spark."

His was a simplified declaration, cooked down to the brown bits on the bottom of a fry pan.

What. The. Fuck.

That "almost had a car accident" feeling hot-flashed from my chest to my knees. I smelled metallic toast. *Am I having a stroke?*

He continued, butchering me with sentences.

"I'm sorry I kept having sex with you. I thought we were both having fun with each other ... ."

I rubbed the splinters on the wooden step with my free hand.

Four years? Gone. Relationships? Irrevocably destroyed. Self-respect? Evanescent. The penny-sized amount of happiness and hope I had left? Titanically placed on his bookshelf of sadistic souvenirs.

More moronic sentences.

"... being naughty together." He had me where he wanted me: a chance to make me aware of everything. A chance *I* gave to *him*.

Wow, this is sucking much worse than I imagined.

"You're joking, right? Fuck, come on, all of this time? You're ridiculous, Jack. Jack. I can't believe this. I can't believe you. I *don't*. I don't believe you." I stood up and walked down to my backyard so I could pace. My mouth hurt. A fireplace smell blew by, and I heard a neighbor call my name. "I've told you before how I felt, right? There, there was always an excuse with you, always. I'm just sorry I didn't see you for what you are sooner. What you were doing...to me. Oh my god...no spark? You have to be kidding! Am I that fucking disgusting to you?"

"Sweetie." Jack never said *January*: never texted it, spoke it, emailed it, or let it out in a wet, alto breath during sex. Jack never said *girlfriend, dinner, yes, come here,* or *love*. His words were *naughty, friends with bennies, no spark,* and *quite honestly never will.*

Sweetie.

My disbelief pressed the red "end" key. Fantastic. Disney and John Hughes movies had infected my unconscious. When I pinned that contaminated unconscious to a lonely dependency on fictional characters, then to my writer's imagination, I was unprepared for the consequence of a fresh, dirty reality.

Jack side-carred more of my emotional and physical triumphs (and failures) than any other man before him. After four years of lasciviousness, faces and necks fused together, cocktailed encounters, sober encounters, thousands of keystrokes (some reciprocated, some ignored) and after I proclaimed every visceral, cognizant idea and sensation I possessed, I was nothing to him. We were bonded only by orgasms.

Fragments of my life dissolved into a rayless hole as I walked back upstairs. He wasn't like me; he didn't know me, yet he would have the world.

Jack. Short Fat Fuck. SFF.

I wanted to die over him. I thought this was love.

He was the Grand Canyon. I was the tourists' spit below.

May 8, 2008 / the next day

I brainstormed.

Easy. Simple. Obviously zero gruesomeness and zero agony.

A painless suicide? *Jesus, I'm a suicidal pussy.*

Nothing appealed to me. You wouldn't know it by looking at me while I drove to Los Angeles for work, but I was sea foam of *"What the fucks/Just kill me nows"* up the bendy 101 next to the ocean's rocky shores. Seals and piers on one side, hills and vultures on the other. California land/seascapes had no effect on my muted flesh with sunglass exterior.

Drive off a cliff? Where? In Goleta? The Cachuma Pass in Santa Barbara had bridges and roads on which a driver could easily overcorrect and outmaneuver. Businessmen, dumbass teenagers, and moms with kids in the backseat died there every year—self-inflicted or not: action-movie-worthy soars into goldenrod prairies where only the demi-mountains, freshwater, and cows knew the truth.

Eh. I didn't want to wreck my car.

Shotgun? Chin, mouth, chest? Too messy. Not a fan of breathing, but not really a fan of ending my life as a contortionist, shoving cold metal in my mouth while attempting to squeeze a trigger. *Seems like a ton of fucking work. Plus, where would I find a gun?*

Xanax. I had a full bottle at home. Chalky peach ovals paired well with white wine, right? How many did I need? Five? Ten? Thirty? Should it be red wine?

Wait. *Garage.* Yes! The old "car running in the closed garage" bit.

Fuck me. I didn't have a garage.

Fuck. Me.

A smart girl leaves before she is left.

— Marilyn Monroe

October 28, 2004 / Four years earlier

Jack wasn't always Short Fat Fuck.

Every few months, I visited my brother and dad in my hometown of Pismo Beach, a couple of hours north of LA. I left seven years earlier— I didn't belong, and never intended to stay. Pismo was a layover, a pit stop before college in Santa Barbara. I was born in Pismo, but I didn't grow up there, in Childless Brad Pitt's or my dad's world. My brother and my dad had their company to run, dirt to farm, and boulders to move. I grew up on the other side of the country, in Chicago—without dirt or a farm—and with a nanny. My mother called her my "governess." I wasn't better than Pismo, and high school was a beachy, corduroyed blast, but pregnancy, a Kmart, one movie theater, and a first marriage by age 23 didn't have the pizzazz I bit nails for.

On this particular Saturday night, my brother (Childless Brad Pitt) and I headed out to the Shack, a blip of a bar facing the 101 at the beach, a mile or two from where the dunes ended and the cliffs began. Uber-popular, the Shack filled a geographical and drinka-graphical void, a vacuum between the pricey resort lounges offer-ing a menu of cocktails shaken and stirred with local and seasonal produce, and the dives sitting closer to the lettuce fields, boasting slogans like, *We have two kinds of whiskey, we don't have a blender, and we don't have coasters.*

With white laminate flooring below and 10-month-old Christmas decorations above, the Shack was hit or miss. Hit: a harmony of decent-looking, cool, conceivably rich older guys, familiar faces, and few girls. Miss: a few meth addicts doused over too many girls. The jukebox was too expensive and the champagne not expensive enough.

I saw the back of his head: a pageboy cap. The hat led to tat-tooed, dough-colored arms holding a can of Budweiser, or was it a mug?

What would a bar serve in a mug?

"That's Jack." My brother pointed as we walked through the glass doors. He motioned to two stools next to Pageboy Cap/Jack.

"Hey! It's been a long time." Jack turned to us and took mental notes of my hair and lips.

"Hey, Jack, what's going on?" Childless Brad Pitt signaled the bartender.

"And who is this?" His blue eyes under the dim lighting switched focus from my lips to my eyes.

"January. Hey." I spoke as we started to shake hands. I pulled mine back and we laughed. He glimpsed my nervous boobs.

"Sorry." My coat was off, and I required vodka. Actually, I needed vodka an hour ago. Childless Brad Pitt poked my arm.

"Jack, January. January, this is Jack. We went to high-school together." My brother had as much enthusiasm in the introduction as he had in pumping gas.

"Hi there, Sweetheart." He raised his can, stood up, and started a conversation with his other barstool neighbor. Distracted by the drink my brother pushed toward me, I took a few sips before I refocused on Jack: an inch shorter than me and semi-stocky.

My Ketel One and soda vanished, and my breath went with it. Baffled and sensing my whole body at battle, I picked at a damp napkin as I abused my limes and overheard Rod Stewart sing, "Stay With Me." My brother talked to his friends nearby; I didn't know many people in Pismo anymore.

What was happening? Jack's Billabong jeans, black metal band T-shirt, and surfer shoes (e.g. Vans, Reef, Volcom) distracted me. A frisson of jet airplane energy fueled me. A flit; a quick pulse more profound than a chill; a reaction so intimate, I stamped it foreign.

And. That. Was. It.

I ordered another. "Three limes, please." My breath returned, and the bartender, Too Tan, rolled her eyes and scooped ice into a fresh glass. I noticed a dark, orange-ish brown ring collecting around her armpits as she cheered on the Chargers in a tank top.

"Three limes, really?" Jack observed as he meandered back to his seat. "You live in LA, right?" He didn't sit.

"Yeah, I'm a writer." I didn't unimpress him with the embarrassing detail I was also Mr. and Mrs. Z's assistant/house-girl/estate manager/empire supporter. He told me about his job. Something having to do with a record store.

He asked what everyone asks: *What are you working on? What's it about? Is it in bookstores?*

Five minutes later

"You're gay, right?" He seemed too chic/modish and his voice too high pitched, not to be.

"Ah, hahaha, no." His smile told me he was single.

"You look like that guy from … that band … Good Charlotte."

"Huh, that's random."

He thinks I'm an alien. Why can't I shut up? I should have the demeanor of a girl who swallowed a Vicodin 30 minutes ago. My new goal: acquire a Vicodin demeanor.

I expected a Kirsten Dunst comparison in return, but all he said was,

"You're a cute girl."

His hands were tough and thick, yet handsome.

Two hours later

There wasn't enough Ketel One, or there was too much, to release me into the weekend, help me enjoy what was taking place, sandbag the impending shitstorm, or alter my entire personality. In Pismo two hours, and I dutifully wreaked havoc on Jack.

"Let's get outta here." I spat sloe-eyed. Jack felt the collar of my leather trench. I looked like *Matrix* Keanu Reeves. "Let's get outta here. Let's get outta here." *Definitely too much Ketel One.*

"Sweetie, I have friends here. I can't just leave." Jack was a coquet who transformed into a rapscallion as I squirmed at the thought of what he thought. Heat reddened my face, and I shed my pink scarf.

I found the owner of the Shack, whom Jack pointed out earlier. I repeated my steps and documented Owner's features: not-well-managed salt-and-pepper hair and a recurring glass of white wine positioned in front of him next to his phone, as if the two were on a date. Not a winery glass either, or one I'd buy at Crate and Barrel; it was one you'd buy in a pinch at a grocery store. Owner always situated himself at a specific corner of his bar. He explained why after we introduced ourselves: "Multi-purpose view of employees, customers, and the cash register."

I asked about the poster near the entrance for a "White Trash Party" happening in a few weeks.

"Everyone dresses up. I wear a mullet wig." Owner motioned to Too Tan to pour me another. I wasn't sure if I liked her yet.

I'm the only twenty-something American woman lush in the history of twenty-something American women lushes who must make friends with, and analyze, every bartender I meet.

"I'll park my Airstream out front. We check out the drunk chicks playing pin-up in front of its door."

Eight-thirty tick-tocked to 11 o'clock, and Ketel One and soda filled me like a bank-side reservoir on the Mississippi. Sozzled January meant impatient and unpleasant. I was done.

Capsized, I walked outside to find Childless Brad Pitt. Jack stood against a railing, talking to his friends. He shifted his gaze to me, away from the crowd of dude losers and a similarly red-in-the-nose girl soliciting a job at his store. Or did she desire something more akin to what I wanted? *I love when you think a boy has left, but he hasn't—not that it made a difference tonight.*

Fabulous. I was going home alone (with my brother) and I would remember all three hours of the night. Why couldn't have this been a blackout drunk night? *Damn you, Childless Brad Pitt. Why did you point out this turd to me?*

"Bye, Sweetheart."

I said nothing, but I thought of him Sunday while driving back to LA. I couldn't place his face, but I remembered the galvanism of an 8:30 p.m. moment at the Shack.

November 18, 2004

I went back to the Shack. Again. Hopeful for second Jack chances, I toasted myself and followed him around like a stray, horny, uncute puppy. Checking for me over his shoulder and rolling his eyes to his friends, he didn't ignore me—but he didn't speak to me. With CIA operative skills, I interrogated one of his friends: a punk, scraggly, skinny surfer who was staying at Jack's over the weekend.

"Hey." Sleepy, unattractive eyes, head nodding. His arms and legs longed for a cheeseburger.

"What are you drinkin'?" A wallet with a chain attached appeared on the bar.

"You know Jack, right?"

"Yep, best friends." Two five-dollar bills passed to Too Tan from his skinny, brown hands, and he ordered shots.

"Tell me about him."

Too Tan dumped ingredients for an "Attitude Adjustment" into her shaker.

"You're cute. Why do you want him? He's an asshole."

"I thought he was your friend."

"He is." Longs for a Cheeseburger downed his shot before his head inclined toward my face. "Don't waste your time."

1 a.m.

I finagled an "invite" to the "after party" at Jack's house. We marched out of the Shack two by two. Me and Longs for a Cheeseburger in one car, Jack and a boyish girl in another. Jack's tattoos shot down his arm from under a short sleeve as he held the steering wheel.

Jack, in all of his fuckwit glory, smiled, nodded, and flirted at his house—a mile from the beach with five guy roommates.

An hour went by. Boys studied their cell phones, girls pretended to gossip in corners, and sweaty hands held sweaty beers as hook ups were cherry-picked before 3 a.m. Jack and Boyish Girl huddled in the kitchen. He finally emerged, whisked by me, grunted in my ear, and grabbed my waist.

It took me a few seconds after the waist grab to comprehend what Longs for a Cheeseburger mumbled in my ear.

"A ride?" As I stood at the kitchen counter, I watched Jack continue to be a good host, now in his living room. Apparently, Longs was staying at a different house—not Jack's.

I realized it was a ploy for sex, but everything else in the house— Longs for a Cheeseburger especially—was subterfuge. He drained his beer.

"Ok, I'll do it. If Jack comes."

"Sure, Sweetie," Jack replied from the living room, while Longs and his chain wallet headed toward the door.

After dropping him and his chain wallet off, an odd and new tension stuck to the gearshift.

"Your house?"

"Yeah, let's head back."

I wanted Jack, but didn't know if he wanted me. After a few blocks, we passed a small, unkempt cemetery. Our eyes met after he pulled out his penis.

"You know you love it."

"Um." *Wants me.*

"Pull over." Was he asking or suggesting?

"To walk around? This is super creepy." While shutting off the engine, specks of my current reality snuck in through my nose and mouth. I couldn't imagine, but I took what I could get. I was bashed by lust and drink.

At least there isn't a cock ring. He looks like the type.

He approached me, and instincts told me to lay back. After he crawled on top of me, we attacked each other between two graves. A blanket from my trunk didn't cross my vodka'd consciousness. Wet and painful sex shimmied our bodies to the front of a tall tombstone. Then a stumpy one. My butt and back burned so I moved him to the bottom. This time the tombstone was under his head: gray, decrepit, and bearing the inscription *Samuel Kennedy, 1919-1955.*

If I ride him, someone might see us. Why am I reading these fucking headstones?

Buttons ripped and underwear buried itself next to loved ones' coffins. I remembered driving by the graveyard as a kid; now it was our temporary mattress. My moistened hair massaged itself in the brown grass and Jack bore into me with a pointed force. He'd already flipped me *back* over. Our mouths opened as if to scream silently, or scream out *kiss me.*

"You are so naughty." He rolled off and twisted his boxer shorts around.

I pulled my jeans up and sighed. I did three things well: drink, fall, and sigh.

"That was fun." My last words for my first time.

Our first time—a christening, perhaps. Desperation, impulsivity, and self-hatred do funny things to a girl with unstable parents, heavy eyeliner and a maturity level of a 15-year-old.

2:30 a.m.

We tip-toed to his bedroom, and I continued my case study inside the subject's own habitat, memorizing the dark red walls, corners, and furniture. Shoes piled and clothes hung in his small closet with cheap slider doors. One wall displayed peculiar dolls from a comic book: mounted and dressed in primary-color costumes accessorized with guns, tools, and capes. He took out pajamas.

"What are these? Dolls?" I tapped on one of the clear, plastic boxes.

"They're not dolls, they're action figures." I laughed and pounced on him to forget the decor. We kissed hard, his tongue and teeth violating mine.

A light tapping.

We parted lips, and I breathed in.

"Yeah?" Jack craned his neck, pushing me away.

Boyish Girl entered, sleepy eyed and suspicious.

"Heyyy," she moaned, claiming drunkenness to the point of being ill.

What the hell.

"Scoot." He nudged me.

What the fuck.

Dumbfounded, I pushed myself off of the bed. Objection didn't seem appropriate since I didn't know him (except for his cock) or her, now stretched out on his bed.

Now, on the other side of the door, a click from the doorknob immobilized me, and defeat overcame me. I pressed my fingers hard into the wall in the pitch black hallway, processing a new depressing reality slithering down my throat like Pepto-Bismol. I was traumatized, disgusted, and without my keys, purse, and Parliament Lights placed in anticipation on the nightstand. Where I once was warm and happy, Jack and a different girl—who smelled like a bar's floor— were tucked in. Warm and happy. I knocked. Opening the door a crack, he peeped at me through the darkness. Boyish Girl lay vertical on my side of the bed, propped up on a pillow, aiming a remote control at a corner where I assumed a crappy TV sat on a crappier TV stand.

"What's up, Sweetheart?"

Is this guy fucking kidding me? "My stuff."

He popped out seconds after shutting the door in my face and handed me my belongings with a kiss on the cheek. I should've walked away right then. Sprinted. Pole jumped back to my cultured, educated, respectable Hollywood actuality, light years away from this ... man, this situation, and this escalating, terrifying feeling after one month of lurking in and around Pismo Beach: Jack wasn't going anywhere, or I wasn't. If he was tougher on me, denying me earlier in the night while making his motives clear, maybe I wouldn't have clung on to a ghost with such palpable appeal.

A lot to ask of a boy who screwed me in a cemetery an hour earlier.

I should've walked away.

3:30 a.m.

I glared at three old hexagon-steel-bolted skateboards in an artistic triptych. The "art" on the wall was a reminder to guests (or maybe only me) that the four or five occupants of the house (surfers, blue-collar guys, students) were desperate. Desperately trying to hold on to their late teens/twenty-something youth—the era coated with alcoholism and nightly attempts at hooking up with girls they knew from high school, or with girls visiting girls they knew from high school.

In a few years, maybe a decade, when the house was a line on their credit reports, the roommates would be numb to the unpredicted fact of how far they traveled from a lost paradise to smaller, more cheerless towns. Children, crazy and fat ex-wives, disappointments, no money, and possibly a blistering venereal disease opened the gates to middle life. In the meantime, other Pismo surfers and their red-headed stepbrothers, the skateboarders, rallied around ignorant estheticians and hairdressers who downed excessive amounts of shitty beer and schnapps, mirroring riotous Russians. Or was it Germans?

Schnapps are German, I think.

Attention to girls who have college degrees: Commitment-phobes and future (and current) losers reside in this middle class, single-family house on a nondescript lane. Extreme danger! High voltage! Fools, enter at your own risk. Tonight I was the ignorant esthetician: uneducated, uncultured, and not unwilling. A preserved cavewoman, defrosted enough to be insulted yet wanting more. Pandemonium of penis or not, I was better than this, but I couldn't move, my forehead impetrating the flimsy door.

"Jack."

"Yeah." No movement.

"Can you open the door?" Footsteps.

"Oh, hey, Sweetheart." He stood there bloated in his pajamas.

"Are you going to bed?"

"She's asleep, sick. Hey, thanks for coming by, though. I'll talk to you later. Ok, Honey?" He attempted to shut the door. Infatuated by his terms of endearment, a murkiness in the air appeared, yet what became clear was I had to persuade and wheedle until Jack came out of his bedroom. Since 10 p.m., I'd hungered for his skin on my skin and wouldn't be denied. The cemetery wasn't enough.

We roamed the house together, him thinking out loud about where we could go for privacy. Slanting into him, I asserted what I planned to do to him. Boyish Girl in his bed was forgotten as he snickered and led me by the hand through the Christmas-lights-lit living room. We plodded through the passed-out legs, arms, and tank tops sprawled on the carpet and into the last available room of the house, and into his roommate Liver's vacant bed: a twin.

We hopped on the bed. He took off my top, and I went for his pajama bottoms. Derailing and intense sloppy kisses.

Breathe deep.

Blowjob.

There wasn't pillow talk or laughter. We didn't explore each other's bodies. The nose, down to the nipples, the navel, back to the nape of our necks, and finally the kneecaps. He wouldn't ask me when my birthday was, or what I'd be doing for the rest of the weekend. Jack discovered I was crazier than he thought.

I admired an experience of marriage without the marriage. Knowing him for 30 days framed a sweetness hidden beneath impromptu sex: He talked dirty, but his remaining senses confided in me. Bedraggled, sweaty, nasty and dissimilar flavors became the burnt ends of pleasure and goodness. A handgrip on my ass or boob, or a fast pounding into the bed was the same as a caress or a waffle/dinner invitation. The contradictions undid a flush so mysterious yet so expected, I begged the desires to last both of our lifetimes. I expected everything from nothing at all, and so I black-jacked the fine-haired moments. My reaction was strong because he had none.

Edging toward daylight, evaporating vodka meant clarity (also due to a punching bag of a pounding from Jack's dick). The dread of this particular encounter ending evoked images of an experience producing the same effect. Last year on a Saturday night, Los Angeles' evenfall exhilaration infiltrated with precision, the dealer was on his way while we popped champagne corks aimed at Model, the party hostess, and her floating tray balancing tall flutes. Then margarita glasses when she ran out of flutes. This made us laugh. An unblemished evening drowned in Chambord and champagne wound down at Sunset Marquis just to wind up again at a strip club. That night, Jumbo's. I say "last year" because this year I lost my dealer's phone number. A good thing.

Jack was the same: Cocaine in the flesh.

He came on my neck in an annoying finality I pretended to enjoy. He also came on a stained, discarded-after-the-fact pillow at which Jack and his friends would laugh about on Monday night as they played Xbox.

Even with the cemetery sex, the rejection, and the kiddy bed, I was there because I wanted to be. I elasticized the evening into 5 a.m. and settled for what it was.

I lay on top of him and admitted, "I like you."

He didn't move a muscle. "Sweetheart, you don't like me. You just want me because you can't have me."

Um, I'm confused. I can't have you? Aren't I on top of you right now? And wasn't your penis between my tits, like, 10 minutes ago?

My blue eyes met his blue eyes. I wondered if he noticed mine with tiny yellow threads and outlined with a hard-pressed indigo crayon. I projected myself into the old movies I watched over and over, inventing expectations from the noirs, stocking-softened blacks and grays, art deco settees and doorways, and '40s fashion. Projection led to inspiration, and I was stirred to change his world.

Of course he likes me. Of course he wants me. Of course I'll have him.

My reaction was strong because he had none.

He was right about one thing, as he would prove to be right about a lot of things: I didn't have him.

———

I went to breakfast the next day with my dad at a local diner a mile from his house. Everything was a mile from anything else. Jack lived a mile from the diner, which was a mile from my dad's. The beach was a mile from my dad's. And so on.

If I sat more than 20 minutes in front of my dad, my face folded in like a burrito. Ours wasn't an estranged relationship; we just didn't have anything in common. He liked sensible men (my brother). He didn't like super-sensitive, creative women (me).

He wanted me to "Find a trade!" Repair air conditioners for the rest of my life, or, "I'll say it again: join the army, Jan. Become a war correspondent."

Maybe we are estranged.

Maybe he wouldn't notice. Coffee quenched the blahs of an overcast Sunday. I'd drive to LA in a few hours, billions of chambers already coalescing in my brain, pencils to their mouths, assisting me in the design of an upcoming weekend in Pismo. Wanting, torturing, wishing, failing, fucking, following, stalking, coaxing, aching, kissing *Jack*. My dad had no idea of the stains of a twenty-something girl flexing her slut muscles while visiting her family for the weekend. I

21

felt my neck: His dried cum was still there. Over bacon and oatmeal, I adjusted my coat. Thank God for thick winter scarves.

December 2004

I celebrated Jack and his bleached impressions in my head while taking a shower, waiting in line at Whole Foods, and at work while picking up Mrs. Z's 10 pairs of boots and shoes at the cobbler. He took over my journal: interminable inky rants and raves about my latest fuckwit on striped or non-striped paper depending on which notebook I took out of a desk drawer. Actually, there were no desk drawers in my house in LA because there was no desk. The 1940s bungalow had built-ins with drawers surrounding a space for a Murphy bed without a Murphy bed, and drawers in a built-in vanity in my closet, and of course there were drawers in the kitchen. Instead of a useful office with organization for miles, my writing utensils divorced one another, choosing to live apart. Pencils in the kitchen. Pens in the closet. I guess built-ins were popular back in the day.

December 19, 2004

Clearly not thinking clearly, I typed up a new Pismo itinerary to a mix of Van Morrison and Elton John on my car stereo. A day mare of traffic started at 5 p.m. with no befuddlement in sight until I stopped at the sorta-clean Santa Barbara gas station I always stopped at. By 7 p.m., the Killers and a dollhouse-sized bottle of wine motivated me further, while driving alongside whitecaps and mussel shoals.

"I'm coming out of my cage
And I've been doing just fine
Gotta gotta be down
Because I want it all
It started out with a kiss
How did it end up like this?"

The sunsets on my left disappeared under different circumstances every time I drove the route. On the dollhouse-wine-in-a-paper-cup-from-McDonald's evening, a computer sputtered out atomic cubes of data in oranges, pinks, and purples.

9 p.m.

"The Shack, again? Dude, there's other places." Childless Brad Pitt walked into the foyer of my dad's house, where I had waited 10 minutes for him to smoke a bowl.

"Any other ideas?" He didn't answer me, just watched as I stuffed a clutch with money, ID, cigarettes, lighter, mints, phone, and lip-gloss.

As with anything, I obsessed over the Shack: Owner, the barkeeps, the drunks, the teetotalers, what drinks they offered, and didn't. As big as a living room, the bar was attached to a ribs restaurant and sat underneath a "Barbecue!" sign, 30-feet-high. Below, like a Shell station, sat a waterlogged but holy piece of property where people left pain and will power at the door. Twenty-one and (up to) 85-year-olds, red-faced and rat-legged, played pool, music, or foosball. Simultaneous endeavors by the clientele and staff resulted in a constant hum above the scooping of ice cubes, the clinks of single malt glasses, and the pulls of beer taps. It wasn't quite a hum—more like a hum on top of a rumble. The bar wasn't a "live your life here and drink on me," storied, beloved, built-from-African-mahogany bar, but it heard the same confessions, depressions, and proclamations when bellied up to.

My brother and I walked outside to a gray mist translucent enough to see stars I never saw in LA. Pismo could have trademarked the fog. It was a rampart to outsiders.

To insiders, Pismo's fog was the mayor, police, and church.

"I'll drive," I told him.

Midnight

"Your brother is freaking me out. Wanna get outta here?" Jack grinned, touched my waist and jacket, and took a deep breath.

Childless Brad Pitt had switched from pumping gas interest to big brother interest.

There wasn't any vodka at my dad's, and my gas-station-wine buzz was gone, so I took visual snapshots: Southern Comfort and Coke and a mischievous smirk on his face. Chiseled. But I also thought *Asperger's* or *inbred* when I looked at Jack for longer than 20 seconds. In a girl's emotionally troubled world, and stomach, looks didn't matter. Boys were soul food.

One vodka/soda and the Black Eyed Peas on the jukebox allowed me time to formulate an answer. Why wasn't I in Hollywood right now? At the Dresden, 4100, an industry party, a Si Sé show, anything with fabulous people, drinking interesting drinks, and wearing or carrying whatever I wanted: heels, jewelry, and a vintage clutch? Anything louder than a pair of jeans in Pismo Beach was akin to walking up to a cop in 7-Eleven and yanking his gun out of the holster. You didn't do it. So, why was I there?

Jesusfuckstopthinking.

"Maybe," I inhaled as I replied. Hollywood and 7-Eleven cops faded as I snapped into focus and realized this might be my chance for cemetery sex redemption. A night in his bed; no interruptions, talking, cuddling, and breakfast.

Jack elaborated into my ear, "I can't tell you how much I want to eat your pussy with your bro standing right here."

Childless Brad Pitt drank one barstool away with his girlfriend, Accountant.

The invitation to "get outta here" gave me something automatic to chew on. As much as I relished in the present, I fixated on the future, and smelled rose petals. Whether it was the next trip to the grocery store, how much money I'd have in a month, or how I would die, I soaked up anxiety like a sponge from rising droplets of circumstance out of my control.

Childless Brad Pitt checked on us over his shoulder. Getting rid of my brother wasn't going to be easy. I told Jack I couldn't leave.

"Why don't you just cruise over when he's ready to go? I'll leave the porch light on." He tugged at the hem of my shirt and walked out. Glowing in my victory and the firm knowledge of where I'd be within the hour, I wondered why he wanted me.

1:30 a.m.

Since we'd arrived at the Shack, there had been some developments: a marriage proposal, one and half fights, and bachelorettes and friends in lace veils fetching chocolate-covered strawberries with their tongues from boy bartenders.

Why are bartenders handing out chocolate-covered strawberries?

The 1:30 a.m. finale was the bachelorette's friend getting arrested, thrown into the back of a cop car with its *oh no* lights reflected on her Maid of Honor crown. The Shack was innocent as much as it was debauched, like a child's playpen for adults, a place to soothe spirits and where, someday, we'd all call home.

1:45 a.m.

Rips Shirt.

I wasn't a fighter; I was a total wimp. Ask St. Croix. At UCSB I *might have* pepper-sprayed a girl in the eyes after she punched me in the head through my open car window. I blamed our mantis-green college years, which stunk of candy apple liqueur and beer, forever flowing in the gutters of Isla Vista.

I possessed a lead conscience. I was fearless. I was impulsive. I was 19 years old.

Today I was 27, still impulsive, and, at times, an unintentional asshole when I spent 9 p.m. to 2 a.m. French kissing Ketel Ones. My bar mates either evolved up to rock star status or for the love of fuck pissed me off. After Jack left, I gawped in boredom around the Shack. Three cute girls flirted with three groomed college guys drinking bottled beer. An 80-year-old sat next to Owner, tilting into his cane and handling a Gimlet: Gimlet Geezer.

Rips Shirt exited the Shack's dingy, single-stall bathroom with a cockiness only a reapplication of lipstick, and third teasing of the hair would bring. She was a petite, middle-aged local who might or might not have been a hooker and who, maliciously and poorly, flirted with my brother in front of Accountant. Too sweet, forgiving, and smart, Accountant paid no attention. "No worries" or "Right on" was all Accountant ever said when encountering douchebags. Her neck dripped with a weekly piece of turquoise jewelry. Her laugh, and stories about her trips to Amsterdam or China, made me wish certain nights would never end.

I walked outside to smoke and check my voicemail.

The "Barbecue!" sign magnified the cheap dye of Rips Shirt's red-velvet-cake-shaded hair while she smoked. I leaned on the prison-yard railing parallel to the front entrance.

"You bought those at Kmart, right?" I pointed to her boots as I hung up my phone.

Rips Shirt didn't hesitate. She threw her cigarette near the can full of butts next to the bar's door and sprang at me. I heard a car whiz by. Fuck.

I had places to be! People to make out with! A bar brawl? What about a sweet comeback? Name calling? Seriously, I have to fight this woman?

As an evolved human being, the only violence I witnessed was on *The Sopranos*. I wanted this to end, so when I had the opportunity to kick Rips Shirt in the face, I refrained. I wasn't physically incapable, but I didn't feel like spending the night in jail. The only punching and kicking I did was in my Tae Bo class in LA.

Since I didn't run, she took her chance and pulled my hair until my roots and scalp developed a sheen of dried white goop I picked at for days. A scrape above my eye, another on my lip, and a torn T-shirt later, two rugby players and my brother pried us apart. I didn't care.

3 a.m.

I dropped off Childless Brad Pitt and Accountant at her house.

"Jan, where the fuck are you going?"

26

I smiled.

In his kitchen, Jack held out a shot of Crown Royal. Nothing matched in the yellow square with '70s flooring and cabinets full of crap that ended with "os." Doritos, Cheerios, Spaghettios (only three of the seven cabinets had doors). There was a display of booze as fully stocked as those tall shelves behind the cash register of a liquor store.

"It's my roommates', mostly." The bottles lined up like a choir between the stove and toaster, below the junk food.

"*Leave your number on the cabinet, and I promise Baby, I'll give you a call. Next time I'm feelin' kinda horny … .*"

Snoop Dogg popped into my head at the craziest times.

"Yeah, Rips Shirt is crazy. I wish I could have been there. I'm sorry, Sweetheart." He straightened my shirt and smoothed my hair after inspecting my head for injuries. I beamed and pretended to listen while I squealed on the inside.

The last drops of liquor atilt, I asked, "Tour?" He laughed and took my hand.

In Jack's bedroom, I forgot about the night he kicked me out to make room for Boyish Girl. He sat on the edge of his bed, hands in his lap, soft, defenseless. I wanted to scoop him up. I stood above him and touched his hair, his face. I kissed him as I would have wanted to be kissed, like on TV, and the way a few of the previous B's had. The smell of his skin: Macy's department store cologne of musk and mint. He reciprocated, hugging me close as we lay down. We slept in our clothes.

In the morning, I liked being in bed, in the new and unforeseen. I couldn't stop the constant whiplashing from staring at him as he slept, and the ceiling. It was an analytical, tortuous night, a first of many that I could recall, but didn't consider. He might lie, he would cheat, he threw/used/played me like a yo-yo, yet he charmed me as I bathed in his fractional sociopathic behavior, and worshipped nothings I construed as somethings.

A shirt straightening, "Sweetie," and head inspection meant I would never ignore his calls or punish him for his unavoidable wickedness. He had goodness somewhere deep inside of him, a goodness

I would nurture and domesticate. Only me. I would walk the coast of California a million times to be able to feel his breath on my neck, his bite on my back. To be near this man.

And. That. Was. It.

I had known him two months.

*I wrap you around all of my thoughts,
boy ur my temporary high.*

— Beyoncé

February 2005

J ack never gave me his phone number. Never wrote it on my trembling hand. Never took my phone from my trembling hand, while saying something stupid (flirty in his mind). The clicking sound from his fingers meant I would read what he typed for days, as if he'd handwritten his name and phone number on 2005's version of a cocktail napkin.

Why hadn't he called? It had been almost three months since I was inspired by the Snoop Dogg song to leave my number on his cabinet, jotted on a corner torn from a *Simpson's* calendar. Rather than wait, I did what any impatient puppy-love-injected girl would do: I asked my brother for his number.

February 8

I zipped around Williams-Sonoma in Beverly Hills, picking out admittedly chic and useful Valentine's gifts for Mrs. Z's staff. Including me. *Do you know how unnatural it is to write your own bonus checks, or give yourself a Williams-Sonoma juicer?*

While on the phone with St. Croix talking about our upcoming weekend, I heard a beep.

805-817-9091.

I couldn't think of anyone I wanted to talk to with an 805 area code, so I focused on the eight minutes I had left to complete the errand. I hung up with St. Croix and held down the 1 key.

His adult, yet high-pitched voice hit my eardrum.

"Hey, Sweetheart, how are you?" he asked, sounding like a talk radio DJ. My hands went sweaty, my stomach shifted inside of me, and my breath stopped.

"Just wanted to see how your winter was going. Hope all is well. See ya around."

Derangements began to dominate me. I hit the 1 key again. And again.

———

St. Croix, my best friend from UCSB, was in town.

Uma Thurman mixed with one of the moms/hot actresses from a Lifetime movie —that was Croix: beachy, cool, a surf beauty with a lawyer's mind. After munching on cheese, crackers, cornichon, and downing prerequisite cocktails making our blue eyes bluer, we perfumed our way from my front door to Vermont Avenue.

"Ugh, I miss you, Dearheart!" We wrapped around one another as the streetlight changed to green on the way to the Dresden. We were at the same height only because I strapped on another three inches.

Los Feliz was a big "T." I lived in the vertical, at the bottom where the movie theatre, Fred 62, House of Pies, the post office, and the Dresden lived. Across the top of the "T," the horizontal part, was

Griffith Park, the Greek Theatre, and steep hills of daydreamable homes regally built on the cartoonishly, twisted streets. Up there, Hockney paintings inspired city planners. Millionaires, nouveau and old, lived in the horizontal part.

"I know! I miss you!" This was the summary of our entire night's conversation while we ran around Los Feliz in taxi or on foot, "crawling" to the Dresden, Drawing Room, Good Luck Bar, The Room, Tiki-Ti, Akbar, and Ye Rustic. We partied well as a unit, but Croix wasn't merely a girl to say, *Here try this,* about our margaritas of mango and persimmon.

It began seven years ago at college in Santa Barbara, in our psych statistics class. After I stopped being annoyed with her (every girl I was friends with annoyed me at first) she was, and still is, forcing the enjoyment out of me, while thriving underneath the flawless and warm skin of wonderfulness and invulnerability. Exams, hangovers, parties, bloody butcheries with/by boys, and graduation swelled to lovelier levels because she suffered or laughed through them with me. Her truth, wisdom and love balanced my anxiety, irresponsibility and love. St. Croix was Christmas morning in girlfriend form.

The penultimate stop for our night in LA was Daddy's on Vine (my favorite bar in LA). The ultimate was swinging over again to the Dres for a Blood and Sand. The ice-cold slushy concoction found only at the Dresden powered the end of the night with brain freezing bravery.

While we perfumed our way back to my house, I yelled, "Watch this!"

St. Croix lit a cigarette as I crossed Franklin to my block and threw my purse on the small squares of grass separating the sidewalk from my apartment. While climbing aboard the retired-for-the-night bulldozer parked in front of my bungalow, I kicked off my shoes.

"Ma'am, get down." *Where'd he come from?*

LAPD Officer X was matter of fact, but cool. No nonsense.

With a flashlight in my face, he reached for my hand, helping me down.

"January! Come on, I have your purse." Croix waved to the cop, and we walked inside. I fell on the couch and she walked into the kitchen: "I'm getting water."

I grabbed my phone and snuck into the bathroom.

"Hey, it's January. January Estlin. How are you?"

Jack crept in somewhere between the Blood and Sand and the bulldozer.

"Yeah, I got your message. My winter is going just fine. In fact, it's the best winter yet! I'm, um, I'm here with St. Croix and we're having the time of our lives, in LA, I'm not sure when I'll be—"

Beep.

"Croix, voicemail!" I walked out to find her sprawled on the couch. "It was his voicemail!" I wailed and threw myself on the floor.

"Here, drink this. So, what is it about this guy? I can tell you from experience—

B2—your success rate with drunken dialing—you *still* drunken dial?"

"I know." I rubbed 15-hour-old mascara from my dry eyes and remembered how she once compared B2 to body odor:

"He's here, he ain't going anywhere, and it sucks, but I'll live with it."

Especially when I hauled her over to his house at the beach at 2:30 a.m., more than once, in SB.

"I don't know, but ever since I met him, I am … I'm fucking nuts."

"You do so much better when you're not insane over them. When?"

"Four months ago, maybe?" *Please.* The exact date. Where the hands were on the clock above the front door of the Shack. What song played through the speakers and how many glasses of wine Accountant drank while beaming under the recessed lighting as she hugged Childless Brad Pitt. All of it formed the structure of my anthem.

"So you didn't learn anything from B2?"

"Ugh, maybe? Maybe not?"

"Oof, you almost want the drama, I think." She noticed my pathology but would never know her friend was the loneliest girl she knew.

I continued, "But he's kind of an ass, and he's in Pismo. It'll end up being nothing."

The next morning we mourned the massacre of the night before over pancakes at House of Pies.

"Jack."

"Jack, ugh. I called him. Why did I fucking call him?" We smelled of 30 cocktails. Croix leaned her head over the table and sipped her coffee without lifting her cup.

"It doesn't matter." I yawned as I said it.

The pies encased in glass behind her, with their earwax crusts, stole my eyes away for a second.

"You always say that. Why?"

Eighty percent of my waking thoughts focused on what other people thought of me. I couldn't move past why. It didn't matter, because I delivered the feelings in tidy packages of "didn't matter." My avoidance of vulnerability backfired because it opened up the possibility everyone could realize how weak and desperate I was. I had been this way since childhood. Twenty years ago, when my dad took me to the beach or San Luis Obispo to shop for clothes, I told him (because it felt good to hurt him) "Dad, you're embarrassing me!"

He strode next to me in his cowboy boots and dust-covered clothes, stopping at every boutique. After lunch we'd go to a department store, too. He rode tractors all day, tended to piles of manure and worms, and lifted boulders. On that day he cleared his schedule because he wanted to buy something pretty for his little girl. No one cared as we walked down the street; passers-by probably thought I was cute and him ruggedly handsome, with Jack Nicholson eyebrows. Most likely, they thought nothing at all.

He took my tiny ivory hand into his smoked and rough one,

"Well, Jan, I'm not embarrassed of you—one day you'll look back on it and you'll feel bad you said that to me." I was a fucking uncool brat from the Gold Coast of Chicago. What did he expect? At my worst, he was at his best.

What did Croix expect? My focus went from the pies to my Diet Coke. *Man, I want pie.* "I don't know why. I just don't think it does. I'm fucked, you know this. I'm fucked up."

She asked me to describe him.

Afterward, Croix winced, her mouth stretched out to its corners, still not getting my taste in guys. I would've bet money she wanted to punish me, to discipline the girl who needed a good mommy-style castigation. In my head, I asked the sticky syrup jug if it was possible I wasn't honest with anyone, about anything.

With her lips on the coffee cup's rim, she announced, "I'm calling him Short Fat Fuck."

March 2005

Confused about men and love, I hoped Jack/Short Fat Fuck would tend to and restructure my inexperience and incompetence with serious intimacy. Mix it up. Surprise me. Fairytale my ass into submission. *Pick me. Want me.*

Any previous vowing, planning, and effort was eating pickled beets in a white wedding dress: chaos-seeking and fucking stupid. Being myself led to reclusiveness. Men wanted soft spoken, gentle, don't talk, don't fidget beyond a smile, and don't make any sudden gestures with the exception of kissing or taking a mint from a purse. Lip-gloss touch ups? Excuse yourself and visit the restroom. Be someone else, but be original. Be the name voyeurs and comrades speak of in secret and of whom their wives are envious. Don't let them know your demons and skeletons. No honesty is welcomed here—and please, be as smoking hot and war-causing as possible. Equally as tectonic as the previous rule: He doesn't want you intoxicated. No falling off of barstools.

I almost always fell off of barstools.

Come on, Jack. Teach me. *I'm ready.* Develop me into the woman voyeurs and comrades speak of in secret. Acknowledge I'm not just fuckable, but worthy of dating. Jack would change me, implode me, then rebuild circumstances, and arrange for new natures and nurtures. I imagined these were issues a late teen would tackle, not a twenty-something, privileged, blonde writer.

April 15, 2005

I replayed *Entourage* episodes in my head when Elvis started to sound like the freeway under my tires. Before Turtle drove Vince and the Escalade into the sunset, I resigned myself to two things: I would start making friends in Pismo Beach, and I would let Jack come to me.

I lost count of how many times I walked through the Shack's doors. The entrance I tore through with angst, purpose, and vodka already on my breath could be confused with an H&R Block office in a strip mall. From the parking lot next door, I walked past the prison railing/cement wall saturated in light by the "Barbecue!" sign. Slouched against it were a surfer with a dog, a surfer on a bike, a surfer smoking, and a surfer with a surfboard. By 10 o'clock, the moat around the bar bulged with a U-shaped river of thirsty roisters.

He saw me, and his head jerked—not in my direction. Ketel One kicked pride and degradation's ass, so I ordered a drink and faked a conversation with Gimlet Geezer and his cane. Coquettishness in place, I finished my order with the three words I had commanded, yelled, and batted eyelashes for at least 10 times a week: "Three limes, please." On a Post-It from the stack I kept in my purse I reviewed my goals and made updates: *Need to make new friends, find my old ones, and befriend the new bartender.*

Bartender was the second bartender I encountered at the Shack. I called him No Name. He figured if anyone knew his real name, we'd all be shouting it non-stop:

No Name! What do you have on tap? Do you have beer nuts?
No Name, can I get change for the pool table/jukebox?
No Name! It's too strong. Can you add more [insert mixer here]?
No Name! It's too weak. Can you add more [insert booze here]?

I respected the theory, but I wanted to know his name *just in case.*

Jack made his way over to me, hoping to slide by. He wore the same sort of outfit from his wardrobe, but this time a bit more 9-to-5; not a T-shirt, but a black button down, still Billabong. I touched the hem.

"What's up?" It was never a question in these sorts of circumstances.

"My ex is here." Jack nodded at No Name.

"Who?"

He head-pointed to a less-chic, shorter, female version of himself.

"Really? She was just looking at me. What did you say to her?"

"All I said was you were really mad at me. You need to learn chill, Sweetheart.

She cuts my hair now, that's all."

"Why am I getting the serial killer stalker glare?" He laughed and went for my boobs.

"I don't know, Sweetie, how've you been?"

"Fab! What are you drinking? Wait, why am I mad at you?"

How dare he parade the night's conquest so close to me while I sensed pre-sex flirting in my ear and along my whole left side? Why did I automatically assume he hooked up with mini-SFF/Hairdresser? He put his hands in his pockets and the moment to bounce approached with intensity. There wasn't a firm no or a firm yes. Ambivalence: a word he didn't know the meaning of but a state I would survive for, pucker at, and allow to delineate years. We'd languish from the term: originating in Germany, early 20th century. Jack would never understand how he emancipated its power to me.

Midnight

"January, he's a *player*," Childless Brad Pitt advised after he and Accountant sat down next to me. I called them one drink after "Wait, why am I mad at you?"

Accountant refreshed my brother and his surroundings. She was a natural choice: witty, down to earth, and un-moody/stable. A single mom who exhibited a poised charm I admired. I envisioned "Will you marry me?" in their futures while she wrapped her arm around

CBP's waist, his face leaning into hers. I needed a boy like her. I nodded and thought of Jack's dark and simple bedroom. A bedroom of a teenage boy from a middle-class family.

"He knows everyone." Accountant ordered chili fries and two Heinekens.

"So?"

"He doesn't have girlfriends."

"I don't want to be his girlfriend." *Lie.* "And what does that have to do with him knowing everyone?"

The eyewitness testimony of Jack being a player was a boring bullet point on a list of cautionary tales excised from my body last October. I defined him as the equivalent of running through sprinklers in the summer of '88 and as earth shattering as a sky dive off of the Sears Tower. Un-boring. I knew what would happen—what *was* happening—and I couldn't stop myself from making a mess on the floor in front of me. He left, walking by in a confident stride with the mini-SFF/Hairdresser, a red bandana on her red head.

"You're an asshole." My un-chilled words followed them.

"Jan." My brother inhaled behind me. I didn't care. I was used to familial disappointments. Short Fat Fuck turned his head to me, also expressing disappointment.

I need to steer clear from this one, he thought.

I remembered this because it was the last thing I remembered. Waking up face down on filthy carpet, hair pasted to my cheeks, I cringed at another lost chance to depict the smart, not psychotic, nonjudgmental, passionate yet kind and aware January. I wiped the crust from the corners of my mouth with a finger and thumb. The next 18 hours busied themselves with dizziness, lightheadedness, and junk food bingeing. He had to see me. Meet me. The loving, warm, and unintentional asshole/vodka spitting girl he kept running into was down there somewhere. The stakes grew taller.

No Name = Jeff.

You know she's waiting,
Just anticipating,
For things that she'll never possess,
But while she's there waiting, without them,
Try a little tenderness.
You won't regret it.
Some girls they don't forget it.
Love is their only happiness.

— Otis Redding

April 16

I called Jack the next afternoon to get his version. "I didn't realize you're an angry drunk."

"On occasion, but I wish I wasn't." I sat on my steps, head tilted toward Vermont Avenue, ever curious about the gurdwara across the street. The distraction lessened the awkwardness of the phone call.

"All angry drunks don't set out to be belligerent. It happens; no worries."

"What are you up to—?"

"I gotta go, Babe. Got a call."

Ugh. I remembered what Childless Brad Pitt told me. *Player.*

I shuddered at my lack of control as I turned into a tumbleweed. A flat, gray mind trip I met only in my dreams, and if written in my journal, decreased the far-awayness, making it too realistic and crushing. Invaded, I swallowed my urges (to call or drive to Pismo *right then*) with orange juice at breakfast, smoked them outside of the Dresden, and shook my head at their strain in evening traffic. My molecules were nourished with the hopes we *would* end up together. I had no proof we would, but I had no proof we wouldn't. I thought like a priest prays. The assumptions (and fantasies) were the hallmark, the final destination of that gray mind trip, forcing me on the ride no matter how much I resisted. I didn't *have to* write anything down. The gray mind trip already passed through the important places: cunt, lips, brain, hands, knees. Not my heart. *Why, that's ridiculous.*

Two weeks later

Again on my stoop, we chatted under a balmy LA night, where I stood and sat and stood and sat three deep into cloudless vodka/sodas, Parliaments in my lap, one in my mouth, a lighter to its end, and still curious about the Sikh temple across the street. We talked about how much I hated him. I didn't. Did I assure him I didn't? I couldn't remember the conversation. Afterward, a flood of loneliness injected into me by way of a punchy needle—powerful, at breakneck speed, and longer than I'd anticipated. A pattern formed: Jack rejected me, then called. I didn't live in Pismo, so my gut seesawed between yin and yang. What was his end game? Was he sweet, vindictive, or as stupid as I was?

June 15, 2005

"Hey, wanna hang out tonight?"

Drunk enough to forget the last two months—and the last time we spoke—I called him.

"You in town?" His tone foretold my future, or at least the next 12 hours of it.

"Yep." I covered the phone. *Jack.*

"Who?"

"Short Fat Fuck."

"Oooh … ." She fell over laughing. *"SFF! SFF! SFF!"* Her chants echoed a group of guys holding red cups around a keg while shouting orders to newbies. *Chug. Chug. Chug.*

"Nice, how are you?"

"I'm good," I replied while giving her the "Shhh" signal.

'I'm greeeeaaaat, Short Fat Fuck!" Croix mocked me, her voice quieting with each word. She emptied her wineglass of a Calcareous blush, preparing herself for a sweet summer of every varietal of rosé. I nudged her off of the barstool.

In Berkeley on business, St. Croix met me halfway in Pismo. After dinner and two hours of *Oh nos!* and *Oh reallys?*, we coddled martinis and slammed shots of Patrón (in addition to the glasses of rosé).

"Where are you?" he asked, pleased. *Love it.*

"Old V. You?"

"Just back from the Italix show. What's going on there?"

"They played in SLO? Not much." My smile widened each time I answered a question.

"What time are you done?" He coughed.

"Midnight? I need to get home early." *Bigger.*

"Ah. Early, huh? Well, cruise over if you're not too tired."

"You sure? Ok, yeah, cool." *Bigger.*

I set my phone on the sticky oak wood edge. I'd never been so anticipatorily giddy. *Disco.*

June 16, 12:30 a.m.

We migrated north to a different bar, Obsidian, in San Luis. A 10-foot-by-10-foot framed definition of obsidian covered one of the walls: A black rock similar to glass.

"We should've started here," St. Croix declared over the techno/hip-hoppy music and chic décor you'd find in a house in the Hollywood Hills house or a Manhattan apartment. We surveyed the 20 or so people in the place before we mined our clutches for gum. Blind obsession would be a phrase to describe my feelings on purses (and ice buckets and stemware). Blind because I had no idea where the taste or aspiration originated.

"Dead, no?"

"It's Tuesday."

Mine: a gold knit lamé that folded over like a business-sized envelope. Hers: black croc in the same shape as her upper arm. A muted cocktail waitress took our order.

"I can't believe this place is in San Luis." My phone rang.

"Are you coming over? If you are, I'll leave the door unlocked."

I snapped a finger at St. Croix. *We need to go.*

She nodded and shot Jack Daniels.

"Cool, I should be down there around 1."

"Ok. Just come on in, Sweetie. I'll leave the porch light on for you."

Favorite. Phrase. Ever.

Midnight

"He'll like you more if you make him wait." Wisps of whiskey hit my nose. According to Croix, it was important I kept Jack waiting.

"This is how it works. It will work."

"What will work?" I switched to water after his call.

"Act like you don't care, and he'll be your boyfriend." False hopes of honey poured over her statement. I took her advice.

1:13 a.m.

"On your way?"

"Yes, definitely. So sorry for keeping you up."

"He'll want you more. Make him wait." Same statement, more Jack Daniels.

2:05 a.m.

I scurried up the walkway toward the porch light and checked my phone. He saw me through a window and opened the door.

"I didn't think you were going to show. Wow, you look good, Sweetie."

A soft, loose, unbuttoned-down-to-my-freckle black blouse, white jeans, and natural looking blonde, highlighted hair, blown out: beachy and flowing around my neck, shoulders, and upper and middle back. I left St. Croix snoring on her bed in our room at the hotel.

"Thank you." I hugged him and noticed he had slippers on.

He pinched my waist and glanced at the freckle—a single, dark brown, hard-to-miss-dot an inch lower than my boobs in the center of my chest. It was the only one of its kind on my body.

"It's good to see you. How's the book coming? Are you dating anyone these days?" We walked past the skateboards.

Dating? Even if I were, I wouldn't admit it.

After a few minutes of *South Park*, we kissed—soft and low at first. A heated, aphotic river overcame me; fed me. All I wanted was him inside of me, where the blood came from, where he fit best.

He spread over me. We spent the next 60 minutes moving, moaning, pushing, lunging, demanding and begging, and reaching for bewilderment. He finished, his tongue superb, never slowing down or dwelling in one tender spot. He worked hard, studying me, completing a task he had no intention of half-assing. Jack clutched my thighs as I clutched the pillow. Inhumanity twisted my mouth, stretching it wider than ever. I screamed, but nothing came out. I pulled his comforter over my face and I came. We were the same person. I sensed where he would go, and I found him. He shook and thrust as I begged for no ending. He kissed my torso before he sprang up like a gymnast and buried his cock so far up inside of me it ploughed through my stomach and out through my back. He bit my neck, shoulders, thighs, butt—and I bit his. From my point of view, I wanted two things: for him to hold my gaze, and to sit up. The latter went unfulfilled as I straddled him.

Deeper, deeper, harder, harder. I wished for the position in the movies. He didn't respond, and I wondered if it was a *Pretty Woman* no kissing on the lips thing. Was he embarrassed because he was uncoordinated and physically incapable? My punishment for being late and for causing a tightness in his chest and neck during the last eight months of his life? After finishing all over my chest and tits (he liked this part) we laughed, our heads falling back on the pillows. The shifting began as he snored.

My face in his chest.

His arm under my head.

My back to him, his arm around my waist, then my hips.

His eyelashes brushed my cheek.

I didn't sleep.

I nudged him to have sex all over again, the second time fiercer—and calmer—but equally orgasmic. I didn't want to be anywhere else in the world: not in Cabo or Fiji, not at a party in Beachwood Canyon, not in some foolish version of an upcoming heaven, and not with any other boy I thought I loved. Every second bonded me to him as I forged a new plan, something to draw him in further, bridging me to him irrevocably.

When morning traffic traveled outside of his window, he gently cupped his hand over my ear.

"What are you doing?" I whispered into the sheets.

"I was blocking out traffic so you wouldn't wake up."

Not knowing what to say, I said nothing. Maybe saying nothing was sexy. I attached that final moment on every single leaf on the branch of a true love I developed. The newly recorded, unspoken, symbiotic, and totally freaking awesome beginnings of an un-love affair.

At brunch, later that day ...

Bacon slices stuck out of our Bloody Marys like burnt, mini-drowning Popeye arms. The viscid liquid appetizers commiserated our miseries. Me: depressed/happy after sex-with-boy-I-love; her: hung over. St. Croix and I continued our conversation from the House of Pies morning in LA.

"I'm stoked I saw him last night, this morning, I don't know ... that's it: I don't know what happens next, that's what kills me. He doesn't seem like he wants me to stay, for coffee, whatever, you know? I mean you're here but ... he knows you're here."

Croix leaned forward and took a sip from her straw, then ran her fingers through her hair: cat-eye blonde, looking fresh and clean even after 10 hours of her face planted into a pillow.

"Jan, I'm sorry, I am. I don't know what else to tell you. You don't live up here. I mean, at least you saw him. That's something, right?"

"Maybe I'm bipolar. Up one minute, totally devastated the next." I felt the breeze behind my ears on the outdoor patio of Lido.

"Is that the one where you dress like a slut, and blame everyone else for your problems?"

I shook my head. "Histrionic." I wanted to vomit. Poop, too.

Poopandvomitpoopandvomitpoopandvomit. Does she think I have histrionic personality disorder?

"I was thinking only bipolar, god, but now I'm thinking I have borderline too, and histrionic. Damn. It's a fucking Madonna album."

She spit up some of her drink and laughed. "What is borderline again?"

"Mood swings, recklessness, unstable relationships, distorted self image, boredom ... there's more." *Fuck*, I thought to myself. *Borderline.*

Croix continued, "I so don't see where you're getting borderline from. But bipolar is mania and depression: highs and lows, right?" I nodded and looked at a couple a few tables away, reading newspapers with their heads down. "It's been awhile since Santa Barbara," she said, then laughed the laugh of someone with a useless degree, same as me.

How could I not have a mood/personality disorder after meeting SFF?

I want you to want me.
I need you to need me.
I'd love you to love me.

— Cheap Trick

July 11, 2005

"Listen, quickly, I need, today, 25 *Vogue* magazines, vintage, from the 1960s and '70s for a good friend of mine from Spain. *Spanish Vogue* if you can find it."

As "Mr. and Mrs. Z's assistant/house-girl/estate manager/empire supporter," I spent half the week, Wednesday through Friday, searching for the *Vogues*. And not just in 90210. In 91402 (Panorama City), 90015 (downtown LA), 90024 (Westwood), and 90247 (Gardena). Surprisingly, or maybe not, it wasn't impossible to locate stores selling old issues of magazines. I called, I visited, and comic-book-store-looking guys unlocked their front doors with burglar bars and let me loose in their warehouses.

"*Spanish Vogues?*"

"Yes. *American Vogue* will be fine, but *Spanish Vogue* would be best. And there is a certain one I want. I will call you later about it. I have it written down. I need them wrapped and brought to me, and then you can deliver them. I'll let you know the address when I call you about that other *Vogue* I need."

After I climbed ladders, stretched up to rusty metal shelving eight-feet-high, waited while the magazines were wrapped and ribboned, Mrs. Z called. *Three hours later.* Finally, on Friday at 5 p.m., I headed to *Spanish Vogue*'s house in Bel Air. *Friday at 5 p.m.* I wanted to collapse where I stood, beneath a parking meter on Melrose. Friday at 5 p.m. was a first margarita at El Coyote in West Hollywood. It was not merging onto the 405 Freeway.

———

I had a fascination with assholes. Emotional "fuckwits." Meeting and hunting Jack was inexplicable, and not so inexplicable. It could be compared to past illustrations:

B1, B2, and B3.

When I favored someone or something, I acted like a lunatic. A child with no game. My own self-fulfilling prophecy, and private sinkhole of unrequited love. I relied on gut sensors: *Yes. No. Possibly.* I was a yes girl, never wavering, immune to healthy attractions and smarter than all the rest. I thought the man I chose to love, to follow, and pursue had to be right one, because *I thought he was.*

Fuckwits breakdown:

B1: High school. A caveman with intelligence. Rich, popular, possibly a psychopathic rapist. We barely dated, and, after sex a few times, he became an unattainable football quarterback who drove a truck too fancy for a 17-year-old. I wasn't a cheerleader, graceful, or easily victimized.

B2: UCSB. Engineered by supermodel scientists. A fall-over good-looking California surfer from La Jolla, Yale alum, co-worker, and friend. I hopped out of bed with a manufactured zest for yachting and a curling iron plugged in on workdays at the yacht club.

Ends of shifts meant time alone. After fellow employees clocked out, we were left behind to laugh and bump into each other on our way to happy hour, hard cider pints toasting away the sexual tension. *Or accelerating it?* Coronas for him. Evenings, before I went clubbing with St. Croix, Dave Matthews Band's reverb drove and crushed temptations sharper and deeper down the back of my neck.

Pints also toasted away the distances between B2's and my noses and chins, but at whatever beachside pub we sat in, the "almosts" and melting sunscreen were more erotic then a potential love scene. At least that's what I told myself as I pined and whined for B2 around Santa Barbara—a pursuit as satisfying and successful as tiling my kitchen counters by myself. Rather than him becoming my college sweetheart, leading to 40 years of surfing trips to Bali and perfect babies, I sentenced myself to five years of phalanxed Saturday nights and death-defying Sunday mornings. My gut gossiped into my ear how pointless my efforts were, but I ignored it. While I waited, I watched B2 date everyone around me. We remained friends. St. Croix hated him.

"He's a dork." She moaned as we ate lobster bisque and cleansed our palates (without knowing at the time we were doing so) with margaritas after a sailing class we took as an elective our senior year.

"I like dorks." I fretted as I made her laugh with my clown frown face.

I guess B2 wasn't technically a "B," but he was critical to the "January is a lunatic/has no game" theory.

Moving to LA after UCSB lit a glamorous kindle. My targets for love changed and improved. *Actually, I don't know if either is true.*

B3: Los Angeles. A Frank Lloyd Wright-ish home in Los Feliz (impressive at 26 years old). Possible descendant of the DuPonts. If he had asked me to eat fire, I would have. While I marveled at B3's work-of-art penis, he read E. E. Cummings to me in bed. His style swayed in directions I appreciated, from "Nightlife Hipster B3" (blazer, collar up, and aged brown suede boots) to regular "every day Hipster B3" (Pumas/belt/not-yet-coined-as skinny jeans).

One night last year, after a few hours with Model, Huge Rock Star, and Ketel One (*three limes, please*) at Daddy's bar, I tracked B3 down at his house. At 3 a.m. we were talking and comparing Thursday nights when the house alarm interrupted us at DEFCON 1. Shouting and thuds of all sizes and volumes followed.

"Holy fuck," he rasped and pulled me into him by my arm, his hand over my mouth.

Holyshitholyshitholyshit.

After listening to a human hurricane for three minutes, I was convinced I'd be shot, execution style, by the fourth minute.

Execution style? WTF? Why did this pop into my head?

Damn you, Unsolved Mystery reenactments.

Oddly enough—and luckily—they didn't race up the stairs hoping to find a closeted safe full of cash and jewelry. Instead, they took everything *downstairs*, including original artwork by Obey (Shepard Fairey) and Banksy, and tens of thousands of dollars of music and recording equipment B3 had invested in, for his "band."

A couple of weeks later on a date at 4100 (a bar) he confessed (while laughing) he'd organized the "heist" at his house for the insurance money. This asshole, who actually used the word *heist*, was proud of his crime, and didn't find anything immoral about scarring me for life. Well, not life. Maybe six months.

As with B1 and B2, my exterior didn't matter, nor did the kind of person I seemed to be in the first hour of meeting me. With every "Three limes, please" I uttered, I suffocated and sunk chances. Layering my drinking with a wild, intermittent, and widely agreed upon (from friends, family, and innocent victims) chemical imbalance and a melodramatic temperament, I was unaware I would be single forever. Unaware because I was too drunk or hung over. Or I didn't care. I didn't know what a first date was, but I knew the names of my children with each of the B's. All of these men—and Jack too—had one thing in common: They all provided an energetic and artificial safeness. Alive, agog, and moronic. I wish I knew about the "guys want to pursue you" theory 10 years earlier.

Thanks, Childless Brad Pitt.

August 2, 2005

Jack was the definitive fuckwit.

I recited the sex in between the sex. *Two-month-old sex*. Each impulsion, remark, glance, and epileptic orgasm cued a redefinition. Shaking my head to a *"come here"* finger, reaching to an astral distance for more wasn't a talent I possessed. When would the normal reactions to or about this person arrive at my front door before I mixed a cocktail and skimmed through my phone for his number? Was I capable? Could I have this? Did I deserve this? A coupling not of cheating and lies, but of maturity, adventure, roaming beaches in the South Pacific, hand in hand, exploring each other, and the world. Brains and hands tattooed with billets-doux.

Too many questions and fantastical planning for a tryst 10-months-old.

I couldn't escape the effects of all of the wallowing and visualizations. I hated myself on Monday, Wednesday, and Friday. Tuesdays and Thursday, I despised us both. Weekends (not all) lasted an unpredictable two days while muzzy and puckered in a Pismo Beach bar. Weeks in between I spent disinfecting the stains of Jack with those Hollywood hipster boys.

August 2005's "move the fuck on" clues would be aplenty, but one in particular stuck out. After a drive-by of his store, I witnessed his staff and friends standing around a smoky barbecue, pokers and corncobs in hand. I clicked "save as your desktop background" on a non-tavern Jack. I hoped I'd see him later in said tavern, and when I did, I relayed the clue to Short Fat Fuck's roommate, Liver.

"You should've stopped by for a wiener!" Liver yelled in my ear.

Jack said nothing and turned his head; he wanted nothing to do with me. Liver was a young Danny DeVito: a Betty Forded roly-poly with dark hair and a beer belly at 23.

August 6
Journal entry

I called him. No response. We hadn't communicated since the St. Croix/Obsidian /cupped-my-ear night. Edging toward panic, I left my dad's house and drove less than two miles to the beach. Ocean to my left, small piles of sand dunes to my right, a camping area behind trees, and a boardwalk in between. I ran, then jogged toward the pier, avoiding the other runners' eyes and their dogs' panting. Sometimes in the water. Every 20 feet I ran perpendicular from the ocean, up to the tinier dunes with skirts of seaweed. I arrived at the boardwalk to litter and sketchy camping families. Such a good workout.

August 2

Back in LA, when I didn't hear from Jack, I exchanged utopias for serious justifying.

In the car. Is he thinking about me?

At work. Is he fantasizing about the sex?

It was official: I hated liking someone.

Was this like, or love? What the hell was going on?

Ten months. For almost a year, I had referred to a strict syllabus of tears, stress, sex, smoking, and alcohol.

After three calls, Jack returned, crossing off the flirtatious, apologetic, kind, and complimentary checkmarks. I understood these virtues one at a time, but as a unit I didn't comprehend. I couldn't electrocute myself out of a sort of mystified shock.

When I favored someone or something, I acted like a lunatic. A child with no game.

I told him I'd call him later, and when I did, he didn't answer. Maybe I did possess some "game." I didn't want game. I wanted a fucking boyfriend. I wanted Jack to be my boyfriend.

I didn't leave a message.

"If I don't want to talk to you, I won't answer," he once warned.

I hate this shit. Agonized for a week? No. The depressive flu lasted three weeks. His quest for convenience meant he would call, eventually. I suckled "eventually" like a cold popsicle slaying a hangover.

In bed that night, I deleted him from my phone. I would re-enter it, always in new ways: full name, initials, first name and last initial, or simply Short Fat Fuck. When "SFF" appeared on the screen, I felt terrible. Not worthy and spiteful. If I wanted him so much, why did I treat him like shit in my mind, or with friends? A loosened moral gauge and insecurities shined bright as my two faces held on to whatever they could—whomever's hands hung low enough when walking past me.

We hooked up a couple of weekends later.

August 21, 2005

Sex bereavement was the new hangover, without the nausea and vomit. While in the shower on day one, I smiled at the soreness in my thighs while the water rinsed soap off of my face. Day two: The hickey on my neck and tiger-paw shoulder scratches in the mirror told me I wanted him to inflict more sex injuries. By day three, paradise zipped up its suitcase.

I'm not sad, and I am not in love with this moron I just had sex with.

I couldn't love or be attracted to or habituated by this person who had his penis inside of me. His tongue taking me over, kissing me hard and astonishing, the sex outmaneuvering the kissing. After two weeks, I went into another shock. Bleakness was next. Why sadness and not a Lewis and Clark spirit for what was ahead? I wasn't attracted to Jack; I was a rogue wave not giving a shit in which direction I spawned disaster. I asked CBP if he'd seen him. He hadn't. He must've been making love, on a date, falling in love, or getting married while I sucked down In-n-Out French fries driving home from work. Why did I care?

August 28

Back in Pismo. I took a half a Xanax and told myself I didn't want to go out. The weekend turned into a Neapolitan of anxiety, panic—and later—doom. I wasn't expecting a call, or to see him, so I typed at my dad's kitchen table, wondering why I wasn't in Los Feliz. I sent an essay to *Cosmo* and continued to work on my novel, *Anti-Fat*.

If he doesn't call me, then I know it's over. I'm so sick of myself. My first superhero power would be to change my personality.

Anytime now, Xanax.

September 6, 2005

Days from turning 28 and bored. So bored I wanted to call the bad-for-me B's and eat pizza. Thank God the only carbs in my house, Saltines, were covered in ants. I slurped Crystal Lite through a straw and wrote. Sent 100 letters to 100 agents and received three responses. Two of them said they stopped reading after the first 50 pages. Rewrote 50 pages.

Later, outside on my front stoop, I watched all of the normal, fulfilled people drive up my street through the palm trees to The White Stripes show at the Greek. As I tapped my cigarette on the trunk of the ashtray—an old ceramic elephant I made in high school—I kicked myself for not buying tickets before they sold out.

I wasn't a pack-a-day smoker (maybe 1/4 of a pack a day) but—like ice buckets and purses—interesting ashtrays caught my eye. Too wounded from weekends in Pismo, I didn't hunt for a cool mid-century piece to flick ashes into and adore like a pet.

Short Fat Fuck/Jack. Jack White. Huh, never thought of that before.

Jack White will probably drive down this street.

September 10

My "birthday weekend" was fun. Did it take place at one of the 20 bars within walking distance of my house in Los Feliz? Of course not. It began and ended at the Shack. On my Central Coast pub-crawl, I downed too many free shots at a decent replication of a London pub called Bankhead in San Luis, and kissed a guy who reminded me of Ryan Gosling. I visited a new destination to be paralytic in: Moondoggies, a honkytonk a few blocks from *Jack's house*.

Wary, Jack stood in a group, again with mini-SFF (I baptized her Hairtrix) and Liver before he slogged over, hands in pockets.

"Hey, Sweetie, you havin' fun?"

"Yeah, but I'd be having more fun if you asked me over." Rotating my stool toward him, my knee wedged between his legs.

"I can't tonight; I have people in town." He scanned the crowd milling about the pool table and karaoke catalog. Soccer moms, cowboys, and eight surprisingly adept-at-singing Asians.

"Are you dating her?" *Hairtrix.*

"What? No, we're friends. I told you that." He inched away.

"Whatever."

He stopped, turned, and waved, ever the sexual politician.

"Need another?" A familiar face behind the bar, No Name, poured Ketel One like my favorite uncle would. I didn't have to stray far from him when I threw the dart hard and missed the bull's eye by a hair. For some strange reason, this prompted a need for citrus, so I ordered a Greyhound and inquired about No Name's second bartending job at Moondoggies. My sobriety gashed again, uncontrollable eyeballs rotated to Hairtrix as she spat something into his ear. They glanced at me. I waved Jack over, and he walked through the crowd without hesitation.

"Dude, what is *up* with your friends?"

"Oh, they know about you, but we weren't talking about you." *Lie.*

I took a clumsy sip and amped up the haplessness.

"So, you can't see me tonight *why*? It's my birthday weekend." I chewed on my red cocktail straw.

"I told you; it's just not a good weekend for me, I have a lot of friends in from out of town, ok? I need to get back over there, Sweetie. Have fun tonight." He backed up.

All of my genres writhed with pain (mind, twat, perfume, vodka) because Jack knew nothing about me, or his power over me. He diffused the situation just enough for a boy who didn't give a shit.

This is just sex, you silly bird. I'll have you when I want you.

I'll call you when I want. Don't make any sudden movements.

"You're an asshole." His mouth unlatched.

"Sweetie, I didn't mean to upset you," he said, facing me.

No Name and dirty highball glasses worked hard behind me.

"Right, I don't understand you. I mean, when it's convenient for you, I get to come over?"

"Sweetie."

I stepped within a few inches of his nose.

"You. Are. An *asshole*." He looked perplexed and regretful. Did I not know another way to insult this person? I disappointed myself as a writer.

"You're a bitch." He did a half nod and walked off.

Something other than an orgasm ricocheted from him.

September 12, 2005

Like NFL clockwork, I called him on Sunday before I drove back to LA. Voicemail after a few rings: I frowned to no one and started my speech.

I wanted to tell you how sorry I am for my behavior last night. I'm not that crazy, but I'm that crazy after drinking. This is not an excuse, but I wanted you to know that I'm not a lunatic trying to mess with your head. This is also not an excuse for my behavior, but the reason I am like that around you, the only reason is … I am seriously … in love with you… In love with you. I don't know what that means, and I'm sure I have never told anyone that before. But I am, and I did.

Ok, I have to go now and drink a birthday mimosa. Again, I'm in love with you and that is the reason I was acting like a fool.

What I didn't say.

If you're satisfied with your message, hang up, or press … .

A chance is all I want. This, I did say. I think.
He called back a few days later.
"I'm so sorry."
After lecturing me on the dangers of overdoing it at a bar, he finished with,
"I'll call you, ok, Sweetie?"
He didn't.

———

"I'm sorry, but I told you," Childless Brad Pitt reminded me on the phone.
Was he a sociopath?
No conscience? No problem!
Manipulator; cold-heart; laissez-faire attitude; confidence man: His idiosyncrasies dampened my cerebrum while shackling Jack and his penis to whatever dignity I had left. I wanted to *be* him.
Two weeks later I walked into Moondoggies. I called him, and he showed up 20 minutes later.
"Truce." He wasn't asking.
My veins varicose with firewater, "Sure."
Definitely a sociopath.

October 23, 2005
Pismo Beach High School reunion. Was I excited about seeing old friends? Bending over shoulders at out-of-focus pictures of babies and balding husbands? Showing off the fact that I no longer

wore a flannel and beanie from 7 a.m. to 3 p.m.? Of course not. It meant a weekend of drinking, tripping, and laughing with all of my old girl-friends and guy-friends. And another weekend in Pismo meant increased Jack pursuance.

The real anniversary was the one-year that had passed since meeting Jack, not the 10 years since I left Pismo for college. By Sunday night, when I hadn't heard from him, I still hadn't left for LA and didn't want to. Hadn't we made headway? My headache from the reunion and three after parties told me I lingered because of him. *No* meant try harder. The last 12 months turned into one big waiting room, where I hoped for an appointment with Jack. When I did see him, there wasn't enough time to discuss where we—he—stood.

In the waiting room, I had ample time to wish and theorize. *Let's start with dinner.* We avoided obsessions if we started with dinner—or would have a year ago. I'd get to know him before the sex, learning he chewed with his mouth open or asked to split the check. If well mannered and generous during the meal (him, not me) he would initiate sex at the proper coupling hour of 9 p.m. Not 3 a.m. If this true-to-life (a total fantasy in mine) scenario would've happened, I wouldn't have glamorized him, treating SFF how I did now; like my own little Jack White. I would marry Jack White in a heartbeat and have five of his kids. Then again, Jack White might be a total fucking tool whose house smells like (and is decorated like) a thrift store. How would I know unless I went on a date with him first?

I drove back to LA and cried. The original tears chastened and corrected. Jack (not Jack White, the other Jack) took over blank pages, my dreams and awakenings, my pee, vomit, and psyche. I loved him inside of me, literally.

November 2005

Still nothing, and I needed answers.

It's been five months since we had sex. The fact that SFF clung to me like suffocating, southern, inland humidity defined me mentally. Five months? Basically a one-night stand delivered me to this point. I couldn't say his name without kicking something or throwing something on the floor of my apartment: tissue boxes, cans of soup, or clothes yanked from my closet. Unbreakable stuff. In the least, I deserved angry Jack sex. *Fuck the shit out of me. Fuck out whatever rotted inside of me, and solve my world.* If I couldn't get answers, I would take his bed. Desperation birthed new humiliations and settlements.

I called him.

"I've been very good. Stopped drinking."

December 2005

We hung out while I was his "good girl."

A few weeks later, in bed, I bit off more gristle.

"What are we doing? Is this going anywhere? I, I … I can't take this."

"Bring it down from a 10 to a 2."

"Bring what down?" I asked.

"Your craziness, Sweetie." He cuddled me closer.

"It's passion. I'm a passionate person." I wore one of his shirts with "I'm a drinker with a surfing problem" stitched on the front in yellow. I stopped listening, preoccupied with how I smelled, or if my stomach was sucked in enough. It was too ridiculous to admit how much of a genius I was at not doing anything at the exact time I was supposed to.

"Well, be a good girl and let's see."

———

Three weeks in the life of that T-shirt:

Week 1: Scrutinized, fantasized him buying it and wearing it, smelled it.

Week 2: Wore it.

Week 3: Rolled it up with a used tampon inside of it and threw it out.

Almost another month, and nothing. No calls.

My compulsions didn't ruin his day, or night, or weeks. Sociopaths weren't ruined. My behavior bit off the arms of occasional nights surrounded by his friends, but the carnage would settle on the ground around him while he drank his one Southern Comfort and Coke.

Obviously, no longer his "good girl," I lost chunks of entire days worrying that he'd found a new ingénue with proportional, nymph-pink nipples to suck on.

January 2006

I was dating. Breaking up, too.

"You're stunning," B4, a producer who lived two blocks away, stammered out loud as we swanned out of the Drawing Room to smoke, me pedaling the beach cruiser he rode to our second date: an inebrious one.

Our first date took place down the street from where we first met, in another bar, Good Luck, which sat on the corner of Hillhurst and Sunset. If Good Luck was Ella Fitzgerald, the Drawing Room was Britney Spears. Not the 1999, school girl, full-of-promise Britney, but the shaved head, a flash of naked pussy exiting a limo Britney. My love for the Drawing Room was unconditional for solacing reasons. A lug nut could've made the Shack comparisons.

In the parking lot, I rode his bike around in 3-inch black/gold platforms before he stopped the bike, lodged it between his legs, and tried to kiss me. A guy advanced several miles with a word like "stunning."

Ok, his face is cute. He's got a style about him.

I'd be seen with him in public, right? I'd be seen with him sober, right?

After he kissed me, I diagnosed him as needing all of his teeth yanked out and replaced with Altoids. I would drive him and while I waited for him in his dentist's office I'd fold and crease the old-timey mustache instructions on the tissue paper from the Altoid can. My dream was only half-fulfilled. A few minutes later at the bar I busied myself with the Altoid activity mustache, after forcing two mints on him.

Damn you, lack of light bulbs in the Drawing Room.

January 7

His two-bedroom apartment carved up the deal like a Thanksgiving Day turkey. Under track lighting and one of those late 1980s white floor lamps with an upside down triangle on top, a tragedy years old hit me, hard, in the throat. How could a successful guy live like this?

I need a woman to help me fix up/clean my shit. Oh god, me?

Papers: boring papers, too—not stacks of scripts, a printout of a novel, or even magazines, but tax papers and whatever other papers are notoriously dull. Years of 'em. File cabinets (why the hell weren't the boring tax papers in the file cabinets?) and a table jutted against the kitchen countertop (not a sexy table with a trunk-shaped chandelier of hanging crystals overhead, but a folding one from Costco with a litter box underneath). I think I saw (and smelled) an aging, obese TV and three computer monitors, a lack of curtains, and an allergy to Lysol. I didn't have to go into the bathroom to confirm *pubic* (Is that not the grossest word in the dictionary?) hair, flakes of skin in its corners and footprints of black grime on its tub's floor.

I strategized.

After the apartment horror show, I drove B4 to pick up his Mercedes downtown; it was a cool old one that ran on diesel, stinking up the air from its tailpipe. The 2 p.m. winter sun radiated through my windshield as I smelled his pits and breath when he opened my car door. What he wore: crusty flannel, cords, and a brown, grayish hoodie underneath.

4 p.m.

"Wanna grab dinner?" I actually wanted to. I needed a night out, a meal at a good restaurant, of which LA provided so many. A night when I thought back,

I can't remember the sounds, food, or the conversation, but I counted the streetlamps outside of the restaurant (four) and the 50-foot palm trees lining the street for blocks, like the Queen's foot guards. Most streets in LA have the foot guard palm trees.

The dinner date at AOC wasn't entirely wretched, but it didn't stop me from meeting eyes with a guy passing by with his dog on 3rd Street.

He leaned in for a hug and a kiss at my door. The sequel of the bottomless, rancid odor left my mouth and nose after 10 seconds.

"I'm getting up at five to work out. Talk soon?"

———

After B4, a revolving door, a grocery list, a to-do list of non-fuckwit LA guys appeared on my caller ID and kept me busy and stimulated. B5 was a sweet drummer from Ben Harper's band. B5 also included: a scientologist, Tobey Maguire's PA, the son of one of the members of the band Chicago, a Capitol Records studio exec/producer, and a tinier-than-me engineer from Paris. B5 was also 10 years of one night stands after stumbly Hollywood nights and a Dolly Grip who never shut up about the latest "show" he worked on where Cameron Diaz's acne *was really that bad* and John Travolta *was really that gay.*

In LA, there are a lot of people and a shit ton of stuff to do. This made dating curious and casual. A guy I made out with on my couch Wednesday night could be my wingman by the next weekend. A few times I found myself in Dolly Grip's old white, OJ Bronco heading to dinner, and a few hours later we'd be surrounded by a dozen more in La Poubelle. Then Paris would walk into La Poubelle, since that's where all of the Frenchies in LA ended up. It was never awkward: As much as they all wanted me, they enjoyed a break. I didn't miss the cozy moments, aside from sex. LA had the Chateau Marmont, orange signs with arrows tacked to lamp posts pointing to movie shoots, makeup artists who had agents, and two weeks of road closures thanks to the frigging Academy Awards. We didn't have grudges and yearnings, third-date sex, promise rings, or first squeezes next to valet stands. Besides B3 there weren't many noteworthy LA squeezes or yearnings. My Friday and Saturday nights didn't end at 10:30 p.m. with leftovers from Madeo's and a kiss under my porch light. LA was home by 2:30 a.m. and eating Madeo's filet mignon over my sink, drunk. That was dating in LA.

January 10

Jack converted into a celebrity. "Fame" was an ordinary concept to me.

Hanging out with famous actors, the latest hot shit directors, or musicians, carries a distinct vibe in LA. Living in Los Feliz, a neighborhood kissing Hollywood on its cheek, I saw celebs at concerts, movies, shopping, at lunch, or in the Drawing Room every week. Nodding to them in lines while they paid for groceries at Gelson's was expected and became the norm. Nights, drinks, peeks, and conversations were supernatural, provocative, easier, and distinctive when I sat next to B-List Actor, Huge Rock Star, and Model at Daddy's.

When I wasn't with Jack, I visualized what his day consisted of, as I did with my celeb acquaintances. What was he cooking for dinner? How was he on the phone with a Verizon customer service rep? Had he ever shouted at one so violently they hung up and used the conversation in training videos of how to handle irate customers? Or was he *so cool all of the time*, purring "Sweetie" to guys and gals in Calcutta?

With addiction came withdrawal and a double screw. Not being with SFF/Jack for a month put me into an unappreciated, heavier phase. During my LA interactions, I never trusted or cared an exceeding amount. Jack became a solution to a math problem I struggled to solve for 10 years: *When will I fall in love?* A surprise since I left Pismo for this exact reason. I wanted a metropolis romance, not an unknown California farm/beach town romance. In Phase 1 of life (age 24-30) I had the option to settle down, get married, and have kids. If I didn't meet my prospective goals in Phase 1, I'd move on, alone until Phase 2 (age 31-38). I'd focus on my career until my mid to late 30s, then try again for a family. I'd be better prepared.

Did he love me and couldn't admit it? He snuck into a pocket—a minute in a day in a month in a year—and he portrayed himself (or

I portrayed him) as the answer to the second question I had been asking for most of my adult life: *Who will I fall in love with?* Failing at math and logic during withdrawals and obsessing, my thinking lapsed.

The 45-minute drive to work over a 7-mile stretch of Sunset reinforced my desire to write full time without distractions—and without the Zs. Instead of working on *Anti-Fat*, networking, attending writers' conferences, I spent 50 hours a week in Beverly Hills reasoning with passive aggressive housekeepers; pointing out dead plants to gardeners; driving a Cadillac to the car wash; picking up clothes, shoes, and purses from Saks; and paying credit card bills. Not minimum payments. It was always the "total balance due," which amounted to the cost of a Ford Focus or a BMW, depending on the time of year.

Oh yeah—and delivering (giftwrapped for $150) vintage *Spanish Vogues* to an $11 million house.

I was eager to make a change.

January 18, 2006, 8 a.m.

Light from the windows glinted on the fruit in bowls on the counters and on the lemon trees near the tennis court, spotlighting and cultivating a hundred grand worth of landscaping around the prewar pool and spa and 25 grand in patio furniture. Patio furniture had another name in that stratum (modular, rattan, loungers, crater, hanging day chair, daybed, exterior lawn furnishings) but it was still patio furniture. The black-cushioned sun rockers and sectionals surrounded the gardens designed after Mrs. Z saw Laura Bush giving a tour of the White House grounds on TV.

I smelled a Lalique candle and Lestoiled hardwood.

"January, I need a charger like this one," she said, pointing to the marble counter and a large, black, Versace dinner plate. Chanel and cigarette smoke didn't distract me as I scribbled with one of the hundred black rollerballs I kept in my office in the pool house. "It is a *charger*, you know that right? Not a dinner plate. There is a difference."

"January, I need—*today*—Lucite (it was always Lucite) book-stands. Three of them. Call Taschen; they'll have them."

"January, my niece is coming back from Thailand. Can you pick her up at the airport?" Mrs. Z's auburn hair extensions hung in her face below a boy waving a blow dryer. I couldn't hear her in the fishbowl kitchen.

"January, can you get my mom lubricant?"

"January, I need you to go to Bed Bath & Beyond today and replace all of my hangers with the ones they sell. Spanish Vogue told me about them. They're maaarvelous." Everything was always *"Maaarvelous."*

At Bed Bath & Beyond, I wouldn't receive a call back from her for a half an hour. I took five pictures, trying to get the front of the box and actual hanger in close ups and in focus. Still no response. I left with five boxes (50 hangers per box).

"January, these are all wrong. Next time why don't you call me?"

I stood over her as she squatted—French-tipped toenails, Juicy sweatsuit—studying the black, velvet hangers of all shapes and sizes. All 5-foot-7 of her, spray-tanned, typical Beverly Hills body from Pilates and Bikram yoga, plus climbing stairs she installed on a hill behind the tennis court. They were modeled after the ones in Santa Monica; she sent me there for precise measurements.

Did you know all stairs have the same measurements?

When I presented the stair diagram, "Trainer already went there."

Back to the hangers,

"You didn't call me."

"I did call you," I replied.

"Then email me. Pictures are best. Put all of this away; I can't stand this mess."

This was a daily occurrence: rushing because she wanted every-thing "Right this minute." When I had an hour left to complete actual business, I'd miss something—a stamp on a credit card bill, an email sent without her consent, or a spray tan appointment never booked. She wasn't a yeller, but she was rude (like, make you reevaluate humanity, rude) intimidating, and condescending while she accepted my mistake and I drug myself through the next-to-nearly-impossible task.

In Pismo I could finish *Anti-Fat*, afford to live at the beach, write at a local paper, reconnect with old friends, possibly lose the Z-produced ulcer, and bolt cut the links of a constant traffic jam. Traffic? Really? One con for LA and 100 for Pismo. What about what was waiting for me right outside of my bungalow door? After I swallowed the Excedrin, I could walk outside to Vermont and into history, glamorous nightlife, and culture. Forever delve into my carefully chosen lifestyle.

I didn't consider the cons for Pismo because the pros sang out like hummingbirds. Dying ones. Soon to be stuffed for some old man's dreadful "summer spent in his garage" project. *Illusioned. Demented. Futile. Sad.*

"January, can you pick up my toe fungus medicine?"

You will do foolish things. But do them with enthusiasm.

— Sidonie-Gabrielle Colette

February 2006

I hadn't seen Jack in a few months, so I sent my brother into his store for recon: a modish (keeping with his modish theme) record store with imports, framed concert T-shirts from the '60s and '70s on the wall, and three aisles of impressive vinyl. I labeled it the baby Amoeba, at a prime location on the boardwalk in Avila Beach, another beach town a mile or so from Pismo.

"He asked about you."

"Yeah, and."

"He says he's never met anyone like you."

"What do you mean? What does *that* mean?"

"I don't know. That's what he said." Childless Brad Pitt was annoyed. He'd been annoyed since October.

"Yeah, this isn't good. Never met anyone like me? What am I, an alien? I don't get himmmm. I don't get this shit. I'm calling him."

"Look, he's into you. He's into it. Take it slow and see what happens."

"What do you think?" I asked him about moving back. I told myself and my brother I wouldn't be moving to Pismo Beach for love. I wanted a change. *Ugh.*

"Don't overanalyze it. Move back. Do it. Hell yeah." My brother believed me or believed in me. I didn't know which.

Everything without him was muddled and at the moment, in the boring dip of the ride at Six Flags. When I wasn't dreaming of him, I bought his music, wore clothes I hoped he would like, saw movies he would see, and huffed his cologne at the men's fragrance counter at Macy's. I cut out a "Surf Peru" article I found in the *LA Times.* I told him when Interpol would be on Jimmy Kimmel. The robotic black-haired boys in suits time-traveled me back to Jack's room with their textured melodies and wonderfully stirring, poetic, puzzling lyrics. *They're kinda brilliant. Under normal circumstances, I'd be stalking them.* Their music meant more to me now. If we were on good terms, I was uplifted, coasting through stop signs, and singing along. When we weren't talking, I buried their CDs in my glove box under napkins, sunglasses, and my insurance card, fearful I might pull over on the side of the road to cry after track 1.

When I wasn't with him, I found ways to be.

February 7

"I'm 170 miles away. It isn't France."

"It's just a rule I have. I've passed up a lot of great women because of it. Sorry, Sweetie."

Jack making it clear to me he wouldn't date a girl who lives far away, was a hint. I never caught on to hints. It was a test, another Eminem-like *"rap, tap, tap,"* but this time on my windowed unconscious, petitioning the gods of influence to do the right thing, the mature thing. The sane thing. The window was darkened. Nothing could penetrate it. Statements hit me with the opposite stick. I wanted his life and to be a part of it. He exuded a mindless, easygoing lifestyle with young roommates, porn-worthy sex, ample play time, surfboards, skateboard ramps, townie chicks, and barbecues. I had peeping Toms, 17 freeways, and decay. LA didn't captivate anymore, whether created on a film set in my head or in reality as hot as the sun. Los Angeles, and unfortunately my beloved Los Feliz, was done. He was up *there* walking on the beach with a girl, in front of a sunset, at the same bars three nights a week, and never in traffic for more than five minutes. The unfair differences made me jealous, unhappy, and decisive. Confused, but clearheaded. The opposite stick was having the opposite effect; I wasn't strong enough to fight it off.

My untamable personality had been unleashed, and it brushed my hair with losses and crying, like riffs on guitar strings. How could I miss something, desire something I never had in the first place? I missed him when I was in LA. Minutes, hours, bedtime fantasies magnetized a needful permanence in Pismo. What did I miss? I didn't know him: not his middle name, not his favorite meal, not one truth from his consciousness. I was a "booty call" nightmare.

When I finally saw Jack, whether at a bar or at his front door, I never stopped being uneasy. With each rejection and torture, I couldn't grow and learn. I was stuck. He's *passed up a lot of great women*: another lodestone of a statement keeping me near him.

Sweetie, you want me because you can't have me.

There weren't fairytales with Jack; he wouldn't allow them.

No meant try harder.

February 15

I left him a voicemail a few days ago.

"Hey! What's up? Just calling to check in and see how things are going. I'm in town—hang out maybe?"

A week passed. He didn't call back. It was simple boy psychology. When it was light, he called. When he associated me with heavy pressure, he didn't.

My brother apprised me of an update.

"He's dating a girl who works at Walmart." *Heavy.*

I knew nothing, and Walmart knew everything. She experienced him, kissed him, barbecued with him; he hugged, smiled, invited, and requited. Haste, determination, and sheer madness ate me for dinner, but a few remaining cells focused on the past, my mistakes, and the burgeoning assemblage of unfinished novellas stacked higher and higher in a library I opened in 2004. Stories with no end, no verdict—yet.

Would a girlfriend really change anything? I had a gut feeling it would not. I wasn't numb to the news—just invincible. I would get him. Have him. Be with him. And that was worth me moving to Pismo. I wanted a simpler life, but when had I ever known simpler? I knew complicated. I knew mess. I knew chaos, and I had the best-kept, secret, passed-down recipes.

Questions fueled action.

Why didn't we hang out during the day?

Why didn't I push for this in the beginning?

Why hadn't I ridden in his car?

Oh my god, these questions are hilarious if they weren't so pathetic.

Forming most of the answers (guesses) wasn't difficult because they were obvious, and I wasn't a dipshit. What I didn't have were the actual facts from the one boy who could provide them. The lack of these simple experiences and feedback seemed unfair, and deserved a penalty. When I was with him, it was never enough. *Jack will help me; make all of this go away.* LA was my France, and those 170 miles prevented me from the having the one thing in my life I wanted. I plucked up everything else before him like a potato chip—in all arenas, not only love, never giving it a thought; taking whatever I wanted, whenever I wanted. My reach was limitless.

But, no! I'm moving to write.

I had known him 16 months.

February 10

"You're moving?"

Mrs. Z sat behind her Tiffany desk set: ink blotter, an uncanny infinity calendar that worked in any year, penholder, desk pad, and paperweight. The White House garden framed her through the windows like a trifold poster board.

Can I get fresh coffee, please?

Sometimes she smoked up there. The desk set was never used.

"I'm finishing my book." I hovered over one of two Louis XVI (XIV?) chairs, fearing I'd be the one who'd split the priceless antique in two with my ass. Mrs. Z's tired and watery eyes opened wide; she wore too much makeup, and never the right shade.

"A book? A book about us?" My eyes fixated on the 25-foot-high ceiling and the catwalk outside of the door of her office, encircling the entire third floor.

March 10, 2006

Jack had a girlfriend, and I packed.

Family photos were filed between fresh *LA Times* and old *Esquires*. I shoved clothes and purses in duffle bags and shoes in black trash bags. I didn't know where my jewelry or toiletries were. My new apartment was an all-white, one-bedroom in the Pismo hills. Similar to Beverly Hills, Pismo Beach had two distinct residential areas: hills and flats. Flats meant dumpier, smaller apartments where, nine times a year, I'd be trapped on my block because of whatever festival or parade was roaring through downtown that weekend. The hills had homes, a park, and a school. It was a smaller-scale Hollywood hills: A few rows of horizontal, narrow, and poorly paved streets housed million-dollar contemporary, white and taupe structures jutting out of bedrock.

It rained. A lot. Every trip I made, it rained harder as I drove north on the 101—to a slight off-ramp after 170 miles, up a couple of ski-lift-steep streets—unpacked each load from my car, and walked up my stairs. I liked privacy, so I picked the hills: an *affordable* place in the hills. My street was high up, at least a 45-degree grade from the ocean. When a tsunami hit the pacific, prepared and cautious folks perched themselves in their cars and campers in front of my house *just in case.*

There was a third option for living in Pismo: beachfront/cliffside. Living against and above the rock faces. No. 3 had no relevance since I wasn't a millionaire.

On the last trip, I delicately packed the last of my ice buckets and stemware in bubble wrap and left everything else on the curb. For $10, a guy working security on a film shoot loaded my mattress and box spring into the Mercedes.

"It's not going to fit." He mumbled in the rain.

Mr. and Mrs. Z offered the boxy-looking Mercedes pathetic excuse for an SUV, instead of the Escalade. Days before, everyone I loved made the fake frown/cry face when they stopped by to help pack a box.

"Why are you doing this?" Friend after friend and neighbor after neighbor asked the same question. I had a speech memorized:

"I have to know, either way. It may be a huge fuck up, but at least I'll find out whether this is for real or if it's an infatuation. I'm not happy, I'm sick of Z, sick of LA. I love Los Feliz, but I can't do it anymore. I need to finish *Anti-Fat*. I can't concentrate here."

Actors, assistants, chefs, impersonators, music execs, club promoters—the people who loved me in LA agreed—it was rough at times. Film reels, velvet ropes, nightlife, nostalgia. The pancake makeup and walks down Vermont Avenue would never mask what made up LA: brutal bravura. After six years, the brutal came into focus first. They also noticed I mentioned writing *last*.

"I can't believe I'm not going to walk by your open door and see you writing on your couch." Model, my neighbor and Huge Rock Star's girlfriend, gazed at and hugged me with her laundry basket in tow. Model didn't look like a runway model; she looked like a runway model backstage before the fashion show, getting her lipstick painted on and hair teased—striking even while doing chores.

"Yeah, I wrote until you dragged me out to Thai food, then the bars. Do you want this back?" I pointed to the dark wood table she gave me a few years ago.

"And you're not moving just for Short Fat Fuck, right?"

I left the table with the box spring on the curb. It didn't fit.

Reckless.
Stuck.
Batshit crazy.
Limitless.
Weak.
Alone.
Alienating
When would I be a noun and not a horde of tragic adjectives?

April 2, 2006

In Pismo, another soldier of my life fell into place: work.

In the Zs' kitchen (I commuted to the Zs from Pismo until the "new girl was trained properly") an Editor from a local magazine in San Luis called after I sent 12 emails over six months, asking him to call me.

"I think I found something for you." I set down the Zs' checkbook, opened the door to the pool house, and walked in the direction of a pergola. I snapped off a tulip.

The magazine blended elements of *Spin*, *Travel and Leisure*, and *Entertainment Weekly*.

"You'd be great for this thing. We need someone who knows the arts, the scene, someone who can dig up unique events, find scoops, and report on the edgier, under the radar goings-on." I hadn't lived on the Central Coast in 10 years, and when I did live there, I went to house parties and bonfires, not art exhibits and film festivals.

"Cultures editor, what do you think?"

Editor wouldn't know or care; he knew immersion and navigating a county's art scene wasn't rocket science. What I didn't realize was that I packed my bags and quit Mr. and Mrs. Z—and LA—for a job paying a fraction of my Z salary.

May 14, 2006

In May, I acclimated. One week before, I finished training my replacement at the Zs and now? I watched the sand move east, dusting the streets with sugary almond powder. I didn't notice the daily fog while I jogged through light drizzles running down my Adidas-hooded head. In my new mornings, I ran south of Pismo, away from the pier and toward the more desolate sandbanks, a constant hum from engines echoing on the sand. Monster trucks, jeeps, four wheelers, and dune buggies hauled ass in a whipped-metal frenzy through the broad and bumpy hills, across the faithful overturn of the strand. The blanched dunes Pismo was famous for were a religion for the drivers and passengers from the valley: not San Fernando, but Fresno. Or is it Bakersfield? Pismo was cooler weather, strawberry farms, trees, fireworks, clam chowder, surf culture, and Mexican food eaten while sitting on the edges of white plastic chairs.

May 16

Another soldier of my life: Jack.

I touched base.

Hang?

No. Way too much drama.

Ok, the Jack soldier not yet in place.

Even with the understanding of Walmart, it didn't stop me from taking advantage of any window opening I could. In the meantime I grew into Spanish moss on its sill. A slutty dipsomaniac with no business handling the intricate mechanics of a window.

May 21 / a week later

"Too much drama" didn't stop him forever; he came over, never acknowledging the fact I moved to Pismo. Walmart lived oblivious in another division of his life.

Through "back doors" (always mine) Jack and I had a lot of sex.

On this particular morning, I woke up with a message on my phone:

"You were drunk and rude."

Opening my eyes to 7 a.m. and a junior hangover, I found signs he'd been in my bed: his smell on my hands, a used condom, and bedding on the floor waiting to be washed since 1 a.m. A shower was a miracle, and I smelled of citrus at work.

"You look happy."

I turned around from my Mac, dozens of emails, and an article on a woodcut artist.

"What did you do last night?" Disheveled Lady Reporter blew on a small 7-Eleven coffee cup, emphasized "you," and irritated me with the cackle of someone who really didn't want to know. Lady Reporter would be my first co-worker/friend.

"Later. Lunch?"

"K."

She picked up a reporter's notebook and her and her haircut wandered outside. It was red, brown, and a few inches longer than a boy cut. Her skin was properly moisturized, making her look younger than 47, but her eyes gave away her age. There was a sadness, too, only seen after her third glass of red. She was feisty, and maybe that's why we became fast friends. Kindhearted with the attention span of a flea. No, not a flea—a flea's baby. A baby flea. Her hearty laugh annoyed some, but resonated through the magazine's underground office.

May 25

Requiring more than a voicemail, and after my Blackberry died that morning, I sat in my old bedroom at my dad's, my hand shaking and sweating into the landline while Jack re-punished me, but gently confided I would be daft not to throw liquor an evil eye and spit hard. The *Winnie the Pooh* wallpaper from 1979 still covered the aged walls and did a good job at peeling away. Was he telling me this because he cared? Would sober January be his girlfriend? Was he dumping Walmart? Would we still hook up?

"I hope we're cool."

"I don't know, Sweetheart. Can you be nice?"

"Yes, I'm so sorry."

"You're a different person when you drink."

"I know. I'm sorry. You're always in the wake of my craziness."

"You said I bring it out in you, the craziness. If that's—"

"It's not your fault. It's just very hard to act normal around you, and even harder when I'm drunk.

"So, we shouldn't hang out if you've been drinking."

I didn't know if he was asking or telling but I had no response to give.

These little five minute, ten minute convos did nothing but draw me in closer. Half-mouth smiles, winks, "Hey, Babes," and comings over became my gold stars. He placed the stickers on my cheek when I behaved and obeyed the three-cocktail limit. Other nights, he required I wear dunce caps in corners, near the electrical cords plugged into neon beer signs. Where I ended up was up to me. The later the hour, the more trouble I caused. I was placed in corners closer to midnight. He gave me my gold stars earlier, like 10 p.m. A to F, back up to A, down to an F, and euphorically back up to A. Stopping altogether didn't occur to me; it was just a quick respite to ride something else, always returning for more.

The times befit nature. Peaks, valleys, ebbs of the tides, and all of the usual mountain and sea metaphors applied to Jack and what we allowed and gave into. Clear signals meant we'd hook up. Less clear or lost ones meant no contact for a few weeks. Causes? Many. Me sober. Me drunk. Him glimpsing my face or tits when he wasn't getting what he wanted with Walmart. Excitement. Boredom.

Along with brushing my teeth and applying moisturizer with SPF 50, my daily regimen included "agonizing overs": agonizing over what Jack thought, heard, felt, forgot, and forgave. As my behavior barometer, he dictated the way I spoke to friends over happy hour at the beach in my wayfarer sunglasses; how I walked down a public street, cell phone at my ear; or how I bellied up to the first bar of the night. I acted (acted out); he reprimanded. He scolded. He taught. He corrected. He rewarded. He denied me, disconnected me, and towed me in after wanting me again. It was a college course in mannerisms and traits: cues, tones, and subtle hints—again, hints I didn't understand or take at face value. Drunk and rude? Of course I was. I learned Jack possessed a sociopathic forgiveness trait; one that I saw right before I took quick late night trips to joy by way of his dick. This trait came with a hideous Halloween mask disguising his "I don't want to stop fucking January" mantra. Being wanted, being loved:

There was no distinction. I wanted him to be my father. He *was* my father.

I considered something else: Did I like this person I tried so hard to acquire, or was I feeding a starvation? I fucking hated him and his horseshit piped in through the luckless distillery where I didn't occasionally arrive, but rather lived. If I was sober all of the time, I wouldn't have had the chance to ransack and crave this person.

I asked "why" about everything concerning him, but the most important "why" wasn't considered. A history lesson lasting 500 years wouldn't clarify why it was Jack who fattened my grips and gripped me. Whats, hows, and whens could decapitate a giant beast. "Why" didn't matter. Even liking him didn't matter—not yet. I'd never move on, love again, or finish anything because I'd be too busy tallying up the whys, reciting them to Childless Brad Pitt, or whomever was still at my side, before dying over them.

Wait, spinsterhood, then death.

Anyone who wanted a "why" from me didn't know me at all. I should've asked "why" *and* answered myself, or demanded an answer. Running, plotting, and "loving" became my summer exercise routine. The routine punched me in the face, leaving a permanent scar as a grateful Jack exscinded me from his daily routine. But his habitual battleship sweetness embraced me after dark.

The conclusion? Jack was a habit I needed to break. Break into a million fucking pieces.

And it was only May.

Dis·remember
transitive verb

1. FORGET

June 3, 2006

The incest began.

I started to seduce Jack's friends. It went both ways: His friends gravitated toward me as well. My inner minx emerged via sex, dating, or a comingling of the two. I blamed the breeding on him. Since I couldn't have Jack in the way I wanted, the problems I faced were his fault—not mine, or the inebriants I consumed like a blue whale. These phantom provocations led me to the top:

Jack's business partner, B7.

He and Jack opened their record store a few years prior; B7 was a renowned surfer. During a long overdue stalking trip to their store, Jack breezed past me.

Every time I see him, why does he have to smell like a minty, ice-cold mojito?

"You look good, Sweetheart." I wore a quarter length sleeved black cargo shirt, boyfriend jeans (before they were called boyfriend jeans: baggy with the hems rolled up a bit) and espadrille wedges with black ribbons going all sorts of ways around my ankles. He kissed me on the cheek. I wanted to wink, but I was the worst winker in the history of modern eye movements. I half-pecked back and told him I stopped drinking.

"That's great, Sweetheart. I'm happy for you."

"So, what's going on around here?" I searched my purse for my phone.

"Hey, you owe me three more boxes of the posters!" he yelled behind me at a truck parked at the curb between his store and the beach.

"Sorry, Sweetie, I need to talk to this guy."

I took a few steps and dialed Childless Brad Pitt.

"I'm in Pismo right now. Meet up?" I stared at a wall of local bands' music, but saw Jack's face.

"You're technically not in Pismo." I turned and faced the voice at the cash register: decent looking, mohawk, 30ish.

Ignoring him, I flipped through '50s-era vinyl. I didn't hear my brother's response.

June 7

The imagined scenario of B7 and I running into Jack and Walmart made my chest thump as I put on my makeup. On our first date, we hit up the Shack and played pool. After the Shack, through an alley I never knew existed, we arrived at an exotic/tropical meth biker bar where I got gut-fucked on mai tais, elevated my ping pong game (loved they had ping pong) and threw up in the bathroom.

I took a deep, "get it together" breath and unlocked the stall door. I wrenched the revolting, ancient fabric towel apparatus: the stained sheet cranked out like dough from a pasta maker. When I finished making the *ick* face, a short, methed-out chick with dry, crackly cuticles shoved a silver business-card-sized camera into my hands.

"Here, figure this out."

My two-week stint as a sober person? Over.

Afterward we sat on my porch swing facing the beach. We didn't have much to say to one another, so I studied his head. His mohawk wasn't of the 1980s London variety. The straight, stylized, dark blonde hair rose an inch or two from his head and was a normal color. It was kinda hot.

"I asked him for your phone number after you left that day. At the store." B7 took a swig of his beer.

"Really?"

After date two, he leaped off of me and started getting dressed. *What are you doing? Get back here.*

The analyzing lasted five minutes; B7 didn't consume me. I pretended a shorter shell of a body lay next to mine. Tall, mohawked, and monotone, I suspected he wanted to be a kind, reactive suitor, but Pismo's surf mentality, and his possible mother issues cheered on his 90-percent jackass/10-percent robot performance. While he put on his clothes in the dark, I studied his silence, then the ceiling.

"I had a good time, did you?" I asked, wondering whether I should get up or not.

"What? A good time, sure." He tied his shoe. "I'll call you."

His hairstyle symbolized our liaison: short-lived. Our month (if that) of dates took place exclusively at bars.

June 10

B7 overlapped with B8.

B8 became my first Pismo boyfriend.

Childless Brad Pitt introduced me and B8, a neo-hippie, at the Shack. In a hazy high-school flashback, I remembered he was one of those curious male cheerleaders: short, tan, zero fat, and zero charm. The mini-Abercrombie model flirted, and we discussed the best breaks and agreed on the best burritos in Pismo while standing in front of the glow of the jukebox, minimizing our facial flaws.

Jukebox knows all of my secrets.

B8 rambled. "Isn't it crazy that back in the 1920s, '30s, even up to the '70s, there's no fat people, not in photos or TV. I don't remember any at least. I mean maybe there were big women on farms pushin' out babies, but nothing like the McDonald's fat ones today."

He must be high.

Zorro's for burritos, and I don't remember what surf breaks because I didn't give a shit. He surfed, but everyone in Pismo surfed.

June 15

"I need to stretch." Outside an Italian restaurant, a few blocks from the Shack, I lit a cigarette as B8 reached down to his toes. On a break from the double date with my brother and Accountant, I watched B8's arms hang at his shins. I breathed in the sycamore air. The quiet, except for the whooshes and hums from the 101, made his stretching awkward. I felt sorry for him. He reminded me of someone who made me sad once. I couldn't remember who.

June 18, 2006

"I sleep naked," B8 informed me, slipping under the sheets and propping his tan head up with a fist.

We did a DVD night at his apartment. He lived with his grandmother—or above her, rather—in a wood-paneled studio a mile outside of Pismo. Before the movie and ice cream, he asked me to stay.

"Alright." My shoes mesmerized and my eyes danced, sending cryptic messages to myself, adding an internal drama and a pop quiz.

What the fuck is happening? I don't know him that well.

Is this going somewhere rapey?

"We're watching a movie, right?"

"Yeah." He let out a *January, I'm not Ted Bundy* snort. "Do you care?"

"No," I assured him. I missed Jack as I reached for a pillow. Everything, everyone else, was *effort*. But who else was I going to lean into, and eventually kiss, while watching *Mr. and Mrs. Smith*? I took off my jeans and wiggled into bed with hesitation. *Right side—my usual at Jack's.* I didn't anticipate sex during a pre-Brangelina film. Original and challenging he was *not* under the sheets. I hated myself when the stoned, relaxed surfer stare masked his face, not caring either way. Poured from a jar, his voice sounded like the salted caramel sauce I made at Christmas time: in pace and thickness. But not in taste.

June 20

An 805 number popped up on my phone as I climbed into bed after a Ziggy Marley show in Avila, exhausted, sunburnt, and sober.

"Hey, this is Stalker, B8's friend."

I sat up straight. "Ok. What?" *Who is this?*

"He told me he's dating a girl from LA, so I guess we're broken up now. I wanted to talk to you though."

"How did you get my number?" I was too tired to deal with this psycho. What was she talking about, broken up?

"I found it on his phone, you kn—"

"Ok. So, you still see each other?" I rested my hands in my lap, putting a light dent in the duvet.

"Yeah, we do. So, you live here now?"

"I do."

"Where?"

"San Luis." *Lie.* "Did you want something? Is everything ok?"

The noises I heard in the background irritated me further. I wasn't her main focus even though *she* called *me.*

"Just wanted to introduce myself, in case we ever run into each other. I'm sure we will."

"Ok, what's your name again?

"Stalker."

"I—thank you?"

I realized no matter who the man was, I was a jealous lover. A week or so after she called me, Stalker showed up while we lay in bed watching TV.

B8 yelled and sent her away. Rolling my lips together, eyebrows moving into my hairline, I thought and comprehended. If she was compelled enough to stop by, then something more was happening. Did they talk? Hang out? She was kind of pretty, her hair perfectly straight and flowing, as she reluctantly ran down the stairs.

Tires. Keys. Eggs. Piss. Acid. What would she do to my car?

June 28

"He's annoying, and too environmental, and I think he's cheating."

"Environmental?"

"Cutting up old beach towels to use as toilet paper. *Beach towels*, CBP."

My brother seemed bored with my complaining. "Cheating? With who?"

"The Stalker chick; she's so friggin' weird, but there's definitely something there. It's just *off*. She calls; she shows up; they're still friends I think. I don't get it."

Childless Brad Pitt and I reached for a rib tip; he shook his head and laughed.

"What?"

"You know she's his cousin, right?"

Margaritas at the Shack scumbled the past few months away on a Sunday night, my favorite day of the week at the Shack: low key, relationship opportunities, and as much Bob Marley and Frank Sinatra as I wanted.

I popped forward, and salt stuck to the corners of my mouth.

"I'm not kidding." He laughed again.

If he isn't kidding, why is he laughing?

"Not kidding? What are you talking about? What the fu—cousins? Who?" I wiped froth from my chin.

Childless Brad Pitt drained his water and crunched down on some ice. His viewpoint was that we could drink, but not together. This rule was probably followed 35 percent of the time.

"B8 and Stalker. They're cousins."

I started laughing. "Come the fuck on. Come—." My head swiveled like a demon's. "You *are* kidding right? Please."

He shook his head.

"He dates her, he dates Stalker, his cousin? B8? I can't believe that, you you've got to be—why? Why in the flying fuck didn't you tell me this the night we saw him at the Shack?"

"I didn't remember until you mentioned her just now, and honestly it didn't cross my mind before."

"Oh, *honestly*. Really? You're an asshole.

"Chill."

"He's an asshole."

"Dude."

"It's disgusting! And weird!"

Owner slid a 20 on the bar in my direction. The only thing he asked was that I play The Cure once in a while. I stood up with my drink and sighed.

I typed F-R-A-N-K. I pressed "One For My Baby (And One More For The Road)." I emptied my glass. I typed C-U-R-E.

I could see my reflection in the jukebox. An alligator took over, and rolled me, then became me. The thick skin shed, unveiling new grayish/green scales from my brow to my throat. Bony plates lined the middle of my back like the Great Wall of China.

Jukebox knows all of my secrets.

"Jesus."

June 30

Over pasta primavera:

"This is going to sound weird." *Sip.* "I'm sorry, but I heard something ... about Stalker. You and her. I'm sorry, this is so ... ."

"January! Say it." He laughed as he said my name.

"Are you guys cousins?"

Embarrassment—maybe one or two percent—flickered on his face before he spoke.

"Yeah." B8 giggled.

We were at the same Italian restaurant we went to with CBP and Accountant. He just got back from surfing Mavericks—just enough time for me to get the guts to confront him.

No big deal, January. The "couldn't care either way" giggle.

"Uh, ok?" Expending every single particle of energy I possessed was my only shot at acting nonchalant—filtering the unattractive part of me. B8 grinned, prideful of another part of his lifestyle immune to consequences.

Sip. "Well, ok … how—" I touched my napkin and took a sip of the honey-hued wine. John Barleycorn bullied the questions out of me.

"She's in love with you, you know that right?"

"What, Stalker? Nah." Leaning back in his chair, a thumb (a stumpy one due to some random thumb injury) and finger rubbed the base of his wine glass.

"Look, she wouldn't have called me if she wasn't still into you. Do you still hang out?"

He took a sip of his red, his smile wider.

"You want to know if we still hook up?" Men who ordered red wine off a wine list were a mystery, and not in an attractive way. The image of his finger running down the two-page leather-bound book and pausing at a merlot irritated me.

"Yes, right now, yes. Are you done for good? Do you hang out?"

My pasta primavera had turned cold and slimy.

July 2006

Why wasn't I dating a winery owner? A pilot? A hotelier?

B6. *You thought I missed a number didn't you?*

I wanted to start this paragraph with an intriguing quote focusing on these themes: *embarrassing pathetic drunk immature desperate mentally unstable.* I couldn't find one. Instead, I'll tell the story of B6 like that episode of *Seinfeld* when they go to India for a wedding, or the movie *Momento*. From finish to start.

I knew what my Sunday would consist of: Taco Bell, my bed, Diet Coke, and 7-Up. At 7 a.m. I waded barefoot through the fog to my car at the Shack. Four minutes earlier I slinked on my clothes and left B6 in his 2-feet-off-the-ground bed.

B6's house wasn't a block from the beach or cliffs. It was *on* the beach and the cliffs. A 10-year-old steel and charcoal accented structure bolted into the rocks and painted a Portobello brown in and around the black railings and chimney tops. There were no shutters. The newest house in the area was built next to a small park, above a secluded cove, and next to a house that looked like a castle.

Back at the steel-bolted house, the biggest, black, mounted television ever built kept me awake from 4 a.m. to 7 a.m. At 1 a.m., B6 led me up to his hot tub on the roof. I felt the chill, saw the stars, and heard the ocean as he went under, went down on me, and came up for air—*over and over.*

Around midnight, lightly gripping cocktails we took from the bar, we walked to his house from the Shack where he threw his arm around my shoulder. I missed SFF so much I closed my eyes, scrunched them into my lips, and silently whimpered. A constipated look. *Can a person silently whimper?*

"I've waited for this, for you," he said as he took a sip of his wine. I looked a block ahead to one of the bird poop rocks with the Pacific crashing into it. *Over and over.* I squeezed and fell into him. The guilt didn't escape me: He was elated, and I was miserable.

Back at the Shack, while he nodded to No Name for another glass of Talley Chardonnay, I asked him for a jukebox request.

"You know, The Cure, 'Love Song'." His flirt smirk (and the sudden interest in my neck of Alfred Sung) were buzzed and hot. His 60-year-old pewter Corvette lit up its parallel parking spot in front of the bar. It dazzled. B6 watched it all night like a mommy in the park with her 3-year-old on the monkey bars. His view was of his car; mine was the same view, but it was to double, triple, and quadruple check to see if Jack wandered in.

Probably around the time he told me about the White Trash Party back in 2004, I knew eventually, one night, frantic when SFF hadn't called me back by 3 a.m., B6 and I would fuck. Predictably, an underwhelming orgasm, if any at all. It only took a year and a half. Even with the salt and pepper, he wasn't *old.* His physique I didn't notice. He met my *"winery owner, pilot, hotelier"* expectations, sort of. For the night, anyway. He had money, and maybe I'd be lucky enough to get pregnant. In nine months I'd be a millionaire, like the pro basketball and football baby mamas I envied. I blame The Cure. I should have been dating *him*.

Owner.

Yep—underwhelming.

July 23

Stalker Cousin emerged loonier than me, and not so much.

She *was* me in some ways: her idée fixe a different boy, but the method pathetically alike. It wasn't simple, white bread stalking, but an unrelenting haunting. Stalker Cousin showed up wherever we happened to be.

"I hit my head." She slumped down next to me after staggering over in sweats and a T-shirt.

B8 and I were at the Shack with friends visiting from LA. He'd been in the bathroom for at least five minutes doing god knows what. I turned away from No Name and his story about an old bartender at the Shack who killed his ex-girlfriend.

"Hey. You hit what?" I asked her.

"I gotta concussion last night, and it still hurts." I touched her head.

"You probably shouldn't be drinking." I slid her beer to my left, in front of the guy whining loudly about his sister who named her newborn son Waxman.

"All I'm gonna say is, 'Wax on, Wax off'." Waxman's uncle laughed a trailer park laugh, and I saw the gap where his back upper teeth should've been.

No Name interrupted and poured him a shot.

Stalker Cousin blubbered into my ear. "You're in love with him, aren't you? He likes you."

I spoke clearly: "I don't love him. Are you insane? I've only been seeing him a few weeks."

Jack.

"But you moved here." She nodded to No Name. I bet she knew his name.

"I moved here to finish my book. It has nothing to do with him."

"A book, really? You wrote a book?" Her question petered out, she bought me a drink, then went outside to smoke. She looked like one of those girls who ran cross-country in high school: brown hair, no makeup, athletic. No boobs or ass, either. Where a firm, plump twenty-something butt should've been, an empty poof deflated in the rear of her sweats.

"You are my hero," B8 cooed as he kissed my head. Outside, my arm left his waist. I ran ahead and hopped on a nearby syca-more stump. I faced the Shack and the dumpy neighborhood sur-rounding it. Behind the parking lot lived white, derelict apartments, which seemed to slant in one direction and whose residents' alarm clocks were men emptying dumpsters at 6 a.m. Behind those resided one-bedroom, one-bath homes with kids' plastic cars and 15-year-old boats parked on front lawns. "Single family homes," I guessed, although I never understood that phrase.

One, maybe two blocks away was the ocean, and B6/Owner's house, and the castle house.

Amused, I asked him what he said to Stalker Cousin as he buck-led her seatbelt in the back of a taxi, making sure she made it home ok. She leaned into his ear, or his into hers. I petered out during his explanation. Sobriety was valuable. Observing from the outside was ascendant, and a good place to be for once.

Sometimes we all hung out, and it was during one of these "more college life than current life" nights I figured it out: B8 *was* sleeping with her. SC rubbed Neosporin on his ant-bitten ankles before they skipped away, dot cottoned, and onto a kid's trampoline in a random backyard at 3 a.m. The odd dynamic aided me during low tides. B8 (and Stalker Cousin at times) numbed and diverted my attention from Jack making sense, and prevented his absence from overwhelming me.

July 27, 2006

"You know I'm a pro at folding, right?" He pointed to the bed.
"Folding what?" I asked.
"My comforter." B8 held up the duvet, twice his size.

"Let's see it."

He burrowed into it, punching his fists into the four corners, popping out to fasten the buttons. Five B8's could've fit in it.

I clapped. "Nice."

My phone vibrated in my pocket.

I peeked in my coat, and *Jack* lit up the screen. I felt like a French fry machine without oil. Pink-faced and mouth falling open, I wondered if B8 saw me stiffen and lurch.

"Oh my god—" I started to say his name as B8 continued folding laundry, head getting lower.

Get a grip. Do not answer.

"I have to get this." A few steps from the bed, I pressed the green button.

"Hey, Sweetie, I'm driving back from SF and wanted to see how you're doing."

He went on to explain that he'd texted me first but didn't get a response, so he called.

When I mentioned B8, I felt victorious.

"Oh, sure, I know B8. We're buds. Tell him hi for me. So. Can you cruise by?"

"Um, can I call you back?"

I turned to B8: "What's texting?"

You've always had [my heart].
You cut your teeth on it.

— Ashley, from *Gone With the Wind*

August 2006

It surprised and embarrassed me how awful I was at hiding my affections for Short Fat Fuck.

"I saw your man out last night," B8 confessed after we shrieked like pigs being hunted with a dull hatchet and a hunting knife, in case the pig resisted being slaughtered with only a hatchet. Most likely we woke his 90-year-old grandma and neighbors. I imagined their heads jerking and recliners retracting behind swollen calves. At their front doors they squinted, hands shielding their eyes from the porch light, wondering what the hell *that* was.

My gaze shifted from the trees outside of the open window to my feet above his head.

You can come inside of me or *I want you to come inside of me.*

With a lawyer's purpose, I moaned one or both of those phrases, into B8's neck/ear.

He didn't respond.

Why do I say this? My concentration was elsewhere, my body another's (never my own unless with Jack) yet I said it as if for that instant I wanted us to be married, trying for kids. I amazed myself each day at how illogical and retarded my thought process was. A boy's un-condomed dick inside of me wasn't enough to feel loved or intact. I craved an ounce of him in me forever, running through whatever parts of my body his cum wanted to travel. Synchronized swimming with my birth control pill. *Not a fan of the word cum.*

Afterward (it was never lengthy sex) I turned over and put my arm over his chest: It was the shade of chestnuts. He smelled like every bath product Trader Joe's sold on those lonely shelves near the cash registers and bottled water: lavender, lemon, mint, tea tree.

"You saw who? What are you—what?" My pulse pressed a mute button.

"Your man, Jack. I saw him at Bankhead. I told him I was dating the girl who was in love with him."

August 15

Jack received the very first text I ever sent. I don't remember what I wrote, but his response was noteworthy:

Jack: Sorry, 8-10 is girlfriend time.

Fucking Walmart. Fucking Short Fat Fuck.

August 20

Thirty seconds after I began forcing dollar bills into the juke to play Bell Biv Devoe's "Poison" and John Mayer's version of "Message in a Bottle," Jack opened the door and held it open. Walmart ducked under his arm: hoodie, perky tits; dark, almost out of fashion curled hair; and shorter than him. A disruption in communication with SFF was the reason I was standing where I was, alone and depressed, vodka/soda and one red straw waiting for me next to Owner.

This should be fun.

He strutted by on the way to the bathroom without a drink.

"I like your hair, Sweetie."

I focused on his shirt collar and the stubble on his chin. "How are you?" My nerves spurt the words out fast.

My body sped up. The rpm's and not breathing wrecked my chance to take notes or plan a reaction.

"I'm good, good. Have a great rest of the weekend, ok?"

An hour later, Walmart's head leaned into Jack's armpit at the bar and sipped a rum and Coke. The Pretenders came out of the speakers, and he caught my glance.

"Gonna use my fingers ... there's no one like me ... I'm gonna make you see."

He mouthed the words as I faked fascination with Owner's story about his mom in Florida. I didn't look away.

He called me a few hours later.

"Well, hello there. Wow, you looked great tonight, Sweetie. And you're being a good girl—not getting wasted, huh?"

Was he just being friendly? Catching up? I trusted nothing this guy said. Cloaked and daggered, I needed daily clarification. Even a simple sentence, greeting, or late-night phone call warranted suspicion. My anti-gut deciphered the awfulness in the way he could take me or leave me while finding Walmart and her cherub face blind and insensitive in an edge city. Did he know her before, rediscovering her after sifting through discarded girl scraps? How did he make the decision? The transition? What is said to the prospective girlfriend?

I couldn't imagine these words coming from SFF's mouth:

Will you be my girlfriend? Want to make it exclusive? I'm game if you are.

I couldn't imagine the questions with *myself*, let alone her.

I horrified myself with what transpired after the conversation and contract between him and Walmart. Barbecues, dinners at TGIF's, or lunch together in the McDonald's inside the actual Walmart while on her half-hour break. Sitting in a filthy booth a family of six vacated five minutes before, her ugly shoes shifted on the floor beneath them. During lunch they planned a visit to her parents in a mobile home park (I'm being polite using the term "mobile home"). Weekends kept them busy: driving around in his SUV, going to the lake, and kissing goodnight.

"Sweetie" tramped its way into my vocabulary. I didn't like this. I fantasized about what he would be like when we would finally be a couple, and sometimes it wasn't as fabulous as I anticipated.

The being together ending me, *finally*, as if this weren't bad enough. I skipped ahead to married Jack/January.

Me, sitting on the floor of our sunken living room. He gets home from work.

Baby in my lap. He smiles. We make dinner together in our contemporary white kitchen with a Subzero fridge. He holds the baby, puts him/her to bed. Sex—a fluid mirror of ardor and love.

Reality.

How fucking exhausting it would be to enforce and carry out interesting sex. *Forever?* Crystal balls revealed Jack requesting a threesome at dinner, a question as laid-back as "How was your day?" Saturday and Sunday nights: digging out a dildo from a bedside drawer. Birthdays, Halloweens, and Christmases: hideous slut costumes ordered online with a wide sneer. No peace. Dips, grooves, and slow, loving sex never heard from or seen again. If I didn't comply and the sex derailed into the mundane, the inexorable cheating would lead to more landmark, blood-bathed events.

As I entered and exited the Shack, Moondoggies, and Bankhead, still blue, I started a checklist: He never slept at my place. He lied. He cheated. I desired truth, kindness, calmness, power, security, safety, and sweetness—all of Jack. I'd seen those parts of him during the hours we spent lodged together, so I knew they existed. Outside of sex, I was on my own, and a low deception coiled around time passing. Jack redistributed attention, sure, but I wasn't what he really wanted: arm tattoos, midget tiny, and stupid as fuck. He banged me when smarter girls balked at the sight of his name on their caller ID, hitting the red key fast. Expressions I wanted or I bestowed upon him weren't reciprocated.

I hated I said "Sweetie."

August 25, 6 p.m.

"What does C-minus stand for?" I asked in a hurry before I took a labored sip of a shitty vodka/soda. Shitty could mean one of three things: too strong, too weak, or not enough limes. I don't remember which one it was. I wanted to be as drunk as 40 billy goats, and for no particular reason.

"Coors Light." The executive editor at the magazine, Editor 1, was preppy, seasoned, middle aged, and cool.

"What do you call Tecate?" I'd never heard of this beer until that night.

"Shit." He took his sips without moving much more than his arm and hand.

He switched to edgy magazine journalism from the world of television news 10 years ago, and now schooled me in lessons five and six of "journalism drinking" at Bankhead. Taped above the cash register was a picture of Johnny Cash giving the bird, "Cash Only" written across it in red.

"Beer, sometimes Tecate, most times not, and Jameson—always Jameson.

That's all you need to know about men in San Luis."

Bottle after bottle stood tall in front of patrons' forearms planted at the bar, on dates with glassed jiggers filled with the russet Irish substance. *Jameson*. Bouncers on their nights off, waiters, local musicians and DJs, college students, and old men sat or stood and proved Editor 1's theory. It wasn't only guys; women drank as profoundly as the men. Ladies cherished their beers and the garnish of a shot waiting patiently at their elbows.

"What about Pismo?"

"I don't know—you would know better than me—margaritas, maybe?

"So, the magazine."

I nodded.

"You're doing a fantastic job, by the way."

As the Cultures editor and writer, I discovered and showcased up-and-coming artists—artists who'd been painting for decades but without an audience—and rediscovered local, legendary artists. Every week I met people and cultivated relationships with readers, movers and shakers, winery owners, writers, and businesses. Every day events took place and happenings happened: art openings, concerts, fairs, fun runs, meetings, camps, plays, fundraisers—all of it taking place across an area of California easily distinguishable on any atlas. My job was to condense the information, add some cool pictures, and hope readers would plan a weekend around what they read in our magazine, while they relaxed outside of a café.

11:59 p.m.

Editor 1 was gone, and I drove home from Bankhead as a lightning storm strobe-lit the sky. Navy sailor drunk, I watched the darkling outer space event from the 101 South, one eye half open and my hand slipping on the steering wheel.

10:35 p.m. / 1 hour, 24 minutes earlier

"Hey, I know you. You work at the magazine, don't you?"

I lifted my head from the glass and rotating 45s.

I think this person is talking to me.

"I'm Vanity Fair," she chirped. I let go of the jukebox and tumbled toward tall, pretty, and a halo. Not Pismo pretty. LA pretty. Her straight, silky brown hair hung down past her boobs, over tan, long, thin legs. It was a quick, tee-lit, but thorough once-over.

Through, to the other side of my four hours of Ketel One, I noticed and loved that she was alone. She was like that one page in *Vanity Fair* where the editors choose a spread of a bunch of curious items in glossy color and in matchbook-sized photos: books, exotic destinations, New York City restaurants, a bench with "call for price" beneath its description. Everything I didn't know about, wasn't aware of, and would probably never see again. She was ... aspirational. Enigmatic.

"Who are you with?" she asked, then smiled as I sat down at her table in the middle of the bar. Bankhead didn't belong with VF, although she acted as if she'd sat on that stool 10,000 times, which she had.

I couldn't remember at first. "My boss. Then an interview."

"An interview for what?"

"This story I'm writing on a jewelry designer—he makes bracelets and rings out of wood, or maybe sandstone? It's in my notes. Be sure to read it when it comes out in a few weeks." Her ensemble came straight from a rack in a tennis pro shop at a country club. VF shot me an inquisitive smile, as if she'd already decided she'd found a friend.

"Who are you with?" I asked.

"I'm waiting for my boyfriend." Vanity Fair sipped something clear. She told me about a local millionaire she started dating a few months prior.

"We should hang out. Tomorrow night there is this great … ."

When she texted me the next day, referring to plans we made at Bankhead, I didn't remember anything except for the lightning storm.

August 27, 2006

Beyond and significantly below the rest of my neighborhood and downtown Pismo was the ocean. The pier, a caterpillar peeking out from the shoreline, completed my diorama from the nosebleed section. Mine wasn't quite a floor-to-ceiling window, or a "wraparound porch" view; 18 inches of wall separated two glass panes. The view looked *simulated*.

After living and visiting here more than 20 years, what smiled at and enveloped me from my bay window, flabbergasted and jolted me. But I still didn't understand why people gravitated toward and obsessed about the ocean. I understood the beauty and stillness, but the notion or motivation was otherwise mysterious to me. Any body of water, really. What was it about not having a backyard or neighbors behind you? Or in front?

Then I remembered something my mother did. In Chicago, when she decided our view of Lake Michigan wasn't "grand" enough from Division Street, she and my stepdad bought a new house. There was no discussion, except for my mother asking, "Phillip, I'm thinking the 10,000 square-foot layout, agreed?"

Four months later, we moved into our obnoxiously "grand" (although downright divine—and flawlessly decorated) high rise across the street from our old house, and directly on Lake Shore Drive. *Across the street.* It did make a huge difference. Sometimes all I had was my bedroom view of Lake Michigan. I guess it *is* all about the view. I understood the stillness not from the waves or currents, but from the farawayness of it.

"I can't believe we slept down here." In pain from the liquor and the hard floor, I went in the bathroom to decrust. Vanity Fair stood at the window, staring out, checking her makeup in a compact, with a phone to her ear.

"Millionaire called."

I met him at one of our stops last night. At the Shack around midnight, he strolled in, dressed in shorts, flip flops, and a grin above a polo shirt. His 50ish body made his way over to VF, where she was perched on her stool, watching and sipping. He didn't give off the fifty-something vibe: tan like a motorcyclist would be. His feet worn, but cared for and strong in his Reefs. He was stoked she'd found a new girlfriend.

Liver and I stood a few feet away at opposite corners of the pool table. My pool playing ability died with each shot Too Tan sent over. At 11:30, I asked him if Jack was coming. I blocked out his answer, probably because I didn't like it.

After a shower, I thought of the pool game, the overstuffed Shack, and I couldn't picture VF drinking or how much. I knew she drank a split of champagne (remember—*shitty* champagne). That showed me she was down to earth. The image vanished of how she held the glass or how long it took her to finish it.

Men of all types paid for the spirits that drove the dangerous outing from Pismo to SLO and back again. Suits, bikers, frat boys, guys with potbellies, bartenders, Owner. Even Liver. None were immune to her and me (really only her) side by side, during a fire drill for our friendship. We passed out on my floor in blankets and pillows I pulled from my bed.

I poked my head out of the bathroom, flossing the lime bits out of my teeth.

"Zorro's?" I suggested the roadside (same road as the Shack) al fresco café down the street from my house.

"Yes," she moaned, putting on sunglasses.

"You guys were so friggin' cute last night. He adores you." I tried to watch my mouth around her. *Less fucks; more frigs.*

Watch my mouth. *Watch your mouth, January. My mother used to say that.*

We sat outside on wrought iron, surrounded by unkept landscape and other hangovers. Twenty-five years ago, Zorro's lemonade/ice tea mixture filled my kiddie cups. The place had a different name back then, but my dad loved taking me to the restaurant for enchiladas after he parked his tractors and trucks under the tin-roofed truck ports.

Traffic whizzed by: un-addicted, successful people with higher self-esteem than I were off to hike Madonna (the mountain, not the singer) or kayak the coves. SUVs with a black metal contraption hooked or fastened on top or on the back secured their sporting goods. The thought of exercise, happy people taking rights and lefts in love, upset me. Morons with mountain bikes bothered me the most.

She secured her "halo," and I barely hung on to my chair.

"He's married," VF admitted as she hung her purse on her chair, while I reached for orange juice and soda. I noticed purses. I never owned a purse like hers, with a strap from shoulder to hip.

"Who, Millionaire? Really?" I wasn't sure if she was testing me and putting feelers out for judgment. Eventually she realized judging wasn't my style. I was too self-centered and flawed to have an opinion. Plus, she was a find—Vanity Fair was easy: easy to talk to, easy on the eyes, and wasn't easily spooked.

"He's going to leave her."

I was a spectator for her marvelous life of requited love, august beauty, and a trust fund.

I want love
to roll me over slowly,
stick a knife inside me,
and twist it all around.

— Jack White

September 16, 2006

At the Roost, a humbler arena, VF and I summarized our weekend we spent at a local wine festival. The day before, we had our pick of the hundreds of indigenous architectural anomalies called wineries, sticking out every mile or so on either side of main roads and highways, dividing the corn silk acreage. They all participated in the event, and the 30 minutes or so at each involved the same activities: tastings, food, live music, shopping. Wine wasn't the only thing for sale; some offered hospital-like gift shops.

Dusty roads led to barn door, family-run establishments. Others welcomed us through the middle of two rows of full-grown, alien eucalyptus trees ferried all the way from Australia. The wineries' gate doors and interior designs were worthy of a $9.99 magazine found only at Book Soup's alley bookstand.

Saturday we spent at Calcareous in Paso Robles, a hunting lodge-esque winery I never wanted to leave. Perched on the side of a mountain (or was it a hill?) Calcareous reigned over its competition below.

Oh, and bocce ball.

I forgot to include bocce ball in the activities list. Every stop had a bocce ball court laid out near a parked tractor or storage shed. Calcareous and all wineries wanted us barrelhouse drunk, buying bottles (cases) of their 2004 syrah, and playing bocce ball. Whatever the fuck bocce ball was.

If I was vain, Vanity Fair wasn't vain at all.

Saturday.

Thirty minutes in, while adjusting the birch wood plate with the hole to hold my wine glass, a trio of updone ladies, shorter than VF and me (because I wore an extra four inches that day) sashayed up in slow motion, as if in a movie when two school cliques meet to fight. No fighting: They were there to admire and fuss. Their pinots rocked back and forth and side to side as they beamed up at VF as if she were Barbra Streisand. Their plate/glass holders didn't have a crab cake resting atop, like ours did.

"Wow, you are gorgeous, Honey. Dear, what do you *do*?" Updone Trio ping ponged between the two of us. Oh the pressure from the Updones! How do you tell three, classy, demanding little ladies what we *do*?

VF: "Well, I'm having an affair with a married man, and live off of my dad's millions."

Me: "Well ladies, I moved here from LA to "write" and to force a guy, who will never fall in love with me, to fall in love with me."

But I loved moments like those, when strangers adored me for no reason, and the conversation ended with a kiss and the exchange of phone numbers that would never be dialed. Those moments, between the regretful purchase of the $20 corkscrew with purple grape leaves for Accountant, glided up to us often.

Sunday.

Summer swung outside as we watched karaoke from the bar.

If Moondoggies was Hank Williams, the Roost was Hank Williams, Jr. The bar, directly across the street from Moondoggies, was cozier than its father and served a purpose when the mood required: fewer people and a jukebox that played Q-Tip *and* Patsy Cline. When Jack didn't appear at one within the hour, I walked as fast as I could in peep-toes to the other.

"I want to sing E-O-11." I flipped through the binder.

"E-O-what? What song is that?" She finger combed and inspected her hair through the bartender in the mirrored backsplash.

"Sammy Davis, Jr., sings it in *Ocean's Eleven*—the original *Ocean's*. No one knows the Brad Pitt one was a remake. I like the lyrics, something about 'foldin' green,' Do you think that's money? I'm not sure what foldin', folding, green is. I like the melody."

"No idea either. Melody? Wow." She laughed. "I doubt they have it. I thought you'd do Sinatra."

"Holy shit." I spoke low and sucked my stomach in.

"What?" VF followed my aim, a few feet to our left. Jack approached, wanting to pass, but stopped.

"Hey, Sweetie, how are you?" He stood expressionless, between us, but a few inches away from our barstools.

"I'm good." He wasn't listening. He glanced at the guy in Wranglers singing "Mammas Don't Let Your Babies Grow Up To Be Cowboys."

"No Walmart tonight/Are you happy?" He turned to me and I went in for a hug to override the odd statement/question.

"Yes, Honey." We hugged like two watchtowers colliding. A vibration dove into my chest from his and he jerked, then I jerked. I smelled him and heard a misgiving in his "yes." He drifted away.

"So that's Short Fat Fuck."

Not wanting to draw attention to my reaction, I murmured yes.

"I like his lisp."

"Lisp. What lisp?" I asked.

"Listen to him next time. He has a lisp." Vanity Fair searched her purse. "Why did you break up?" she asked.

I held my wet glass with both hands, debating if I should tell her he lived a few blocks away from where we sat.

"We didn't. We weren't actually, technically ever … together."

"What does that mean?"

"We weren't a couple. We didn't go out."

"So, you've never been on an actual date with him?"

"No. I guess not. Not technically." A loathsome statement, under a spell of hard questions. "I know, it's insane."

It wasn't that I hated VF asking. What took my breath away—and me away from my temporary sanity—was the fact I now was forced to pause to remember Jack was just in my airspace, and how I was without him, indefinitely. I ordered another vodka/soda and shot back the current one, with my eyes closed until an ice cube chilled my top lip.

"January, you're joking. Him? That guy? What do you do when you're together?"

Talking about the Jack situation was as natural as taking an unholy, bilious, and nefarious shit in a church's pulpit. When I glossed over who he was to me; what we were behind closed doors, I admitted defeat or I avoided it. I didn't know anymore.

"Well, we haven't hung out in a while, but what do you think we did? Before I moved here, we'd hang out on a Friday or Saturday night when I came up. Not a dinner-and-movie thing. He never asked, and I didn't ask why. Maybe that's not true. Maybe I did."

"He never asked you out? *Out* out?"

I gave her a shrug and a "What do you want me to say?" unspoken response.

"I get it. I felt that way about a guy once. Before Millionaire. I'm so lucky I met him soon after, and the feelings for the other man went away. It's the hardest thing in the world when they don't want you back, but he has to like you. He still calls, texts, wants to see you, right? How long has this been going on?"

"Two years, almost, and I agree, on some level he must, but he has a girlfriend now. It's cool; I want to date other people. I am dating. He drives me nuts, but—I don't know."

"You can do better."

Forty. *At least.* That's how many times those four words were spoken to me. I tried to defend Jack in the ways I wasn't better than him: pointless. No one believed or understood. She said she did, but she didn't really. VF couldn't understand unrequited love, rejection, or landing a better guy as an aspiration. She always got the better man. Except it wasn't the "better man" to her. It was *the* man.

I told VF what I told maybe two of those 40 people.

"I'm in love with him: totally fucking in love. I can't explain why or what it is." I paused and thought of something new.

"But I can explain what *it isn't* or who it wasn't. Ok, when you saw or met Millionaire for the first time, there were other men there, right?"

"We were at a baseball game, so yes." She had perfect posture.

"The nervousness, the smiles, the attraction, the wanting was directed toward a specific guy, him, who you had no idea existed up until the second you saw him at the concession stand, or wherever you were. No one else was even an option for you."

She nodded.

"When I met Jack, there were other guys there—at least 10 I could have mingled with, talked to, hooked up with, but the point is, when I think back, they didn't exist. There was no one else. It was only him and me. It's like, ok, this is my mom and dad—an unerring fact. And this is SFF: the man I want to stand next to for the rest of my life. An unerring fact."

Vanity Fair's eyes widened in shock as she sipped her drink.

"And the sex; oh my god. Maybe that's all, *all of this*, is: an addiction to the sex. But when he just hugged me right there." I pointed to the corner of the bar:

"I changed at that moment. Every time he touches me, I change."

"Wait, did I introduce you?" Introductions wouldn't have made a difference. VF would remember him forever, but he'd never remember her.

Jack and his buddy walked to the other side of the bar, did a shot, and headed out the back door into his night: so cool and so together. He had Walmart. My lack of lip-gloss crossed my mind when I recalled the hug.

"I've never ridden in his car." My eyes didn't leave the back door when I told her the most inconceivable detail.

"How is that possible?"

I faced the mirror behind the well bottles, and I knew. I didn't belong there. So, we left.

September 17, 2006

By 6 p.m. my work's end-of-summer party wound down and Lady Reporter and I trekked up the stairs of our publisher's beachfront house.

"I've been looking for you." As we exited through the glass doors with starfish knockers, I turned around to see the bass player from the party's band. Lady Reporter didn't stop.

Packing up his instruments into various faded black and battered trunks and wrapping cords between his shoulder and hand, he grinned for a split second and raised his eyebrows.

"You were good. How long have you been playing?" I stepped closer.

"This band? Three years."

"Nice." I pointed to the Led Zeppelin sticker on one of the cases. The boy of normal stature, with gold-blonde hair had a face that reminded me of the lead singers of The Fray and Coldplay. It made B9 more appealing.

"What are you doing after this?"

Love that question.

"I wasn't sure yet. Maybe the Shack for one more before I head home."

"You live in Pismo?" He finished with the cords and shut the cases.

Standing still, I nodded, choosing not to follow him while he loaded his truck with the rest of the band.

"Well, I'm finished here; wanna go together? Grab a beer?"

Soft-spoken, B9 proposed a place I *hadn't* been Brahms and Liszt in, "Let's hit up 75-Footer instead. It's a dive in Avila."

7:30 p.m.

"Black and tan."

"Whoa, nice." B9 acted surprised after he asked me to guess what beer he ordered while I was in the restroom. Two layers of dark and light beers settling in a woman's waist curvy pilsner glass were unmistakable, considering how many boys I drank next to.

He dominated the conversation with facts about his music, birth-place, and family. I drank water. He licked his lips—not in a gross way, but in a way that suggested lust, and toward another level of liking me.

"You know, you're stunning."

That word again.

"No, I'm not," I promised him as I bit on my straw.

"Everyone in here is staring at you."

"No. They're staring at *us* because we aren't bearded fishermen." Hunched- back, tan guys in recycle-bin-blue T-shirts with feet as big as rotisserie chickens, chatted in sets of twos down the length of the bar. Their dark brown legs and flip-flopped feet hung over the sides of their stools and I couldn't believe how quiet they were. We were the least wrinkly and tan people in the bar, and the loudest. Actually, I was the loudest.

September 2006

Work reached an interesting status in autumn, and after five months, the unknown became less unknown. I meandered through the local arts scene in downtown SLO, up curved roads to wineries in Paso Robles, on college campuses and in small blue-collar homes or mobile home subdivisions covering a 75-mile stretch of the 101. The more expensive homes surrounded themselves with a womb of trees, the rustlings of civilization nearby. Grassnuts, dried leaves, and those ball-bearing-sized, prickly starburst weeds that come out of nowhere lay at my feet and clung to my shoelaces. Sitting in theaters, I developed a skill for scribbling in the dark amid audiences of 60 or 6,000: Articles and profiles assembled at home on my living room floor, in front of my office computer, at bars, artists' studios, galleries, or on a bench outside. Questioning famous writers passing through town, attending high-school musicals, poetry events, gallery exhibits, and witnessing courageous and lame flash mobs ruled my days and evenings a few hours before vodka/sodas would.

September 26

Hippie.

I envied Hippie. The college-aged reporter breezed into the office a couple hours after most of us arrived, not knowing where she left her computer, notes, wallet, or flash drive the night before when she wore her Russian fur cap, rising a foot off of her head. After a day of roller skating around San Luis from bar to bar, she never seemed to be hung over, as if hippies were unflappable with regard to hangovers. Most admirable was Hippie's purse: crumbs of Ritz crackers and a joint awaited her inside a purple fabric tote. Her style could be summed up with two polished nails and pink knitted leg warmers running up to her muscular knees.

January.

I couldn't leave the house if all 20 nails weren't manicured and pedicured, my purse chosen and jam-packed, and hair blown-out. My huge leather hobo bag (one of three I owned—and those were the brown ones) contained:

- Bright orange wallet so I could find it. It held: ID, cash, spare car key, two credit cards.
- Three mesh bags, each the size of a paperback book containing: hand sanitizer (two), tampons, nail files, bobby pins, Tums, Airborne, hankie, gum, Altoids, Tic Tacs, handy-wipes

(three kinds: Burt's Bees facial, antibacterial, and computer cleaners), Band-Aids, lotion, floss, Advil, small mirror, Zycam, Crystal Lite packets, tissues, Aquafor, lip-gloss with SPF (three), Chapstick with SPF, sunscreen, nail clippers, concealer, another spare car key that would start my car (the other would only open a door).

- Sunglasses and pouch
- Post-Its
- Small notebook
- Reporter's notebook
- Pouch with pens, pencils, Sharpies, and highlighters
- Febreze

Hippie and I Moulin Rouged at Bankhead after work on occasion—always spur of the moment. The 45-minute sessions were simple: elbows sticky and hands wet, each not approving of the other's drink: her Tecate, my usual. Toned from biking, tan from zero SPFs, and sporting a boy haircut, she could care less about me, my face, my clothes, or how much I weighed. I bought the first round, and although she didn't seem spongy, a Tecate and Jameson met her wide eyes and outstretched hands. She tried to make me laugh, patting me on the head, pleased she had me as her own one-woman audience. As if the hats and roller skates weren't enough. Her mission? Graduate from community college, make enough money to feed her hamsters, and ascertain how many years she could get away with wearing mukluks.

I was bubbly and blonde— someone who had yet to outgrow her numerous nighttime pastimes developed at UCSB while maintaining a non-Pismo wardrobe: not expensive, but terribly resourceful. Most at the magazine didn't know what to do with me, and some didn't like me. Hippie and Editors 2 and 3 were at least five or six years younger than me, and I was 29. Intern 5 was at least nine or 10 years younger. I didn't like Intern 5.

Rugby.

Oh Rugby. Another engineering feat from the supermodel scientists. He worked at the magazine off and on, and was finally back from Aspen. Hippie, Lady Reporter, and myself caught up with him at RatOnRug's (the magazine's entertainment editor's) house.

"It was sick. I had the uglies every night, hooked up with old ladies in mansions, and got busted for punching some dickfuck after he threw salsa and a basket of tortilla chips on me."

"Chalets, not mansions. Aren't they chalets when they're in snow?" asked Lady Reporter.

"So, did you work?" I recaptured what I missed: his loose-hanging cargo shorts, nice feet in Reefs paired well with his hands, and a "Beauty is Boring" T-shirt. A face and physique I wished for on top of me. Tall with wide, understated, laid back (archetypal, classic, model) muscles—as if he never stepped through the doors of a gym, and never would. As if he was born that way. The lighter caramel tint of his hair matched his skin and face: a blown-up picture of advertising on the wall of Abercrombie & Fitch or a building in Times Square. We became instant friends.

"Yeah, at a weekly, and at the restaurant where the chips and salsa fight happened."

Three words for Rugby: *Impregnate me please.*

Everyone drank heavily. And by everyone, I mean everyone at work and everyone I met through work—and not always for the greatest of reasons. Already gold-headed dinners and movies gave way to even golder-headed happy hours. Happy hours Wild Turkeyed themselves into side trips to pinball-machine-lit, smoke-filled, meth-addict-infested bars. The bars were always on side streets I never knew existed.

Everyone got baked, too. Weed was puffed in between bar hops and capped off nights. Bedside Jameson shots and a toke on the bong weren't uncommon at 11 p.m., midnight, or 1 a.m. I tried my best to keep up—and a few steps ahead of a hangover, of which mine were vicious. I never smoked weed.

September 29

"Ahh, holy hell!" Yelling and burping up a bacon-wrapped something, I set my triple Greyhound (in a plastic cup) on the wicker shelf above the toilet.

"What?" RatOnRug shouted from the backyard, drinking around the fire pit with 20 others at another barbecue. Greta, the cat, bolted out the same window facing the backyard, toward RatOnRug's voice. RatOnRug was a fatter Steve Buscemi.

"Holy shit. It's a dead rat ... on the rug. On the fucking rug."

"Yeah, it's Greta. That's what cats do."

RatOnRug hosted my birthday barbecue and the Rugby homecoming. Croix flew up from La Jolla. We leaned and sat and drank, laughed, and flirted around a bonfire in the backyard. Earlier, Rugby asked me what I wanted for my birthday.

"I wanna play one of the drinking games I played in highschool. None of this beer pong horseshit." Rugby coordinated with RatOnRug's roommates and set up three card tables for an Asshole tournament.

Rugby was thoughtful.

He surprised me with CD's at work.

"You have to hear this chick, Amy Winehouse." Rugby dropped the disc on my desk and walked off eating a burrito.

"Here. Raconteurs. Jack White's new band." Rugby stood over me at my desk teasing me about an article I was writing on an art festival that showcased art made from wine: paintings, assemblage, and watercolors.

"I guess you'd call them 'winecolors'," he offered.

"Ooh, JW? I love you." I swiveled in my chair and inserted the CD into the computer.

Another day, him, his hoodie, and board shorts met me halfway to our office in the parking lot:

"This guy's insane. I can't even pronounce his name. He does Bowie in French. Seu something. Maybe not French. Whatever. The shit's badical."

"You just said that? Badical?"

"And you're Beautical. I made that one up last night, zambon-ied (drunk) after a match with The Lushingtons (fellow drunk Rugby players)."

Back at the birthday barbecue, RatOnRug and his roommates spread out prosciutto-wrapped asparagus, cheese-stuffed jalape-ños, 10 things wrapped in bacon, guacamole, crudité, tri tip, beer, Ketel One, and Jameson. I asked him if he read Dr. Atkins' book in preparation.

Hours later, stuffed, and far along the Ketel One trail, RatOnRug and I rested low and slurried in lawn chairs,

"Thanks, Rug. This was fun." I patted his dog, Wassail. I gave him an extra thank you/wink combo through the fire for taking the time to buy diet tonic water.

"You know I masturbated to you three times yesterday," he confessed.

He didn't notice my shitty winking skills.

Croix hooked up with Rugby in between the prosciutto-wrapped asparagus and me passing out on his couch. Him living a block from Bankhead meant I slept on his couch at least once a month (six times so far). I loved it when girls I loved, fucked guys I loved. It comforted me. Two people softly—or not so softly—uniting behind a closed door 12 feet away, expanding their "love," and releasing it onto me.

September 30

Jack, still not single, called me at 4 p.m. and didn't leave a mes-sage. He called again at 1:30 a.m. and I answered to a vulcanized SFF.

"I just wanted to show you how it feels," he said. I didn't remem-ber the rest of the conversation. I rarely remembered any of our talks, vulcanized or sober. Dither gave way to deafness. After throwing my covers to the side, I hopped out of bed and ran over to the red cal-endar I kept in a drawer. I kept track of every time we slept together with a single letter, tallying the days and calculating averages. This wasn't sex, so I marked the square inch with a little black dot, distinguishing an occasion of him drunken dialing me.

October 3

As he moved my head backward and forward, Jack let out a contrived moan. "You don't like giving blow jobs do you?"
Omg.
"No, no, I do. I think, my mouth is just dry. I'm sorry."
"No, what you were doing was fine."
The funny thing was, I liked sucking his dick. I would do anything for him, attach my mouth to anything he wanted me to. He ate me out like a pie-eating contest champion. Pleasing him, surprising him, impressing him: These verbs were to become my new cardio routine.
Cinnamon candy, a "how-to book," or is there a class I can take?
A few hours later, still embarrassed about my performance, I picked up my purse, and while he leaned down to put on his slippers, I set a wide link of black plastic on the nightstand.
I walked to my car parked a few houses down the street.

The next day

It performed its duty perfectly: I heard his car, then spied him parking in my driveway. I quivered as he walked up the stairs with my bracelet I left on the nightstand. This was "Afternoon Jack." *I don't think I've ever seen "Afternoon Jack."*
"How are you, Sweetie?" We hugged quickly and made our way across the knotty wooden-floored living room.
He took a call, and I busied myself writing in my office consigned to a small room off of the kitchen in what was probably once a pantry. A desk sat beneath shelves displaying my purses and shoes. Stemless wine glasses, hard-to-find champagne flutes, martini glasses sized to fit an ounce's worth of martini, interesting gold carafes, and ice buckets acted as accessory bookends. Every few months the collections multiplied like a litter of kittens.

"Who's that?" he asked, pointing his stubby finger at the wall.

"That's me. I'm probably 2 there." Did he think I was cute in the candid black and white photograph taken by my uncle?

Afternoon Jack didn't stay long: the lint on his shirt, the unshaven hair on his face, the crust in his eye, and his off-white teeth were in a hurry. His details were emphasized in the sunlight, not in an effulgent way, but in a non-fictive way I wanted more of.

He didn't leave empty handed. Operation Bracelet ensured he'd be stopping by, so I bought him two kinds of cookies at the farmer's market: peanut butter and chocolate, both homemade—not by me, but the old man selling them. Writing his name on the thin, white paper bag in black ink mimicked an orgasm.

Pressing together in a final two-second hug sustained me for days, weeks after, while I accomplished nothing. I wished he'd never leave. His black T-shirt bartered the pain of last month for fireworks, as if watching Jack White in a recording studio.

"Thanks for the cookies, Sweetie."

Add to shopping list: lubricant.

October 6, 2006

"I'm at a poker game. Fold. Oy." I set my cards down, stood up from the table with my drink, and roamed out to the balcony hugging the cliffs in Millionaire's living room.

"Where do you think you're going?" Accountant won another hand and simpered and hooted as she collected the pot. I held up the Parliament light and mouthed who was on the phone: *B9.*

She followed me. We were social smokers. She punctuated witty, easy-to-listen-to stories about work and my brother with thin, tobacco-colored (obviously) cloves. I bored her (although she never told me) with one Jack theatric after the other while smoking Parliaments. Even up till then, she knew nothing of B9—except that he was my latest diversion. Accountant or I won most of the hands because we were the most competitive and had a clue. VF didn't care if she won or not; she wasn't as invested as us or as histrionic as me (*not* the personality disorder). Her interests rode parallel to

Millionaire's. A sexy, pleasing frontage road. She tolerated all else with tepid enthusiasm.

VF half-whined, "I can't figure out the call/blind/check stuff."

"Use instinct and know what beats what." I didn't understand call/blind/check either, but I had a poker face.

"B9, come over!" Vanity Fair squawked to my hand as she threw her chips down in the middle of the octagon table with bumper pool underneath. Bumper pool: very '80s.

"Sounds like you're having fun, you wanna hang later ... after your game?"

Texas Hold 'Em was Texas Hold 'Em for one hour at the monthly game VF hosted: an inventive attempt at increasing our desirability and a brand-new setting to achieve a daxxled state. Instead of furrowed brows, dealt cards, and big pots, there was bellowing and gossip:

No way! Where? When? Are you serious? She did? He did?

Girls weren't built for poker.

"Yeah, come over. I'd love to see you."

The last couple of hours of Ketel One and tart lime juice footloosed a two-year-old surliness caused by Jack. I walked into the kitchen for more ice. I laughed, pleased with myself as I pushed an ice bucket into the ice machine thingy on the front of the fridge. B9 planned his evening around me, drove to where I was, used gas and thought of me for 1,200 seconds. Much like my third vodka soda of the night, The Fray's lead singer streamed a buoyancy into me.

"I'm 20 minutes away."

Midnight

With my back to the front door, my hand on the knob, he thrust me into my house by my hips. With his warm mouth, his lips as supple as mine, he exacted ease and an unexpected skill guiding me to the bed. I led him into the kitchen.

"Drinks." I said as I set my wristlet on the counter.

I wasn't a thrift store junkie, but when I had a free half hour—and remembered to—I trudged through a church owned shop with

10-foot-high mazes of "not gently" used golf clubs, washer/dryers, and mixing bowls. The handbag pile was usually on top and in the center of a clothes rack: lustrous black patent leathers, white crocodiles, brown and green pythons, and tattered boot-like leathers suitable for the Shack. I greeted Lido or Obsidian with black cigarette clutches with gold trim, silver art decos with jeweled clasps, scorching and glitzing in all sizes and genres. I'd find what I was hoping for, without knowing at all. She'd be a renegade in her surroundings, compact (unless it was a tote or hobo) and stunning. Under $10 and she made the insides of my finger joints sweat. It was ok if I spoke as if my purses were women. Guys did it with their boats.

"Sure," he replied. Nordic complexion and a low-key sexy style pushed himself up onto my kitchen counter and watched me.

"Heineken or Belvedere?" I asked, stepping out of my heels.

"Heineken." Before I reached into refrigerator, he spun me from behind. His hands traveled my face, pausing at my neck and ears, lightening around my hairline, a romcom move I loved. Jack never touched my face.

I pushed him down on the kitchen floor.

The Next morning

"You don't smell," he pointed out in bed. I turned over to B9 staring at my left arm.

"I better not."

He laughed. The white sheet lay below one of my breasts.

"No, your armpits. Most girls I know smell there."

Way too early for the word armpit.

He climbed on top of me and made out with my boobs until he kissed me all the way to my freckle.

Scents were regulated for every hour of the day, occasion, event, and tryst. B9 was Dolce at night and anything from Fresh at breakfast. Fresh sold lemon, sugar, and grapefruit perfumes I ordered online every few months, during one of my many temporary vacancies I filled with shopping.

11 a.m.

"Sex and bacon. I'm a happy boy."

"I'm glad." B9 draped his arm over my shoulder, and I wrapped mine around his waist, the way I saw in paparazzi photos of celebs in *US Weekly* and on TMZ. Leaving Zorro's, we dressed like them too. Me: hair down in beachy, loose curls, aviators, black leggings, riding boots, gray knit sweater with elbow patches, neck wrapped in a black pashmina, and a white tank top underneath. Him: Strokes T-shirt, worn black boots, and a fitted black leather, yet casual, jacket. A boy rock star ambling down a Greenwich Village street the afternoon after a show at the Beacon Theatre.

"You were amazing last night." A recap of the kitchen floor sex followed his comment into my neck. I appreciated it since I had no idea what he was referring too. I glanced around at his twenty-something butt in his perfectly hanging jeans. If I looked up from my plate of waffles and noticed a couple like us, I'd be envious. I would want to *be them.*

Unfortunately for B9 (and the rest of the B's) rather than falling in love with them, I pitied them. The B's weren't prepared when they saw stars in my blue eyes and fireworks in my hair, the shade of a bushel of hay. I was with them, but somewhere else, embedded with poison—a measured, methodical viper. Boys knocked on my outer shell, smelled it, put it in the palm of their hand, but didn't investigate the rot beneath. Or they chose to ignore it.

I'll have a blue Christmas without you.
I'll be so blue thinking about you.

— "Blue Christmas"

October 10, 2006

Work and co-workers sucked. Well, one co-worker sucked. Others were dumbasses and idiots at times, but I took a cue from Editor 1 and shut my mouth, sometimes.

Say nothing. Have no opinion. Acquire that Vicodin demeanor.

Editor 3 and I were embattled: neither of us able to decide if we liked each other or couldn't stand one another. She was one step above me, which meant she read my articles first. We shared one of those felt cubicle walls meant for pinning post cards, a note reminding me I was having drinks at 5 p.m. with an artist, or a "100% Virgin!" button from a local olive oil producer. Nothing ever stayed pinned to it.

Like a marriage, our pay-checked union whipped around corners each month, and also like a marriage, we attempted peace and compromise when it suited us or if we came to work smiling that day. If we weren't ignoring each other, we hung out in groups, at photo shoots, or in front of drinks. Her coffee order was implanted in the "my pet peeves" section of my head because on many 8 a.m. mornings we dragged ourselves a block north to Café Adeline. Editor 3: no foam, half sweet, soy macchiato fuck me now, extra hot, foamy, caramel drizzled. Venti. Me: iced coffee. *What is venti?*

As for ignoring, our silence wasn't for any particular reason. Usually it went like this: In an editorial meeting when one of us had an opinion the other thought was fucking stupid, we'd rotate our chairs back to our computers after the meeting ended, neither of us wanting to kickstart the conversation. Normalcy returned and awkwardness disappeared once we re-bonded over a previous editor's mistakes in the latest issue. She lived with three cats and dressed like an Iron Maiden fan from the '80s. Nothing could hide or change her personality. On those walks to grab coffee I pretended to be interested in stories about her cat claw scratches and adult softball league. *Say nothing.*

She grimaced at her first Bloody Mary at the Shack, switching to piña coladas. *A piña colada?* That said it all.

I nicknamed her "Nazi."

October 18

"Editor 3, your breath. Are you sick or something?" Lady Reporter's unfiltered personality, and voice, had a lisp.

My throat clicked, I shut my mouth to muffle a laugh, and swiveled around in my chair. Nazi had a B4 level case of halitosis. It amazed me everyday. How does someone with breath like that have friends? Go on dates? Kiss?

LR, hastily dressed in mom jeans and a button down shirt from Ross, worked the crime and political beats. Our friendship blossomed two minutes into our first session at Bankhead. Easygoing and not expecting much from me, if anything at all, Lady Reporter loved to drink—not just at Bankhead, but at all of the bars I loved. I couldn't say that about Vanity Fair. In between dinners of steak Cobb salads, chicken fingers on vinyl stools, and inordinate volumes of vodka and wine, LR chafed me into a sleepwalker's stupor with talks of murder investigations, underground meth houses, and corrupt politicians. When the rims of our glasses met, we spoke of nothing else (with the exception of Jack). I knew little about her kids, where she lived, or her favorite kind of music. Lady Reporter served a purpose, sleeping it off below me on my bedroom floor, when Vanity Fair traveled out of town with Millionaire or when I anticipated my upcoming behaviors (or locales) wouldn't suit VF's tastes.

She didn't have time for music because, as with most dedicated journalists, her vocation was her pastime. I worked at a magazine, but in no way as a journalist. Sure, I received tips: an antiestablishment art show, a new pinot festival, or a last minute, open-air theater production. I pitched and researched stories. As a variant of a journalist, reporting on the arts culture was more like being a really charming publicist. Or social chair. Some artists became dear friends as I admired their work; others I couldn't recall a month later. Anchored to my desk chair, under eye-drooping fluorescent lamps, didn't gratify me. Scribbling away at city council meetings or in a victim's family's front room, then braiding facts and research into concise and interesting copy took a special individual—a dedicated, talented person—not a lazy procrastinator. Lady Reporter hit hard. I puffed with edges.

October 26, 2006

"She's out of town (Walmart). What are you?" I stood in his doorway, posing as if being attacked from above.

Idiot.

My upcoming Halloween costume's showpiece was a flock of black feathered, realistic looking crows I found in an old Hollywood costume shop. They clung to my hair and down my arms and back with twine and bobby pins.

"*The Birds.* Hitchcock?" I was asking not telling. He still thought of me as an "alien," another noun/adjective he typed into the notepad in his phone, the only kind of notepad he used. I was filed under, *Things JE says that I do not understand.*

"Oh, ok. You look really pretty."

South Park, pillows, kissing, Interpol, leopard skin blanket, black sheets, a cup of water. Me on my back till 7 a.m., militarily prepared if I farted in my sleep. I earned a large blue ribbon for prowling into his bed with crows attached to my head.

November 2006

Blow jobs. *Bamboozling* blow jobs. Scarring Jack's brain with my mouth was my goal for November—not writing more pages per day, reading Halldór Laxness, eating more salmon and broccoli at dinner, or cutting back on Ketel One and drunk driving. My ambition was to become excellent at sucking dick.

"I need, I'm here for, uh, I need, my…"

She cracked a mild smile telling me I wasn't the first person to walk through her store peep-show nervous. I parked on a side street and blacked out for a minute as I walked into Pismo's version of the Pleasure Chest.

I forced the words, "oral sex," lowering my voice to almost nothing at the word "sex." I leaned on the glass counter showcasing nipple clamps, butt plugs and Ben Wa Balls.

Ben Wa Ball = two, small, weighted marble sized balls on a retrieval string.

Oral was all she needed to hear.

"Lube. Lube is your new best friend, darling." Jack would date this salesgirl: double D boobs, black hair, red lipstick, acned complexion, and biker boots. She pointed to a rack next to the cash register,

"We have sugar free and different flavors. They're not bad tasting, and you can totally swallow it."

A week later …

I snatched the bottle from under my bed.

He laughed.

"It's strawberry flavored." He didn't care. Not only did he taste good, but I could maneuver my workspace: deeper, covering more surface area, utilizing different parts of my mouth and body, traveling from the penis to the balls, to his taint, asshole, and back to his shaft. I didn't want to stop and when I squeezed harder he groaned like a bear and rolled left, limp.

I saved the routine in my repertoire.

"Your bj's have improved, Sweetie." I kissed his inner thigh. "I think you just needed lube."

I guess the "bj" wasn't improved enough for him to stay over.

November 12

Vanity Fair and I wanted a counterbalance to our bendering, so we began a volunteer cleansing. Rather, we repeated one. A ballooned and thriving trust fund in place, VF didn't work, and already chaired three local philanthropies. I helped out at the local senior center and at their sister building, the Pismo Bingo Hall. I sold the skinny, smoky ladies daubers and "scratcher" tickets and collected their buy-ins. In between bingo nights, I visited Pismo residents in their homes: shopped, read, watched TV, played cards, talked, slept—whatever they enjoyed during the 60 minutes I sat on their brown couch.

"Jan, can you go to Thrifty's and pick me up mint chocolate chip ice cream and shaving cream? Gallon size."

Thrifty's? Are they still around?

Sergeant Major's brown couch occupied a busy thoroughfare between Pike and Main streets in a rundown apartment complex I lived in with my mom when my parents first divorced. The kitchen painted in a Gulden's mustard yellow with the inoperable sliding glass door was a museum for the World War II photos he snapped in combat with a 35 mm camera. The medals and plaques prided themselves on their smudge marks and dust.

I asked him what else he brought home from the war.

"Scars."

While staring at the 3-by-10-foot backyard, I stood at his sink, scooping the ice cream into a bowl. I smelled Play-Doh, circa 1982.

Childless Brad Pitt and I played out there.

Sergeant Major forced me to eat two scoops ("You can handle it.") while we watched Judge Judy and he boasted, "I killed Germans. Italians. I even killed the French." The prostate cancer patient and former paratrooper had the hair and stature of Ernest Hemingway, dressed in Levi's and cowboy boots. I fetched him his old man LL Bean slippers before I left.

November 13

SFF called me two times Monday. My mistake was texting him back Tuesday night.

Jack: Yea, Walmart wasn't too happy when she saw your text.
Me: You called me, asshole. I was returning *your* call.

He promised her: Made a pact to forget my number.

I went home, lay down in my bed, and closed my eyes for the next 19 hours. A few days later, I fucked B9 and visited newer, cleaner barstools, and a few faithful ones. I distracted myself like a Dorothy Parker character.

November 20, 2006

He called and mentioned problems with Walmart.

In my un-Jack world, I enjoyed dating B9. Movies, dinners, wine tastings with VF and Millionaire, watching him perform live, having normal relationship sex, and believing Jack held on to other boobs and thighs, eons away in a starship. Or at least across town on a crappy mattress, house, and life.

Jack "mentioning problems with Walmart," was the freakin' problem. He called hoping for a friendly ear, not hoping to hook up. He tricked and conspired with words and conundrums, not sex. A situation with SFF not defined by sex made his phone call harder to bear and it made our contact mature. Real. *Emotional.*

No, no. This wouldn't do. I required a Hazmat suit; whether in a bar, on the street, or in my bed asleep at midnight. A mini suit for my cell phone, too. Protection in all forms: technological, physical, emotional, and geographical. History dictated I needed protection from myself most of all: a life-size firewall. History also dictated that his "problems" with Walmart were temporary. Throughout the remainder of 2006, I was occasionally a found morsel on his plate, brought to SFF's mouth by a moistened fingertip. Then I was a crumb, effortlessly flicked away.

Even with B9 at my side, and the flicking of me from his finger, my Jack radar never broke down, sometimes verified at the "One mile from everything" diner, fork deep in waffles. On more than one Sunday I glanced up for a sip of coffee, and he drove by my window facing Main Street with Walmart in the passenger seat; visor down, fluffing and fidgeting with her big hair.

Did they sleep at her house and now were on their way to breakfast?

I'm surprised they don't stop here.

What am I saying, they don't eat out. They're going back to his place to eat Pop-Tarts.

So, twilight hours had to be snakebitten and compulsorily graveled to survive another round of "this:" the back and forth. The pounding of vodka over ice began, and Ketel One, limes, and soda formed tornadoes in the fly-over states. Then?

Annihilation.

December 22, 2006

It was the holidays and I wanted a life of fiction.

Pride and Prejudice (the film with Keira Knightley, not the book) and *The Notebook*. Even *The Wedding Singer*. Beguiling and unrealistic plots teased and touched nerve endings. Scenarios tucked me in and hugged my solitude close. I learned things from the characters I turned to when no one else, or nothing else, would help. The "back and forth" had stalled between Short Fat Fuck and me.

"It's over, I swear."

"I told you not to hook up with him."

Homicidal Bloody Marys stood before me and my brother like Catholic prayer candles. Christmas bonuses meant a higher caliber of venues to be inabstinent in.

One floor below the hotel lobby, in Lido, the bartender pitched us his debut screenplay about chefs who played baseball. The entire west side of the property jutted toward the ocean, with the "in every photo" wedding grass between. Bars in hotels were my favorite; the proximity of beds evoked a sense of home and family.

Winter meant an exceptional intensity of jewelry. The gold statement necklaces, cuffs, and bangles caught their breath when reached for from under my bed. The array hibernated in Hermes boxes. Now they would sunbathe. I didn't own anything from Hermes; I only had their boxes. Here's why:

Mrs. Z opens gift from friend.

Mrs. Z tosses box in garbage.

January rescues the box that looks like a fancy version of a $20 box from the The Container Store.

One of my gold pinky rings didn't stand out at Dolphin Bay Resort (where the restaurant and lounge, Lido, resided).

Christmastime in Pismo was epic and smelled of revelry, pine needles, and developing pinots. Wineries promoted parties, art galleries hosted parties, friends invited you to parties, work organized parties, bars spread parties by word of mouth, and parties had parties. Evenings with friends and family, tiny gifts left at my doorstep or bigger gifts delivered to the office, hors d'oeuvres and wine, and weekend brunches left me with Mele Kalikimaka on the mind, bringing forth temperatures naturally folding me into a man's arms. Lots of chocolate too.

"We're doing this now?"

My brother wasn't my usual accompaniment to Lido. Vanity Fair and I often pinched stems of $15 glasses of wine or ate mussels there. With anything in life—whether fancy, cheap, chill, or oceanfront—everything had reason for appeal. Moods decided where we ended up. Ketel One tasted the same on every sooted, glass shelf I faced. The Roost didn't have Ketel One, and Lido had zero soot.

Childless Brad Pitt took off to meet Accountant and I reminisced and scrutinized the last year. When not at the magazine, an art opening, a pops festival, watching a movie, or volunteering, I laced together different boys and beverages, professionally. B9 was a precious metal at the time, but lace he did. Bars and boys: a twinned theme achieving nothing but destructive gratification (momentary). A lifestyle elemental for so many years it sutured my folded arms to the mahogany. For 20 years I glamorized whiskey shots sitting before guys in dark suits, and martinis held to lips by ladies with gloves, hats, and flexed pinkies. Every movie had the foreseeable scene of the lovesick drinking at a bar:

"Give me your biggest, loudest, dirtiest Long Island Ice Tea so I can drown out this misery."

Without coping skills I memorized the line, rehearsing the scene from the script whenever it suited me, but especially during the unsuspected spanks on the ass of my life. Reality wasn't my friend.

Struggling with polar opposites, I bounced from id to ego, depending on Jack's predictability, girlfriend, or lack thereof. From the old textbooks I'd cracked to get a psych degree at UCSB, I recalled long passages, predispositions, factors, and symptoms. One set of symptoms stood out: racing thoughts, mood swings, anxiety, low self-esteem, agitated easily, and some suicidal stuff. I remembered what Croix and I discussed when we were in Pismo. It all sounded very familiar.

A second set of symptoms, and a term I discovered (not from my textbooks but from Robert Greene's book on seduction) was "Anti-Seducer." Symptoms: crushed if ignored or rebuffed, lavishes praise and falls in love with a person quickly and without knowing them well. The theory lit strike-anywhere matches against my arms and hands, and my wallet containing crisp vodka cash.

Well, goddamn.

"Seducer"—minus the Anti—would be my (hopefully) second superhero power: a birthright inked on a hidden crest.

VF snuck up behind me for her own 5 p.m. aperitif and bought a round. In front of the horizonless gray sheets of sky and water, soft live music played a few feet away, and an office holiday party wound down in a booth behind us. For work, I picked out a secret Santa gift earlier at a local shop that sold mediocre housewares and ugly oven mitts. Childless Brad Pitt, VF, and my dad's presents were wrapped and ready to be opened.

Jack and I drifted apart in time for Christmas. In fact all of the B's scattered during the holidays. Somewhat untrained in boyfriend gift giving (pre-SFF B's bought gifts for me, not the other way around) I sunk into my own unreality in Pismo. *What should I buy for him, him, or him?* While pricing rooms at Dolphin Bay, the wine glass sped up its intervals to my lips. I envisioned Jack (not B9) in a $400 a night room, 24 hours of us, and foiled boxes of delight.

I stuffed stockings full of the best gifts, scenarios, and fantasies. I was a fabulous non-girlfriend.

Katz·en·jam·mer
noun
\□kats□n□jam□(r)\
plural –s

1: the nausea, headache, and debility that often
follow dissipation or drunkenness
2: distress, depression, or confusion resem-
bling that caused by a hangover

January 10, 2007

" I 'm going to write a story about YOU! About this whole THING.
You guys are fucking imbeciles, Crazy fucking imbeciles … im-
beciles! I didn't *dooo* anything … anything … anythin … ! Shit fucks.
All of you Shit fuuuucks!

I flailed about as the deputy attempted to hold me steady on a
mat, process me, and document my fingerprints. Although shitfaced,
I noticed *his* hands shaking.

125

"Anything. This is, jis fucking bullshit."

"Ma'am." Ink, lasers, x-ray or lights, I blacked out for the following series of events. Reliving the half hour of booking and mug shot photo shoot was as necessary as a needle shooting into my gums before a cavity fill. I assumed the half-hour time frame.

"Do you want to be separated?" Barefoot, I flailed less.

"Separated, from who? Yers! Yes. Fucking separate me … what is sep … ? You guys better … money, my stuff … If anything … missing… ."

The badge handed me a blanket, directed me to a cell across from the other drunk tankers, and nodded to more mannequins in uniforms.

"When will I …?"

Three deputy dipsticks severed me from other female DUI'ers and meth arrests, with mild success. I screamed and threw the one item I could use to keep warm, the thorny piece of fabric, on the floor. At 5 a.m. I passed out on pee stains and weeks-old gray patties of Bubblicious on the ground.

Ten hours earlier

The year 2007 wasn't jumpstarted by my finest hour. Before I talked back to cops and demanded an attorney for a public intoxication arrest, I crawled pubs with Vanity Fair, Lady Reporter and friends in town from LA.

Old Vienna for happy hour.

Second course: the Shack. Vodka, miniature bottles of the shitty champagne, and zero calories from actual food. Super 8mm flashes of Owner and Liver's faces. Through murk, and stupidity, at 12:30 a.m. we chose to relocate. I would give anything to hear the conversation or see a video of this conversation.

Second course: Moondoggies. One or two more lefts and rights and I could knock on Jack's door. No matter how tile counting I was, I carried this knowledge with me like I carried my driver's license, packed safely in a zipped, isolated pocket in my purse. The danger sat in sleep mode, quiet and still, like a golf course sprinkler. Water could start spraying in all directions at any minute. All of the sprinklers I knew began a *chickchickchik* at 3 or 4 a.m. Prime time for knocking on Jack's door.

Vanity Fair had the right idea and went home as LR, my two remaining LA friends and I climbed over each other and exited the cab. We befriended strangers, karaoke bashed, and hurtled our asses into the walls, booths, and barstools. Bits of cognizance polka dotted the blackness. Very few bits.

What I sort of knew, in possible chronological order:

1. Met an older couple, became best friends, and possibly date rape drugged by these new best friends.
2. Spied Jack, Liver, and three unnamed cohorts. A side dish of girls, not including me of course.
3. Gave ice-cold scowls at SFF and girls.
4. Walked in the direction of Jack before he separated himself. He was sweet and surprised I was hanging with whomever he saw me with. I didn't know who he was referring to.
5. I apologized for calling him. "You didn't call me," he replied.
6. Minutes later a fight broke out between him, his friends, and me.
7. Screamed at Jack. Call him Short Fat Fuck. To his face.
8. All of Jack cohorts' and girls' jaws dropped.
9. Jack's jaw did not drop.
10. Kicked out of Moondoggies.
11. Raised hell in bar parking lot where Jack followed me. There's a split second burned into my mind of him – his face full of concern and sorrow.
12. Cops arrived.
13. Arrested.
14. Unwillingly flung inside of the cop car, landing on a cold, vinyl backseat.

What I didn't know:

1. Was I read my rights?
2. Where the *F* were the two remaining LA friends and Lady Reporter?
3. Was I kicked out of Moondoggies for a specific reason?
4. Particulars of mine and Jack's second conversation/verbal assault?
5. Why did he follow me outside?
6. Did he call the cops?
7. If he didn't, who called the cops?
8. Does B9 know?
9. Where do I send apology notes to cops/deputies/Moondoggies' employees?

The next day, 8 a.m.

Before I passed out (and woke up) in the county jail, I pleaded with PPD Sergeant for a phonebook.

"We've been more than accommodating to you miss."

My brain recalled no phone numbers. I couldn't remember last names of my closest friends.

His number taped to the receiver, a bail bondsman I drunken dialed didn't answer. Calling from the metal phone in my cell at 3 a.m. reminded me of a recurring dream. I often dreamt about a need to dial 911. About to be killed, raped, or robbed, running, dodging, and hiding in corners, I shook and failed to match up my fingers with the buttons on the phone. Portions of phone numbers—611, 211, or 411— were victories, but 911 eluded me. Over and over I tried, hung up, and started over before finally waking up.

In a small offset area, I read a bus schedule and thought of B9. *Hate myself.* I turned around and sat on a bench.

"How are you doing?" Olive Skin asked the question so gentlemanly, as he inched closer on the grimy bench, grinning, and aggravating me. Cement was the featured décor element in jail.

Olive Skin was a few years older than me.

"Just peachy." I fake smiled and sighed at the thought of the two-hour wait before the 9 a.m. bus arrived. The makeup around my eyes and bad breath stopped bothering me three hours earlier. My cheeks still shimmered. I didn't want to talk to anyone, especially with a see-through plastic bag as my purse and cheap stilettos on the floor next to my jiffy feet. At this level of hung over, I laughed as Olive Skin walked off. I let out a self-pitying whimper, remembering Jack from the night before. As a suicide bomber of love (and life) my behavior and drinking imposed traumas. My reactions had victims.

February 5, 2007

"There she is." B9 greeted me at my car. *This* phrase, from a boy and followed by a smile, beat sex with a stick in the dirt.

For two years I loved Jack with an unwitting foot on my neck while I seized, cried over, harassed, stalked, and fucked him. Every time he turned me over I saw more of him by way of his bones and boner. When the calls stopped and the sex lulled, leaving my diary incomplete, I didn't deserve him then, but a chip of me hoped and I set goals. I'd adopt that Vicodin demeanor, and after I duplicated the aura he possessed, he would know, and then I'd be his, and I'd be perfect. Until then, I let arrested dogs lie.

2007 became one of those years in which I would recall half of my Friday nights. By February I had a smeared-lip-sticked, crooked-eyed mug shot, and a boyfriend.

It was his birthday.

Avila Beach. A hillside, oceanfront hamlet, with barely a zip code, perched in between Pismo and SLO and only accessible by a two-lane road with sulfuric springs on one side and a Buddhist temple on the other.

Avila was fried clams. The lagoon behind the beach, near footbridges and a ninth hole provided me another playground when I was a kid. The first time I beachcombed Avila's bars as an adult, I zoned out at the lagoon for a long time before the 20-year-old memory returned.

Oh, Lagoon, right, right, I remember now. How are you, what've you been up to, Lagoon?

Decent concerts; golf; wine bars; and champagne bars. There was a wharf where VF and I drove on a rickety pier to meet dates. We ate and drank over the ocean and swimming fish. This was Avila Beach: a taxi ride away from civilization. Two lanes and Ketel Ones meant I didn't drive to Avila that much.

"We dubbed it Trente Ans." B9 sang into my ear.

"What's Trente Ans?" I asked before kissing him, hard and deep, but not long.

"French young lady." Beard Angry spoke but didn't look at me when I sat down next to him at a picnic table. We'd met a few times. When I drove up to the cottage a few blocks from the lagoon and a second, non-rickety pier, a bottle of Maker's Mark statued itself on the table, with its oozy blood-red adornment.

It was a small gathering. Beard Angry was B9's best friend. The scoop: an older guy with a roughed-out black beard who stitched bitter, temperamental, and sensitive patches to the back of his jacket. Whether the jacket was puffy, leather, or denim I couldn't tell, but it—he—belonged on a Harley.

Stephen King Jr., B9's roommate, stood near the fire and didn't say a word. In the dark I could make out Stephen King's long lost son stoking embers. A dead fucking ringer for the writer: facial structure, mouth, eyes. I mean, it was the very first thing I thought of when I met him for the first time. *So that means it's true, right?*

B9 wore a fedora and thumbed a ukulele. We kissed again. His kissing, *every time* he kissed me, defined to me what kissing was. SFF didn't kiss that well. I repeat, SFF *did not* kiss as well as B9.

"Come with me," he requested, and picked up his tumbler of bourbon.

Inside, I canvassed his ramshackle of a house and the wall above his dining room table.

"David Hockney," I commented, leaning closer to the painting.

He nodded.

"*A Bigger Splash*." He seemed impressed I knew the title. "It's from 1967. I heard him speak at LACMA once. He's one of my favorites," I told him. Hockney captured the soft flesh, sky and water tones of a simple subject. A typical pool day in the backyard of a modest, sleek modern home with two palm trees. The pool, diving board, and splash took up the half the painting, the splash being the most intricate part of the piece. Picture Palm Springs.

"Wow, I never knew the name of it. Anyway, it's a remake. There's a guy in San Luis who does 'em."

"Art forgery; very cool," I said as he played his ukulele and nudged me into the kitchen.

"So, did you get everything you asked for?"

He poured me a glass of wine. "The guy from that tasting room down the street recommended this one. My dad gave me this outrageous Strat from '54. But no, not quite everything I wanted."

"You didn't?" I met him in front of the kitchen window, placed the ukulele on the kitchen table, and heard Beard Angry hoot when we came together.

"You want your birthday present?" He whispered *yes* in my ear, brought my hands behind my back, then led me down a hallway.

He's so hot. Ok, cute. He's cute. Maybe he's good looking. He's ok.

Before lying on the bed I attacked his mouth and cock like a heroin-shooting porn star, fantasizing he *was* the lead singer of The Fray. He lifted my dress and fucked me hard, fast, and unromantically. We did the same routine, in reverse.

"You're the best girlfriend ever." The entire seven minutes was expected. The sex was symbolic more than anything.

With one hand over my shoulder, his other picked up the wine from the kitchen table. I adjusted my vintage coat with a mink collar, and we walked toward the fire.

"We motherfucking christened the party." I couldn't look at B9 when he announced this.

"Best girlfriend ever." Beard Angry spoke, but, again, didn't look up.

"That's what I told her."

Stephen King Jr. handed B9 two sticks. "We need marshmallows," Jr. told us. He hated the alter ego I created, tolerating me as he ate the Oreos he kept in his corduroy coat's pocket.

Beard Angry twisted the zoom on his camera.

"What are you going to shoot?" I sat down by the fire.

The French wine lingered on my tongue for a long time—longer than local wines did.

"A girl gave me a blowjob the other night and I smoked the entire time." Beard Angry spoke while he took a picture of me through the fire. It perplexed me when people didn't answer my questions, but started a conversation about something completely different.

I laughed. "You're joking."

"I shit you not, I lit up as soon as she started." He smiled.

"She didn't say anything? That's disgusting by the way."

"Why? It was gnarly." He smiled wider, shot a whiskey, lit a cigarette, and handed me one.

"You found your fedora," I said as B9 walked over with another bottle of Maker's Mark and marshmallows.

"How was she?" Stephen King Jr. asked B9.

Beard Angry snapped another picture of me through the fire.

The next day
Journal entry

I left my Blackberry in my car last night! I can't believe this but I don't miss him. (Short Fat Fuck.) For once in the last eight months, I won't go into Moondoggies. I don't have to. Don't feel compelled to. Thank god. So over that place.

April 19, 2007

Compelled.

Not 86'd from Moondoggies for life and after a cooling off period of a few months, we (VF and I) sauntered past the taxidermied lion in the display window.

The window belonged in the entrance of an old barbershop, where everything stayed old on purpose. In addition to the lion: a dusty, cruddy checker board; sewing machine, and decades-old St. Patrick's Day beads. All of it was nailed to the wooden window seats on either side of the Moondoggies door. Maybe Moondoggies used to be a store with a storefront, or an actual barbershop. Otherwise why would there be a display window? Bars in Pismo had no rhyme or reason like they did in LA.

There was no other rational reason for Vanity Fair and me to walk through the door other than Jack living a few blocks away. No Jack, no Moondoggies. *Bad girl.* In the same way I placed valuable break-ables in my car, haphazard in the backseat or trunk, challenging them to smash into pieces or endure the ride, I panted for the rush of caus-ing a problem and finding a solution. My tolerance for re-humiliation stunned and my "learn the hard way" agenda, like Jack, fucked me over. I *never* learned, so the last cliché needn't apply. Solutions were illusionary. *Hence, walking back into this ridiculous place.*

Lightened from less vodka and at eye level, I spotted a booth on the opposite side of the bar.

"It was long, but I loved the piano." VF faced the lion from her side of the booth.

"I still don't get what the conductor does." I felt stupid for admit-ting it, even after writing articles about the local symphony.

"I've been arrested for that," VF admitted.

"Really, drunk in public?" On the way to Moondoggies we didn't stop talking about the four-month-old incident, the latest front-page gossip of our lives. My life.

I couldn't believe it, though. She was *demure.* It made no sense.

"Yeah, it was humiliating at the time. I was young. The cops have nothing better to do here."

"I know, right? You would never be arrested for that in LA. V, it was so embarrassing. Especially with SFF. How he saw the whole thing, I think. And the fines, fuck."

"They just do it so you don't hurt yourself or anyone else. It's preventative. Are you doing community service?"

"Yeah, since I'm already helping at the senior center, I'm hoping I can increase my hours and avoid most of the fines. At Bingo."

"Is it weird being back here?" VF plucked the straw out of her drink.

"No ... kind of? I don't know, as long as it never happens again. Three is my limit, watch me, k? Don't let me have more than three. Ok, this is a Red Bull, but still, no more than three after this. This will be practice for us. Who knows? I may not drink ever again, but it feels right not to drink tonight."

"Got it." She saluted me.

I checked out the crowd. My sight landed on Jack with two girls.

"Look." My head tilted one inch, in slow motion.

He and the two girls vanished behind an olive-skinned dude.

"Hello there, lovely ladies. Hi crazy." A few seconds later the olive skin dude hovered over our booth. He directed the "Hi crazy" greeting at me. The tall, not fat, not thin, dark-haired, and goofy-grinned guy slid into the booth before we reacted.

VF and I locked eyes, and I smiled in fear and embarrassment. *Do you know this guy?*

"You don't remember me, do you?" He asked me.

"Um, no I ... ." I got nervous. Really nervous.

"You told me you were "peachy." He added air quotes to peachy. "A few months back."

"Peachy? What? Wait. Oh my god, in the waiting room. Why were you in jail? You were arrested, too?"

"Defending you, actually. The shitty part is I was arrested the night *before* also." *Olive Skin.*

Olive Skin's elvish grin prompted a thought: *My life might be a lot more interesting after tonight.*

"You're kidding." VF's straw fell out of her mouth. "For what?" She asked him.

"DUI."

On cue, I glanced over when Jack and Walmart's heads swiveled, finally landing on us; a concerned half smile tacked to his face.

"Ok, that sucks. What's going to happen there?"

"I'll pay a fuckload of fines is what's going to happen." He turned to Walmart, who held up her drink while Jack tapped on the glass,

Hey, you're right; that's an ice cube in there, honey!

"So, you're into Jack, huh?"

I shook my head.

"You were pretty outspoken about it that night. I get it—girls dig him." He straightened his back and looked at VF.

Another person to reassure with a lie: "I'm not into him. But yeah, I kind of remember. That was vodka, though. There's nothing there. There was never anything there."

"I'm just saying, he's a smart guy who has his shit together. Most of us don't. Not like him. You know he has a girlfriend, right?"

"I realize that, but I don't have a thing for SFF, for Jack, so I don't care."

I thought they broke up?

He wouldn't shut up. "My theory is like that saying, 'In the land of the blind, the one-eyed man is king.' Anyway, girls love that shit. That's Jack—or SFF you said? What is SFF?"

VF explained with a smirk, "He's short, he's fat, and he's an enormous fuck." I loved hearing this because she hardly ever said fuck.

"SFF. That's fantastic. Better than anything we've given him. How'd you come up with that one? But I'm glad to hear it, that you don't have a thing for him." He stood up. "Be good little lady."

"January." I took a sip of my Red Bull and smiled at Vanity Fair.

He bent down and his mouth closed in on my ear. "I know."

Olive Skin exited and hopped over the railing of the deck, and I watched the entire group make its way toward Jack's house.

Jack reached for Walmart's hand.

1:15 a.m.

After parking my car, I patted myself on the back for being cool and for not being legless by way of Ketel One. Tasks, events and chunks of time could be recalled: driving for and taking care of my friends; meeting boys; remembering people's eyes, hair, or makeup. The smells coming from the bar floor at my feet. The fun didn't last a death-to-my-debit-card 10 hours.

Not watering my tonsils and watching the people who regularly watched me, confirmed what Olive Skin said about the one-eyed man. King—or queen—didn't describe me, but possessing tempo-rary control in an area of my life not involving my family, work, or rela-tionships gave me satisfaction. Underneath satisfaction lay potential. The potential reentry of Jack.

My phone rang.

818?

"Hi, it's Olive Skin."

"Who?" I locked my car and walked upstairs.

"Jail. Olive Skin, from jail. I just saw you at the bar."

"Oh, hey! How'd you get this number?"

"I asked Jack."

"I'm sure that was an interesting conversation. And I *am* really sorry about the whole jail thing."

"It's cool; it wasn't your fault. Can you hang out tomorrow? Dinner?"

"Um, yeah. Sure. You live here?"

"No, I live in LA, but I'm here for a few more days."

"Oh, cool. I work in LA too." Six months ago I reunited with Mr. and Mrs. Z. They hired three assistants to replace me, I trained three assistants, and three assistants quit. It wasn't some monumental con-versation. It was almost like I was expected to come back to work if one of my replacements failed. I didn't need a lot of convincing. I commuted a few times a month, hating every minute of it, but the money was worth it.

Having a bi-county love affair could stifle my gloomy days of searching for Jack. Like moms and daughters and fathers who vow for a loved one in a press conference in front of trees and posters and under clouds,

"I will search for him until the day I die."

Instead, I should have proclaimed, "I just want to prevent this from happening to someone else."

June 2007

"And the award for the most difficult orderer, ever ... ." I teased Olive Skin (B10). He recited the entire menu to me, asked 10 questions of our server, and ordered two thirds off of the two pages of plastic. We had been dating for two months, so I was used to his intensity, even when ordering edamame and sashimi.

"You say that now, but when you try the Dynamite, you'll seriously go out of your mind." He warned me.

Earlier, we met at Barney's Beanery in West Hollywood after one of my Z work days ended. There, my gut went sour knowing B10 had asked me out and his best friend didn't—or even worse, didn't want anything to do with me. More of B10's friends stopped by our booth. I forced myself to make it through the night and cry later at Mr. and Mrs. Z's.

One of the friends was gay and bitter. *Tightly Wound.* I never saw him again, and I couldn't tell you about the shape of his eyes, or if he had nice teeth, but I remembered he worked as a pathologist and drank Corona, which seemed weird. The Corona part. A gay, bitter, Corona-drinking pathologist with too many muscles and moles. Muscular, gay, Corona-drinking pathologist guy brought more fear and tension to the evening. I lifted my arm to signal a waitress. Lighting myself up like a firefly would repress the sourness and make this evening less horror movie-ish.

Back at his favorite sushi joint, on a side street in West Hollywood I had never been on, we sat on semi-uncomfortable seats at the bar as he ordered double rounds of shots and beers. I grabbed his knee.

"Ew, no. Wine for me, I detest Japanese beer." An exasperated face kissed me.

He pulled back and his hand swept over my mouth, "You know that night I was supposed to leave, head back to LA? I stayed after I saw you in Moondoggies. I got shit for it, but I'm happy I did." The bottom half of me warmed.

"I can only guess how Jack reacted to that. He probably doesn't care." I sipped my wine.

A word to define B10? *Mercurial.* Fun, flowing conversation; better (than most of the B's) sex; and a distraction from his best friend, all with a sub rosa context. I wouldn't learn about the sub rosa parts until later. Occasionally, after the fun, *whoosh*: He spat out a temper, worse than mine. B10, upset by the stupidest shit, then apologizing after 24 hours, reminded me of another man I knew. But B10 didn't have Jack Nicholson eyebrows or dirt on his boots.

B10 gabbed on and on with the chef long after we ate our last dishes and I lowered my head to check my Blackberry.

"Come here." He touched my hand and kissed me. With a tender effort, he patted my ass before getting up. He texted me lovey-dovey crap from the bathroom while I paid the $200 bill.

Two hours, later we stumbled out of Canters, then he hugged me for 10 seconds and threw me in a cab. For some reason, I noted the length of time he held on. As drunk as I was, I counted to 10. After I snuck in the Zs' house at 3 a.m., hoping Mrs. Z wouldn't hear the alarm, he left a message on my phone telling me *not* to call him back because I'd only irritate him.

A few minutes later, he texted.

B10: What r you doing drunken dame?

July 2007

Back in Pismo, my mind screened a volleyball game of the B's and an uneasy, familiar tide carrying me out to Jack.

I never responded to B10's "drunken dame" text. In fact, I hadn't talked to him at all since the taxi outside of Canters. I looked forward to seeing him, but didn't know when he'd be back. He was an ass, but when he held my hand or touched me, apertures filled. Still, I wasn't blown away, or bored. B10 simmered at medium heat.

B10 once told me, "Maybe you and Jack are too much alike." I wondered if Jack and I *were* related. In the mirror, a part of him stared back. Usually his blue eyes flashed, then I cackled before I could pin down why.

A few days later ...

I texted B10 while cement grapefruits ripened, peeled, and secreted their acids in my belly. I lit a cigarette. Had he moved onto another "drunken dame" to fuck and order sushi for? He wouldn't be the first boy to stop calling without warning. An image came to me as I smoked: my old Reef flip flops on the passenger side floor of his Jeep, left behind one night after I put on black suede platform pumps.

"Are you ok? I'm worried." I texted him one last time.

I can't tell you what it really is.
I can only tell you what it feels like,
And right now it's a steel knife in my windpipe
... the wrong feels right ...
High off a love, drunk from my hate,
Here we go again.

— Eminem

July 5, 2007

805-817-9091.
Ugh.
"Hi, it's Jack."
"Hey."
"Did I catch you at a bad time?
"No, you're fine, what's up?"
"Olive Skin passed away." *B10.*
Long, long pause.
"What? Wait ... oh my god." I froze.
"I don't know much. His mom is here now."

"Oh my god, what happened? Was it pills?" I thought back to when I gave him a Xanax or two.

"I'm not sure, I have a lot of calls to make. Talk to you later, Sweetie."

My head shook and my mouth hung open as I imagined his mom or dad checking his phone for clues and finding my messages, then my flip-flops.

July 9

I decided not to attend the memorial in LA. After, Jack asked me why: "It was sad. Why didn't you come?"

"I don't know … I just … I couldn't."

I couldn't eat or attend funerals, but I could get tanked.

At 3 in the afternoon, I was one drink in, and VF was 10 minutes away. We hadn't seen each other since it happened: she was away all week with Millionaire in Sonoma for the Fourth of July.

I prayed for his family and prayed he didn't suffer. Wakeless on his gray couch in LA from a handful of pills after a few days of not taking pills. *Sounds peaceful.*

Vanity Fair showed up.

"What happened? Jack called you?" She sat down with a forlorn look.

"I don't know."

"January, this probably was going to happen eventually. I thought you said he took pills."

"Yeah, but I didn't know to what extent, and we don't know if that's what happened. I'm just assuming."

VF fidgeted with her vodka/cran and purse strap. I could tell she wanted Millionaire next to her.

"He told me he was high for like six years straight when he was married. Went to Thailand, screwed, and snorted drugs off of hookers. Went to the Playboy Mansion, drove a Ferrari. High the entire time." I pushed my glass toward Too Tan. I pushed it farther. Finally, she cleared it away.

The sushi night was the last night I felt them, the B10 flutters.

"I can't believe I'll never see a text from him again."

"Have you talked to Jack since?"

I cried, mumbled and started to forget, until words and thoughts stopped forming altogether. Too Tan picked up the Ketel One bottle and fed me.

A taxi was in my future. And puking.

July 12

For a couple of weeks at work I checked incapacitation, catatonia, and hysteria off of my bereavement to-do list. I couldn't pick one as I buried my red and blubbering face into anyone who would let me: bosses, wives of bosses, the receptionist, my brother. I texted Jack every day, scared of the never endings. Even in "real life adult stuff" terrible times, I didn't stop inserting myself into whatever circumstances I fit.

Did he hate me? Does he blame me? I'm still scared of him. Scared this might end us.

"January, get some rest." Editor 2 pushed me out the door. "Work from home or don't work at all. Don't worry about anything right now."

Editor 2, deputy editor of the magazine, was consistently nice to me—partly because he was my boss, but his niceness included fair and decent, which helped in a pinch with Editor 3's antics. His presence forced the kids to behave and he understood my writing, quirks, and my humor. Married with kids, Editor 2 was further along in life than myself, and years younger. Not a hippie, but an amalgam of hippie and one of those Renaissance fairgoers. In baggy jeans; loose, untucked dress shirt; and flip-flops, his unintentional disorganization was stoked with a MacBook, and a quiet corner in which to work.

2 personified a married-for-life man. In 30 years, his wife and he would be the rare couple with a mid-life crisis nowhere in sight—not idealistically happy, but focused and stable. His office, which he rarely used, kept itself filled with stacks of papers and magazines piled in milk crates.

Editor 2's could fool you: a savvy, professional individual on the inside, with a kind, surfer's aura. He didn't surf. In meetings with the five or six of us in editorial, he laughed and slipped a ring off and on his finger as he listened to pitches, updates on stories, or Hippie's tale of why she had a black eye and a scrape on her arm after Burning Man.

"It's a 'fiddle with ring' my wife makes me wear so I don't lose the actual wedding ring," 2 explained at a meeting about an upcoming special issue. He then told Hippie she spelled her name wrong on an Op-Ed piece she wrote about the city councilman/planner who decided four Walgreens within a 10-block radius was a proper use of local real estate and in the citizens' best interest.

That was the last meeting I remembered before B10 died.

The rest of July ...

Horizontal for so long, my left eye slanted farther down than the other. In order to even them out permanently, I stretched open both eyes every morning. I don't know if it worked, but I looked in the mirror at symmetry. My bed head lasted through October: a flattened circle of hair at the part where a yarmulke would go. The hair smooshed and spread out like grass under somebody's butt after a concert in the park. I learned fast how to tease it with a comb.

July could be broken up into categories based on the movies or television I watched.

Week one: *Beverly Hills 90210* reruns. TV on, not watching, hysterical, and scared.

Week two: QVC. Soothing in the background. Numb, no emotion, and not ordering the stone cookware, argan oil that would change my life, orthopedic shoes, or 90 ounces of Philosophy body wash. The box at the bottom of the screen listed everything at $19.95, which they claimed was "under $20."

Week three: Not sure. Lifetime, probably. Facial movements and answered phone calls reemerged that week.

Week four: *AbFab* and *Trailer Park Boys*.

Also week four: *Weekend at Bernie's*. At this point, I smiled and read an *US Weekly* without wanting to burn it in a trashcan.

Salvation by television. I had no contact with SFF.

Jack didn't blame me or hate me; he would have to think of me to have an opinion.

I didn't get out of bed for a month.

August 2007

Grief hunted August like a lion tracked a zebra, devouring its prey after capture.

Even when out of bed and vertical (from 7 a.m. to 2 p.m.) I couldn't make decisions. Driving home after work, I couldn't go home, I couldn't go to the grocery store, I couldn't grab a coffee with friends. I imbibed. I remembered. I wrote. I discovered.

I found out B10 was dating another girl at the time of his death. A subdued jealousy landed near my stomach, but with no one to react to, fight with, or accuse, I didn't wallow for long—although I hated myself a little bit more.

I remembered he didn't like flip-flops, which I lived in.

Shoes

"I can't stand the strap between my toes." He wore Tevas, prompting me to dry heave. After he wore socks *and* Tevas during a visit to Pismo, I intervened.

Outside of Zorro's, he changed clothes next to his car door, into more Jack-like gear. I stood and watched, wondering why he hadn't changed before he picked me up.

"Your 'ex *lovva*' picked this stuff out." Skateboard-ish, black button-down shirt, black Vans, and dark jeans. My stomach twinged.

"I was at his store the other day." Lurch.

"I approve," I told him.

Sex

He pulled me to the foot of the bed like my gynecologist does while I'm in stirrups and his face skyrocketed straight through the middle of my legs.

We fucked well. Going and going, orgasm after orgasm.

One time, he had to get back to LA for work, but he couldn't stop finishing and starting up again.

"I still have to go back to my mom's and pick up my dopp kit." He blew raspberries on my behind.

"What's a dopp kit?"

He never told me.

B10: My mom kissed me goodbye as I was driving off. I flinched because my mouth probably tasted like your twat.

Blackberry/Cell phones

"Get that thing away from me." Referring to my Blackberry's flashing red dot alerting me I had a text, email, or calendar reminder.

"Are you serious?" I asked while we sat outside of my house on lawn chairs.

He took a swig of the beer I kept for him in my fridge. "I don't like electronic lights near me. Near my brain."

Mattress

We broke my bed, twice. The mattress, elevated by cinder blocks and stolen milk crates, gave way. The last time we ever had sex my un-box springed mattress collapsed fast to one side.

"You need to fix this, get a box spring, for Christ's sake." I told him I was lazy and too busy. Childless Brad Pitt bought me one for my birthday.

Temper

He texted, "When, where?" to my invitation to hang out but 85 percent of the time it preceded nonsense.

He ramped discussions into frenzies:

We debated *The Sopranos* or *The Wire* for best TV show of all time. During a Tarantino debate he preferred *Kill Bill* to *Pulp Fiction*.

"*Kill Bill* is rad, I'll admit it."

"See," he added.

"*Sopranos*, for sure though."

"Have you ever seen *The Wire*?" His voice went up an octave and a decibel.

"Not every … ."

"Exactly, you haven't seen the entire series."

"Ok, but … ." I started to respond.

Mistake.

"You reject. You're a fucking … ." The words came through the telephone so easy and swift and without provocation. Stunned, I gently hung up without making a sound, and listened to more of that same nothingness. He called back after a few seconds, apologizing.

Just like my dad. My mother, too.

It was exactly like the stillness, breathlessness, and terror after you hear gunshots. "Way too close" gunshots.

If you've ever been exposed to such a thing, that is.

Vodka

"Belvedere is ok." I agreed.

"Ok? Every 'best vodka' list in the world says hands down, Belvedere."

"I like Ketel One, what do you want? We're arguing about this? You really want to school me in vodka?"

One night at my dad's house while picking something up from my brother, I happened to be on the phone with B10, during the vodka debate (before vodka it was a Hitchcock movie). This time my dad overheard me defending myself—and B10 through the phone as his octaves and decibels increased, again. I tried to pacify B10. My dad was pissed.

"No, Jan, no. That isn't right. Get fucking rid of him." I shushed him.

After the call ended, my dad wanted more details. "Who was that?" He didn't give me a chance to respond. "I'm telling you, I would end it." I didn't have to.

August 14, 10:15 p.m.

Some people I could imagine dying. Some I wished dead. Others I believed to be immortal: the Zs, for example. Surfers, skateboarders, and body boarders I dated in and out of consciousness. Larry David. I couldn't imagine him dead. Or Jack White. I couldn't picture Jack White old *or* dead.

B10 wasn't the first guy I dated who died unexpectedly. The year before, I went bowling on a double date with a girlfriend (whom I don't speak to anymore) and two guys (whose names I can't remember). My date was hot—Antonio Sabato Jr. hot—if you're into Antonio Sabato Jr., which I wasn't but it made the evening bearable.

A few months after bowling, Antonio took a punch to the head outside of the Shack on a Saturday night, fell onto a cement curb, and into a coma. He was dead by Wednesday.

Jack finally called to tell me there was nothing to tell me. We talked about B10, the funeral, and what his mom claimed was the cause of death. I never found out.

"Are you with Walmart?"

"No, going solo tonight." He paused.

"Are you propositioning me?" I asked.

"Yeah, come on over. Haha, we don't need to go down that road, Sweetheart."

In my living room I froze in front of the window, ocean, and moon.

He rattled on. "I was kidding, I don't want to encourage bad behavior, make you drink again. You're doing really good."

"I didn't—don't—drink because of you. I drink because of me. I wanted you whether I was drunk or not."

September 2007

My mourning of B10 ended with two loud bangs. Well, one and a half.

At a noontime Dolphin Bay Resort summer concert, sun glistened over a sea of sunglasses. VF and I strolled the walkways bending through manicured grass behind Lido, and through invisible rows in

147

front of a stage of reggae music. Our heads tipped back pale yellow margaritas and our attention went from this to that: the crowd, the concert, the headlands, and the rock islets layered in mucky blacks and whites from hundreds of years of bird poop.

Groups of three, four, and five talked, held perspiring cups and smudgy wine glasses, and bobbed their heads. Most overlooked the sapphire water, the butterflies flying from shrub to shrub, and the live music. Vanity Fair and I caught up with at least 40 people in a Little League sportsmanship "good game" way. Each step brought on a new *Hi* and business card exchange. Some even shouted a "Where have you been!?" over the wind and music.

We were so *formal* at a reggae concert. Where was the running up to and hugging? The blabbering and table-crashings? It wasn't B10's death. We always put forth this suave, businesslike persona. I think VF liked to keep her demure distance from others. When I was with her, I did the same (to the best of my ability).

For my first outing since B10 died, I wore a silky, buttery sleeveless blouse with a long drape front section down the middle and slits up the sides. With a skinny white pant, my outfit served its purpose on the hot day with a sea breeze.

I liked cute clothes: trendy when necessary, but classic. Things had to last, but I wasn't comfortable in only one stapled trend. That's why I shopped at H&M whenever I had time after work in LA. The clothes and accessories were inexpensive, gorgeous and everlasting. I never edited closets because most of my wardrobe I revisited, and I didn't have a lot to revisit; I didn't own 30 pairs of jeans and 75 pairs of shoes. I owned probably five pairs of jeans. Shoes, maybe 20, of which I wore half.

On reggae day, I carried a vintage clutch, wore a wooden block bracelet, and flats, appropriate for grass walking. Not Louboutins. Clumsy and spill prone, I didn't dare purchase $100 tops, or jeans, or even pricier shoes. Louboutins didn't pair well with dribs of pinot or morsels of Brie.

It took me 10 minutes to spot Jack and B7 (and his mohawk) hunched over a large round table 20 yards to our right. I didn't bother mentioning it to V. They sat with other surfers, goths, and those other girls—*oh what are they called when they have tattoos of Marilyn Monroe, vintage scarves, and poofs on top of their heads? Rock-a-billy? Yeah I think that's it. Is this his type?*

I wondered if he recognized me behind my cat-eye sunglasses. He drank a Bud light, the only one he would have. During my second cocktail, he turned his head in my direction. After my second, he walked up to us.

"Hey, Sweetie, you look great. Hey there, how are you?" He said both of his hellos at once. Vanity Fair didn't respond. We hugged.

"Great. I'm good. You?" I scanned his outline as I talked, and I smiled at no one to his left. I held up my glass: "Good, we're heading this way." I pointed behind him. "Have a great day, ok?"

"Bye, Sweetheart."

———

By 4 p.m. I was wearied on my couch, keeping one foot flat on the floor to slow the spin. B7 called. B7 came over. Too smashed to have sex, I puked while he guzzled a Tecate he brought with him.

"I'm gonna get going."

Is he already in the frame of the opened door or is he still in the kitchen?

I heaved the toilet (and *into* the toilet) wishing, then unwishing he would hold my hair.

After a nap on my floor the welcomed, pesky, corner red light blinked at 7 p.m.

Jack.

By 7:45 his wide chest pumped up and down, and his hands shoved painful pressure into my boobs, pushing them up, toward my chin. Walmart didn't matter when the second boy of the night, her boyfriend, strayed into my bedroom. I didn't want to think about what the neighbors thought, but I did. Same went for B10.

"I'm going to count down, I'm almost there," he moaned with heavy breath.

Count down to what? Why doesn't he shut up?

"10, 9, 8, 7, 6, 5, 4, 3, 2." *Pause. Grunt.* "I came, Sweetie."

A vision of a rapist, and a porn star, radiated itself onto the ceiling. He plopped down next to me, his arms falling behind his head.

What was wrong with me? What was wrong with him? I hated us.

The next morning, after a shower, I craned my neck in the mirror trying to find out why my back stung. Three, inch-long, pink nail scratches on each shoulder blade. I bet those rock-a-billy girls craned their necks to find the same marks on their backs—not from Jack, but from stupid tattoos. The girls pretended a cat, jaguar, or some other animal inflicted them.

What was wrong with me?

I learned to live half alive.
And now you want me one more time.
And who do you think you are?
Running around leaving scars,
Collecting your jar of hearts.

— Christina Perri

September 10, 2007

10:30 p.m.

Every time I think he's gonna call, he does.
We discussed the weekend already gone.
"Went to the lake."
"Walmart, too?"
"Nope."
"Vanity Fair and I went hot air ballooning for an article I'm writing."
"Nice, who's Vanity Fair?"
"You met her the last time I saw you."

"Oh yeah, she's cute. That was nice, Sweetie," he replied when I mentioned our last night together.

"What are you up to now?" I picked at a cuticle.

"Sunburnt and relaxing."

I texted him an hour later because I needed more than a phone conversation.

Me: I still have the scratches you left on my back.

He didn't respond. I hoped Walmart snuck a peek at his phone and saw the little bubble and asked *Who's JE?* She knew me.

September 11

"You taste good." He licked my ass, taking a bite, sparking a body shudder. His tongue grated by back, leading his teeth to each shoulder.

I wonder what he's like as a boyfriend. Where did the condom come from?

He pulled his pants off, and we threw them on the floor. The sex killed me. Killed my cunt and any chance I wouldn't hold onto his neck a bit longer. I was sober.

Another plus to not becoming bar tuned: I remembered elements of us: how his sweaty head smelled; if we spoke or held hands while we fucked, if he looked at me. He never commented on my smells. Sociopaths didn't smell. I loved when a guy greeted me with a silent inhale. They'd comment on the bergamot, musk, and sandalwood and adore me in whiffs.

To counteract infrequencies, I wrote an article about his record store, and we went from disquieting to must-have. I gave him space and let him contact me first. I calculated averages as I bought a Diet Coke before work. He lived a few miles away; a year ago, there were 170 between us. Either way, I saw him just as often.

September 13

The news ticker exploded on my Blackberry.

Jack and Walmart broke up.

"She betrayed me. I'll never talk to her again."

I didn't care on what floor of the building truth lived. In bed that night, I pawed at his shirt, wishing he was naked so I could assault his skin directly. After pleading for everything, I cried when I came.

September 14

Jack: what are u up too
Me: chillin. What about you?
Jack: just got home. Feet up relaxin. U at home
Me: lol. Good for you. No I'm not at home.
Jack: where u at
Me: LA.
Jack: what for
Me: Work.
Jack: oh, well have a great weekend
Me: u too babe.

September 14, 4:30 p.m.

Me: hey-I'll be home in a bit. My plans changed. If u can hang call me
Jack: what time
Me: sixish
Jack: ok I'm at party for a friend tonight. Ttyl. Drive safe
Me: will do

6:25 p.m.

Jack: u home yet
Me: ah yes, just got out of hot shower
Jack: naked
Me: yep
Jack: can u stay that way
Me: of course

6:45 p.m.

Jack: cxl that idea till Sunday
Me: alright but I can't promise I'll stay naked until then.
Jack: haha ok.

September 16
    Jack: what are u up too
    Me: hey-working…u?
    Jack: in slo? Chillin
    Me: no Pismo.
    Jack: at ur house
    Me: yep.
    Jack: be right over
    Me: nooooo.
    Jack: I was kidding anyway, but why?
    Me: just can't hang today sweetie sorry. I want to see u though. Call me later in the week.
    Jack: lots of work to do?
    Me: yeah. And some other shit too…too much to text.

He called me on both phones.

"What's up?"
"Not much. So you're busy, huh?" *He salivated. Love it.*
"Yeah, on deadline. And I have a date in a few hours." *Lie.*
"Not even for a quickie?
"You know, I saw you."
"Me, oh yeah? Where?"
"You and Walmart, in town."
"Oh, you silly girl."
"Oh, you silly boy."

September 23, 2007
    During my first glass of wine at Old Vienna, a German beer garden kind of place, I watched a kid behind the bar in the kitchen with an iPod on his arm. A dishwasher. He stuffed a slice of an onion and pepper pizza in his mouth, which made me laugh because he stood under a big red swastika.
    Kidding.

Dishwasher chewed with his mouth open under Germany's flag and a 5-foot long, distressed, framed advertisement for Wernesgrüner. During my second glass, Dishwasher mutated into a dead ringer for Shia LeBeouf. I instantly wanted him.

I reeled B9 back, out of necessity. A refreshing deviation from the offscouring from Jack and the incest clusterfuck of B7.

Old Vienna was beer and skittles, my favorite non-LA bar, but categorized under "Infrequently Visited." I blamed the SFF radar. A petite, warm-wooded bar space with tall booths along the wall of the front entrance. I loved those booths the most. On the same strip as the Shack, the stucco building faced the 101 in front of different dumpy houses. It was always beachfront quiet outside at 1 a.m., when I traipsed outside, my clothes reeking of pilsners and sausages. All of the bars saturated my hair and jackets with different scents: smoke, fry oil, seafood, barbecue, beer, and alcohol (obviously). The bathroom door taught me German. "Herren" meant men/gentlemen; I couldn't remember what woman meant.

"Hey you." B9 strolled toward me at the bar, a polished baby mahogany that sat six.

"Hey." He kissed me on the cheek.

I had been there at least a half hour. I liked to get to places early, get comfortable and a teeny bit buzzed. I lived for sitting in front of a glass half empty when a boy arrived. I wanted an empty mind, and for now, empty except for Shia LeBeouf.

"You look great. Do I need to catch up?" He pointed.

"Thanks, no, I just got here."

He ordered an Oktoberfest beer.

"Yeah, we're playing … ." Three words in, and he soured my wine with his soft voice talking about nothing interesting.

I texted SFF when B9 headed to the bathroom.

9:40 p.m.
  Me: hey.
  Jack: whats up

Me: want to come over?
Jack: working late
Me: call me if you want when you're done.
Jack: ok

An hour later

Jack: u still up?
Me: yeah
Jack: u up for awhile
Me: I can be. I want my lips on your...
Jack: oh snap

Another half hour later, and a switch from wine to vodka

"So, how's work?" He asked me. Earwax was about to fall out of B9 left ear. I wanted to pluck it out.

"It's good. Doing a cover story on the music awards. You're nominated, aren't you?" I chewed on my lime and took three sips the Ketel One/soda.

"Yeah. It's cool *Obsidian* puts on an event like that. Should be fun. We're gonna do a few new songs from the new album." I stepped outside to smoke.

Jack: U up
Me: yes I am
Jack: u want me over
Me: absolutely

He called me a minute later.

Two minutes later a big rig's horn blasted over the 101. The warmth hit me as the door shut behind. I walked over and stood next to B9's barstool.

"Well, I'm gonna take off."

An hour after that

He grabbed me by the neck with one hand, a lightning bolt hitting a zip line from his mouth to mine, different from before and in a couple-like way.

"You said 'snap' earlier. That's hilarious," I laughed hard when I said it.

He placed a hand above my chest to feel the vibration of my whole body laughing. "How's your bro and dad?"

"Everyone's good, you?"

"You datin' anyone?"

Yes, but I want to be dating you. Do you know what dating is? Is this dating?

"Yes, you?" If I said yes, I seemed less attainable, happy, and not obsessed with him. If I said no, I was available and vulnerable. Either way ...

"I'm taking a breather after you-know-who."

October 2007

B9 didn't vanquish totally; he was the slow wind I needed but didn't want. The biggest problem: The idea of B9 was far more exciting than B9 himself. Alcohol *had* to be involved; without Ketel One and soda, or a beer for him, we sat around wooden tables with crisp smiles, rimmed by 5 minutes of mechanical chatter about the view, weather, or his latest show or instrument mastered. I was trying to drink less so basically I was now losing a boyfriend because of sobriety. *Is that irony? Seriously, I'm asking, because I really don't know. Seems like it could be.*

Toward the end, on our last date at dinner, then the Shack, our harmony faded out completely with each drink unconsumed, before we gave up and walked to our cars. B9 should've been *the* guy because I'd have a fruitful and meaningful life with him. He'd end up producing and recording music in LA, we'd live in Laurel Canyon and make love until a musical prodigious, handsome, modest, polite boy appeared and then a girl who'd become a CEO of Apple or Spanx in 40 years. The logical fantasy didn't include career plans for myself. I didn't care. I'd be a mommy. He represented the best of both worlds: creative, kind, not a player, soft, but with a chipped edge. Maybe all of the B's were like this. Sobering. Correct. Boring.

Boring was brilliant, but made me want to put my head in a toilet, then a guillotine.

October 3
Random, embarrassing journal entry

It's 7:30, totally wish he'd call. I'm hungry but won't eat ... I should have gone running ... fuck ... that pizza and ice cream was so good on Friday. That's all I want to eat. I would, and could, eat a whole pizza every day. Depending on the day, I might throw up after. But bulimia is a lot of work: the timing, water, soda, use two or three fingers, don't eat bread, eat ice cream, eat Cheetos first so you know when you're done puking. So much to remember. ex-lax is easier.

October 12th to 14th

Jack and I talked on the phone and texted more. He came over for a third time: Outstanding sex/weird conversations. Upping my game meant being cool and uncling-y outside of bed.

If I see him out, be nice, but get away fast.

Faster than he can.

The self-discipline didn't last. I boiled over and drank from a glass half empty: the other half filled with charcoaled vodka and dissolutions for garnish. Dirks stabbed me, and what I didn't have. He never took me to dinner, I never rode in his stupid car (SUV?) yet other activities connected us.

At midnight in front of *South Park*, I craned my neck to the left and we kissed. I wish I could describe more romance. Candles. A bubble bath? Possibly a candle, but I didn't care about the blurred lines of "romance." No time! I had only a few hours of Jack. When I pictured a fantasy, the events edged closer to domestic violence than love. Standing, shoving, and taking off each other's clothes: film footage edited into my sex life. The shoved-up-against-the-wall scenario never happened.

The few seconds he rolled on top of me were forgettable. He took off my jeans while I lay on the bed, but bras and tops were my responsibility. Our sleepovers halted: not a gradual or subtle change. Not that there were gobs of them to begin with.

"No sleepovers, sorry Sweetie." Seeing my bra on the floor eroded something in me, I wasn't sure what.

"That's cool, I wasn't planning on it. I have a huge day tomorrow."

"Ok. Good Babe. You know, Walmart might stop by or call."

October 26, 2007
Journal entry

Hate him. Being distant. After almost two weeks, I texted him. He barely responded five hours later. How does someone "barely respond?" I told him to call me when he can. I have to stop this once and for all because I want to fucking kill myself.

October 28

Jack: What r u up too

Me: Supposed to be writing/working but I'm being lazy. What's up with u

Jack: same here

Me: nice

Jack: wanna

Me: ?

Jack: u free for a bit

Me: no. sorry sweetie

Jack: Too busy?
Me: never too busy for that. But I just can't.
Jack: ur monthly friend?

Good lord.

Me: no, that wouldn't stop me either.
Jack: so u have company
Me: I love having sex with you. U are a wonderful guy. But you coming over for an hour and then leaving…it's way too hard for me. not good for me. I want more, and I know you can't give that to me.
Jack: I understand. We should just b friends so u don't hate me.
Me: I could never hate you.
Jack: good then we r friends, have a good night and get some work done. TTYL

Want to kill myself.

in·cu·bus
noun
\-b□s\
plural incu·bi \-□ bī\

1: an evil spirit believed to lie upon persons in their sleep and especially to have sexual intercourse with women by night
2: nightmare

January 2008

Last year taught me nothing. Ok, it taught me one thing: Don't get arrested.

Jack's new year's pastime? Texting me pictures and videos of his penis. In one gem, he jacked off on instant replay: a spout of cloudy off-white, up close. His comforter and headboard in the background. Horrifying, not an aphrodisiac, and expectant of an "LOL" from me. No, not candid pics of him at the lake or him and his friends, just dick pics.

Me: LOL! ☺

He was a moron.

Like any other creative thinking person in love, I imagined the everyday stuff in between the pornography: Jack paying his bills, making dinner, biting into a banana or brushing his teeth.

His sweet and caring side showed itself a few times a year.

Jack: Did you see the moon? Go and look.

I looked out my car window. The albino disc glowed, suspended just above the tips of the hills. Yards from his house and a mile or two from my own freeway exit, I pictured him in front of the mirror shaving and dressing in surfer/skater boy attire. After I got home while unpacking my trunk in my driveway I wished for a change in atmosphere or temperature in the next 30 minutes. It was Saturday night. Date night. I would have done anything for him to just, simply, *ask me out.*

After the moon text, I was forgotten.

Instead that night in Moondoggies, he'd meet up with the skank he texted after my moon text. I imagined her name. *Amber? Crystal? Laurie? Stacey?*

⎯⎯⎯

At 8:45 the next morning, my phone chimed on the way to a beach run,

Jack: make it home ok from LA?

January 4

After a hooking-up hiatus, Jack brought over a cock ring for pleasure.

"Whose pleasure?" I asked him. I wasn't into porn props; they would cheapen our time and that was not acceptable. I was nuts in the sack, up for almost anything, but I had a wholesomeness threshold, and the roadblocks began with threesomes, orgies, and certain sex toys, if any at all.

"Yours, of course. You've never used a vibrator?"

I shook my head and slid under the sheet. Then he spoke the words all girls love to hear,

I only have an hour.

I made a face to no one in the darkness because each time we made love I anticipated him with unknowns. A dense sadness and sense of loss inevitably cuddled with me longer than he did. I knew the outcome if we weren't at his house.

"You're in for a treat." Twenty minutes later he walked out of my bedroom door.

January 5

I asked him if Walmart suspected.

Jack: um, maybe this is getting to be to much for u?

Me: I meant … I'm sorry. I didn't mean anything by it

Jack: No its cool and u r right. I just don't think I can have sex with only one woman my entire life

Me or her?

January 15, 2008

He came over. After I sedated my nervous dorkiness with Xanax, he came in my mouth, and I swallowed.

"My little cum muffin." He pulled me closer, then on top of him. *Still hate that word.*

I sensed fleeing. I applied pressure to his lap, a silent, physical, sensual prayer for him to remain in bed and violate me all over again. Nope.

"Ok, see you soon? Maybe next time your house." *Single? Not single?*

"Sorry, Sweetie. No sex on the home front for a while." *Not single.* The back of his shirt and jeans sprinted out the door.

I was a concubine. No, I was less than that.

February 10, 2008

Jack again. In bed, the kissing descended further and found a rhythm as we fit together, snuggled and watched TV. He kissed my head, twice. I hadn't seen him in a month. Tender and semi-slow didn't hold out for long: he crammed his dick up my ass so hard I traced his actions back to my gay theory—but then I came like a jackhammer while he went down on me. He came and transported me to wistful mania.

But, I didn't hear about his life; we didn't speak or catch up. My body wanted time more than sex. I overflowed with anecdotes and ideas, holding a wanting to share. As a reporter doing a story on Jack, the elusive source, I asked questions but rarely received answers. Now my whole life smelled like him, his cum. My hair, my bed, the house.

Wait. I smelled something else besides Jack.

"So, you're not staying."

"Do you want me to?" *Hell yes.*

"Um, I don't … ." I sniffed again. "What *is* that?" My head whipped around as I checked out the room.

That's right, sociopaths don't smell.

He tied his shoes. His heavy hand grabbed the doorknob.

Was it coming from me? I sniffed my armpits. *No.* I looked down. My top sheet had a stain. I smelled the fabric. I put a hand on my behind. *Oh my god.*

I got out of bed and turned the lights on. Poop was on the walls, the headboard, and even on the bed skirt. *The walls—what the fuck?*

Was the sex and canoodling because of the time constraint? I promised myself I'd obsess later.

I had a poop situation.

I texted him the next day after spending $30 on Lysol, bleach, and paper towels.

Me: Thanks.

Jack: What? For that good luvin?

Me: Um, no, you didn't smell it, you must have.

Jack: What.

Me: poop! There was poop everywhere. you fucked the shit right out of my ass. My walls were covered in shit. Poop!

Jack: oh no way, sorry. LOL. I've heard of that happening tho.

Me: It was a bitch to clean up. Walls, ceiling, all bedding. A mess.

Jack: Sorry sweetie.

Note to self: white bed not ideal when boys are in it.

February 27

I found out the fuckwit hadn't been with Walmart since December. I read somewhere most couples break up between December and February. I assumed that's what happened. He invited me over, which required another Xanax since the last time I mentioned his bed, he made that annoying home front reference. After we watched TV, fucked, and talked, I left. No news and no idea what these latest developments meant, but I drove home clam-chowder-in-a-bread-bowl happy. I didn't deprive myself of him, and no willpower was worth the spectacular sex.

March 2008

I never knew when another B galloped in on his white horse. An opportunity of hope and an adequate distraction arrived suddenly.

B11 was a night swim in a turquoise pool: refreshing. Also, level headed; normal job; never angry, bored, or vexed; wasn't an addict; had green eyes, a sensible car, and preppy clothes.

Let's define preppy here and now: Solid color, knit, crewneck sweater (and/or old button-up sort of dress shirt—each too big) khakis or "slacks" of some sort and not the smartest choice of shoes available at the simplest of local stores.

B11 *was* his knit sweater. He made sense, maybe the most of all of the B's. He was a staff writer/reporter at the local weekly and we touched base over a fundraiser we were both promoting. A few days later he emailed me.

I concentrated on B11, our plans, and my perfume. My non-Jack dates formed a pattern: normal-sized men, decent looks, in the beginning stages of success, and they *wanted me.*

First date: watched and cringed at *No Country For Old Men* while eating popcorn and flinching, then slamming into one another every time Javier Bardem came on the screen. I did the flinching and slamming. We paused outside of the theater in Pismo and found a deserted main street and a two-hours-old fog. He kissed me under a flyer taped to a light post advertising a barbecue/concert at a park. His face fit his preppy look: not at all ugly but not at all hot. It didn't matter. I didn't remember the kiss.

"Ok, how terrifying was Javier Bardem with the weird oxygen tank thing?" I wanted to discuss his hair too, but stopped myself.

"Yeah, straight to the head. I've never seen anything like it." He stuck a straw in his Coke.

I sighed. "Those first words, Tommy Lee Jones said, like narrated in the first scene. 'Be there in 15 minutes,' about the prisoner going to hell. I think I'll be obsessed with Tommy Lee Jones for a while."

"Or Cormac McCarthy." He added as he scanned the menu before ordering for us at the Chinese restaurant.

"Right." I smiled at him while he ordered carbs. *Great.*

"You're funny," he said. "Funny" January meant unique, hyper, and/or full of trivial opinions. After the middle-aged waitress put the chicken chow mein on the table, I excused myself and cried in the restroom. I cried for a night's worth of respect to give a guy who bought me dinner and offered me more than his penis. B11 picked me up in his sad Toyota. Sad? It shouldn't have been. His Toyota was a miracle and, literally, more than Jack had ever given me. I prayed for anything but Jack as I cried over the sink.

Hey, jackass! That last prayer's been answered! Anything but Jack is here!

I cried for myself; for my monumentally lopsided, invisible priorities. The tears didn't work; they made me pissed. Revenge-drinking pissed.

March 15

On our fourth date, we went to the Roost.

The Roost kept up with the region's rustical feel: an old pool table in the back and a smoking porch with unemptied tin buckets playing dress up as ashtrays. Similar to the general store a block away or the ice cream parlor next door, it blended into its Main Street locale where parades passed through and kissing booths stood annually. You'd expect Harleys, although there wasn't a huge biker presence on a daily or nightly basis, but on certain Sundays in October, motorcycles waited two-deep for their riders to polish off whiskey and tri tip.

B11 ordered a Sam Adams. "They don't have Ketel One, is Stoli alright?"

He turned to me again, "Three limes, really?"

I laughed and nodded as a sloppy tonk sang a gospel Elvis tune.

"This place is cool, and a live show. Not bad, right?"

Fingers squeezed limes, hand picked up glass, glass met lips, glass met bar. I dwelled on the crying from our first date, objectives, and current situation. Did I want to be *here* right now?

Knit sweater is good, but I'm not attracted to good right now. After the glass hit the counter, the vulpine part of my brain evening-dreamed about three objectives: *Squirrel myself away, text Jack, and be in Jack's bed by midnight.*

"I want gum. Do you want gum? I need gum." I picked up my purse.

"7-Eleven's a block away, we passed it on the way here. I'll be right back."

"Ok, no, I'm good. But are you sure? I bet they have mints or gum here, behind the bar." He pointed to the bartender.

"No, I'll just be a sec." I sprang off my stool before B11 could get his attention.

On the short walk to Jack's house, I called him. No answer. He texted me back.

Jack: Where are you?

He greeted me in pajamas and a hard-on. *Kidding.*
"Well, hey there, you look good." He kissed me on the cheek.
I explained to him why I was panting.
"Wait, he's at the Roost? You're crazy, Sweetie. You better get back."
"I don't want to get back."
After we fucked a few cups of coffee into me, he crawled to his side of the bed. Ten minutes later the bartender looked up from washing glasses, "He bailed about a half hour ago."
I wasn't a broken, unrequited person. I was careless, weak, and evil. I was the manipulator. I was Short Fat Fuck. I was nothing.

April 5, 2008

Our foreheads and bodies pressed together. He brushed away a sweaty strand of hair stuck to my face. He didn't normally touch my face. Seconds earlier, we came thunder fast while he impaled me on the wall above my bed.
Don'tmoveohmygoddonotmove. My hands became ghosts when I pulled harder and moaned into his shoulder blade. *Dontfuckingstop.* He ground my insides into a fine dust.
"Do you know how amazing you are?" I asked him as my lower body deflated.
"Yeah, the sex is pretty awesome with you, Sweetie."
He left, and I rolled over to my down pillows and fell asleep on his smell. The next day, my bedroom smelled like Tide, his cologne, and stale sweat.

April 6, 2008

I was late. In a half hour, I was meeting B11, Vanity Fair, and Millionaire. B11 believed my outline of improbabilities regarding the other night at the Roost.

"On my way to the store my dad called me. I had to race over there. I'm sorry."

"It's cool; I get it."

Today's phrase was "Day Drinking." I cheered on the simplistic afternoon like I was at a USC game. I defied consequences until the next morning when I woke up to a purse full of crumpled, smeared bar tab receipts. It wasn't only the discovery of the number on the subtotal line—and the hour I lost pissed off at myself. It was the tips coming after. $20 here, $50 there, and always 30 percent or more of the bill jotted down on that troublesome *add tip here* line. Was I the only one who drunk-tipped like George Clooney leaving a poker table?

Is Clooney a big tipper? He seems like he would be. Ok, I'm calling it: Clooney's a big tipper.

Me: Black nails with a cherry shine seen in sunlight, white wide-leg linen pant, a navy and white striped sweater, and canvas wedge sandals. Very Nantucket. Except for the nails. I relied too much on wedges in Pismo. I was sick of wedges. I wanted to wear flip-flops, stilettos.

Concealer below the eyes and around the nose. Bronzer, mascara and lip-gloss. After a long sip of a Calcareous cabernet, I saw it. Sitting on the carpet in front of my floor-to-ceiling mirror, I bent my head to the left and moved closer. *Shit.* The mark went from dark to light then light to dark at my pulse point.

Sequins of frothy ocean water rolled past me on the 101. 50 times in my rearview mirror, I re-applied and recoiled (smiled) at Jack's plum lip print on my neck, a thumping little purple Earth. At Lido I attempted to keep the right side of my face away from him.

"You having fun?" B11 asked, putting his arm around me.

After a couple of hours, full bottles of wine in the center of the circular table thanked us for emptying them, and my fermentation took B11's hand. I leaned over to a light kiss. I sighed and gazed west.

Dolphin Bay was the place you, anyone, or I would get married: a resort designed for a purpose. The sprawling, closest thing Pismo had to a ritzy resort in the area had a saltwater pool with a view and 100 feet of shamrock-green grass acting as floor seats before a stage of cornflower brininess. Water was so bright in certain sections and lines, I would bet pin money it would be warm, but the Pacific in Pismo was always cold. Palm trees tilted into the buildings and sky-scrapered the sunset. Cabo came to mind on the walk from Lido to the pool and out onto the lawn.

As our glasses smudged, dried, and became wet again, I noticed red wine settling at the corners of B11's lip.

"How are you doing?" His hand went to my knee when he spoke.

I smiled and took a long sip. "I'm good, good. Isn't it gorgeous out?"

Vanity Fair and Millionaire basked under the sun, giving us slices of the umbrella.

"Orlando Bloom stayed here when they filmed *Pirates of the Caribbean* in Pismo," B11 reported. He looked like a professor's TA.

"Oh, that's right. In the dunes?" V liked B11. But her anti-facial expression didn't change as she spoke.

"Millionaire, how's business?" I asked. He developed oceanfront properties, and according to VF, owned about 45 miles' worth of shore up and down the Central Coast. He smiled and stroked her thigh.

"Why? You ready to settle down, buy a lot?"

"Yes. Yes I am, in fact."

"I have the perfect location for you."

Millionaire left his wife and kids in 2007 for Vanity Fair. The almost unheard of outcome of the cliché would've been fucking unbeliev-able, if not for the fact, I witnessed the transgression. Before the secret was out, he slid laptops under her front door and surprised her with clandestine trips to Big Sur. VF recapped unimaginable experi-ences in a hot tub nestled in secluded forests, breakfast, and serious relationship-y conversations on a balcony overhanging those infa-mous jagged edges. Now they went everywhere together: dinners, baseball games, parties, walks in the park, and errands to Rite Aid and Trader Joe's. At events she (or we) attended or volunteered at, he showed up a couple of hours in. I imagined their conversation that morning, about the meet-up, and envied how he kept his word and showed up.

"Poor guy. I wouldn't leave him alone last night." She had all of him. The gamble paid off.

We paid the bill; I left the tip, and waved to a few friends on our way out of the hotel. VF mouthed to me about the Earth plum. I walked behind, and then around our group to keep B11 on my right. *Or is it my left?* Vanity Fair whispered, "Right," and her and Millionaire took off for dinner elsewhere.

"Shack?" B11 nodded in agreement.

B11 adjusted his arms over chili cheese fries on the tall table in a corner by the fireplace and foosball. He wasn't smiling. I waved to Owner.

"You look like you want to fire me or something. Like you're my boss." I laughed the laugh of someone buzzed enough to ignore reality.

"I have to know this is going somewhere." He said it softly and looked away after. *Did he notice the Earth plum?*

I inspected my surroundings while trying to form a thought. The lighting was no lighting at all. Being in the Shack in the daytime was unsettling and wrong, under these circumstances; tense, serious, and grown up. I wanted to go home. I wanted to see Jack.

"Ok, I'm sorry, but sex … I 'm just … ." I successfully fended off sex with B11 since *No Country For Old Men.*

"No, the sex part, I get. But I wanted you to come over last night, and you flaked." Ah yes, *the don'tmoveohmygoddonotmove, ground me into a fine dust* night. I looked down quickly so he wouldn't see my eyes roll into the back of my head in memory.

I didn't want to hurt this person anymore. The wounds weren't deep, the timing ideal. *For who?*

Un·re·quit·ed
adjective \☐☐n-ri-☐kwī-t☐d\

1. Not requited: not reciprocated or returned in kind, as in love.

April 15, 2008

He roared into my Spandex-covered body. I pushed him away. "Let me shower."

"Nope, I love you dirty and sweaty." He sucked on my neck.

I love you! Ha!

He raised my sports bra over my head and lowered my pants, throwing me on the bed. He entered me from behind as he cupped my boobs. *I* focused on my orgasms. Jack was an unstinting philanthropist every time we hooked up: A salaciously juicy paradox. However egotistical and sociopathic, he worked his white ass off until I was satisfied. No other boy did this for me.

He came "hard" and wanted me to watch.

I wished he could be excavated from my brain. *Guy-is-a-jerk neurosurgery, the first of its kind.*

He rolled on his back, thin horror-movie-slit eyes veering over to me.

"I love to please you." I hugged his chest.

"Me too." He said before he started to sing, "Baby Got Back."

"Omg, I love you … I meant I love … ." *Nervous dork laugh.*
"I know what you meant."
So in love. Hold off on the neurosurgery.

April 19

Jack was single and lying about it. Still.
I couldn't sleep.
The lameness, the lying, the constant mindfuck game of Clue he played with me had skills of sandpaper, then a vice. I texted him, wanting his input because I had no idea what to do. He admitted to them breaking up but still wouldn't fall asleep in my bed. I finally asked why.
"That's a couples' thing, Sweetie."
Again, how could I feel so strongly for someone who didn't reciprocate or even understand my predicament? *You want what you can't have.* The idea teetering on banality seemed destructive and scientifically inexplicable. I did have him in a way. Thanks to Walmart: Walmart instituted the Dumb Boring Girlfriend Syndrome.
D.B.G.S. was my philosophy for men, but specifically and currently about why Jack would most likely, never be my boyfriend. Jack, and most men, wanted a partner in life they can manipulate, lie to, get away with things. Jack admitted he needed more than one vagina to fuck. But his need to operate all of the puppet strings was as constitutional as the white blood cells in his bone marrow. So, savvy people like him live with the disease of the Dumb Boring Girlfriend Syndrome (Walmart) and treat it with "On the down low, thought provoking, additional pussy side project" (me).
Remember, men want soft spoken and gentle. Don't talk. Be the name voyeurs and comrades speak of.

I would be the one with the power, not him, another fact I didn't know. I liked advantageous manipulations more than I liked truth. A bullshit detector had been implanted long ago, a microchip an inch deep into my thigh. Like my SFF radar, I honed instincts—and not because I was smart; most of humanity was easy to read. What they said, facial expressions, their eyes (biggest indicator) their reactions, their pauses or quick responses condensed into a nifty report I glanced over when necessary. All of the data informed me who lied, manipulated or what they thought. Was I proud of my theory, of my recognition of what was alarming, unhealthy, and a waste of my time? Of course. Would it deter me? Save me? Teach me? Prevent me? Cure me? Change me? Did it matter?

May 7, 2008
Here we are: At the point where Unrequited began.

"I'm sorry, I just don't feel that way about you ... and I quite honestly believe I never will. I just don't feel that spark."

Before that generous offering, Short Fat Fuck also informed me, *"I thought we were fuck buddies."*

After a bomb of a statement like that one, charred bits of myself absorbed only useless data when it came to Jack.

Disregard what I said before. I didn't hone instincts. I was motherfucking gullible. I was dumber than all of them.

May 8

"Don't feel that spark" rubbed me raw, but I made a commitment to help Vanity Fair at a fundraiser the month before. She didn't tolerate my flake rate of 75 percent and opposed the last year of my life with a vengeance. The looks she shot me through her long brown hair, sunglasses, and creamy skin terrified me, and I didn't want to hear what she might have said out loud. Even if I was a big girl, and she wasn't my mother.

On the Avila golf course, we served hot bowls of butternut squash ravioli and plastic cups of pinot to old coots, the regular drunks I saw around Pismo who had more money than most drunks, golfers, and up-and-comers in their 20s and 30s. Every event in the county highlighted one central element: Wine.

- Savor the Central Coast (Featuring 25 wineries).
- The Taste of Pismo (Featuring 26 wineries! Take that, Savor the Central Coast!).
- Day of Epicurean Delights (Took place at the Castle house—near B6/Owner's house and features 27 wineries! Take that, Taste of Pismo!).
- Central Coast Wine Festival.
- Pinot Festival.
- Pinot *and* Paella Festival.
- Paso Robles Wine Festival.
- Roll out the Barrels. *Get it?*
- Beer Fest and Oktoberfests (Yes, wine, too.).
- The Art and Wine Tour.
- Avila Beach Oyster Festival (Yes, wine, too).
- Battle of the Bartenders.
- Margarita Battles.
- Bloody Mary Battles.
- Martini Battles
- Sommelier Battles.
- The Romance of Reisling.
- Passport to Wine Country.
- Atascadero Lakeside Wine Festival.
- 5K Vines to Wines (Run a mini-marathon *and* get well-heeled!)
- You can even get wasted on the "Wine Train"—Woo-hoo! Wine and motion sickness.

Or maybe it was the other way around. Pismo and the neighboring towns were known not only for wine, but food, booze, and "Battles" in general. No wonder everyone who lived there was basically an alcoholic or wine obsessed.

It was like Croix told me once, "It's like living in Jamaica: You can't *not* drink the rum."

Under our tent at the 16th hole, I checked my Blackberry and phone.

"I want to call him." I sent texts to all of my contacts, except Jack. They were full of typos thanks to my QWERTY keypad and not wanting to use a manicured fingernail. Vanity Fair wasn't a text-aholic. She partook in a few of her favorite pastimes: sunbathing, people watching, and the combing of her hair with her fingers.

"Jan, don't."

She sat motionless, except for her mouth, and dressed in a mini-skirt and a polo shirt made for women like her: 24-inch waists and C/D-cups. Another "tennis-pro-shop at-a-country-club" outfit. She pulled it off.

VF reached for her mojito, conveyed to us every half hour on trays balanced on the palms of rugby players. The silver platters sizzled. Ours wasn't the unluckiest lifestyle, and today defined a typical Sunday: fresh air, booze, golfers, and boys. The beach somewhere to our left or right. But on that Sunday I lived in shadows: filling in gaps with enough cocktails to flood my beloved Lake Michigan.

"January, no Jack today."

I hadn't brought up the "spark" shit. My undeveloped pain gave me a break. Maybe I'd get laid: sexy waiters, a bartender or a security guard? Her advice was useless, unbeknownst to her.

"Oh my g ... look." I pointed toward the ocean, in the direction of where a golf cart approached our tent at 30 mph.

"What are they doing?" I set down my Blackberry and conversation with Rugby.

We had ravioli ready and the wine poured. Were they that hungry for the ravioli? I stood up and set their utensils and napkins by their food. Ten feet from our table, the two guys and a girl slammed their cart to one side, then the other, and flipped the golf cart, forcing the windshield out and hurtling toward the green. I ran over.

The thirty-somethings stood up laughing, flipped the cart right side up, and drove toward the flimsy piece of fiberglass. They didn't eat their ravioli.

I still remember what I wore, like a last meal. Wide legged vintage gray pants with a hem hitting the tips of my toes, a long tank top, a jean jacket, and old-school Vans.

Vanity Fair didn't look up.

May 10, 3 p.m.

VF and CBP marshaled with nightsticks, directing me like a jumbo jet.

MOVE THIS WAY. THIS WAY. NO! NO! NOT THAT WAY!

"I just don't feel that spark." Sweetie. Sweetie. Sweetie.

My world was blowing up into particles of filth and metal because Jack was being distant. We couldn't play games or participate in our regular tennis match of back and forth; we didn't know where the tennis courts were. Or he knew and wasn't sharing. Jack and I wouldn't stand under flying saucer court lights the size of loaves of bread, casting the ground in yellow whites. Under its unflatter he wouldn't shout a river rapids of nos, Sweeties, and anymores. I wanted him to. I needed more than the "Don't feel that spark." Did I?

Decision made. *I'll do nothing.*

Nothing didn't last. After I heard from him (I couldn't remember if he initiated contact or I did) I thought of analytical tangents. Dumb as a cattail, I demanded to know *where this was going.*

"I will never, ever, want you" was not enough.

After the ravioli/golf cart idiots day, I went home to no one, and into some sort of shock. A deadness. No phone calls; no texts; no B10; B9; B8; B7; B6/Owner or B5. Not even sex with a random wealthy golfer to send this denial rampage into the underland. I ruined everything I came in contact with.

No. Not ruined. *Neglected.*

6 p.m.

Me: I'm going to give you some space...which I think is what u want. It just seems I want one thing and you want another. And I keep waiting...and nothing changes. And I don't understand why. I am not exactly repulsive. Anyway-when you know what you want - let me know. *Cattail!!!*

Me: I guess I'm not needed anymore-you probably have five girls on your mind.

Jack: Just taking time for myself. No girls at the moment, to be honest. I am working on sharing my feelings.

With whom?

I couldn't remember the last time I wrote his initials in my forsaken red calendar.

After we stopped texting I did write one thing down,

Will I ever *neglect* Jack?

May 11, 8 a.m.

"I'm sorry, I just don't feel that way about you."

Me: I'm going to give you some space

Oh my god—let it, him, go!

Jack: I'm going thru a lot of stuff. I want 2b a better bf.

More horseshit piped in.

Jack: Can we talk in a bit.

Me: Just know I think you're amazing. I deserve a chance after all of this. All of this time I've known you.

Jack: I care about u. ur my friend

Me: Fab. No more texting ok?

Jack: k. Have a good day.

"No" meant try harder.

I would have done anything for you.

I want to die.
I thought this was love.

May 13, 7 a.m.

The last week was a montage, the ones I loved in movies. A 20 second scene accelerating the plot and featuring the main characters cleaning a house, making over a girl, shopping for a new wardrobe, putting together an emergency survival kit for a zombie invasion or whatever impending catastrophe tilted in their direction. The soundtracked sequence with fast, pop music comforted me while constructing a new backdrop of possibilities.

"Don't feel that spark" clipped the montage from its reel. Without the backstory, solution, and the comfort, the last few days were just scenes of a really bad slasher movie.

"I'm sorry, I just don't feel that way about you...I never will."

With the deadness worn off, I began a medieval breakdown leading to swift thoughts of death.

Drive off a cliff?

Shotgun?

Xanax?

Car running in garage?

Almost a week later and I still hadn't decided on a method.

There was no in between, no question (except how I would do it) which told me suicide was way to frighteningly easy of a choice.

Unloved/Unlovable/Not capable of loving anything/Not worthy. Realizations of certain characteristics I possessed did the decision making for me as I drove at 7 in the morning. I hated this time of day, and I hated the night before this time of day, knowing I'd be driving to LA instead of lying in my soft, white bed. I drove without coffee. I didn't touch my CDs or volume knob. I broke one of my cell phones

179

in half, cancelled its service, and threw it in a McDonald's trashcan. I called AT&T and informed them January Estlin was already dead and I was her sister tending to her affairs. They believed me. Now it rested in peace on top of half eaten Egg McMuffins in Santa Barbara. I didn't cancel my Blackberry or throw it away; I needed it so Mrs. Z wouldn't get suspicious.

I emailed Childless Brad Pitt and VF, shrieking, but only in words. Then silence.

I drove closer to an abattoir for stupid little, needy sluts while I ran errands in west Los Angeles.

Abattoir = another word for a slaughterhouse. It's pretty, right?

I couldn't remember what I wrote in the emails.

3 p.m.

Petrified, I sat in front of the Container Store in the Grove, reiterating plans on the phone to my brother.

He called me 10 times before I answered and spoke in a grinding-his-teeth tone.

"You can't do this, January. You can't, you can't."

"I have already decided; I am nothing. There is nothing. I don't care."

"Jan."

Childless Brad Pitt, a non-emotional organism, started to whimper. I smelled Panda Express and Cinnabon. My ass was sore from the metal bench.

"I don't care," I repeated.

"Over Jack? Fuck that guy! Wait until you're back and we'll talk. Wait *one* day."

"It's not just … I have to go."

"January, wait."

"I'll call you in a bit." While I willed myself to do the last task asked of me, purchasing 14 Lucite magazine slipcases for Z, she called.

"Hi, how are you?"

I sensed something was about to happen. Shop for *more* Lucite crap?

"How are you?" Same question, happy voice turned on. "Constantly let down by my assistant" voice off.

"Good!" I managed a smile so my voice would change. "Just leaving the Grove, on my way back to the house. The magazine holders weren't that bad: $11 each, I think?"

"Ok. Ok. Well, I received a call from your brother." Happier voice. "Then your father."

Fuck.

"They said you told him, emailed them … ." My finger went to my temple.

Don't say it.

"January! January."

"Mrs. Z."

"January. Stop. Breathe. Think about this. No guy is worth what you are talking about. You are a wonderful person. Amazing." She laughed. "Now come on."

"Z, I just don't care anymore. I want this." I could not believe I was having this conversation with my *boss*. With Mrs. Z.

"Nooooo! Move back here. Move in with us. Move home."

"I can't. Honestly, I don't want to work for you anymore. I would be working at *LA Weekly* if I moved back. Hunt for Lucite crap every weekend and live in a pool house? Hell no."

What I didn't say.

"You're right, I know." *Lie.*

"You tried it up there; now it's time to come back. You need a fresh start."

5 p.m.

"January!"

Round two.

Mr. Z shouted my name as he walked through the front door with the pineapple knocker. I gritted my teeth at the sound of his bag dropping and his feet stomping. His tone wasn't what you would expect from a mogul.

This is so fucking humiliating, and it's starting to interfere with my plans.

Mr. Z appeared in the doorway of the pool house as I typed on the mega iMac cautiously resting on an architect sawhorse desk. The glass top could withstand the computer, the keyboard, and that weird, angled square mouse pad Apple provided, and even those I placed over felt. Desk fundamentals—penholder, stapler, and in-box—would have scratched it on day one.

He picked up the weird metal mouse pad. I started to snivel and turned around, hit by the scent of his driving-home cigar.

"Look, do you want to force him to love you the way you love him?"

"Yes, yes." I prattled through freshly rubied lips. "Yes". I looked away and rested my forehead on the glass.

"I'm sorry babe, but it doesn't work that way. You don't want to force it. Give him some time to want you, and if he comes around, that's great, and if not, well, you can't kill yourself. We need you." He began his own unrequited love story:

"I dated her before Z. Insane, I loved her, I asked her to marry me. We lived together. It was a mess, but I dealt with it when she dumped me. She started dating a friend of mine, in fact."

"How?"

"How did I deal with it? Six months in Europe."

I sank lower.

He was idiotically and indecently rich, bred by sumptuous, creative thinking parents who purchased an open-ended ticket to London, first class. Indecent and idiotic wasn't the problem; a lack of a creative thinking mother and father was the problem. I couldn't exactly call Mommy for travel money. She was probably in London herself, recuperating from a full organ rejuvenation surgery.

My dad would burst out a one-note "Ha!" over the mentioning of Europe, "Get the fuck out of here, Jan. Try visiting Jim Beam instead."

Jim Beam? Did my dad know me at all?

Talking to the two most level headed, yet zany people I knew flicked me in the forehead with a couple of hours of non-Pismo realism. A busy, rich, trainer-toned wake up call. I left LA sprinkled with a quarter teaspoon of Miracle-Gro in my hair. A fertilized slap in the face or love tap on the head. Too much of a coward to fail or succeed.

Flick, sprinkle, fertilize, slap, tap.

May 15

"It's so final," Vanity Fair told me in her kitchen.

Home from LA, I had at least two people to convince I wasn't totally deranged and *was* a total chickenshit: Childless Brad Pitt and VF.

I drove to her house in SLO and dreaded punishment. Vanity Fair, regionally my favorite person, carried with her mountainous, intimidating expectations. For the last couple of years, she latched onto Technicolor January: a façade of a cute dress, flirty disposition, pumps, and vodka dehydration. She never saw me like this: drained and dressed in cords and a T-shirt, no purse, no smile. A wreckage with car keys. She smelled my platinum knots boycotting shampoo and leave-in conditioner and tinged with the aroma of failure at killing myself.

Over a boy.

"What happened?" Neither one of us sat the kitchen table.

"Nothing." Where I stood, I blocked part of a sunflower painting. Something I would never hang on a wall in my house.

"Something must have happened, did he say something?"

"Spark."

"Spark? What spark?"

"He told me he'd never go out with me; he doesn't feel the same way. Didn't feel a spark. A fucking spark. That's what he said. All I wanted was a chance, that's why I called him."

"January, you kind of knew this already: he's an asshole. It's been building up to this. For so long. You have this crazy, messy back-and-forth thing, and it's not good for you, or anyone. You'll meet someone else. Just *move* on."

"I don't want anyone else." I turned and started picking at the frame of the stupid sunflower painting.

"I get it. You asked and he answered. You needed to know, and he told you. You need to listen to him." She fiddled with a container holding her spatulas, spoons and whisks.

"J, look, you have to get your mental stuff straightened out, or, or I don't know about hanging out anymore."

As with St. Croix, there was no nervousness with VF, no anxious race to plan topics of conversation, no sporadic thoughts of, *Ugh, I don't want to go out tonight.* I *always* wanted to hang out with Vanity Fair.

"I'd hang out with you every day if I could." She would say.

I was destroying all of it. Nodding, half-crying, "I know, I know, I'm sorry, I'm a disaster. I don't blame you for not wanting ... ." *Why is this about you now?*

Draining faster, I wanted my bed. Bent over and fiddling with my keys, I was ready to go, but wished for a different response before I left. A hug? If a large spoon and pints of Häagen Dazs weren't available soon, another heartbreak would puncture me like a saline drip. I had to succeed at suicide to get sympathy.

I know that now.

May 16, 2008

Writer rejection grounded me, would make me appreciate success.

"Dear Ms. Estlin, We're sorry" revolted me, but made me laugh at the sadism of my "profession." I hadn't written much in the last month.

Jack's rejection one-upped suicide; it was assisted: a small, blood-spattered and avoidable assassination on repeat, exploiting the fact I had no idea how to stop the slaughter. I wanted him to know what he did to me.

Me: Can we talk. Maybe next wk?
Jack: can we be friends?

Me: I don't know, I just wanted to see how you were doing.
Jack: I am ok. U?
Me: u don't really want to know, I'm sure. Are you working it out with Walmart?
Jack: we r friends but I do miss her to be honest
Me: she'll take you back, be well
Jack: I don't think she will but u be well too

I baited him. I didn't know what else to do.

Me: I do want to be friends. But did you even wonder how I was doing? If you really considered yourself my friend you would have called me since we spoke
Jack: u told me not to. I was respecting your wishes.
Me: you didn't hear from anyone what happened?
Jack: No sweetie what happened?
Me: I'll talk to you about it some other time, I don't want to ruin your weekend. I'm glad we talked/texted.

Within seconds he called three times from his house and cell. I didn't answer. The re-orbit, while making me ill, was loved and as soothing as the ideations from a week earlier. Another tier to my trifle of a mess. May 13 became a prologue. Jack's rejection didn't deter me; I appreciated its sustenance. I didn't know how a person could be this damaged. Or if I was worth fixing.

May 30, 8 p.m.
I had a feeling he would text me

Jack: Hey there, you want to talk still
Me: hey how r u
Jack: good and u?
Me: I'm over it....
Jack: What happened
Me: Don't worry, not prego.

Jack: farthest thing from my min…although now I'm thinking it!
☐ I'm concerned tho

June 3, 2008

People who have suicidal ideations (fantasizing about hanging yourself from a ceiling fan) don't follow through.

Damn, I didn't think of the fan one.

When I emailed VF and my brother, the words locked up the fact I *wouldn't* kill myself. Suicide was too serious and downright sad to be attention seeking, but held up a sign to my loved ones something was dire and amiss. I couldn't cope on my own anymore. Plus, if I was dead, I would never watch *Weekend at Bernie's* again.

We were going to talk. After much cajoling, he was on his way over. Not cajoling on his part, but on mine. I didn't want to talk to him anymore, about *this* anymore. By email and text, on paper and as a writer, the words broke with waterfall force. Talking? Expressing serious thoughts to a male human? Out loud? Speechless. Wreck, nervous, sounding like an anxious asshole, a tape-recorded version of myself I was forced to hear. I couldn't stop myself from thinking how sexy/cute Jack was in his DC shoes and Volcom shirt. I didn't want to talk to him; I wanted him.

"I was going to end this."

"End what?" He fidgeted concern.

"This. I couldn't take it anymore, so I was going to … ."

His eyes widened then became the horror-movie slits. "I'm very sorry I did this to you. You don't deserve this. You need to find someone that respects you."

Almost the worst thing he could say to me.

"Right. I don't know what else to tell you. After that 'spark' comment I lost it. You just killed me." I couldn't say the exact truth.

"What spark … ? Oh, Sweetie, I didn't mean … ."

"It doesn't matter, it really doesn't. Because I will be fine. It's cool, I just can't really ever speak to you again … and ignore my texts if I text you."

He started to cry.

What did his *I didn't mean*, mean? Wait, he's *crying.*

I cried into my pillows as I prayed for forgiveness, from my family, from god, for myself, and that this would be the worst I'd ever feel again.

I texted him a few minutes after he left:

Me: I am here for you as a friend. And my intention wasn't to make you feel worse. You are amazing-you really are-and you deserve the best. Be kind and gentle to yourself. if ever in the future you think you would want to hang out with me again-for whatever reason-i'll be here.

Jack: Thank u sweetie. Again I am sorry

The "Ignore my texts if I text you" rule was broken within five minutes. Nice!

I wasn't boundless. I didn't know who I was, where I was, or what I was supposed to be. I didn't know my part or my role. I made mistakes and I expected to make more. Was it the beginning of the end or an eye-opener?

June 5

Jack texted me again to see if I was ok. Glances at my Blackberry offered my imagination new, albeit remakes of fantasies of a ride in his car or an invitation to a barbecue in his backyard.

"Don't feel that spark" floated up and away like a sky lantern in Thailand introducing the heavens to new ideas, people, and wishes. *Just. Like. That.*

I was blessed, but I wondered if I was cursed as well. I was too stupid to know what those lanterns were truly meant for.

*If I had a pistol I would have shot him—
either that or fall to his feet. There is
no middle way when one loves.*

— Lady Troubridge

June 7, 2008

"January, I'm going to say you're probably bipolar: bipolar II, not I."

A Buddha statue watched over Dr. Disorder's plush office: dark cherry woods, the *DSM IV*, and five fake plants. He sat behind his desk, and I sat five feet in front of him on a club chair. On the table beside me, *1,000 Ways to Relax*.

"Ok." I reached down to my purse at my feet and started tearing up. "That's not good. Bipolar, there's a difference between I and II?"

"Think of it this way: With bipolar II you might buy a boat."

"Buy a boat? What? I hope to god I don't buy a boat. I get sick in the front ... ."

He handed me a tissue box.

"No, not what I meant. I want you to visualize this. Being bipolar II you might buy a boat—this is hypothetical. Of course you won't buy a boat." He paused. "But call me if you find yourself at a boat dealership. With bipolar I, you will buy that boat, and you will buy it naked."

"Ok, no boat. But I have borderline personality disorder too, right? I have a degree in ... ."

"No borderline." When he took the cap off of his pen, he paused again.

It's not a "cap" if it's a fancy, metal, inkwell sort of pen is it? Should I call it a writing instrument?

"I really thought I had borderline." I focused on the dust on fern No. 3.

"Stop reading your old textbooks."

Throughout this I couldn't say Jack or SFF. He was "the boy," "the guy," "the asshole." Hopefully I never referred to him as a man. The boy with blue eyes, the same as mine. When grasping my thigh, he vanished particles of pain.

Otherwise, I had no trouble talking: "After a hundred men in my life, mostly sexual, nothing felt, feels like this. I can think of three instances where I had strong feelings for guys, but nothing like this. It ended and I moved on, eventually. One of the main reasons I'm having trouble stopping it. I can't."

"Now is the time. Start extracting yourself from the relationship. You have to start thinking in terms of 'I'm more worthwhile than this. This isn't a good way to spend my time.' He, the stress, is interfering with your everyday life, is it not?"

My eyes, nose, and tissues nodded for me.

"The truth is, a breakup is never easy, and the attraction will be there. It would be careless on my part to not realize you are human and your reactions aren't going to be 100 percent healthy in the beginning. It will be easy, practical, and accepted by your peers to continue on as if what is happening between you and him is tolerable.

"Actually, I'm losing friends because of this, it. Him. Me."

"See? Then there is no peer pressure to continue this fairy tale. The fairy tale doesn't exist. You have built these fantasies in your mind. He's caused you anguish, a sort of relationship with no boundaries, one extremely harmful to your mental health. I am going to help you. It is why you're here." Dr. Disorder wrote on his leather bound legal pad.

He thinks this was a breakup.

"What about your drinking?"

My best ditzy blonde face.

"We've talked about this. I know you don't think of yourself as a typical alcoholic, but like your father, you are high functioning. You make it to work on time; you pay your bills. With the exception of the public intoxication arrest, you don't get into trouble. However, when you do drink, 75 percent of the time, the consequences are magnitudinous."

Ooh, good word.

"Whether it's bingeing, losing consciousness, a drink after work, it's within the same context for what it is you do so well, and so detrimentally. Drinking, and a propensity to abuse alcohol, was inherited from your father. We will address those issues at a later time. Or *in time* I should say. Let's get back to my diagnosis. Bipolar Disorder is often misunderstood. From what you've related to me about your mom, the abandonment issues from Chicago, the volatility of your father, and the lack of an environment without a normal structure set forth by your parents, you were almost guaranteed this disease. Without love, and by that I mean positive, consistent affection, compassion, and proper discipline, many individuals often show a number of symptoms falling under many umbrellas of the large umbrella of psychopathology.

"Right, like, instead of talking to me about it, they punished me and thought I was dumb. It was insulting, I guess. There was no in between. If my mom found out I had sex, she'd start screaming 'Abortion! You must have an abortion!' She didn't ask about condoms or who the guy was. It was, 'You are going to fail." My dad isn't as bad. But in other areas, he's frigging insane too."

"January. Your parents are broken. They were afraid so they responded in the best way they knew how—by indulging you and handing off responsibility to others. And I'm taking about your mother in that regard. But your dad as well, is guilty of that. He was your dad for three months a year. But, they surely don't want you to make the same mistakes they made in their own lives. Their parents were broken. It is a trickle-down effect."

"I'm never having kids."

"Don't rule anything out. You would be a wonderful mother. The sensitivity you possess is innate. Your instinct to attach and ask for and give love comes naturally. You desire love more than anything. It is a good thing. Now it is about finding the balance between fixations and healthy boundaries in relationships with men. Between the worrying, the severe depression, and your manic episodes—and there only has to be one of those—I think you would benefit from medication. You worry a lot. Again, that tells me bipolar."

"What kind of medication?"

"I'll get to that in a minute. Right now, let's focus on the other half of your treatment. Medication is essential, necessary, and it will balance you—your moods, agitation, and anxiety. But you need other activities for times, hours of the day, when you're not working or sleeping. And in saying that, an important part of your treatment, your daily ritual, is rest. So keep that in mind,"

"K."

"Do you volunteer?

"Yes."

"Good, start there. What about cultural events: art, plays—you write articles for a magazine, correct?"

Where is the clock? I hated not knowing if we had 30 or five minutes left.

"See a theater production without having to write about it. Go to movies. Go with girlfriends. Go alone. Another thing ... . "He made a 'c' with his finger and thumb and repositioned the lens part of his glasses. "By no means should you consume alcohol while taking the prescribed medications. The ones I am prescribing to you today."

This time Dr. Disorder wrote on a prescription pad and handed me five white pieces of paper.

Five.

"I will see you in the hospital if you do. And your stay will not be a tonsillitis, ice-cream, private suite sabbatical at Cedars type of facility. You will be in lock down. You will not have clothes. You will live in a paper gown. Pay attention to what I am saying. One more thing, and then we're finished."

More? I recalled the non-alcoholic beers I saw in refrigerated aisles at the store, squeezed in at the end next to the mirrored panel. I hated beer. *Do they make non-alcoholic wine?*

"You need to stop contact. Absolutely no contact with this man. Write a letter and file it away. Don't give it to him."

"And you're sure I'm not gonna buy a boat?"

July 2008

I hadn't touched *Anti-Fat* in months. The bones were there: It needed a few more scenes, additional development of two characters, and I hated the ending.

Keep submitting, promoting, emailing, selling, prostituting to make sure this book ends up in someone else's hands besides myself and VF's. Write, write, write.

I opened the file, rolled my head around in a circle. The right side of my neck was sore. Writing was the easy part. Landing a literary agent and consequently selling a book to a publisher? A drastically different, degrading, dreadful experience, grew rapidly into to a monster tyrant of a 6-year-old. I wrote for seven years while trying to sell my first book, *Twenty Something and Blonde*. I was done.

My pill bottles stood strong on my kitchen counter.

The rundown:

—100mg of Zoloft (anti-depressant).

—250mg of Clozapine (anti-psychotic—now called the less monstrous term of "mood stabilizer").

—400mg of Lamotrigine (again "mood stabilizer").

—.5-1mg of Xanax

—5mg of Ambien, as needed at bedtime.

I opened two other projects I started last year. "Projects" because I didn't know what they would end up as. Then, there was last of my Blonde series, *Thirty Blonde,* and finally, *Soulcrusher.* Two more novels. Jesus.

I remember bipolar disorder:

Racing thoughts, hopelessness, mood swings, anxiety, low self-esteem, agitated, and some suicidal stuff. My very own domain of disorder.

Before I clicked the X in the upper right-hand corner, and pushed away from my desk, I checked Kohl's, Wells Fargo, and Denny's websites for job openings. *I can always call my mother.*

Jack: U doing ok?
Me: I'm ok babe. How are you?
Jack: I'm hanging in there.
Me: do u want to talk later? I'm going into my office now.
Jack: Have to work. Thank u though
Me: staying busy is good. I hate that you're upset
Jack: I hate that I made u upset
Me: its not your fault. I'm ok. Don't worry about me. It helps talking to u
Me: (later) Why don't you come over to watch a movie. Unless it would be too weird for u. It would take your mind off things! I know u work late tonite...

I don't remember what he said.

July 5

Walking into the Shack, the evening colors ahead dimmed the skies with red, topping a beachy white: a Mark Rothko painting.

"It feels like a Bloody Mary night." VF wasn't enamored or hindered by my sobriety. I agreed, drinking vicariously through her throat as I adjusted my ass on a stool. Owner waved from a safe and solid eight seats away. Too Tan suggested a Virgin Mary. Her

14-ingredient concoction apparently won an award last year (at the Bloody Mary Battle!) and when I took a sip I knew why. Sublimely delicious. I slurped and watched her make two rum and Diet Cokes. She smiled at me.

The virtually non-existent sting of awkwardness of seeing B6 didn't result in any dangerous reaction, but the not drinking helped. I probably wouldn't fuck B6 again. Whatever. Bars and nightlife provided fun whether Charlie Sheened or sober (sober = designated driver). My clearheaded powers expanded if a new B happened to walk by whatever throne I sat on, laughing with my friends or smoking outside. If my capriciousness and nuance intrigued a B, it guaranteed at least a month of dates. A hospital seemed worse than jail, so staying yards away from alcohol took much less effort than wits kept when I inhaled vodka and limes.

———

The Tuesday before the Rothko night, in the very teetotalling climate of a Coffee Bean, Vanity Fair sat across from me at a window table, facing Pismo's version of an "Outlet mall." In front of the wall selected to exhibit atrocious seascapes (locally painted in the 'plein air' style) she stiffened.

"What did he say?" She peeled the lid off of her cup.

Her question effected me, warmed me. I mattered to her.

"Pretty much what I expected, and a bit that I didn't."

"What do you mean?" Her smile hadn't arrived, the relaxed one I missed.

"He thinks, I mean I'm, he diagnosed me bipolar."

Her eyelids closed as she blew on her latte.

"It's a 'mood disorder,' he put me on medication, I already feel a difference, I mean, I thought it was much worse."

"I've definitely heard of bipolar disease, disorder. It's still pretty serious right? I remember reading about manic depression when I took a psychology class online. That's what they used to call it I think."

I sighed. She leaned in.

"I'm so sorry, really: I'm sorry this is happening to you. I'm proud of you though."

She smiled…a little.

"I hope he told you to stay away from him."

———

By the time the Mark Rothko disappeared, I was locked in a bath-room stall.

After sailing into the port of flirting, he made his motive clear.

"Ok, Sweetie, but it's just sex. Nothing more." I hung up. Maybe the meds hadn't taken effect yet.

His honesty caused me the most grief. His respectful, spit smart, brave, straightforward reaction was 100 percent admirable, sort of. Too bad his truth fell on a flawed woman: satisfaction didn't find me, no matter what I did. I was crestfallen with a shelled surface, lost and stupefied; Vanity Fair sat co-pilot. She'd never know.

You need to stop contact. Absolutely no contact with this man.

11 p.m.

"Your pussy's so tight. I love that."

Did you hear that, mattress? He said love again!

Desiring death over life and notions of murdering my soul, could not crush, sweep, challenge, or squash this saga. I couldn't quit. I didn't fight until the death, I fought through, with agony as my shield, dragging it in the dirt behind me. As long as my eyes were open and Jack breathed air, I owned my chance. I would grow old and alone, and I didn't care. I lived in a town of nothing, so what else was I supposed to do? I settled.

I couldn't foresee a time when I didn't want his sheets under and over my body, his doorknobs in my fists, his TV tuned to 248 light-ing up our backs while we had sex. Jack survived for me as some obscene, enjoyable form of cancer, infecting me while pleasing every cell of me.

I wasn't done with Jack.

July 10
> **Jack**: hook up?
> **Me**: Abso.
> **Jack**: no strings? No freakin out?

> *Fuck. How stupid am I, and how annoying is he?*

> **Me**: U still feel like u want to hook up with me? I mean I actually can't believe it. If some guy told me he tried to fucking kill himself I'd cut his ass off.
> **Jack**: I cud have sex with other girls. I enjoy our naughty time.

July 12

July seemed to veer down, then up. Like Thrill Hill. Thrill Hill Road ran along behind my dad's property line; a quarter mile section of it as attention-getting as a medium-scary roller coaster. At one point you couldn't see past the hood of your car on the descent. I ran/jogged/walked it on occasion.

July 16, 2008

> *They're best friends.*
> "I love her." *Walmart.*

At 7 p.m., always on his drive home from work, he explained he couldn't add me to his Myspace page because of her.

> "You don't want to see all of what we do together, do you?"
> *Myspace—are you kidding me? I wasn't on Myspace.*

By 9 p.m. I threw shit, again. Again, nothing breakable. In my kitchen this time: a box of tissue, air freshener, hand soap and mail whacked to the ground, in one fell swoop from the back of my hand. I saw it on *The Sopranos*. One of Tony's mistresses decimated a clothed table and a beef tenderloin. Then she threw the roast at his head. He didn't like that. Her choreographed and artistic tug of the centerpiece inspired. Gripping my counter, I breathed torture in and out, and reached for the freezer door.

Sex started to project depressing and upsetting images into the corners where my walls met and up the ceiling like a midnight movie. In Avila Beach, as a kid my dad and I swam at a local pool. With his cowboy hat on his head we floated on inner tubes, watching old western films on a huge stucco wall on the side of the concessions stand at the far end of the pool. My dad never took his hat off. I didn't want to associate this with that, but the water outlining my inner thighs in the sulfur-scented pool entered me as Jack did, my back sweating into the feather bed.

Why was he doing this to me? And why weren't the meds working? Helping, fixing, reducing, radiating, remastering. They helped me in other parts of my life. Was sobriety fucking me over? Let's face it, not drunken dialing should have reduced our contact by 90 percent. Then again, sober sex with Jack magnified the sex by a million. Even the sex with the disconcerting images on my bedroom walls.

Then Molly Ringwald in *Pretty in Pink* came to mind: "If someone doesn't believe in me, I can't believe in them." I gave him three days; Then I had the chance to do something I almost never did: what Dr. Disorder, or anyone, told me to do.

The next day I begged him to let me be.

"I'll leave you alone."

I don't want you to leave me alone.

I sobbed into my bed and wailed into the walls. I was torn.

July 18

Me: NO ONE gives a shit you LOVE your fucking girlfriend. Did u love your precious Walmart when u were fucking me? Or all of the other girls? i don't give a shit. YOU THINK I do, but I don't. Remember that...you asshole...and liar. Two things you will always be. Hope walmart knows that.

Jack: let's drop it move on hope you are ok

Me: Easy for u to say.

July 19, 2008, 8 a.m.

To: jack_aka_sff@gmail.com
From: Januaryyy@yahoo.com

You can't imagine how much I don't want this. I am not one to give up-on anything. But I have to be fair to you and myself, and stop obsessing. You were right...I can't talk to you anymore Jack, at least not until I get my head straight and my shit together. I wish I could just fuck you-bc I really don't want to give that up. But it was never just sex to me. Even from the first times we were together-you gave me a sense of comfort and warmth that I desperately needed-and was searching for...you touched my soul, and that is powerful.

I know you don't reciprocate what I feel-or even understand it. I also know I have made a lot of mistakes, showing you the worst parts of myself. And I am so sorry for that. We never officially dated but I got to know you...and I remember liking you from the first moment we met. You've taught me so much these last few years. You helped me to grow up. its very hard to let go of something that feels so right and wonderful and passionate...something that I want so badly...something that makes me so happy...But I have no choice. I'll say it again...if, down the road, you want to have sex, And date, then I hope you would give me a chance to show you how wonderful I can be, and how I would add pleasure and goodness to your life. Either way, thank you for always being a friend to me. You are truly, truly special. –j

Same day, 1 p.m.

Jack: Can we be friends?
Me: I don't think so.
Jack: Maybe when you're ready.
Me: I thought it was pretty clear in the email-I can't be just friends. I don't want to be just friends. Its not possible for me. That's why I can't talk to you anymore...
Jack: I know that. I meant hopefully in the future we can...

Me: that is up to u

Jack: well have a great day and I will leave u alone.

August 2008

I couldn't believe I lived here. Why? How?

Driving to Pismo from LA after working for the Zs became a crescendo of a melodramatic hell. Passing through Goleta: worry and regret. The tunnel telling me Buellton was coming up: anger. Santa Maria and its farm dirt in the air: terror and tears. Wine grapes and the machines harvesting them rested in the valleys, but even a blossoming wine industry wasn't as interesting as a year or two ago. The miles decreased, my face shrunk, and my thoughts bred offspring. Pills stopped the crying, but with nowhere else to escape after the drugs wore off. Friday and Saturday nights and happy hours spent high as an Oregon pine, were no longer an option.

Even though Childless Brad Pitt hated Jack and wanted me to have nothing to do with him, he told me he saw him out and Jack told him he missed me. Missed what? He didn't miss what I missed. Why did he tolerate my shit? Why didn't he behave, and not talk to me anymore, keeping his "texted" word? Because he didn't care enough not too? Because he craved me as much as I did him? I believed in his skin, tattoos, hands, hair and the soul, which became my Xanadu: the hell where I lived. How could Jack bang, fight, lick, smack, sweat, kiss, and annihilate me and not believe in any parts of me? Weeds sprouted in the sidewalk cracks, and with each fresh clover, a dewdrop of brilliance diminished. Tattoos faded into mistakes and his knuckles exposed tales of treachery and heartbreak. *Finally.*

September 3, 2008
Journal entry

For the first time since I moved to Pismo, I wasn't dating anyone—or anyone memorable, anyway. Summer took off in a seaplane, and shockingly, so did some of my loneliness. I think the preoccupation with Jack fucked up chances toward mundaneness, marriage, mortgage, monogamy, and monotony. The M's. I kissed the M's goodbye at my front door two years ago. I'm hopeful though.

September 7

Jack and I did what we did best: He came over, then came on my tits. After shutting my bedroom door, something he never did, we fucked liked Neanderthals until the next hurricane warning lit up the news ticker. Tickers gave me a headache while I read them at the bottom of the TV, passing over the Samsung emblem, slow, but guiding me out of the evacuation zone. I surrendered.

I thought about Walmart.

I attempted to separate our thing and their thing. I prayed his optimism and joy depended on nothing to do with her. His eyes were blue marbles. Emotionless. The daylight through the blinds highlighted his sideburns. I formed a small smile and stared out the window.

I needed a catalyst to throw me over the fence, compelling me to run from the hockey-masked SFF.

Maybe it meant something.
Maybe not, in the long run, but no explanation,
no mix of words or music or memories can touch
that sense of knowing that you were there
and alive in that corner of time and the world.

— Hunter s. Thompson

September 14, 2008

Thank god for Vegas. Seriously.

A lobotomy wasn't as effective as a weekend three hours of Red Bull away (from LA, not Pismo) where I wore the thinnest pinned stilettos, gambled like a sweaty degenerate mobster in black loafers, drank like Amy Winehouse and Charles Bukowski's baby, and snorted throat-dripping lines of coke in a Hard Rock Hotel bathroom with four new best friends. I'd giddily rub off any one of those from the to-do list I wrote in eyeliner on my hotel bathroom mirror.

Not this time.

This weekend I traveled to LV to deliver milk and cookies.

30-years-old, knocking on doors with cookies for a living. *I was a well-paid Girl Scout.* I made $35 an hour to drive the boxy Mercedes SUV full of party supplies, silver trays, boxes of chocolates, wine Mr. Z elected from his cellar, Dom saved in the fridge in the gym and their luggage. Anything Mrs. Z figured the hotel butlers wouldn't provide in one of their villas or didn't want to haul on the plane. On the second-to-last day of my trip, I hand delivered fancy Beverly Hills cookies and condensating milk jugs resting on three silver carts with two butlers. I checked all of the guests off my list as we walked to my room. Except for one.

Cress Reiter was a pain in my ass.

Cress Reiter. A few years ago, Mr. Reiter complained to Mrs. Z he "heard" I was rude to a saleswoman in Gucci—on Rodeo of all places. A Hollywood super-agent had nothing better to do then email Z, bitching about my attitude. Did this guy even have balls? What kind of name was Cress anyway?

"Z, this is a store whose top priority, and for their own entertainment, is to be rude to people like me. I walked in there and ... ."

She put her hand up and took a sip from a Versace cup on top of a Versace saucer.

"I don't care. You represent me, and you represent Mr. Z when you are at work. It's that simple." She had the rare gift of reprimanding without yelling. From then on, when I saw Cress Reiter's name in Z's emails, his name on a guest list, or his kids' faces on a Christmas card, a rigorous irritation took over. I couldn't imagine a bigger douchebag. His kids were super cute.

This weekend Cress Reiter didn't stay at the Bellagio where the other 30 guests had comped rooms; he had to stay at the Four Seasons.

"He's staying at the Four Seasons, guys. I'll have to get them to him another way." I handed each of them $40 and headed to the hair salon.

"We'll leave them in your room, ma'am."

Under a blow dryer and with champagne in hand, I double-checked my bipolar plan. I stopped all meds the week prior except for the Zoloft, and brought Xanax, which helped with hangovers. At 9 p.m., I put on my black wide-legged tuxedo pant, a black silk mouth-watering pleated dress, black patent leather, closed toe sandalettas, and a huge black cocktail ring. I didn't intend to look like a peroxided witch escaping a coven in New Orleans. I walked through the casino, toward the restaurant.

"Whoa, January." Mr. Z was used to my customary assistant apparel: T-shirt and jeans or a top and jeans or a T-shirt and a cute jacket and jeans or a T-shirt, cords, and Converse, or flip-flops (a "yikes" for Beverly Hills). Black wedge boots if I walked anywhere between Canon and Roxbury.

"Doesn't she look fabulous?" Mrs. Z exclaimed after she walked over and hugged me.

"We never see you like this; you look great, babe." Mr. Z squeezed my arm. I spied on the guests in clusters of three or four standing and leaning on one foot or the other next to the dollar slots. Before this, most of them were just names on a cookies and milk list.

I fidgeted and stood alone, self-conscious because I worried it would be misunderstood as to why I attended the annual weekend party celebrating another year of Mr. Z's moguling and climbing home-made stairs behind a tennis court. The low-key meal included grandiose interpretations of appetizers at TGI Fridays.

Mr. Z sat across from me.

"Z, Pure tonight?"

"Definitely J, I'm calling the guy now, put his number in your phone."

"Pure? You're going to Pure?" Someone was standing behind me.

I turned around to the voice. Handsome. In shape with help from a trainer. Early 40s representative sample of a put-together, show-business type. Head down, double fisting his Blackberry. He spoke but didn't look up. I knew him. *How did I know this guy?*

"January, take Cress with you."

Oh lord.

I expected to go to Pure alone; I went anywhere alone. bars, restaurant patios, movies, shopping. I wrote best this way: have a conversation with a stranger, discover a character's name in a bartender, and make tipsy phone calls. I planned on traveling alone, too. What were the odds I'd have a companion who had the money and yearning to visit the same places? Islands called to me: Fiji, Jamaica, anything in the Caribbean, Ireland. Parts of Europe seemed unreachable. Thailand and Vietnam? Again, I was carried away and motivated by the islands on the Internet, in magazines, or in movies.

The last time I was in Pure, I was alone, for half of the night. One of my oldest friends, Abbey, a sophisticated and addictive (addictive to *me*) gay boy, lost me after we ate steak cooked in front of us in a Japanese restaurant at the Hard Rock. With two more shots of Don Julio in hand, we migrated. By migrate, I mean we walked from the Mirage (our next stop after the Hard Rock) to Caesar's (and Pure). Never, ever, again.

An hour later, he got tangled up in the net that was the mayhem in front of the club. I worried for 10 minutes before I spent the rest of the night and the next morning around a low-to-the-ground polished black table, drinking, laughing, dancing, and smoking. At 1 a.m. my hostess, Apricot, asked if five 40-something Canadian businessmen could sit with me.

"Of course!"

10 p.m.

"Let's go." Cress kicked the back of my chair.

I picked up my cocktail, and we walked past Mrs. Z's table. She stared at us in a way I'd never seen her stare, and flashed a *"Why the hell did Mr. Z put these two together? But have fun!"* expression.

Non-Pismo smells coasted from his jacket, or neck, to my nose. I glanced down at the carpet, up at the rafters or at the people as they passed us, but not at him. I'd already tallied the dark hair, tailored black suit/sport jacket, the whitest Etro dress shirt I'd ever seen, bowery pants, Berluti shoes, and a watch—not sure what kind. A live, walking glossy page out of *Esquire* swaggered next to me, and through my unconscious.

He wanted to gamble before leaving the casino, which gave me time to run up to my room, dab Dior on my neck while syncing sips of vodka/soda with whips of my mascara wand. Twenty minutes later, I sat down next to him at the blackjack table—the $100 minimum blackjack table.

"Don't let me gamble more than 10 tonight."

I lit a cigarette. "10,000?"

He nodded.

"That's hilarious." Sinatra's "Luck Be a Lady'" wasn't so loud I couldn't hear his next question.

"You smoke?" The question came from the corner of his eye as he shuffled his chips.

"I do when I'm in Vegas."

He smiled.

"I quit last year. Actually I didn't quit. I just stopped one day. I love it, but I can't stand the smell." *Shut up January.*

"So, no more than 10,000. Then my wife won't … ."

I didn't hear the rest of what he said as he ordered us two drinks from the panty-hosed cocktail waitress.

"Hit that." I pointed to his cards. "Where is your wife? Is she here?"

I knew he was getting divorced. I read the news in an email to Mrs. Z from his ex-wife.

He had an ace and waved me away with his hand as if to say, *I know what I'm doing.*

"Ex-wife." He let out a half laugh and slight grimace/sigh. Whatever he did was sexy. Polished. Professional. Distinguished. An entire man, maybe even a species, I had never encountered.

"You have kids, right?" Cress tossed the dealer a tip.

He faced me for the first time. His head jerked back and he nodded and smiled.

"They're amazing, they're doing well."

He scrolled through pictures on his phone.

"Your son's an artist, right?" I knew this because I spent many of this kid's birthdays scouring LA for the latest, yet least expensive, art supplies: a gift from the Zs. I never understood what "latest" meant. What changed about paint, paintbrushes, or canvas in the last 100 years? The Reiters drove me crazy way before I met Cress.

"Henry, yes, he's the artist in the family, and Tallulah loves animals, clothes, typical girl stuff." He won the hand with a blackjack.

"Tallulah, I love that name." I put my cigarette out and checked my manicure.

"*Lifeboat*." He took his Blackberry out of his inside jacket pocket as he said it. Inside jacket pocket? The B's in Pismo didn't know an inside jacket pocket from a seashell.

"Yes *Lifeboat*, that movie's insane. I can't believe Tallulah Bankhead wasn't ... ."

He stood up before I stopped talking.

"You ready?" He picked up his chips and took my hand. If I could have eaten the way he smelled, I would have.

11 p.m.

"You know, you got me in trouble with Mrs. Z once." We hopped into a cab.

Head in his Blackberry.

Was Pure too personal, unbefitting, and transparent of a place to be with Cress, whom I didn't know and who would report back to the Zs? Could I relax? Go crazy? Flirt? Dance? Do coke? Be a megalomaniac self-indulgent goddess, working hard for the next day's hangover? Ok, no blow, but still. I wouldn't know for sure until I drank from several bottles placed in front of us and after at least 10 cigarettes. Long after my shoulders relaxed and I danced to hip-hop/techno and rap. Until then, I hoped he'd do wingman things like babysit cocktails, order drinks, watch my purse, check my lips for gloss, and pay the tab, which wouldn't be much considering we were comped the VIP table. "Wouldn't be much" meant somewhere in the $500 to $1,000 range.

"Caesar's, please. January. Why aren't we walking?" He turned to me and brushed a hair out of one of my eyes, then wrapped his arm around my shoulders. "This is my wife, you know. We were just married." *Ok, he did that fast. Oh my word, the way he smells.*

"You two get married today?" Cab driver had an eastern European accent.

"We did." I played along, tilting my head to his chest and smiling wide.

Cress squeezed, "Honey, I'm so deliriously happy."

The cab driver turned around, "Where's ring?"

11:10 p.m.

"Walk, are you insane? I'm in heels, and I've done that walk before. It's like, over a mile." Out my window, the Strip was queues of striped neon candy behind the counter of a sweets shop.

"In trouble? What were you talking about earlier?" His phone was at his ear.

"Last year I returned a scarf you'd given Mrs. Z, and you told her I was rude to the girl at Gucci. The salesgirl."

He laughed the laugh of someone who didn't remember.

11: 31 p.m.

We stood near a tall fake marbled column, surrounded by 5,000 square feet of hedonists ready to occupy the next five hours with concepts so alien to their Monday-through-Friday lives, anarchy was guaranteed. Frat boys, Latinos, Hollywood types (businessmen: old, young, and in between) celebrities, old men fish out of water, and women masquerading as hookers, most holding yards of frozen, sub-standard margaritas. Some had their arms up, rocking out in the front row at an Aerosmith concert, mouths open, eyebrows up, trying to get his attention. "His" being the doorman/list guy, barricaded by five apocalyptically burly UFC types.

"You talk to him." Back on his Blackberry.

I texted the Pure manager a half an hour earlier.

"Done."

Cress handed me a hundred for the tip.

11:55

It was dark, not a revelation. What surprised me was the way Pure smelled.

Lemons, vinegar, and air conditioning—upscale air conditioning. Mopped, distilled, and dusted from vomit, wine, liquor, sweat, cheap perfume, smoke, body odor, contaminated carpet, and bathrooms. The nightly collections of blood, skin, coke, and gin avoided us. Like they never existed.

A familiar song shot out from the walls and ceiling. "I heard this on my drive here!" I half shouted into his ear.

"I'm not lovin you, the way I wanted to.
I bet no one knew, I got no one new.
I know I said I'm through, but got love for you.
But I'm not lovin' you, the way I wanted to.
Gotta keep it goin', keep the lovin' goin'.
Keep it on a roll, only god knows.
If I be with you, baby I'm confused.
You choose, you choose."

He nodded. "It's Kanye." I loved he knew this.

We continued through a series of stairs and gates; one, made of wrought iron, stood as big as a redwood. He informed me in my ear as he followed, "I'm an investor." I wouldn't have believed him, but I saw his name on the monthly statements at the Zs, since they were investors, too. Slipping his phone down the sexy pocket, Cress stepped in front of me, took my hand, and led me to the first bar. Dark, set back, stoked to be a first stop, and obligatory to people who weren't pre-table service drinking. Men handed back red, pink, brown, green, blue and clear drinks to ladies and their already broke guy friends, as if to say, *Take one and pass the rest back*, two minutes before a pop quiz in high-school.

Lips mouthed Kanye and went wide as they took their first sips.

Pure consisted of levels, and those levels had colors. Black, red, silverfish gray, electric blues, and white, illuminated with Hollywood cerise. Two more girls joined us. I loved a bigger crowd, but they came with tingles and questions. Was one a girlfriend? Someone he wanted to fuck? *Why did I care?*

"January, this is Assistant 1 and Assistant 2."

They are immaculate and my feet hurt.

"You're gorgeous," Assistant 2 shouted.

Cress raised an eyebrow, smiled, and looked at his phone.

"Are you kidding? *You* are gorgeous," I replied. We started chatting and sat down at the table/booth in the black-and-red level. When I pressed the end of my cigarette in a silver ashtray in the shape of half-moon, unmistakable, charming cocktail hostess legs flounced toward me.

"Apricot!!" I shot up. The same hostess from the losing Abbey/Canadian businessmen night at Pure.

"Love! How are you?" We hugged, and she nodded in approval of Cress.

"My boss' friend." I rolled my eyes as he talked on his phone.

"You'll need vodka then."

Our table sat below black and white porcelain bathtubs, pods for the pin-up girls go-go-ing, spinning, and dancing in the rafters. The mystique of the first hour added to the intensity and uniqueness of what was happening. Like a 1932 foreign movie I watched in European Cinema 101 at UCSB: I didn't understand any of it, but it was meant to be experienced and dissected. Vessels of vodka, gin, and rum as tall as toddlers paraded by with air traffic controller timing. Mixers: silver and glass carafes of Diet Red Bull, fresh orange, grapefruit, and cranberry juice. Apricot wasn't just our director and friend, she was entertainment. In between a booze run in a pretty tame black outfit for Pure cocktailing, she leaned down,

"Listen to this, this happened to two of my friends last night: Walking home after a girls' night out, they passed a graveyard and stopped to pee. Sally had nothing to wipe with so she used her underwear and tossed it. My other friend, Jane, found a ribbon on a wreath and used that. The next day Sally's husband calls Jane's husband, pissed off: 'My wife came home last night without her panties!' Jane's husband replied, 'That's nothing, mine came back with a card stuck between her butt cheeks that said, 'From all of us at the fire station, we'll never forget you.'"

Our heads tilted back to the raven-haired bathtub girls.

"I'm the type of girl to look you dead in the eye ...
I'm a Wonder Woman, let me go get my rope ...
If you see us in the club, we'll be actin' real nice ...
We ain't here to hurt nobody."

"I love this song!" I screamed to the Assistants as we danced in front of our table.

"It's Timbaland." Cress stood up and moved closer to me.

"I know." I told him as I sung along.

"He's a client, look." He rolled through his contacts and held up the screen.

"January, you're probably the only white girl who knows who Timbaland is, and who is a fan."

I sat down on a high-back chair next to our booth. "He remixed Nina Simone on one of his songs."

He raised an eyebrow.

2:20 a.m.

"Come with me." Apricot took me by the hand and waved the others to follow.

"This one just became available."

We went straight to the top: white. One of the most coveted tables in Pure, positioned with pride among rows of ottomans; chairs; beds, and chaises, bathed in pink and diamond blues, tinting the ambience with futuristic, cosmic tones. For the second or third time in my life, I was exactly where I wanted to be. Nowhere else. Cress slid closer from the other side of the couch.

"I want champagne." I wasn't sure if he heard me.

"Vegas should end with champagne." Cress flagged down Apricot.

End?

He twirled the flute around my head like a crown before he handed over the Dom. Assistants 1 and 2 took their final steps toward a shamrock state with glasses of black-imbued vodka and nibbled on the strawberries left behind for Cress and me.

"It's black! Black *vodka*!" 1 thrust the bottle at 2.

Cress and I stood hip to hip, watching the crowd. This newfangled instant with him, a glorious speck of the night, brought with it hesitation. I turned to the other half of the candescent, white tulle and Lucite booth.

I told Cress we were going to the restroom.

The Assistants and I pow-wowed in the bathroom that could've been a hotel suite. The girls were enchanting and cool, and had worked for Cress years ago. *I love it when girls are nice.*

We lounged on a huge black and white daybed.

"Don't do it. Go home, back to your room. But don't hook up with him." 2 lectured me and swallowed her last drops of Dom. 1 hoisted a shot of the black vodka to her lips. I drank water while women in groups of threes and fours drifted in and out.

"Uh, I don't feel good." Assistant 1 started to moan.

"What doesn't feel good?" I turned around and Assistant 2 was gone.

In the next room, a mini Pure with stalls, I held her hair and rubbed her back while she threw up.

"Are you going to hook up with Cress? I think you should. He was looking at ... ."

"Earlier you said not to" She threw up again, half of it on the floor.

"Oh my goooodddd." 1 moaned a familiar moan.

"Don't worry about it. Don't fight it. You'll feel better."

3:20 a.m.

"Is she ok? Where's 2?" Cress looked up from his phone.

I held her waist and yelled over the music, "She bailed. I think we're done. You want to take her back to her room?"

"Of course, come with me."

Cress and I tucked Assistant 1 into bed at the Hard Rock and laughed our way outside. He held my hand in the taxi to the Bellagio. I was pixilated, but not enough to forget the way his strong, not-too-soft, hand touched the top of mine. Assistant 1's words clanged in my ear as we sat quiet in the cab. At 3 a.m. things weren't slowing down on the Strip, and I remembered he wasn't staying at my hotel. We exited the cab in front of the valet stand. I couldn't remember if we touched then, but at the hotel entrance, he held his hand above my head while holding open the glass door. In the lobby, under Dale Chihuly, we stopped.

"Ok, well, I'm going to head... ."

I stopped talking when he touched my hand, then my waist, and then my face. He drew in a lip, then two, the creases and curves of my mouth engaged by his. I hung on a second longer than he did. He pulled back.

"Your eyes are a different blue right now." He pointed out.

I was graduation-day sober: the sober that never leaves you on special occasions like weddings or 21st birthdays. No matter how much Ketel One and Red Bull you drink.

4:30 a.m.

I changed into a T-shirt, brushed my teeth, and gargled Listerine.
Fuck me, my feet.

In bed, I touched my lips and smiled. An episode of *Seinfeld* went dark brown.
Shit.

My eyes opened to his damn cookies lying next to me on a pillow.

I called the Four Seasons. "Cress Reiter's room please." *This won't work. He won't answer. He's using a fake name like John Wayne or Lil' John.*

"One moment, madam."

"Hello?" I heard a rumbling. *He answered he answered he answered.*

"Hey. Cress, it's January." I fiddled with the lamp next to my bed.

"I have your phone."

I laughed. "I know, I have your cookies and milk, and I'll probably get in ... ."

"Come over." I couldn't remember if he told me his room number or the hotel operator did.

I put on jeans, perfume and grabbed the bag of chocolate chip cookies off of the bed. In the cab, in the dark, I ignored the pangs of regret and fear, in salute of gluttony and giddiness.

He opened the door in his robe and took the cookies.

He was five or six inches taller than me.

"You're nuts." *Was he regretting this too? Did he not want me here?*

"My feet hurt, do you have any Band-Aids?" I took my shoes off and stood in front of him. He was so ... *handsome.* He looked like the guy from ... I couldn't think of it. From a TV show about lawyers I didn't watch.

"Band-Aids?"

I pointed to my shoes.

"Check the bathroom." He went over to a couch with the cookies. In the Egyptian marbled bathroom as big as my living room, I glanced at his toiletries. His hotel amenities sat quiet where the maids delicately placed them before he checked in, mini bottles of Kiehl's men's lotion and soaps unopened in the corners of the long, smooth vanity with two porcelain sinks.

"These cookies are ridiculous."

"They're from that place in Hollywood. I trucked them all the way here from LA."

"You drove?"

"I drove." I peeked out at Cress from the bathroom. I couldn't believe I was watching Cress Reiter eat cookies. *Dylan McDermott. That's the guy. But thinner and less actor-like. Like an ... an agent.*

Maybe not Dylan McDermott. He really doesn't look like anybody. Just himself. How am I going to describe him to VF?

"No luck?"

I shook my head, walked back to him, took off my jacket, and sat one seat away from him on the couch.

"Have one. You had to give these to everyone who came this weekend?"

I nodded. "Butlers helped me deliver them. With milk."

We both started laughing.

"It's late. And I kind of ambushed you."

"Well, I'm assuming your phone is something you need."

"How did you end up with it?"

He reached over, setting the cookies on a table next to me. My gaze followed him like a cat's. Cress pulled me into him with an arm around my neck and then his hands on my face. His minty breath hit my nose before our mouths came together like a Magritte painting.

———

"I put it in my jacket pocket." *The sexy pocket.*

The next morning I couldn't sleep with Cress' arm across my stomach, dreaming in a thin snore that heated the back of my neck every other two seconds. I decided that was one of the best ways to wake up.

My feet were numb. *Stupid shoes.*

I inched away from him and wobbled over to my Blackberry on a table by the couch, and television. He entered his number and email, and never gave it back to me. Cress turned onto his stomach.

I walked over to him and decided not to get back into bed. "I can't sleep," I whispered, touching his back. The clock on his night-stand told time, and today's noun: *reality.*

"Wait, it's 3?" My hair felt like straw.

I imagined the Zs lounging in white linen clothing at their poolside striped canvased cabana, wondering why the hell their best friend hadn't made an appearance, and their assistant wasn't answering her phone.

"They pump oxygen into these places. That's why you can't sleep." Cress grumbled into his pillows. I hated this part of Vegas: the waking up and leaving. Closing time.

"I have to go." The sun framed the blackout shades, cocooning us in the room painted gold and beige. I didn't want to step out into the unapologetic sun, a hung over taxi, and alone up to my room at the Bellagio. I thought of the crowds hobbling quiet and tired out of Pure:

I lost my purse, where are my shoes, I think I broke my (insert: finger, wrist, nose, tooth) my room or yours, who are you?

"Back to work?" He turned over and watched me put on my jacket.

"Oh, I hope not."

With his hair spiking out everywhere, he stood up, put on his robe, and followed me to the door. A quick exit was a priority before he saw me *after* a night at Pure. At the door his hands went to my shoulders, pulling me back. A couple of breaths on my neck, and I clenched my purse.

"Go get some Band-Aids."

Hot as a fever.
Rattling bones.
I could just taste it.
… it's not forever
… it's just tonight.
Your sex is on fire.

— Kings of Leon

September 17, 2008

"**E**stlin, did you find Band-Aids?" He waited in the Admiral's Lounge for his flight back to LA.

"Hey, hi. Yes." I was driving drowsy back to Pismo when he called. The smile on my face remained for a few seconds after I spoke.

"That was fun. And I'm still eating these cookies."

I'd never see Cress again. Well, that's not true. I'd see him again: on a picture I'd find on Mrs. Z's camera, from the hundred or so I was asked to burn on a disc from next year's trip to St. Barth's. Or I'd see his kids, smiling and leaning into Mickey Mouse at Disney World, arriving in a pile of the Zs' mail, in the form of a holiday card.

Sorting through bills and magazines, I'd remember Vegas and feel more emptiness and loneliness because Cress thought of me as a weekend fling. He had kids, an ex-wife, and work to fly home to. I drove home, less evolved, to Jack. Not even Jack—to my *desires* for Jack. Cress dated models and actresses with movie star boobs, zero stretch marks, and unspoiled personalities. Not a thought or opinion gracing their heads with hair impeccable from when they woke up at noon, because they were filthy rich and didn't lead a snooze-button life.

Delight, curiosity, sadness, guilt, hung over: There was a lot to process while driving on the 15, past the diner a hundred yards off of the freeway surrounded by nothing but sand, rocks, and cactus. I meant to stop there, but never did. When I did stop for gas, I contemplated a room at the Easy 8 on the other side of the freeway. *Is an Easy 8 nicer than a Motel 6? No hairs in the corners of the tub? More pillows beds?*

As soon as I shut the motel door behind me, I wouldn't be tired anymore. So, I climbed back into the boxy Mercedes with silver trays, carry-on-sized suitcases, and uncorked bottles of wine blocking the desert in my rearview.

October 2008

The last few weeks began to extinguish Jack from my radar leaving nothing other than some veins and fleshy bits of muscles. But, I was no cardiologist.

How about a fucktard? I could be a fucktard, no problem.

I wasn't sure if the interruption stemmed from Cress and Vegas, but Jack and I not being together started to make sense, somewhat.

"I wish I was with you. Caesar's is my favorite; I've never been to Pure. I would've loved to have met Cress. I like his name." Vanity Fair, hands in her lap, sat at a formal tea, rather than a bar.

"Yeah he was cool. You know what place I love, but didn't get to this time? That Russian bar that only serves vodka." I sighed at the thought of a whole bar space dedicated to hundreds of varieties of vodkas.

"Red Square. Yes! Don't you need a winter coat to go into one of the rooms?

Millionaire and I did that on one of our trips."

I agreed, "I think so. I love that place."

VF galvanized two rounds. *Club soda and three limes please.*

Jack texted me a few minutes later; he saw us at Moondoggies but we didn't see him.

"Don't talk to him, don't answer." She tried to take the phone.

"It's a text." I typed.

"I know but I like you with Cress."

"You don't know Cress—and he's in LA, and I'm here. He's friends with the Zs, for christ's sake. You can't imagine the women he's surrounded by every day at work, at parties, events, every-where. Non-stop, sophisticated, beautiful LA women." I breathed out despair.

"Have you looked in a mirror lately? And Mrs. Z saw what Jack did to you. She loves you. She won't care if he makes you happy."

"Cress doesn't make me happy, I don't know the guy. And you so don't know Z."

"But you like him, right?"

I pinched her cheek. "Shack?"

11:45 p.m.

Jack: Where'd u go

Me: Shack.

Jack: haha us too. Who was that guy u were talking to?

I liked the fact he noticed me and who I talked to in the bar, and that I didn't notice him. But this was nothing new. We never hung out when I saw him out. Our camouflaged lover-ship bequeathed me head nods, manslaughter by jukebox, and texts after the fact. You'd think by now, four years into this, we'd have hung out beyond his benighted bedroom. At bars, Jack surrounded himself with a bunch of people, a mix of guys and girls, and even though he reminded me they were his friends, my mind wandered.

3 a.m.

I didn't like waiting. A few hours after we migrated to the Shack, nothing remarkable happened except when I drove V to her house she fell out of the car, an uncustomary cigarette clipped to her bottom lip. She turned to me like a vagabond, leaning out of the car door while we sat in her driveway.

"Cress."

I went home and waited. I changed clothes, then changed clothes again. He claimed he was stuck in a vehicle he wasn't driving.

I don't believe him. Or this. Did something better come along? I can't believe anything he says.

I sat, sober, on the edge of my bed, watching TV and the walls.

4 a.m.

At first I didn't know if he wanted me to stay, but I wanted him to ask. We talked. His record store wasn't doing well, which was stressing him out. He touched me after sex, and kept touching me—my back, shoulders, hip. As I lay there, adjusting my boobs, I thought of what he told me a few months ago,

This is a "couples' thing."

Soon after his body listed into mine, he snored and itched his nose. I distanced myself, taking up one small edge of the bed, and I wasn't sure why. We fucked like animals, in the realm of a lady I saw on one of those taxicab confessional TV shows. She cleaned her huge dildo in the back of the cab while relaying to the driver she received, a few hours earlier, the best birthday present her husband had ever given her: A gang bang with five black guys. The disturbing image popped into head once in awhile.

I couldn't sleep in his house.

Cress.

Jack White. Jack. Jack White. Jack.

Cress.

Jack lay his hand on my shoulder. My reaction to an after-sex gesture I never felt before was sadness and confusion. Arm across the belly, sure. Arm under my neck, of course. This was a different awkwardness. I remember a few years ago, our faces couldn't get enough, not wanting to turn away from each other. Or the benign biting: one of my favorite Jack talents, him pushing my hands down, giving himself control on top of me, mild bites to my face, chin, and neck. How could Jack *not* love me? Not settle down with me? He always came back to me: his stress reducer, the standby, the smokin' in the girls' room girl who broke all of the rules, knocking them down with my tits, lunacy and need for control. What about the next time we fuck? What's the protocol? Are sleepovers ok now? *That was hardly a sleepover.*

I'm going to start making decisions and not ask for permission.

At home later that morning, I wrote his name on the date in my calendar and looked at May's page. *May 13.* I was tired.

How much easier life would be if I moved. Back to LA.

October 20

"Your pussy tastes so good, but it always does."

He never said I smelled good, only tasted good. During "pre-going out with our friends Saturday night sex" at my house, he repeated the same thing while fucking me.

"I like the feeling of my dick sliding and grinding against my finger."

That's his finger up my asshole, in case you're wondering.

Jack didn't lick or eat; he *gnawed.* Lips and teeth worshipping my clit.

I can't remember what kind of lips or teeth he has. Full? Thin? Crooked? Yellow? Straight?

As if greedily licking into oblivion a double-scooped ice cream cone, he never let up, as he's grabbed, pulled, and pinched my tits and nipples. Gently and then not so gently. For a short guy, he had long arms. Long and strong. They didn't match the other parts of him.

During the gnawing, I wanted to take a picture of him, his hair and its sandy, soft, mink fur feel. My orgasm, on the high side, didn't contain the guttural, pressurized ache, then explosion, as when he was inside of me.

"I sweat so much with you." I didn't reply, concentrating on maneuvering his blocky body upward and my hands holding his ass. He wanted to feel me come, and I did. I force-thought strange images in order to make myself come. Him on top of me during the best sex of my life wasn't enough.

I want to suck your cock. I will do anything. Anything for you.

"You liked that, huh? Stay there." While perpendicular over his bed on soft lines of blacks, reds, and leopard skin, I noticed the entire room was decorated the same way as he arrived at my head with our strawberry-flavored, sugar-free lubricant in hand. I had a few seconds to come back into reality. Then I caressed his balls and bit them so hard I hoped they'd burst.

Silence. His restraint wasn't surprising while we made love. An "uh" here or there, a slap, but I didn't hear him moan, scream, or say my name. He didn't flail about. He didn't move his arms at all, really—not just in bed. I assumed contentment when I crawled over him. He bit my ass before I lay on my back and he dug a little sandcastle up inside my pink throbbing clit. I came again so hard, I grabbed his soft big ass while bringing his dick back into my mouth. The sandcastle night was the best sex we ever had. I ever had. I wanted us to come at the same time. It turned me on when he came. I loved when I could moan with his moans, move with him.

Was there any doubt as to why I was in love with this? This man, these ins and outs, ups and downs of elation and humiliations, earth-quaking my emotions? During an archaeological dig neither him nor I had any intention of pioneering, the humane and wonderful bits of me crumbled away. My complexion ruined while blitzing my way through my gingery years, his cum binding me to whatever this was, then dissolving. Nothing remained but stained sheets and an abused Blackberry.

Hours after he left, or I left him, I disappeared for a few days into his lingering scent, an echo of bliss. Smells I lived for; small, simple treasures I preserved in jam jars in the kitchen and in shampoo bottles in my shower.

Why can't you look at me and want me the way I want you? How can you look at me the way you do and NOT want me the way I want you? I wanted more from the guy who had empty pockets. He would never stop. More whys. A circus tent of why's above me. Yet no protection from the storm brewing, undetected, about to come down.

A toxicity showering all over me.

October 21
   Jack: you likin this weather
   Me: Yea, the weather has been crazy. Cold.
   Jack: K, stay warm. Goodnight

Punk ass twerp cocksucking dick.

   Me: Thanks, have a good week.

Later that night ...
   Jack: what r u doing
   Me: Working. Whats up, how are you.
   Jack: working naked?
   Me: Noooo. Actually at my office. Major deadline.
   Jack: Naked later? Touching yourself?
   Me: omg does it always have to be about sex?
   Jack: Sorry sweetie, just messing w u
   Me: Not to sound harsh, but you'd have a better shot at getting what you wanted if you asked me in a different way. But I think you know that.

The two sets of texts meant he had a plan. In fact, the plan went into effect when he said goodnight in text No. 1. Text No. 2, "What are u doing," meant the first plan flew away like a fly trying to escape from a swatter.

November 2008
   I complained. I tried to stay positive; when I nagged, he punished: flipping me over vigorously and sticking his dick up my ass. Some positions, some sexual situations I begged for with my eyes or

my hands. In rare and memorable seconds, his face would freeze into a statue and his eyes emptied. He wouldn't do the movie move: me on top, him in a crunch and hugging me, my hands through his hair. His hands smoothing my back.

Human sexuality class at SB taught me to communicate in bed with a partner. I couldn't: talking didn't feel correct or natural. I knew what his answer would be.

That's a couples' thing, Sweetie.

November 2

Jack: Are you up

Me: Yeah

Jack: You shouldn't talk to me 'n e more'. I have issues. You shouldn't want to be around me. Something is wrong with me. Sorry I am drunk

Me: Go to bed.

Jack: I just need to be held.

Me: You do?

Jack: Yes I do. I just miss my friends. I need them all of the time in my life. Sorry, I am drunk.

Me: They miss you too, I am sure. Don't worry. Everything is going to be ok.

Jack: I feel better. U rock. That is weird.

November 5

He asked me to come over and told me I could "crash there." I loved making him wait. He put water by my side of bed and lit candles. Could this be it? Time to take this somewhere?

Where was Walmart?

Four years to the day as I drove to his house. *Four years* since we first met. He didn't know four years from four weeks.

"Huh. I thought we knew each other longer." The living room was big, with a good-sized TV and two framed surf movie posters on the walls. Two surfboards stood guard in the corner, lit with strands of Christmas lights. After we watched *The Happening*, we laughed, played, and he gave me the most amazing massage without my reciprocation. I'd rather buy him a gift certificate to a spa. I was too clever to spend my Jack time doing something a girlfriend should do.

"Here, walk on my back."

"You're kidding me."

"It'll be a huge relief. I hurt it rock climbing." He did a belly flop toward the carpet.

"Um, ok. I'll do it, but I'm warning you I'm heavier than I look." I took off my Vans. I had to wear Vans around him, as if wearing a particular brand of shoes would increase my chances of him becoming my boyfriend.

"Shut up," he teased as he put his arms above his head.

I walked on his back, and then it became clear: I was *bored*.

A sampling, a practice test of all I asked for, wanted from Jack, ended up being an "*Eh.*"

The whole of this thing wasn't as thrilling when the hours between 9 p.m. and midnight felt like "dating."

"Are your roommates here?"

"Yeah they're asleep, I told them you were coming over."

I knew when his roommate Liver, a mechanic, was home and I knew when he wasn't sleeping, but passed out. Liver was one of the few people in the world I witnessed being as swacked as myself, bowed over an ATM in the Shack, bills spitting out at him, red, and drooling. The last time I saw Liver, he shoved me toward No Name, slurring "Round, now" into my hair.

The proximity of myself, Jack, and his roommates stimulated me. Like I was one of the girls in their "We're just friends, Sweetie" clique I ogled so many times on Friday nights.

Liver blared loud Johnny Cash while we had sex. Between that and the Interpol, I left Jack's house with a week's worth of dejection sung to me by talented, black-haired skinny guys. Liver never opened the unlocked door to Jack's bedroom. Another mysterious circumstance occurring to me while we watched *South Park*.

Jack walked into the kitchen, and I snuck a few clicks with my Blackberry's camera, capturing our shoes side by side under his coffee table. In his room I dropped something on the floor and glanced under the bed: feng shui with one red box dead center. I didn't have a chance to ask or contemplate what it held. After sex, I tossed and turned, eventually waking from a two-hour slumber to roosters cock-a-doodling a block away.

November 7

He hadn't texted all week. My red calendar contained pages of blood spatter instead of a murderous sexual rampage commemorated with a swift roll of a pen. Rejection was a cramp: coming and going, doubling me over for a couple of days, telling me something happened, or I took too much ex-lax. I exploded into a burst of tears. How many times would I cry? Why had we started up, started speaking again after last May, chain linked through semen, death, and self-loathing?

I finally texted.

Me: Hi, how are you.
No reply. So, I reacted, at 8 a.m.
Me: I know you don't give a shit about me but you having me over and not calling for a week is not cool. Why are you doing this to me? Either leave me alone, tell me to fuck off, or be a man, and show me some respect. It needs to end, or go forward. I feel like you're testing me, and the waters, but i'm failing.
Jack: lets talk about this not on text. I wasn't trying to make u feel that way at all. I have had a crazy week at the store and my parents. Can I call u later…what time?
Me: are u back with your ex?
Jack: no, I swear on my mother, not at all.

November 12

Over the next week, we talked every day and texted at night and in the morning.

I told him I wasn't feeling well, and he asked if I needed anything. The next night he asked me what I wanted from him. He was *just wondering*.

Me: I don't expect anything so don't stress. *Lie.*

Wtf? Why didn't I tell the truth, expand and find compromises? I felt more subdued in my craziness for Jack.

I thought about Cress.

I like intelligent women.
When you go out, it shouldn't
be a staring contest.

— Frank Sinatra

November 13, 2008

"Estlin. When are you down here?" Cress sounded attractive and succinct.

"Hey! Next week, what's up?" I fell on my bed when I heard his voice.

"Hold on a sec."

I got a hold of myself and tried to remember anything I could use for small talk. Kids, Vegas, the Zs. I despised small talk.

"Hey. How are you?" His tone mellowed. My ear melted into my Blackberry.

"I'm good, I'm good. How are you?"

"I'm good. Um ... ." He paused and I laughed nervously, blacking out for a couple of seconds.

"I have tickets." I heard two people talking and what I assumed was his office door closing.

I interrupted. "What kinda tickets, ooh, speeding tickets? I *hate* those." Lying down switched to pacing.

"No, dork. Lakers. They're at home next Thursday. Will Z let you out of the house?"

"Um, yeah. That sounds fun. Ah, eh, the Zs, shoot, I don't know if I want them to know we're hanging out. They don't need to know, right?" Pacing led to cleaning my kitchen sink.

"In Vegas, Mr. Z asked me if I "hit that" after I told him we were together until the next morning."

"Oh my god. Good, you didn't tell them what time I actually left your room did you? Wait, what did you say?"

"Nothing. Mrs. Z gawked and yelled, '*NOOO!*' as if, '*Not my little January!*' Don't worry about Mrs. Z. It's a Laker game. If you want, I can tell her."

Was a date with Cress a good idea? Bad? Hanging out with him in Vegas was one of the best nights of my life, and his call was unequivocally uplifting. I didn't know how Mrs. Z would react. She was possum crazy.

Cress didn't like small talk, either.

November 15

We texted; we didn't text. Hurt and alone, I abused him digitally. He came over and stayed one hour and made sure I knew he wouldn't be staying over. I felt like a whore and didn't care. I didn't have the energy to care. He left in a bad mood (no idea why) and I turned back on a TV show about the morbidly obese. It was becoming impossible to be pleasant. I wasn't easy going, perky, positive, or happy enough for him; his influence on my emotional problems and my personality was an excruciating side effect of what we'd created. *I bet this is where a dumb, boring, girlfriend comes in handy. Just shut up, smile and spread your legs.*

While deleting him and all of his dick pics, I asked myself and told myself so many things: small mental duels. *I wanted more. Was I still bored? Does he still want her? I wanted a companion in him, but does he still want to know what I want? Keep it light. Be nice.* I hated him, but I wanted to know long before I heard from him. I wasn't a Gemini; I was a hundred Geminis fighting for no. 1, scratching and climbing, and canceling each other out.

I wasn't good enough for Cress.

November 16

VF and I were at a sushi bar when I saw the red flashing light. "Cress."

Cress: Estlin. Thursday. I'll pick you up.
Me: Hey, can we meet instead? J
Cress: you're scared of the Zs? don't be. drinks before?
Me: Sure, L'Ermitage?
Cress: 6.
Me: k.
Cress: it will be fun … don't be scared.

With plenty of effort on my part—respecting our time together, no flaking on plans—Vanity Fair and I were in love again. It wasn't her role in our lives to be my constant cheerleader. We munched on the pre-sushi cucumber salad on the wooden plate.

"Finally." Pleased I embarked toward something, anything substantial with someone else, she asked questions.

"What does he look like?"

I glanced down at his name on my phone. The one Cress typed into it when he took it at Pure. Then he put it in the *sexy pocket*.

"Um … basically the standard, clean cut, Hollywood show business type: tall, thin, but not too thin, dark hair, perfect skin tone to go with the dark hair, good clothes, even better shoes. A little like Adam Levine, I guess, but taller, not rock and roll. Wait, not Adam Levine. Lemme think. God, when I describe him he sounds perfect. Like the perfect guy. I don't know, you'd think he's cute. I think." I didn't bother bringing up Dylan McDermott. She'd have no idea who that was.

"Who's Adam Levine?"

"Maroon 5."

She proceeded to give me a detailed, strict set of instructions on what not to do at the Laker game.

Don't have sex with him, sleepover, or give him a blow job.

Don't bring up Jack/SFF.

Don't cry.

Wear lipstick, not just lip-gloss.

Don't pay for anything.

Don't get drunk.

"What about kissing?" I asked VF.

"Kissing is ok."

"Should I call him after to thank him?"

"Oh my god no. Do not call him after. Under any circumstances."

November 19

I took a quick shower at the Zs, added jewelry, smoky eyes, and Alfred Sung on the neck. Every guy I ever came in contact with—even at the grocery store while I decided which size of vodka bottle to buy before a night out in LA—went ballistic over the sweet, woody, balsamic scent. I sifted through my luggage for the black clutch I remembered to bring from Pismo. I waved goodbye to the house-keeper as I ran out the door. Exhausted, but not sleepy, I drove to L'Ermitage in front of the setting sun and upcoming glow holding on to Beverly Hills for a few more hours. Streetlamps wore holiday deco-rations, and parade banners of twinkle lights traversed Wilshire at each intersection. The Writers' Bar in the hotel was absent of uncom-fortable and drunken decibel levels and featured dim lighting, and an ease I hoped would deter a panic attack, during my date with someone other than a cretin from Pismo. I left my car with the valet, hoping I was early, and walked into the warm, white space toward the contemporary bar. The smell of Bulgari arrived at my shoulder 30 seconds later.

"Hey. When did you get here?" He was still Vegas/Esquire Cress as he sat next to me, but this time closer to Agent Cress. Everything about him—his glasses, his smell, his mouth, what he was saying, increased my pulse. A very sexy, stylish, and handsome nerd. Or dork?

Looks never mattered to me. Even though I called SFF SFF, he was cute and not *exactly* fat. Jack/SFF was the product of immaturity, rejection, and anger. The nickname SFF allowed me to actively pursue, study, and converse about him, without ever saying the word *Jack*. The few times I said Jack out loud in public, or during a particularly heated month, it was as if my tongue was set on fire and the flames were stomped out at the same time. It was a visceral experience, saying his name.

I didn't know what type my type was until I saw it. Types were invented by screenwriters. My type sat next to me in The Writers' Bar. Cress was an episode of *Entourage*, or more likely a character. Guys behind the scenes representing the beautiful people didn't have to be beautiful, but in LA, even guys walking around with their Blackberries, 1st assistants, and 2nd assistants uphold a standard. They weren't potbellied insurance salesmen, put it that way.

"Scotch, please. What would you like?"

Hi, I'm a freak and a horrible drunk, so I'll have water. I ordered wine. *Five sips max.*

"Have you been here before?"

"I lived in LA before I moved to Pismo and came here a lot back then. A departure from the east side."

"Los Feliz?" I nodded. "I go there occasionally for clients."

"I like Los Feliz because it's spread out, not like sardines off of Melrose."

"The magazine, how is it?"

Did I tell him where I worked when I wasn't at the Zs?

"It's ok." The wine glass was as big as my head. "I'm writing, so that's good."

"Why Pismo?"

I bored myself with the story of my book, how I left LA to write, and how I was from Pismo. "I've been writing for eight years."

"What's the title?"

"Anti-Fat." I nervous laughed. *Four sips left.*

"Anti-Fat? I guess I have to ask."

"Ha. It's about a girl who works in the same office building as a Leonardo DiCaprio type. He's a good friend of hers. So is his mom. I might use his name; I'm not sure yet. Anyway, he has a serious public relations problem, snafu, whatever, and he needs a nice girl to round out his reputation. Repair it. So they start hanging out. And it goes from there."

"We need to work on your elevator pitch."

"Elevator pitch?" *Three.*

"Astonish me in one sentence. Describe the plot of your novel as if you had 30 seconds to sell it to me in an elevator." He advised me on the legalities of using an actual actor's name.

"Did you finish it?"

"Yeah, a while ago. Now it's about a literary agent." I glimpsed my shoes—suede, open-toed booties—becoming nervous about falling at the Staples Center. I hoped he liked what he was looking at.

"Ah, yes. Nothing happens without us, does it?"

I laughed. "No, I'm learning, it doesn't. But I can't write when I'm doing all of the other stuff: letters, sending out proposals, finding agents, emailing, research. I want to create, but I can't because all of the other stuff is so overwhelming. It's harder than writing. Writing is the easy part."

"Ok, you ready?" He took my hand and we left in his car for downtown.

8:35 p.m.

At halftime we stood at a tall table in one of the clubs where Cress was a member.

"You've been?" I asked.

"Both. AFI and the TCM film festivals." He swirled the ice around in his drink.

"I'm obsessed with TCM. I won't ask about Cannes."

"Really, TCM? Cannes isn't bad. Usually people ask me about Sundance or Tribeca."

"I know, it's crazy. I studied international cinema in school, and after watching

Pedro Almodovar, and *Citizen Kane* for the first time, I went psychotic."

"What's your favorite?" He asked as he took a sip of his scotch.

"Classic?"

He nodded.

"Probably *Sunset Boulevard*." I paused.

"So, how are Tallulah and Henry? Are they doing ok?"

"They are." He gave me an odd a smile I didn't try to decipher. "They're rock stars."

"How old are they?" I rubbed the side of my water glass with my fingertip.

"Tallulah is 13, Henry 10. But they're tough, I can't imagine what it's like for them."

"What happened there?"

"With my ex-wife? We … I knew less about her but realized more. She wasn't … she became something I didn't want to be married to anymore, put it that way." He leaned on the table. *Fucking Bulgari.*

"Most things in life are complicated but that is hard. But I get it. I mean what your kids are going through, at least. You seem like a normal, (he laughed) even-keeled sort of guy, a good dad, so you're probably making the transition easy for them. It's how you react to them, not how they react to the divorce. Well, of course that matters, too … but you know what I mean."

"No, you're right. I try. Your parents are divorced?"

I nodded.

"You need another." He moved closer and touched my glass. I was relieved he didn't ask about my water drinking.

Another agent looking type spotted us and stopped.

"Reiter, yo." Agent 2 checked me out as Cress turned his head toward him.

"Bennn. January this is Ben, Ben, January."

"How are you, um, January? Not a name you hear every day. This guy boring you to tears? If you wanna have some actual fun, come up to the suite with us. Reiter, why aren't you up there?"

"We work together." Cress moved toward me. "We're going to the bar for a second and talk boring agency stuff. Will you be ok for a minute?"

"Definitely, go." He lifted his hand from my wrist. While alone, I carved the last two hours into a stone tablet. I didn't know if I was going to make it through the game without attacking him in the stadium. I studied other girls in the lounge and compared outfits. I held my own in black skinny jeans with the same color leather stripe up each outer leg, and a gold statement necklace Mrs. Z brought back for me from London. My blouse was a smoke white, airy, chiffon button down, with long, roll tabbed sleeves. I tucked it into the jean a bit and left it unbuttoned just enough. I looked tall and fashionable, but not overdone at a basketball game.

Cress placed his drink in front of me from behind.

"You have to try this. Their margaritas are great. Like the place in Vegas we went after Pure."

My head soda-popped at the memory and I grinned (probably like an idiot) "That's right, I forgot about that."

Ben smiled at Cress and turned to me.

"January, it was wonderful meeting you."

10:30 p.m.

"Ireland." I named a destination.

"Two Christmases ago." Cress drove toward the hotel.

"St. Lucia?"

"Honeymoon."

"Eh, ok, Spain?"

"Last summer with my kids."

"Fiji? Bora Bora?"

"Not yet." *Hmm, someplace he hasn't been.*

"There's, like, 300 islands—mostly uninhabited, I think." I opened and shut the clasp on my purse. In that second I couldn't believe where I was, and how *delightful* it was, and pure. *Pure.*

"Beach, water, sand, nothing. Fiji sounds relaxing." He lowered and relaxed his voice like a beach bum.

"I used to have a Fiji fund."

"Seriously?" He glanced over at me and moved his hands to a different position on the steering wheel. The way Cress drove his car was attractive.

His hands: I noted a firm handshake with Ben at the Staples Center. I vaguely remembered from Vegas—his hands weren't harsh on the palm side but weren't weirdly supple like some guys'. He didn't have fingertips shaped like grapes, thank goodness. He had a thinner version of John Goodman's hands from 20 years ago. Don't ask me how I know what John Goodman's hands look like, but I watched enough *Roseanne* episodes to remember them: strong, handsome, and what I would want touching me.

"Yeah, in one of my drawers in my closet in Los Feliz." I wanted to take his photo.

"What happened to the fund? Did you ever go?"

"Nope, I spent it at L'Ermitage."

He laughed.

Then we laughed about the refs, the four-beer-deep fans falling over one another in the stands, and the celebs (his friends and clients) sitting near us, courtside. I tried not to focus on time, but I did. Six months ago, one side of my mouth went up to my nose and my eyes wouldn't *roll*, they would unhinge and burrow under my dark circles when I heard his name. Today, right then, I was in his car. Cress Reiter made me laugh, smiled at me, listened to me, flirted with me, and crushed me with charm. An hour earlier, he bought me a hot dog and Diet Coke. He took me on a date, introduced me to people, and wanted to be around me. *I rode in his car.*

"It was hilarious how the people in back of us thought you were Kirsten Dunst."

I nodded. "Someone else said something Upton; do you know someone, somebody named Upton?"

He looked over at me. "I do, and I get why they said it." He moved his hand on the steering wheel again and smiled.

"Are you going back tonight?" West Hollywood tinseled behind us and the ficus turned thicker, greener, and taller as we drove into Beverly Hills.

"Yeah, I have a deadline," I told him.

Cress left his car with the valet and walked with me into the lobby, his hand on my back. I wanted to stay and at the same time I wanted to go and kneel over my carvings on the stone tablet, reliving the entire night on my drive home.

There was no magical equation to my self-constraint; Cress could've been the cause. Staying over, doing whatever we would do, didn't feel right. A pivotal moment like this one, dictated future moments. It required a simple, respectful decision, however excruciating. Nine times out of 10 I sent myself thank-you notes when I disrespected the men I dated, and nine times out of 10 I was drunk. I shunned my addictive, afflicted half-brain and thought before I spoke.

"That was really fun." My car pulled up and we walked outside. Cress tipped the driver.

"I'm following you." I hoped he couldn't hear my whole body, featherlight, increasing tempo in beats and measures. With his hand on the car door, I noticed his hair was classic: straight, short on the sides, medium/long length on top, baker's chocolate brown. I didn't look at his eyes; I looked at the chin, good teeth, lips, the handsome shave and not-too-groomed eyebrows.

"You don't have to."

"Yes, I do."

11:20 p.m.

I inhaled the collar of his pea coat.

The Zs' cars were gone, but for someone who wanted Lakers night on the down low, I was being an idiot. Under the porch light with a fountain to our left, we stood on the latte-colored stones. He took me by my lapel and I raised my head. I couldn't wrap my mind, even loosely, around the warmth and satisfaction when his face bent down to mine. His lips paused at my mouth and he pulled me in by my back. The kissing slowed down. *Faster.* We went underround, then his mouth went to my bottom lip, and then the top. I kissed him the same way. His hands lowered to my waist.

"That was our first kiss."

"What about Vegas?" I asked.

"You don't remember Vegas, and you smell like lemons right now." He smiled as he whispered into my mouth. He brought my left cheek into his hand. *Fast.* When both of his hands touched my face, our kiss slowed and I held onto him by his arms.

"I remember Vegas. Wait, lemons? Is that bad?"

"Opposite of bad."

He's five-feet-11 or six feet.

One hand still holding my chin, his thumb on one side of my face, the rest of his hand on the other, he stepped away from me, and his expression was where I wanted the evening to end. With *that look* on his face.

"Be good." He let go.

"Bye." He left me, and the fountain.

I could barely maneuver Mulholland.

I rode in his car.

Spark.

**Life is a shipwreck, but we musn't
forget to sing in the lifeboats.**

— Voltaire

If you're going through hell, keep going.

— Winston Churchill

Wait, they don't love you like I love you.

— Yeah Yeah Yeahs

December 5, 2008

On my drive back to Pismo after the Laker game, through a descending pyramid of cold temperatures, I realized *I didn't think about Jack at the Laker game.*

I didn't text Jack on my way back to Pismo.

I hadn't seen Cress in a few weeks. We talked and didn't text much. Not tying Cress to a flashing red light on my Blackberry made him dreamier, like we were closer than we were. More real.

"What's the music on your voicemail?"

"'Moonlight in Vermont.' Sinatra. I was about to change it to one of his Christmas songs."

"What's going on in Pismo these days?"

"Well, let's see, work is good, the Zs are nuts."

"Are they riding you?"

"Always. It's cool; I enjoy it."

"Seriously?"

I loved the fascinating creatures who were the Zs. My desire and need for their unconditional love grew from the fact they gave me what most couldn't: attention. I wanted attention as much, or more, than I didn't want rejection.

"It's never dull, I'll tell you that."

I needed a delicate way to ask Cress who he was dating. I tried a casual tactic.

"I bet you've been dating models and actresses since your divorce, right?" I hated it as soon as I said it.

"That's funny. They're nightmares to deal with in business; I can't imagine being in a relationship with one."

I had to let him come to me.

January 4

Back for more. Was Walmart out of town? Her pussy not tight enough for him this week? Did they break up?

Let me call January! I was "JE" in his phone.

He wants to talk. He's confused.

He came over and we did everything but talk.

"You've missed the sex, huh?"

Ick. I didn't know this person, a boy I had salivated blood over. A week into the new year and the sex was off kilter, awkward, and disappointing.

Why am I still doing this? I imagined sad scenarios.

I asked if he was staying over

"Huh?" He lied like I breathed. Those few seconds in between "Huh?" and me repeating the question scissored the night.

I turned around to an urgent hanger situation in my closet.

I had no idea what my end game was going to be.

January 10

Since I couldn't drink, I "ran."

Diet Red Bull, smoke, run, smoke.

Like always, I ran/jogged/walked. I stretched down to my Nike shoelaces while I did a yoga pose I learned from a DVD. With my feet together, my arms dangled in the seaweed and sand, prompting my spine to crack. A few vertebrae popped while I held my core, abs, and glutes. Forget endorphins after exercise—endorphins were for happy people. Endorphins gave me more anxiety. While I walked back to my car, the sand hung on the pavement, next to pickups with surfboards sticking out of their beds. It constantly shifted and resembled the all-purpose flour I watched our cook in Chicago throw down on the counter before he rolled out pizza dough.

The yoga pose/all-purpose flour day was the last time I ever smoked.

January 15

Jack: How are you?

Those three words moved me into gaga-land.

Jack: We'll talk soon, ok

Me: We don't have to talk unless you think there's something to say.

Jack: Well, I don't want to hurt your feelings.

Me: We never talk. I can take a hint. I'm beyond hurt feelings. I guess closure is just something I'm never going to get. I've accepted it.

Jack: I guess you want something from me I can't give you. Honestly I thought u knew it was a friends with bennies sitch.

Me: You guess? U thought? U don't even know. U think I want you to be my boyfriend? You're fucking crazy if you think that. *Lie.*

Jack: Well, I'm sorry for not asking. What do you want

Me: I want you to be more clear. If you're dating or fucking other girls I need to know so I can move on.

Friends with bennies. Asshole. I thought we were fuck buddies. Blowhard.

Ten minutes later

Me: All I've ever wanted was to hang out w/ you. And be a part of your life. I am not dumb, I don't expect to be your gf. But I deserve consistency.

Jack: ok. Well consistency is tough right now to be honest. I am dating a little to be honest.

Me: ok then thanks for being honest.

Jack: Not dating a lot bc I'm busy but that is the truth

I sobbed.

Jack: i am a little scared of you freaking on me again but that isnt the reason

Me: That's how u hurt me. by calling me, then blowing me off. And lying... Its happened so many times I've lost count,

Jack: I swear I was w my mom. How did I hurt you

Jack: r we ok then

Me: No, I'm not. But I will be.

Jack: What wud you want me to say. I am sorry

Me: Good bye.

Jack: Forever, or tonite

Don't answer. Don't put thumbs to keys.

Me: Forever. You were honest and that's what I wanted. I can't be what u want and you can't be what I want.

Jack: but can we be friends

Me: No, I don't think so.

Jack: Wait I'm confused not friends forever yes or no

Me: Not friends. No we cannot be friends. I care about you unconditionally so I guess I'll never not want to talk to you.

Jack: if that's what u want

Me: Its not what I want of course not, but you leave me no choice.

Jack: u have to make that choice then.......ok i guess

Me: Don't act surprised. Don't pretend u didn't lead me on. Or didn't have feelings for me. Because I know u did. But someone came along that seemed better to u, skinnier, or more stupid....or your ex decided she'd start fucking u again, and u tossed me out like trash. U don't give a shit about me or my feelings. All u care about is you and your cock. And I may have misbehaved before but only because I've been so hurt by u. Why didn't I listen-why didn't you let me listen and remind me – you never felt a spark for me. You asshole. A spark. My life is defined by that spark. And if u cared even a bit about me, u wouldn't have given up, and ignored me after that. U would have forgiven me. Anyway, like I said before - goodbye.

Me: U r a fucking liar. Stop texting me. U got off easy. If uever c me in publoic walk the other way. Asshole. I will kill you.

Jack: That is a threat. Seriously?

Me: Don't ever text or call me again

Straight up violence: a new rung I hadn't yet met on my descent. That's cool. I could live with myself if he were dead and buried in the cemetery we fucked in years before. He deserved that piece of shit cemetery. The arrested developmental boy strung me along as foreplay. Me: a damaged distraction. A time passer with nice tits and a vagina that tasted like spun sugar.

Me: One more thing-go to fucking hell. U mother fucking prick. Fucking ruined my life. I hope every girl u ever try to bang knows truly who u really r. A fucking sociopath.

Jack: I feel bad u mistake this for love. i swear i wont send nemore

January 17
Almost the end

Still crying.

He felt bad I mistook what we had. That I mistook "this" for love.

It's ok, it's ok, I told myself at work, in the shower, putting groceries in my trunk. I moaned and blubbered into toilet paper as I peed. Nothing pushed me faster to a pizza/potatoes/ice cream epidemic then nervous breakdowning on my toilet.

If I was in this much pain, I must be on his mind in some way.

I begged for amnesia or a brain tumor before we ended up a feature story on *Dateline* and *48 Hours*.

The end began as I thought of Cress. Thankfully for the last month, I didn't see him. He went to Disney with his kids at the end of last year, and stayed busy with awards season. Thinking of Cress made January (the month) extra absurd and heartrending. Swollen with so much hatred and poison, I couldn't imagine any man bringing a smile to my face. I prayed for SFF to develop dick cancer and I lit candles in St. Mary's for erectile dysfunction.

I would have done anything for you, Jack.

January 22, 2009
The end

"You have a fucking *girlfriend*? Are you serious?" I texted him.

Who was this girl on his Facebook page?

Wait. The girl I stared at (stared *through* in a stupor) on Facebook looked familiar. I saw him with her once, years ago—oh my lord—it was the mini-SFF.

Hairtrix. His ex. *She cuts my hair now, that's all.*

The stem of my thick martini glass without a martini almost broke off. The last drops of my late evening cyber-stalking cocktail splish-splashed one way, and I tipped my head back fast, wishing the vodka would stop and rewind time.

Ten minutes earlier

Less snockered, I stretched out on the floor with my laptop and unblocked his name for three minutes on Facebook. Big, fucking, Ketel One mistake. Broadcast across 17 electronic inches in blaring 2D was Jack's profile picture: her and him in their Halloween costume as farmers. A straw hat and overalls, her with some Daisy Duke monstrosity and two braids of brassy blonde hair hanging over her shoulders. Their grins hurt me with each visible tooth. I ran to the freezer, shooting him texts the entire way, like blanks into a haystack.

To get to her FB page, I had to go through his. The caption under Hairtrix's profile pic read, "Never say Never."

She never thought they'd get back together. How did he fuck her? How did she fuck him?

The juice from my limes corroded the night air. Back and forth was no longer. There would be no argument. *I'm sorry. Why? I'm sorry. Who? I'm sorry. When?* Jack never called, texted, explained, or made an excuse. *I'M SORRY.* Two words, three if he said *I AM*—which he wouldn't have. All caps. A brave apology text (text!?) signaling me to place *this* in a box and tie up this entire *thing*, with a smooth, shiny red bow. *No, a black bow, definitely black.*

I compromised and bargained.

He has no problem being in my life and not being together, but he is also a sociopath who has no feelings and has Hairtrix. I can't have him in my life unless we are at least dating. And that is positively not an option and hasn't been, ever! Maybe in time we can be friends. I'm miserable because I can't call him, text him, see him, and fuck him.

He whipsawed me with Facebook and the stealth assurance I'd never have him like she did. Jack was all set, but what was I supposed to do? What *do* I do when the one thing, person, revelation who brought wholeness, comfort, happiness, and love, is ripped away? Years-long experience of ambivalence: a desired and expected gravitational push and pull between two people, finally said, *enough.* The push and pull: *it* said enough.

The hatred and devastation did nothing but push me away on an ice floe.

They were a couple.

In a relationship with...

Blondes make the best victims.
They're like virgin snow that shows up the
bloody footprints.

— Alfred Hitchcock

February 2009

*J*anuary 4. January 4. January 4. I rubbed the paper on my red calendar. I cried into the little box, into the last day we had sex.

I was a tornado. I puked hurricanes.

I was Jodi Arias. There were no more tears for him.

Swirling eddies of vodka, pills, fattening food, and tears. Vortexes corralled other vortexes. They joined forces with the eyes of other storms far out into the Gulf and Atlantic and castrated my heart first, then everything below the neck. Fuck the heart; my *brain* was mauled into mush. He didn't have a heart—and possibly, neither did I. The heart had nothing to do with a whirlpool of circles and left and rights I navigated.

The turbulences would strip away my stupid thought process and even stupider clitoris. Before this could happen, I escape-slept and slipped into a case-hardened shell, then I remembered I wanted to die over this guy less than a year ago when he told me he would never want me. Here I was again, foolish and cowering in the same corner in my house, taking false shelter. Or was I?

"Don't feel that spark" meant truth in all forms and deserved a suicide (not a suicide attempt but an *ideation*). We spoke after the "spark" talk, and he consoled me, lessening the pain of what we caused: an exciting and interesting distraction and twist to spice up our lives and sex life.

Even after our last set of texts, turning to violence, we probably would have eventually hooked up. But a new girlfriend? Another betrayal dumped over my head. An epiphany. A cliché. A lie overlapping our time together, and tangible, Facebook proof he never lied to me: He would *never want me.*

He would *never want me.* Is that a fact? What if he was testing me since last November? He asked what I wanted and I buried the answer deep down, avoiding the truth. Something told me to react that way. The unexpected sleepovers toward the end. It was an audition. A final look-see. *Whatever, it's a theory.* I was too tired to revisit any of it. It was over. If I waited another year, or two, for his latest relationship to end, the first half of my life, Phase 1, would be worthless. Who knows how long the worthlessness would travel into the second half, into Phase 2? If I lived in total rejection, allowed it, followed it around, depended upon it, it didn't matter if I thought of suicide in any instance of my life; I would become a scarecrow in a killing field.

He would have the world.

February 7

I dragged myself over to my dad's. I breathed in patience in front of the wide, white, ranch-style house shaped like the sideways "L" in Tetris. There was the house in front and workshops, barns, and truck ports behind that. "Behind that" meant "out back." *Out back.* That's what we called it. I treasured its 20 acres as a kid. Summers from the '80s consisted of stomping on certain patches of dirt, sitting under a specific tree, or hiding behind a corner of one of the truck ports while I played tag with my brother. As I rode my ATV or in the front bucket of my dad's bulldozer I didn't just see, I *smelled* the vista of painted hills, and lettuce fields stretch a mile out in one direction. In the other was a forest of eucalyptus. Nine months in Chicago of bad, wrong, despicable, and unchangeable slipped away. As a kid, I waited for my patches of dirt and bucket rides all year.

I inhaled when I turned into the H-shaped driveway. I don't remember exhaling.

"Hey, Jan," was his jovial greeting. Sitting in front of the TV, on his couch (no one else sat there) his lifelong white hair mussed inches above a huge potbelly covered in a stained flannel shirt. My dad was always happy to see me. For two minutes. Start the count down.

I dropped my purse and cried in front of a brand-new audience.

"You know, Jan" (He *never* called me by my full name—in fact he loathed the name, I know this because he told me so).

"I once heard a Texas fella on TV—he was about your age, the same age as this boy you like. Fella was on death row ... ."

My shoulders fell. "Dad, I don't ... ."

"Shut up and listen to me for a minute. Anyway, this asshole killed his entire family: wife, kids, even the dog. Can you believe that? A dog?" He pet his German Shepherd, Cabe, around his ears. The giant, hairspray-straight ears stuck up like two taco shells.

A rifle smirked at us from above the fireplace. On the other side of the house, a sawed off shotgun separated my sleeping dad from his bedside lamp at night. I knew where the guns were, I always knew.

Why didn't I remember the guns last year?

I drifted back into his death row murderer story.

"He said he only married his wife because she was tall. That's what he said. He was short, so if he married her, his kids wouldn't be short like him. Maybe that's what this boy, this SFF, Jack, whatever, wants: a tall girl."

Same day, 5 p.m.

I would never, ever stop the repining wrapped around my entire existence, cauterizing me at the head. If I didn't ask, in the end I would be alone, with a fuck buddy.

I opened the door, dropped my purse and sprinted toward my freezer.

I filled a large glass with ice for the Grey Goose someone had given me for Christmas. I didn't want to unfeel or feel *better*. I had one glass and threw up in the sink. Ok, no more vodka.

At the deli a few hundred yards from my house, I browsed ice creams. French doors of freezers with four or five columns and at least 10 rows of ice cream: gallons, pints, and miniature pints. *What is a mini pint?* I scanned gelato and frozen versions of candy bars. *What is gelato?* I grabbed three flavors of normal sized Ben and Jerry's, and double caramel chocolate bars on wooden sticks.

I drove south to Jack in the Box and spent $19. Fries (two kinds, waffle and curly) two tacos, jalapeño poppers, fried mozzarella, chocolate cake, and a cheesecake slice in case the chocolate cake wasn't enough.

A few hours later the grease and preservatives wafted up to the ceiling and lingered in my living room. After another Lifetime movie and a few odd but satisfying *Friday the 13th* films, I changed clothes and spritzed myself with perfume, but didn't shower. I hated cleaning myself with a swell in my stomach. The next morning I flossed, scraping out leftovers by swiping each side of each tooth, flicking bits of fat and sugar into the sink and onto the mirror. I walked soiled square food containers, packets of Ranch Dressing and ice cream empties downstairs to the trashcans near the driveway.

For the next three weeks, my workouts included reaching for the remote and driving here and there, but mostly I lived motionless, in a sedentary state. I gained 25 pounds in three weeks.

By the way, gelato is motherfucking genius.

February 8

I practiced my addition and subtraction. I acquired a tenacity, living three miles from this guy/maniac. I broke promises to myself. Burying myself in my pillows and pain, stalling, not fleeing, and bleeding came easier than freedom. Short Fat Fuck should have had a warning label—but I wouldn't have bothered to heed it. Boredom equals an unimaginative, lukewarm hell. So does un-boredom. I needed distractions from the most demoralizing and wonderful memories I encountered with a boy *or in my life*? Memories (and the actual experiences) pierced my psyche and took me on a roller coaster ride I could never bring to a halt. The safety bar cinching my waist wouldn't save me. Jack wasn't the cause; he was a symptom.

Cress.

Cough medicine commercials were difficult to watch. A brunette with a bob leaning over her husband with a spoonful of blue stuff on my 27-inch flat screen propelled me into writhing fits. Flicking and whipping my head left-to-right, like my Yorkie used to do with a baby lizard in her mouth at our winter house in Florida.

Driving, showering, putting on shoes with shoelaces—everything caused me pain or became a chore so monotonous I saved it for another day. Another lifetime. I wore flip-flops constantly. When I saw his car in parking lots and at stoplights, I probed my sunglasses and swollen face in the rearview mirror. The singular thing that held me together and made me whole was the fact I had sewn myself into his life and bed. Now the bed was gone. It was all gone.

Brainsick, I wanted to know what wasn't my business. Were Jack and Hairtrix heading over to the Mattress Barn on Saturday afternoon or decorating their house (trailer?) with postage-stamp-sized art above the couch, as only imbeciles would?

Artless assholes.

Planning a possible RV retirement? I would read about their marriage on Facebook. *The SFF/Hairtrix wedding.* My on-call she-demon emerged to slash tires, shoot knobs, then deadbolts off of bedroom doors. But first, I'd download the pictures and videos I had of him jacking off. A social media gangbang posted along side his wedding announcement. I wanted these choices and outcomes to take over my world and allow me to pass through corridors with a handgun in my belt. I wanted to text him, fuck him over, scare him, and be scared of him. *Am I the maniac?*

Cress.

Home alone with no supervision, I lived in isolation because of my drama, like Howard Hughes. Incarcerated, I climbed trees and chewed on limbs at the intensities. Where and when would law enforcement be ready to arrest me for bloodthirst? Jack and I needed punishment. I relished actual incarceration forever if I could carry out a fingernail's worth of pain he caused me.

February 9
Journal entry

I went back on FB. Pink bike for her, black for him. Beach cruisers. A '"tat" on her upper arm, somewhere I would never have one. That is what she would call it, tat. Beers, smiles, friends. Jack/Short Fat Fuck/the cocksucker was fatter. I didn't know him anymore, save these self-destructive searches on Facebook for any changing of last names. I heard that sort of statement all of the time from people, "Oh, I don't even know him anymore." The cliché sounded like bullshit. My heart beat like a jackrabbit, yet my whole body burned black at the sight of Jack. To win, I had to do the opposite of blackness: jump and play and love through the velvety times.

It wasn't bullshit. I didn't know him.

February 13, 2009

"What would you have done if you weren't an agent?"

"For work? Oh, let's see, flight attendant? They have it pretty good."

I giggled.

"I like to cook. Probably a chef. I have hundreds of cookbooks, and I try things every so often for my kids. There's not a lot of time to devote to it, but it's something I've always wanted to improve upon, take classes."

"You're good at everything you do, aren't you?"

"I know I'd be good at one thing."

"What's that?"

"You'll find out when I see you again."

February 14

I rose further from my coffin-height existence. The meds (increased doses) were working again, and the soft, foggy forgetfulness started; I drove around and didn't obsess over Jack's likes and dislikes or the music I loved because of him. Interpol went in the trash. I wrote *SFF* on January 4 in my red calendar and placed it under the silverware tray in a drawer in the kitchen.

I couldn't remember what he did when he had an orgasm. I couldn't remember how sex began. *What is the order? Do we rip each other's clothes off? On the bed? Hit the wall? How long do we kiss? When does he turn on the music? How many times does the CD play? When does he get a condom?* Those small steps toward sunshine didn't mean I missed him any less. While I healed, missing him became a slap across the face every two seconds, followed by a kiss. The incessant nonsense wasn't Jack's fault—not completely. My weaknesses existed long before the Shack; he happened to be the unlucky dude on the barstool: human lighter fluid. Now I wanted to strive for something more than hangovers, limes, and SFF's cock aura. I wasn't 31. I was 13.

February 16

"Are you attending the women's meetings?" Disappointed, but not surprised, Dr.

Disorder listened without expression.

"Yes." *I wasn't. I told myself I'd go if I had an urge to drink again. I know it's a stupid plan. Whatever.*

"I feel better, and I haven't had a drink since last month." Me coffee, him scribbling.

Back in the club chair, looking at Buddha, I explained my slip.

"The Facebook night, correct?"

"Right."

I was trying to decide if Dr. D was one of those dudes who, if I saw him out in public would be dressed as a hippie. Sandals, shorts, bad haircut. I already knew he had bad haircut. When I thought of his Saturdays and Sundays, I saw Tevas and socks.

"Keep in mind, it is simple genetics. Your dad and your grand-father were heavy drinkers, and—I think you told me—" he read his notes. "Yes, your great grandfather was an alcoholic as well. I have told you before, with the dosages you're taking of these psychotro-pics, this will not end well if you continue to drink. 'This' meaning many things, an all-inclusive term for your overall well-being and sobriety. Continue with the meetings. You're doing well, but you need to do better. I understand slips. Let's see if you can avoid them in the future.

How are things going in other areas of your life?"

"With?"

"Overall moods."

"I'm good. I feel good—better than a few weeks ago."

"Good, and you're taking your medication. Same time every day?"

"Yes."

"I strongly suggest a few OA meetings, too. I know the bingeing is a rare occurrence, but it can't hurt. This new man you've referred to, what is happening there?"

"Good. He's amazing actually, but I didn't want to see him while this all was going on."

"Understandably. And that was smart of you. You are doing both you and him, and his family, a favor by taking things slow. It would be a disservice to his children not to. I'm proud of you and your progres-sion. This new relationship is a huge leap for you. I'm not 100 percent in favor of it. I hope you take it slow, in fact, take everything slow. But it is a step toward greater, healthier experiences. With your previous relationship, the situation wasn't structured in a way that supported your sensibilities. Taking your time with him enables you to sit back and observe: 'Is this too much for me? Am I experiencing similar feelings I felt in my previous relationship?' If you find yourself losing perspective and control, stop and reflect so you can choose wisely what your next step will be. Your next step shouldn't be to reach for the bottle or another man. Communication is key. If you are having issues, or a relapse, call me, or talk to the new man, if you think that will help or if he will be open to a discussion."

"Any advice for not acting like a freak?"

Dr. Disorder smiled. "Try to remember this new person in your life is not the person who broke your heart. Go into this with lessons learned. Be kind. Patient. And if you're going to continue to use Facebook, do yourself a favor and block the former boy's profile. Again."

February 18, 2009

Over the last couple of weeks, Cress and I talked a lot more, when we he was south and I was north, after he made his kids' dinner and they were with friends or on their computers. I observed him from Pismo as a father, one so attentive and warm, sometimes he seemed like a mother more than a dad. We compared affections. He followed and collected more of the up-and-coming and "it" artists filling the pages of art magazines or exhibiting at Art Basel. I didn't stop blabbering about Matisse, Hopper, Hockney, and Pollock or the photographs I obsessed over of Gloria Swanson and Marilyn Monroe.

"Frank Sinatra, photographers, art deco anything. Anything from the '30s, '40s, maybe early '50s. I love *Grand Hotel, Holiday Inn*, anything Hitchcock."

"You were born in the wrong decade."

He asked me to have dinner with him on Saturday night.

Asked me.

When you hold me, I'm alive.

— Rihanna

February 23, 2009

"That was so good." I put on my black fitted blazer as Cress handed me the valet ticket. H&M helped with presentation for our first date since the Laker game.

"Told you. January, give this to him, please." He walked away to make a call. Thirty seconds later, he caught my gaze, and widened his eyes. They were brown.

He walked back.

I don't think I've ever dated a guy with brown eyes.

He continued his phone call while looking at me. It made me palpitate.

"No. Yes, set it up. Thursday is good, eleven. Ok. Three. Friday. No and no."

He ended the call, smiled down at me, and pulled me closer by my satin lapel.

"And why haven't I seen you in three months?" Not angry, judgmental, or demanding answers, but killing me with a smile and a concerned look from those serious yet uncomplicated brown eyes. I swallowed and my throat felt like it wasn't going to man up and verbalize, in a normal, non-dramatic tone, my fucked up excuse (s) for the last few chapters of my life.

"God, I know. I'm so sorry, the last few … ." My head fell and I spoke carefully into his chest. "It has nothing to do with you. I want you to understand. I don't want to hurt you and I'm—."

"Come home with me."

I nodded into his coat.

While Cress and I drove on Sunset, I opened my window to what I deserted in 2006. For the last few years when I worked at the Zs I didn't venture out of Beverly Hills, so I used the drive to rendezvous with the current arts, styles, and smells sucked from my awareness. The brown bricks, gum-and-spit-covered sidewalks, tour trailers on Sunset, sensory overloading billboards, black and red buildings with sticky floors, and musicians who might not sound familiar but would win a Grammy someday. The beauty of LA was in the anticipation: evening hours stretching into an early a.m. Booze, cigarettes, and hot pink Corvettes while stepping over stars on the sidewalk before gliding into a club, lounge, dinner, or movie.

Cress' gate wouldn't open, so we ran up to his front door where he punched a code on a small black box with a lid.

"Come on." He took my hand, I smelled his cologne and primrose or oleander, or whatever perfumed pre-spring LA. A raindrop hit my eyelash when he led me to the burnished front door.

I so need to buy stock in Bulg—

I took two steps before my face slammed into the frame.

I yelped.

"Oh my god," he laughed. "I'm … are you ok?" He touched my nose.

His house could have been the sister property to the Koenig-designed Stahl house, an unforgettable architectural mirage. Up in the hills, rectangular windows ledged out into the city, like a skywalk.

"This house … ." I said as I thought of Julius Shulman's photo of the two ladies in white, legs crossed and chatting with one another and ignoring the 1960s view behind them. Los Angeles at night reflected through the floor-to-ceiling glass windows. I hoped an entire wall in my future house would display Shulman's photos of California architecture: matted (white) and framed (black).

We stepped inside. *"The Holiday."*

"What holiday?" He asked as he took our coats and draped them over a bench at the entryway.

"The Holiday. The inside of your house looks like the house in that movie."

In *certain* ways. The open foyer led to four areas: the living room, a less formal living room, the pool, and kitchen. Beiges, whites, blacks, woods, pops of a cerulean, and oranges and reds (my guess was the last two colors were inspired by his children). Contemporary furniture and ottomans. Onyx trays looked as if they'd been painted just seconds before, while other trays looked like crocodiles had died for them. Over the dining room table a two-foot wide dangling sea urchin chandelier said, "I'm ready for my close up, *Architectural Digest.*" Throws and piles of books from Taschen: art, film history, architecture, ones covered and containing Avedon, Duchamp, LaChapelle, Penn—and those were just the ones I saw. They rested on anything strong and wide enough to hold them. Framed vintage movie posters of *Giant, The Public Enemy, Double Indemnity, The Great Escape, Rebel Without a Cause, Citizen Kane,* and *Thin Man* stood eight-feet-high and hung among a few modern pieces and abstracts.

"Wait, do you have a room with a wall of DVDs?" I asked him.

I followed him into the white and chrome kitchen.

"Yeah?" He thought I was crazy. He grabbed two glasses out of a cabinet.

"See! Just like in the movie." The walls and doors leading out to the pool were unlike anything I'd ever seen. Actually it was one door. One 12-foot-tall curved, steel framed glass door that revolved like doors in a New York City office buildings. But only one door rotated 360 degrees, allowing ease of access to the living room and pool area. Under the lights, hooker green grass outlined three quarters of a rectangular infinity pool. Straight out in front of us sat the Los Angeles motherboard: a background lit with bright, blurred street lights, brake lights, roofs, windows, and spotlights. The perfectly organized beacons, miniscule spark tips from Fourth of July sparklers, wouldn't dare extinguish.

"This is … amazing." I told him.

An abstract lion's head sculpture hung above a phone.

Is it abstract if I can tell it's a lion?

"Yeah, I did ok." His ex stayed in his house in Beverly Hills.

"Where are Tallulah and Henry?"

"At my parents'."

He offered me water; I shook my head and hopped onto his countertop. *Esquire* moved closer.

"Next time, we'll watch one of the DVDs." He put his hands on either side of me.

My fingertip reached for his belt.

"We're doing this?" I didn't recognize this faint, little voice coming out of my mouth. *Anxiety and self-doubt, get ready.*

"If you mean going out to dinner and talking in my kitchen, then yes, we're doing this." *Set.*

I rubbed my forehead with my hand, stopping at the hairline, making my "I'm on a deadline face."

He touched my arm, his head bent toward mine, hoping I'd look up. *Go.*

"You want this? Me? You, this—it's intimidating." I looked around his house. "I see your life, and I … ." He took my hands, held them down, and came in closer.

"I want you here, and whatever you need to do, *want* to do right now, I will do.

You are ok here. I'm not an asshole, I promise. I'm not a douchebag."

"No, I know." *Did I tell him in Vegas I thought he was a douchebag?* "But you like me … want me?"

His head bent down and we touched foreheads. "I don't think you know how lovely you are."

That killed me. I took his face, then wrapped my arms around his neck. We kissed the kiss that no doubt preceded sex. I spoke into his lips, "I just hope, for my sake, you suck in bed."

He laughed at my comment, turned around, and bent down. "Come on."

"Are you crazy? I'll break you."

"Stop."

Breathtaking photographs hung on the staircase wall and up to the second floor hallway: Sokolsky, Eggleston, and Norman Parkinson spied on us as he piggybacked me to a set of double doors at the end of the hallway. I wanted to stop and study the photos I saw online: women in bubbles over Central Park and the backs of old ladies smoking in a diner. His were *not* printed out on photo paper from an HP printer and hung in $6 frames. Mine were.

Two more stylish photographs hung above a table near a door. "Your kids are so beautiful."

Along the dark floors, my head ticked, counting seven more doors lining the hallways: entries to what I assumed were his kids' bedrooms, bathrooms, linen closet, and an office. A divine, black damask wallpaper covered the walls. He backed through the doors to his room. Whites and browns bordered a cloudlike bed on steroids below a gray, tufted headboard climbing the ceiling.

He let me down off of his back and turned around.

"Thank you for tonight." I hated I said this, but I didn't know what else to say, and I needed some words to cut through the heat. His mouth came to mine.

"You're welcome, Estlin."

I sat on the bed and touched a button on his shirt. He shook his head,

"No."

I leaned back and rested on my elbows. Over-the-knee boots. Jeans. Black knee socks. Blouse. I couldn't stay still. I thought I was going to pass out. I felt like my mouth would start chattering like it did when I built my snowman in Lincoln Park in Chicago.

Another attempt at one of his buttons.

He shook his head again and took off his uniform of Prada, John Varvatos, Rag and Bone, Ralph Lauren, and what looked like a vintage Rolex. I tried to help him one more time. His chest, his body, was another damn page from *Esquire*. He never took his eyes off of me. When he lay on top of me, my body let go, and pulsed heavy.

Midnight

"We boogie boarded, ate fried clams. I played outside on his ranch all day. I watched *Adventures in Babysitting* every day one summer, and all of the *Friday the 13th* movies another. My brother and I played in hay lofts, barns, rode around on four wheelers, camped in the backyard." I told him stories of summers with my dad in Pismo before I was a teenager.

"Sounds fun."

"It was. He was drunk a lot, though."

"Your dad?" We faced each other, one of his arms on my hip, the other above my head.

"Sometimes. And a complete asshole. Actually, he's an asshole sober too.

Sometimes." I chuckled.

He laughed. "Wow, I'm sorry I'm laughing, because it's sad but the sober asshole part was funny. What about your mom?"

"I was raised in Chicago, but her and my stepfather traveled when I lived there."

"But you were born here?"

"Right. My mom and I lived here for a few years after I was born, then she remarried and we moved. I came back to finish high school and live with my dad and brother. But Chicago is home too, like Pismo."

My closemouthed shy side was percolating, and my whole body started to tense up, again. Next I'd giggle like a 5-year-old, mention his ex-wife, or ask him how much his house cost. I nuzzled my face in a pillow, trying to find the strength to have a normal, flowing, grown-up conversation.

"Your bed is insane."

"So, you and your brother didn't grow up together?"

"No."

"I have a brother. That would … I can't imagine."

"It was the agreement they had with the court. I was a year old, but I'm sure it affected him more than it did me. I have no idea. It wasn't good for anyone, for a long time. My mom didn't like me, never wanted me around. I think I reminded her of my dad. Ok: Sad time over." I straightened the sheet and gently asked, "What about you?"

He laughed. "Boring. From LA, parents live in Coronado, went to Stanford, then law school."

"And your brother lives in LA, too?"

"Yeah, he works at Warner Brothers."

"Wait, you're a lawyer? How did I not know that?"

"No one really knows, outside of work. It's helpful there." He yawned and drew a figure eight from my hip to my waist.

Pause.

"Are you mad?" *Why do I bring this up after he yawns?*

"Mad at what?" His hand stayed on my waist.

"With everything: not visiting sooner, not seeing you since the Laker game."

"Well. You live up there, and I'm here. We aren't a 20-minute drive from one another."

That statement scared me. "God, right. I mean … It's not going to work is it?" A familiar unease turned me on my back.

"What isn't? This? You? Here?"

"It's just. It's …"

"It's, and I'm pretty sure I know what 'it's' is, going to be a fine tuned piece of machinery."

I laughed.

"Something made in Switzerland. Indestructible."

"You feel that way? You already know this? About me?"

"You're a rare thing, January. I don't pretend this isn't reality. I live in a world of percentages, but I also deal in chance. I knew you weren't single—or didn't expect you to be—when I met you in

September, or even at the Laker game. In fact, when I saw you, that face, I thought, 'Hmm, interesting. There's no way she doesn't have a boyfriend.' But I want you. I like you."

"But are you mad?"

"Look at where you are. If I were mad, would I have done what I just did to you?"

His dorky comment relaxed me. "I don't have a boyfriend," I reassured him. Cress inhaled and pushed my hands up above my head after he lay on top of me. "You sure about that?"

"I like you, too," I murmured into his neck.

I thawed completely.

———

"Noooo." He tugged on my arm when I slid out of bed.

On his back, his head popped through the duvet.

"Bathroom." I put on John Varvatos from the pile of clothes mingling on the floor, sighing and crumpled.

Nice to see you down here. Did you see what went on up there?

"I like your socks," said the pants.

"Wow, you're beautiful," the belt said to the bra.

Hope to see you again.

Cress was asleep when I folded myself into Pratesi and warmth.

At 4:30 a.m. I stirred awake when he moved his head. I faced him before he opened his eyes and reached out for me. Making love with Cress was incomparable: his body under me, over me: the actions, expressions, where he took me, where I took him; where our thighs, arms, hands, heads, and lips started and stopped. By 6 a.m. I changed, something switched in me, and not only for the hours it would take me to drive home, or for the next 24 hours or until I went to work on Monday. The alligator released me, almost. Finally, a normal crescendo associated with my sex life: dinner, kiss under a porch light, and in bed by 10.

On my stomach I listened to him breathe and went over the last six, seven, eight hours in my head: a series of tremendous, palpable, movie stills; easy, comforting, light, fun, and at times serious and dramatic. Not sex. Hypnotism.

I'd never had the best of both worlds at once. Lovemaking and sex. No sadness, no loss, no "taking off." The weight of him, the movements from his body beside mine, allowed me to sleep. No more unease. No more insomnia in the wake of, or wait for, SFF.

An hour later, or it could've been 30 seconds later, an arm wrapped around my waist and his breath met the base of neck. My mouth fell open; I was soulless, not sentient, until then.

"You're beautiful, Estlin." *Ok, then.*

A belief is like a guillotine, just as heavy, just as light.

— David Hockney

April 8, 2009

C ress was the beginning of *something*. I couldn't deny that. But I continued to fume in Pismo. At work. I wanted a promotion. Or I wanted a chance at a new position: features writer.

Editorial had few commonalities. A few months ago we grew spiflicated on a ferryboat during a movable buffet dinner, rocking back and forth on the top deck while I showed off my Dramamine wristbands to the table. We barbecued and celebrated birthdays and pre-Thanksgivings at RatOnRug's house and convened at Bankhead to discuss the magazine. Beer and Jameson ran those meetings.

Come to order.

The congruity dwindled among some of the staff. Meetings grew tenser, shorter, and on Thursday nights we no longer loitered under a heat lamp on a smoking patio.

9:30 a.m.

Editor 3 hammered nails into her keyboard. After a week, no one mentioned the features position, so I spoke up about what I thought I wanted and deserved. Failing wasn't in my sphere of thought. Sure, with men I was a total fuck up, but at work I did a decent job. When Editor 1 hired me, he inventoried a list of qualities he wanted. In summary: someone to take the arts section to the next level.

"You're a breath of fresh air," he declared from above as he motioned for me to come upstairs. He was now long gone.

The last time Editor 3 and I hung out was a few days after Halloween, last year. She asked me why I didn't dress up,

"I thought about it, Uma Thurman from *Pulp Fiction* would be cool, but I'm just not into it." I wore one costume (*The Birds*) in the last 15 years. I could barely put on socks most days, let alone shop for a black wig.

"I'd thought you'd dress up like some silent film actress." She ate her maraschino cherry and smiled.

Statements like those meant she "got me," which wasn't the easiest thing in the world to do. I loved her in that moment. I wanted to love her. Editor 3, rotting cavities and all, impressed me with her ruthlessness.

Memories of 3 and I that no longer mattered:

Crying at the Santa Barbara Bowl when Jack White left the stage. Baking cookies for the hell of it in the magazine's break room oven. The crown she placed on my head one morning, made from wild-flowers she found on her way to work.

Those memories still mattered to me.

9:40 p.m.

Say nothing. No one likes, or responds to confrontation.

My morning meds provided a 5-minute window that made me jittery and talkative (brave).

"Hi, can we talk for a minute?" With Editor 1 gone for a few years now, I met with 2 and 3. 2 and I were always cool. No longer partially embattled, Nazi and I were in full battle.

"So, I just wanted to talk to you guys about the lead features position. What's going on with that?"

"We're giving it to Intern 5."

"Oh, fuck. Oh wow." My hair was tight: the bun, the headband, everything felt constricted.

"We didn't think you wanted it, honestly, and with your schedule ... ."

The Zs.

"Are you kidding?" I looked at Editor 3, "I've told you so many times since you told me you were quitting two years ago, and every six months since. Because I have another job, I'm being punished for that?"

"Absolutely not." They looked at each other. *Tighter.*

"You're giving it to someone who has 10 years less experience, who knows no one in the area, and doesn't even technically work here? An intern? I know everyone in town, I have a degree in art history, I've written for 15 years. How can you do this?"

I looked harder at Editor 3. "It's because you're friends with her, isn't it?" I was the fat, old guy in the shitty suit with a box of crap and a fern at 4:30 p.m., heading out the door. Not retiring, but being passed over: a goddamn office cliché at 30-years-old.

Lady Reporter left months ago, making the dumb fuck mistake of sharing sourced material with a married, rival reporter, unsober, after she fucked him. Editor 2 walked her out of the building.

Editor 3 wanted the idea of me to make her life a bit more interesting, but in the end she didn't like what I threw around a room: good smells, bubbles, honesty, charm, drama, and a mellowness she didn't know would come in a few more years. She didn't care if I was a breath of fresh air. 3 spewed out her book smarts like the dialogue in another one of those foreign films I didn't understand but had to endure in college; but her writing printed out more potent than Valium.

Nazi envisioned specific outcomes for the features section of the magazine, and I didn't live up to her standards—nor would I be considered in the planning. She wanted someone she could control, whom she could dictate and create,

"I'll have 100 little soldiers under me, to mold," she once said about opening her own private girls' school. 3 didn't want me because I wasn't like her. I wasn't odd enough: I didn't possess those bony plates lining the middle of her back like the Great Wall of China. Little did she know.

My personality factored into their decision more than I realized. We all had attitudes and weekly freshets of anger in our dungeon. I yelled and insulted in meetings, asked for things I would never get, demanded to know why my words were edited out of articles, and cried outside with a cigarette on the creekside rock wall. Not to make excuses, but we all did that in editorial. Opinions were our culture, the personality of the magazine (unbiased when necessary, of course). We weren't bank tellers.

A felt a tinge of sympathy from them as I blocked out their excuses. No promotion, no job, no Jack. Editor 3 needed a dentist. I now believed bad breath held the key to success: her secret to attain all she ever wanted.

April 19

Maybe I should've kept my mouth shut. Then I thought of Cress and *Anti-Fat*. Even though I was seeing Cress more frequently, and I would be at his house within the hour, my mind was a prairie of savannah grass. Moving past or focusing on something else daunted me.

"You know that's it, right?" Mrs. Z put the salary idea into my head as she ate a grapefruit on a Friday night while I finished up work. I considered the money factor. *They couldn't afford me.* I made five times as much working for the Zs, yet working at the magazine wasn't about the money. It couldn't be, and anyone in journalism would agree. I wasn't a journalist, but the theory held the same logic.

"Really? You think?"

"Of course! It's always about money. They couldn't afford you. How much do you make there?" Her opinion soothed me, a bit.

With Cress, the book, what did I want? To stay *here*? *Am I being presumptuous factoring Cress into this?* I wanted more effervescence and less castor oil. I couldn't attend another play about AIDS or bitter maids or one more disastrously loud musical about the life of Elvis. Or figuring out a way to say a local artist who used text and animals in her "abstract" impressionistic works was forward thinking and the next best thing. 3 was the cunt version of Jack. She knew many things, but not the meaning of loyalty. 3 never answered the question about Intern 5. I told myself I didn't want the job. Faced with the choice of adopting a conformed, fake cheerleader persona or getting the fuck out, I got the fuck out.

April 23

In my cubicle—while I thought about Jack White, Cress and banana bread— Beard Angry and RatOnRug stood next to my desk. Beard Angry became the staff photographer last year. RatOnRug had written for the magazine for 10 years.

"You're really going?" Disappointed but not surprised, they threw stuff into the box with me.

"It's time, I'm fine." I threw out a new box of business cards and tiny photos taped to my monitor. Printouts of words I used as story titles, an abstract painting an artist gave me, a magnet from the Hearst Castle. Rugby walked up.

"Fucking Editor 3," RatOnRug theorized, looking at Beard Angry and Rugby.

"Let's go." Rugby stayed in town and worked as one of the magazine's investigative reporters. He rode a beach cruiser to meet sources and interview local cops and dated only ugly girls. If you saw him on a date, you'd look around for Rod Serling smoking a cigarette. I still slept on his couch every once in a while.

Rugby and RatOnRug picked up my boxes of crap and walked me to my car. When I shut the trunk, Rugby took me by the arm.

"Wait … ."

In front of Bankhead's mahogany bar (this time American) I turned my stool around and observed stress-free drinkers and smokers on the patio. Warmer weather meant the beanies and Uggs plaguing the town during the winter months dissipated. RatOnRug and Beard

Angry bitched about Editors 2, 3, and Intern 5. Rugby took a sip of his beer and told me about the Christmas sweater he found at Goodwill the day before.

"I'm definitely going to wear this one to the office party. You have to see it, it's sick." He wore a different one each year and made another sad face when I told him I wouldn't be around to see it. Rugby patted my back. I'd miss it. I'd miss him.

Why have I never fucked Rugby?

The boys switched topics to the impending move of the bar itself, into a new, bigger location a few blocks away.

"Here." RatOnRug placed three shots of Jameson on the bar, one for each year at the magazine. He sat down between me and Beard Angry and their Tecates.

"Oh, hell no."

"Do it J-dog." I persuaded them to drink my shots, while Rugby ordered another. Then I remembered why we never hooked up: Rugby slept in a twin bed. A mild turn-off, but so damn perplexing. Who sleeps in a twin bed after the age of 12?

All four of our heads turned to the left, then right. I snatched up my water as the 20-foot long, finished, and course grained lumber serpentined out the door.

"You know, Billy the Kid bellied up to this bar, like two hundred years ago," the bartender with a metal bolt through his nose informed us before he marched outside with his colleagues, pallbearers for 200-year-old American mahogany.

It looks like a really sad parade float, I thought.

Everything changed; everything ended.

May 11, 2009

The ocean performed an opera for us.

The bad best friend in me neglected VF the last couple of months. We hadn't talked or stayed silent. All this time I trusted her with my shame, and now there'd be less of it. I hoped she accepted my innate flaws. The way she looked at me, listened, and reacted told me we reconciled, but I wondered. I prayed she realized SFF was gone for good.

With fur on her tongue from a few glasses of champagne, Vanity Fair commented and asked in one breath, "I love your jewelry, you're moving back to LA, aren't you?"

"I think I have to, V. But I don't know for sure, yet. I love you. Nothing changes."

"Cress," She choked on his name as she cleaned her sunglasses.

My unspoken response: *You have Millionaire.*

———

Time became my food and booze. Human biology allowed me to feel pain. Human nature allowed me to choose how long, how abysmal, or how dismantling the pain would be. Some people like me choose to sit back on a smoke-permeated couch and die a few cells each day, numbing the throes while at the same time letting the furiosity take over. Pastimes included trips to the liquor store, bars down the road, or meeting up with the fellow psychologically sick.

Most went to work. They needed money to finance slow deaths, but hated their jobs, collecting sick days as trophies. Work might care, and probably did. After quitting, being asked to "resign," or being let go, the dying raped the welfare system for a while. Others pulled themselves up by their bootstraps. I didn't. *What are bootstraps?* Survival, growth, and finding original, logical peace made the most sense as the practical choice, after putting my hand to my face, shielding people from my mental health issues for so long.

Some are chemically choreographed to never have a happy, calming, normal, "throw the football around with dad and get a hug from mom" moment in their lives. Heredity is not a choice. Mental illnesses are often misunderstood and ignorantly placed on a shelf in a lab in Minnesota with the H1N1 virus. The blackness of 23 hours and 45 minutes a day demolishes the sick and those around them if they aren't medicated. Ask anyone who lives with a schizophrenic or someone with chronic depression. Ask a mother whose 11-year-old is bipolar.

For the last year I woke up to my pills. Five prescriptions stood on a 6-by-6-inch thick plate of glass I found at a thrift store. No longer in my kitchen, the three-inch tall paddle-swinging disciplinarians shot discerning looks from my bedside table, while I lay buried in fluffy white pillows.

"*Get up,*" *said Zoloft, Clozapine, Lamotrigine, Xanax, and Ambien.*

Like butter, pills were *everything.* They smoothed over the blue-prints, mine, placing paperweights at each corner, allowing the architecture to breathe and appear less daunting. Was being bipolar taboo? Yes. Did I care? Maybe 80 to 95 percent of the time. There was a range to my self-consciousness, but I was sure a lot of LA folks took Zoloft. Lately, movie stars, authors, journalists, and athletes were fast becoming poster children for bipolar disorder—like it was a *trend.* I never forgot how dangerous showing weakness could be. The putting my hand to my face would continue, but not around the people who needed to know. I let them in on the secret and tried not to be a baby. Tried to be courageous. I repeated the phrase *Grow up* alone in the car.

The months detached the soulful Jack recollections from whatever horrendous structures I created. In the debris left behind, the remnants had an order to their delirium. I focused on improving myself. I slipped on my Nike running shoes more. Beach runs (still mostly jog/walks). Back on the elliptical, no carbs at night, whole wheat, egg whites, kale, water. More nights at Bingo and a homeless shelter in Hollywood during my weekends with Cress. *What the fuck can you do?* I ran. By June I shed the weight.

I still needed my alligator—or his skin at least—before I committed to Cress.

Jack hung on to the structure because I did. Bipolar, alcoholism, promiscuity, temper: They sent me off into his arms and a hold so powerful, if our love came true, I wouldn't have survived its transfixing reality. He didn't concern himself with what I was.

I *was* Zoloft and Clozapine. I *was* the bootstraps.

Jack knew all along what I wouldn't know for years.

That sex will melt your face!

— Kramer, from *Seinfeld*

May 19, 2009

"I'm not coming down this week, the Zs are in Europe." I drove home from an interview at an artist's studio in Avila Beach: a yoga-loving, eighty-something, lady dynamo painter whose influences were Matisse and Léger.

"Ah, that's right." He wanted to take me to The Black Keys concert at the Hollywood Bowl.

"Where are you right now?" I parked in my driveway.

"Leaving a meeting." I heard the *ding ding ding* from his car door.

"Are you working this weekend?"

"No, it's mellow. No kids."

"Oh, really."

He laughed. "Are you thinking Pismo?

"Why not? Have you ever been?"

"Pismo? Eh, let me think."

"Or I can just see you in three weeks when I'm back in LA."

"Which exit is it?"

May 22, 5 p.m.

Cress wasn't an asshole, but he did work in Beverly Hills. He lived in one of those houses shown between the scenes on *The Real Housewives of Beverly Hills*. The camera flies overhead and pans in on decadent neighborhoods in Bel Air, the Palisades, Malibu, the canyons or hills, then zooms in on a *particular* house. I always paused the DVR and rewound and paused it again to get back to that exact moment to study the house a bit longer. Pipe dreamt masterpieces with windows and pools with no end. He drove a Porsche and a Range Rover, and made his living as a dealmaker, a broker, a listener, a seeker. Our vastly different echelons needed to be considered. Weren't the majority of LA couples of this persuasion?

Thinking about my league status, I went from nervous to a conniption fit as I looked in my closet. An hour before he arrived, I stood in the mirror and nitpicked my black, weaved, short skirt with a glittery and gold metallic pattern. The bottom half of me looked like the front door of an art deco building. Four inches of T-strapped gunmetal held me up.

How's my skin? Annoying. Everything else? Kind of annoying.

My apartment.

The living room with a view, my bedroom, and a kitchen didn't fall under the embarrassing category, but practicalities fucked me. His Kiehl's and Bulgari did not belong in my bathroom with no counter space and an old pedestal sink.

His Prada and Armani would be strewn on the floor, which is where they'd have to be—not a result of rhapsodic sex—but because I didn't have a dresser. My closet was the size of a phone booth. What I did possess was a cool, faux leather white couch from Target; a mirrored coffee table from Pottery Barn; five staggeringly small, framed reprints of Steichen, Eggleston, and a few old movie posters; a flat screen with Wii; and a rolling rack Z had given me. I wasn't rich or cloaked in Chanel, and I wasn't sure if he knew or cared. Of course he knew. I worked for the Zs and wrote for the fun of it. Independent in the scariest way: no help from Mommy, Daddy, or Stepdaddy anymore.

I heard a car door slam, and I rubbed the edges of my jaw. The sound of a fast trot up my stairs, two at a time.

His chin touched the top of my head when we hugged.

"You look good." I went crazy seeing him in jeans, T-shirt, a light escape jacket that looked expensive and again out of a page of a men's magazine, and Converse-looking sneakers I knew to be Prada. This guy's *clothes* besotted. Finally, the Louis Vuitton weekend bag (a *keepall* in his league).

His hands went to my waist as he leaned in fast to kiss me. One, two, three. His hands went to my face. One, two three four. *Oh my god.*

"Hi." I let go. "Ok, so, the tour."

He held on. I couldn't stop smelling his neck while trying to stay cool. I was born uncool, I would never be cool. I made the mistake of thinking.

Candles. Clean sheets. Poop.

Candles. Ok candles I can handle. I have a Jo Malone one around here somewhere. I took it from Mrs. Z's stockpile last Christmas.

Sheets? He'll sleep in my bedding from Target; what choice does he have?

Oh my god, poop! When and where will I poop?

"Your place is great." Cress walked around, surveying the photographs and art on the walls, pointing to a picture of Frank Sinatra given to me from a friend who worked at Capitol Records. Friend: one of the B5's.

"I've never seen this one."

"So." I stopped near my couch.

He walked back to me and pulled on my belt loop. "So. I mentioned to a friend of mine I was visiting my girlfriend up here and he mentioned Lido or Dolphin Bay. Have you heard of it? He said it was nice."

Girlfriend. Girlfriend. Girlfriend. Girlfriend. Girlfriend. Girlfriend. Girlfriend.

"Yeah, yes it's nice. Gorgeous views. Do you want to go there for dinner?"

"Of course you've heard of it. I booked a room."

I walked into the kitchen and glanced down at the faded, lemon laminate floor and thought of his house. His life. I was having trouble swallowing.

"A room for you?"

"What? No dork, for us." Cress walked toward me.

"Oh yeah. No, right, of course." I brushed past him, and he stopped me.

"Sound like a plan?"

I need that Vicodin demeanor right about now.

Girlfriend. Girlfriend. Girlfriend. Girlfriend. Girlfriend. Girlfriend. Girlfriend.

I ran to my room and packed a bag with my best everything, arranging the Agent Provocateur lingerie on top. A weekend with him in a hotel made me dizzy, but I was a bit confused. I took a deep breath. Why could I possibly be annoyed? How? *Grow up.* Grow the F up. *Take it down a notch. Roll with it. He's not a jerk. He's not trying to hurt me.*

Vicodin demeanor! Vicodin demeanor! Vicodin demeanor!

Leaving my room, I made a decision: I wasn't going to overreact to a change of plans. I wouldn't say one word, and I'd accept the plan for what it was. Man liked woman, man did something special for her. His *girlfriend.* The weekend meant something to him. *Holy crap.*

7 p.m.

We walked through the giant glass doors and checked in. I pointed with my head toward the beach. While our bags went to the suite, he draped an arm over my neck and shoulder, and I led him to the back of the hotel. Elegance and stunning scenery weren't anything new for this guy.

He regrets coming. He hates this. Fucking Pismo.

Jesus, stop thinking.

"Ben was right. This is great." Eight illuminated spouts of water flowed into the pool. We faced the sun, almost done for the day. The coastline was 30 years old to me, but in that pocket of time, familiarity wasn't familiar at all. Similar to the instant surprise and confusion of a déjà vu experience, everything circling around me—the ocean and cliffs, the lighting, the sensation of my feet on the ground, and the size of objects—shifted. I saw the panorama of it in a different way and not for long. The unknown scared me: Would everything go back to normal? I wondered why it happened. Unprecedented, it lasted longer with Cress: soothing, mind stirring, and arousing.

After one Flying Aeurbach cocktail at Lido for Cress (strawberry, basil, mint, lime, jalapeño, and moonshine—we were curious about the moonshine) and an appetizer, he had me against the wall in our suite.

"Pismo." He kissed me all the way to the edge of the bed.

"Pismo." I laughed and moved back a step.

"Hi."

"Hi. I'm going to change." He dropped my hands and took off his jacket.

In the bathroom the size of my apartment, I heard muffled movements from the bedroom.

I double-checked the mirror before I walked out: black love slip, satin ribbon straps, and French plaits.

My rear end isn't bad I mumbled as I turned around and craned my neck to the right. My lips were ok too. Everything else made me sigh. The lucent black mesh covering my body shouted out the loudest from my boobs. I spent a week's salary on it.

Taking off his watch and looking at his Blackberry and iPhone on the bedside table, he didn't notice me until I stood between his legs.

"Oh. My. God." He found my eyes, "I hate it."

His eyes went to my breasts and back to my eyes as he touched me. His hands stopped at the top of my thigh, then slipped under the hem. I helped him take off his shirt, shoes, and jeans. He hugged me and lifted me to the bed with an ardency. I couldn't have imagined, created, written about, or dreamt of the revelation taking place in a hotel bed in Pismo. Slow, steady, but not too slow, he took off the lingerie with grace and precision. His head rose from the bottom of the bed.

Get up here. Esquire obeyed.

We didn't know the geography: I was his and no one else's, especially not a little surfer boy's, who lived a mile from where Cress twizzled me into dementia. We made love, and we fucked—not equal amounts of each. More of the former and, at times, neither. We laughed deep and throaty chuckles, the sort of laughter heard from under bed sheets.

"When you're on your back and you laugh, the whole bed vibrates. I love it." *Seriously, he says the cutest stuff.*

He scooped me up and I slithered onto his stomach. At an unguarded point, I couldn't stop myself from saying his name, my throat clicking into a slow fall, then fast into a whimper. I fell down on top of him and rolled on my back. He came to me and kissed my freckle.

"Are you ok?"

I didn't answer and sat up, reaching for his neck. I begged him to push his body harder, deeper into mine, without begging at all. His face dove into my chest. His hands went to my face, and my hands met his arms and back. He brought our arms above my head. I couldn't dissect all of what we did because I wanted to enjoy specific snapshots as he used his entire human potential to be close to me, to do *this* to me, and to allow me, us, this experience. We let go into necks and opened mouths and when we did we sounded the same. He sank into me.

He didn't move. I laughed, he laughed.

He pushed up a little and looked at me.

I stroked his cheek. I didn't want to stop touching his face. A new face: relaxed, content. There were no "count downs." I was no longer an "anti-seducer." I was the opposite.

We kissed like fatalists, and everything slowed like Georgia air.

Midnight

I tried telepathy to see if he was having as much fun as I was, thinking to himself,

Oh my god, the sex is incredible with her or *I came so hard with her.*

277

I theorized Cress' inner thoughts weren't that vulgar but maybe in all guys' heads the intensity of their orgasm was something to consider. I replayed into my pillows the different ways he touched me throughout the night and into the early morning, following me wherever I went, making contact and keeping tabs.

"I have one word for what you are wearing—or wore—January: carnal." I lay on top of him and sighed.

May 23

"How do you like Pismo so far?"

"It's not bad. I've only seen the freeway, a big rock jutting out of the middle of the freeway, and the hotel, but it's very nice."

Vanity Fair and Cress held their wine glasses on the outskirts of guests asking for another pour and more crab cakes. Millionaire and I breathed in at the same time and met eyes as my boyfriend and his girlfriend studied one another; contemplating and judging. She judged. She was serious. He wasn't, in his James Perse white shirt, light Atworth jacket (another word for a guy's cargo jacket) and jeans so bloody perfect on him, I wanted to lie in bed and watch him walk around the hotel room all day. Hipster/agent/rock star Cress was in town. *Esquire* Cress wasn't far behind.

We sat at an outdoor table at Lido with Childless Brad Pitt and Accountant. The 50-foot celluloid screen sat smack dab in the middle of the lawn that separated the ocean from the hotel. Bottles of wine and food were displayed on tables amid the impromptu outdoor movie theater. I was relaxed on two levels: Cress and my brother bonded over Stanford (CBP went there also) Dodgers, poker, and Guinness. Cress and Millionaire bonded over bonds and good scotch.

"Yeah, I like this hotel. We come here a lot, Millionaire and I. January, too." Vanity Fair and Cress didn't purposely end up alone at the bar, but VF found an opportunity. They walked outside and toward the ropes separating the pathway from the cliff's edges.

"This outdoor theater thing is cool. Sitting outside, big screen, movie, wine..."

"How long have you lived in LA?"

"All of my life. And you're from San Luis Obispo?"

"Yes." VF glanced at Millionaire. "So, what's Leonardo like?"

He laughed at the question he was asked most about one of his biggest clients.

"He's cool. Smart, down to earth, loves his mom, his grandmother."

"So. January."

"January." He glanced at me and smiled. "She's growing on me."

VF was beginning to understand his relaxed style and sense of humor. She aced a barbed, yet subdued, wittiness.

"How so?"

"You know, she sees what no one else does. She'll say to me 'look up' or 'look over there' and when I do, there's a piece of art, a garden, or the architecture of a building we're in. She sees art and beauty in everything—and not in a pretentious way, in a cool way. A unique way."

"You don't look up much, do you?"

Cress laughed. "No, sometimes I don't. January is wild, she's a riot, but she's also low key. She doesn't care if sports are on TV, she doesn't tell me what to eat, she doesn't care if I go out with my friends. My kids want to be around her more than they do me. She doesn't annoy me, put it that way. I think she likes having space, and easily gives it."

———

"I've never met anyone like her." The history behind this statement startled her. She knew the phrase well, and she hated it.

"You're going to take her away from me." Vanity Fair and her halo watched the sunset, her wine glass empty.

8 p.m.

Matt Cross played guitar behind us as we ate dinner in Lido.

"Vegetables." He barely touched the spinach next to his sea bass.

"No. Hate them. My mom tried and failed to get me to eat them." He sat back and asked, "City or country?"

"Um, both, I guess. There's something unaggravating and easy about living here.

I always want to have a house in Pismo."

"Your dad is a cowboy; you're clearly not a cowgirl. What did you say? Your dad lives on a worm farm?"

"It used to be a worm farm; there's good money in worms." I started to crack up.

"He does well?"

"He does well."

"Estlin. Pismo." He leaned in, crossing his arms on the table.

"Pismo. It's paradise, can't you tell? Haven't you fallen in love with it?"

We laughed. *We laugh at the same time, the same volume, the same length.*

"Why do you live here?" He eyed his scotch. "I mean, why did you move?"

"To write, to finish *Anti-Fat*. That's all I wanted to do, but Z needed me, so I worked for her, and at the magazine."

"Did SSF have something to do with it? Vanity Fair mentioned him earlier."

Fucking VF.

"What happened there?" His glass sweated into his cocktail napkin.

"*SFF*? Jack?" I wasn't good at playing dumb and was pissed I had to. This guy expected truth and decency from his girlfriend. Inappropriate, unnatural, and damaging described this conversation about a boy who tore my soul in two. Why did he want to know? Commercials or TV shows portraying some asshole talking to their date about his/her ex at dinner made me feel sorry for both of them. Wasn't there some rule against this? *Think before you speak. Be brave.*

"Well, what do you mean?"

"Jack? That's his real name?"

"Yeah, Jack. Um, I don't know?"

"I'm curious, especially after she told me what SFF stood for."

"Ok. Um, I loved him, and he didn't love me back."

"Did you move to Pismo because of him?"

"Honestly, I don't know. I think it had to be a part of it, but there were other reasons."

"Why do you think he didn't want you?"

I laughed for a second. "Well, I think he did, in a way, but not enough, I guess. I was probably too much for him: dramatic, annoying. I'm nuts, you know how I am. Or maybe I was nothing to him, ever. But I was different with him. Everything was different." I didn't want to go any further.

I was a drone. Closing in on him, circling his life, not quite destroying everything, although I probably came close. Simply, his was a love I was not prepared for: the unrequited kind. Couldn't handle it. Getting what I wanted would have been worse than being unrequited. I'm a loser, aren't you glad you met me?

"And you had sex all of that time?"

Eeh. I took a sip of my water and nodded. "And that was pretty much it. I feel stupid even talking about it."

I focused on the white tablecloth and a mound of pepper near the grinder.

"But you dated, right? You went out. I'm just trying to understand this."

"We never went out together. Technically. he … we were never officially a … ." *Shut up January. Shut the fuck up.*

"Wait, what? What do you mean? He never took you *out*? On a date? Dinner? How is that even possible?"

I shook my head. "I know, it's crazy, but like I said, it was *different*. I was different."

Beyond Cress' head, the bartender fanned out a pile of square cocktail napkins with the bottom of a rocks glass. During the pre-dinner cocktail, he pitched Cress the same screenplay he told my brother and me about in 2006: a film about chefs who played baseball. The cocktail was a "Euphoria:" gin, Saint Germaine, lavender, and lemon. I wanted him to drink it more than he did.

"I don't get it."

"What do you mean?"

"I don't see him, or any guy, not wanting you. And you are not nuts, dramatic or annoying."

I thought of something odd—I thought of Cress. While looking at him and talking to him, I was there, in that moment. I wasn't pre-occupied with self-hatred, self-pity, lip-gloss, my hair, or the other people in the restaurant. Nor sex with him. Just Cress. The human being, hard worker, dad. Sensual, sublime, and totally and wonder-fully natural. I could have cried. I realized what this new feeling was. It was happiness. *Happiness.*

"He's crazy." He reached inside his jacket for his wallet.

The *sexy pocket.*

"I told Vanity Fair I'd never met anyone like you." He made a casual gesture. He didn't swoon or lean in for a kiss. He signed the tab's receipt, smoothed his black suit jacket.

"She said Jack said the same thing about you." He stood up

An ice cube melted in my mouth.

We stood on opposite sides of the elevator, facing one another, expressionless. We held hands but didn't talk in the hallway on our floor, the fourth. He unlocked the door and I set my purse on a table. He took off his jacket and walked toward me, undoing a button on his shirt. I helped him.

"I've been meaning to tell you: your shoes tonight." He looked down. "You are a genius."

He noticed my shoes. Love that.

He bent down a few inches and looked at me while we pulled off my gold belt. With our faces on the same level, we lifted the knee-length satin dress over my head and I heard, felt, and saw Cress realize I wasn't wearing anything underneath.

"No Agent Provocateur." I stated the obvious.

He pushed me upward, kissing the parts rising in front of him.

I took his shirt and threw it. We wouldn't know until the next morning, it wound up in the fireplace. I kneeled and took off his pants. Belt thrown, shoes, socks off. Weak, terrified, and beatific.

Low and fast he said, "Come here," and pulled me into him. I pushed him as he pulled me harder into the nearest wall, the one facing the ocean, next to the fireplace. In the same realm of how his mouth devoured mine, I embraced him. His face showed pleasure, satisfaction, and sexiness. I let him go and sat on the bed. He stood at the edge. I obliterated the rest of his clothes.

Happiness didn't vanish in eight hours (or less) like it did with Jack. With Cress the emotions, and everything they permeated, remained. They were elevated for months. Maybe they would be forever. I thought of what we must look like from the outside. If I saw us, I would want to *be them*. I thought about it again after we made love, and I loved what I saw: A dream, coming true.

1 a.m.

"Would you move back?" I heard our breaths, our voices, and the waves outside.

"Where? LA? Sure, when my book sells and I can buy a house in Los Feliz, and I don't have to drive anywhere. Then I'll move back." He drew a line along my arm.

"You should."

"Should what?"

"Move back."

"Cress … ." I stopped breathing.

"I have something to tell you." He propped himself up on an elbow. "The friend I was telling you about, who told me about this place. He's a partner, an agent at CAA. Ben. You met him at the Laker game."

"Oh right. What did … ?"

"I gave him the copy you gave me. He wants to meet about *Anti-Fat*."

On my back, I turned my head to him. "What?"

"Jan, the book is good. I had to let someone read it who could help move it along."

My head fell. "Cress, you showed them *Anti-Fat*? Is that even ok?"

"This is how 90 percent of shit gets done. He loved it, and his girlfriend found the manuscript at his house, read it, and *she* went crazy. She'd been following the blog."

———

A few hours later, he faced my back from a foot away. I couldn't sleep, excited at the possibilities of Ben helping with the book but I couldn't stop thinking about dinner. I wanted Cress to have immunity from the aging, disgusting pain of Jack. But I trusted he found the information he wanted. I was still *happy*.

"I don't want you to sleep with him anymore." I closed my eyes, sighed, and turned over. *That face.* The Laker game face, the face he left me with, next to Mr. and Mrs. Z's fountain. When he stepped away, letting go and telling me to "Be good," he held a serious expression: stern, yet wanting. It told me, "I will know you for the rest of my life."

I wasn't insulted or scared. What he said hurt because I gave him a reason to think and talk about Jack, again.

"Cress." I moved closer. "I won't and I wouldn't. I would never do that to you, I would never … It's over and, has been since January, I wouldn't have been with you in March if it wasn't."

"And he does want you. You said earlier you weren't sure. He did and he does. I don't understand. I want to tell you to not do a lot more, but I don't want to sound like an asshole."

"It's ok. Tell me whatever you need to." I hoped my arms would calm and protect him. Even his hair felt serious and sad. It made me sad. "I will do anything, absolutely anything. And I don't want you to understand it. It's another world compared to now, what I am, to this. You, this—it's wonderful. He was never wonderful." My hand went from his hair to his face. He moved with my hand until it cupped his cheek and half of his mouth.

"If you have to understand it, what I—it—was, I'll explain."

He fell asleep with his head on my stomach. I was sick I had to utter his name. I never wanted to think about Short Fat Fuck again, let alone talk about him. I remembered Cress touching my back when we stood up from our table at dinner. His hand holding me there, but hardly touching. That spot at the base of the spine, in the little curve. Finally, I cried.

Happiness.

So in love.

May 24

Shape-shifted from the last two days, exhausted and sore, I took my last shower at Dolphin Bay. I loved the thinness after sex, my body lighter and svelt. The brightness in the bathroom lit up my body and not in any way I wanted to witness. I heard the door open while I washed my hair. I rinsed off my eyes to his sly smile. When he hugged me, the water from the rectangular shower head cascaded down his back.

"Good morning," I whispered. My hand traveled below his chest. Hands, arms, legs, tongues biting, necks, lips, back and forth, laughter. There was always laughter with Cress. He pushed the wet hair off of my face, lifted me, and held me up against the windows facing the ocean.

Always against me-love it.

The water expanded and acted like the wind or rain: we smeared and pushed it off of each others faces, out of the way, without being bothered by it. This wasn't the first time I had to stop myself from screaming out how much I loved this person. I screamed a lot of other things instead.

Twenty minutes later, we faced the window, one of his arms was strapped to me like a diagonal seatbelt, the other above my head. Partly moaning and breathing heavily, I kissed, licked, and bit the part of his shoulder and upper arm my mouth could reach. When I edged back, his face went to my neck.

"You are incredible."

"Cress." I turned off the water.

Resting my forehead against the window below his arm, I felt his mouth move on the back of my neck.

"I'm falling in love with you."

He kissed my spine. He was so warm. I didn't respond. I wanted to hold those seconds still for as long as I could. A silent comprehension. My body moved—maybe an arm went up to his hair, and I turned around to kiss him, but before I did, I didn't have a lot of time to remember the tone of his voice, the volume, how many times I felt his breath on my back. How each part of his body reacted to mine. But I did. I memorized all of it, like my fourth-grade self did, when I stood in front of Seurat's *A Sunday on La Grande Jatte* **at** the Art Institute in Chicago, and learned about Pointillism. Cress was more than memorization. He had to be comprehended.

Then a flitter of,

Falling in love with me? How? Why? Is it the sex? Is that why he wants me? Am I just a vagina to him? Is that love? What is love? I don't fucking know. Dude, he didn't say he loved me, chill the fuck out.

The B's, and SFF, were a rigorous workout combining my vagina, destructive and rebellious behavior, and bushels of vodka.

It wasn't real. *Not real life.* This might be real.

Afterward we ate eggs on the terrace and laughed. Eating in front of Cress was getting easier. I ate fast and who knew what that looked like.

"You're a riot, Estlin."

I stood up from the table and walked over to him.

"Thank you for this weekend." His hair and skin were still warm from the shower and he wore his adorable and hot, but nerdy, Zegna eyeglasses with black rectangle frames. I didn't know yet when he needed them and when he didn't.

Instead of talking about his declaration in the shower, I left it alone. He knew.

Driving up to the valet standpoints under the semi-circle roof to boys in khaki shorts and blue polos. Stepping out of his Range Rover, together. Walking through the doors with chrome swirls and into the hotel, holding hands. Nothing ahead but reveries and lips of blue water pearled with moonbeams. Jack broke loose and headed west; setting us ablaze quickly, but five years slow.

Those were the best parts of Dolphin Bay.

I used the bathroom outside of the restaurant the entire weekend.

July 2009

My mouth tightened and stretched to the corners of my lips. Sitting in his office was not how I wanted to spend my Tuesday morning.

"You are lucky. You have a brain that "had your back" as they say. Instead of veering toward an anti-social personality, or psychopathy, you got off easy." Dr. Disorder got a haircut.

"Easy. Really." I glanced down at *1,000 Ways to Relax*. I was happier. *Relaxed*. I didn't want to light the book on fire when I looked at it.

"Bipolar II is treatable. Yes, you got off easy. With that being said, I'm not saying your parents didn't or don't love you. They do, but unfortunately for you, they did not have the tools to carry that love through, and guide you to healthy relationships, boundaries, and life experiences. All of this combined has brought you to this point, and brought you to previous, less productive and less positive points."

With Mr. Reiter, Cress, you now have healthy boundaries, and the tools to successfully maintain those boundaries and in turn, a loving relationship. The abandonment and separation anxiety, those issues may still pop up, but as long as you continue with your treatment and therapy and check in with me every three months, you will do fine."

And no boats.

Fly the ocean in a silver plane.
See the jungle when it's wet with rain.
Just remember till you're home again,
You belong to me.

— Patsy Cline

October 6, 2009

"Good for you. That's great, you're back! We will work it out. Work Saturdays maybe? We need you for our empire."

"Ok." My nails scratched the legal pad I held while I found a stage actor's courage. "Maybe I want my own empire."

"Ah. Oh. Well. It is a terrible time to train someone else and ... ."

"There's more, I mean, it's not bad. It's a funny story, actually." I laughed the worst, most unappealing laugh I had. Mrs. Z stared at me as if I were choking. "Ok." She held up her Blackberry to answer an email while her hairdresser straight ironed her hair.

"I've been seeing Cress—hanging out with ... ." A fake smile pursed her lips. I felt stupid.

"He's great January. I don't know what else to tell you. Good for you."

I walked toward my office, writing a to-do list for the day.

"January."

I focused on the lines on the yellow paper.

"Turn around." I turned around.

"Mr. Z and I already knew about you and Cress. I knew in Vegas when both of you told us you 'got back to the hotel at 6 a.m.' I knew then. Stop writing. He called me the day he took you to the Laker game. It's fine! We love you. We love Cress. Relax."

November

It had been almost 18 months since May 13, 2008. Therapy and drugs put into gear a kinder life, escaping into days with more self-control and a sobersided sanity I kept in my purses and clutches. Planning to kill myself was another disconcerting "from my past" fact I would always be digging out from under one of my fingernails. *My kids will have a mother who once did that. A mother who's bipolar. A mother who's rebuilt, like an old car engine.* Kids as fucked up as I was. Then I thought of my mom-friends who used to be strippers, had orgies, and were, without a doubt, undiagnosed depressives. They seemed to be "happy to be in a minivan" perfect moms. Most of their kids seemed well adjusted.

It sounded insane. *Killing myself. Killing myself.* I began to forget the silly girl who overreacted. Overreaction: it was almost a religion. *Taste red, see red, act red.* I hoped the pharmacy I placed on my tongue a few times a day led me out of the overreactor's house of worship.

A completeness began to run through me, alleviating me, reserving a point in my life: and what a lovely point it came to be.

December 14, 2009

My scents for Cress were Dior at night and Jo Malone in the daytime.

At Bacara in Santa Barbara, while visiting friends, I didn't skydive, paraglide, Parasail, or kiteboard. I didn't want to shop for antiques. Cress didn't care. We went wine tasting (I spit my wine in rusted urns); drank water with cucumber and lemon brought to us on silver trays by pert, college-aged waiters; ate delicious food; and slept on king-sized bed chaises under a black-and-white striped cabana. Cress' board shorts hung *Surfer Magazine* low, and he couldn't help pulling on the side string of my black bikini. Before we fell asleep in our hotel room, we ate the warm peanut butter cookies the maids left on doilied plates in the middle of our bed.

Walking down the hallway to room 1967 after dinner, Cress thrust me into the wall, held my eyes for three seconds, leaned in, waited, and kissed me. His hands never touched me after that, settling above my head, his forearms on the wall. In sync with his mouth, I kissed him harder.

Inside, I threw the hotel card on a table. Cress followed me to the living room.

"Take off your clothes." His lips left my shoulder in slow motion. I raised the Chloe dress over my head and bent down to the Louboutins, the red outsole a reminder of the January/Jack expanse. Example: 2004? Vans or $45 date-night shoes bought at a department store or Target. 2009? $800 (Ok, $1,200) Christian Louboutins.

On Melrose at Agent Provocateur the week before, my eyes went into the back of my head when I *thought* of wearing the midnight merry-widows for my boyfriend. The lidocaine injection's sensation wasn't only between my hips, below my pelvis, or at my pelvis; the pause in sensations went all over, and I was a rubber snake. That pressurized ache would come back, along with a quiver, which disappeared after a few seconds: Most times only sex or masturbation quelled it.

He lifted me and wrapped one arm around my waist. Into the back of my neck: "You are so beautiful right now."

"Cress, I want you to fuck me." I didn't recognize this super sexy, totally in control, sober woman, cunningly purring words over my shoulder.

I couldn't feel anything above my hips when he picked me up with one hand, carried me to the bedroom, and swung me over to a chaise near the bed. I squealed and then my voice washed away.

When he sat down, it was hard to look away from him, and it was hard not to. Standing in front of him, he smoothed the mesh and silk along the thong and corset. He unclipped the right garter, then the left. Determined and a little serious, Cress pulled my bottoms down. He moved lower and kissed above the bit of hair I kept there. *Lower.* I pulled him up from his seat and in the sexiest move from my repertoire, I held his gaze and walked backward to the bed. He followed, a devoted man to a majestic girl. The ceiling came into view.

On our last night in Santa Barbara, Cress read a Cormac McCarthy novel, and I lay engrossed in the birds outside.

"I saw on your computer when I looked up the address for dinner. You have files—pages—of just words?"

"Yeah, crazy right?"

"You're such a writer, and a hooligan. Tell me one." He touched my back like a mouse click.

"Duende."

"What the heck is a duende? Wait, I've heard that one."

"You are. You're also a lulu of a guy. This is my orangery. You slaked the thirst in my heart."

"Oh my god."

"Katzenjammer!"

He tried to muzzle me with his hand.

"Apple-polish!" I moved his hand.

"Galley-west!" His hand went back over my mouth.

"Twee! Bluestocking!"

"Oh, two that time. Unless tweebluestocking is a word."

Cress and I had developed a few different ways we laughed together. This was movie-night laugh. We're in the theater and there's a truly hysterical scene in the movie. We turned to one another in the dark and laughed into each other's faces, not looking at the screen. I missed the next few lines, but remembered his face, lit up by the daytime scene in the movie. Sometimes I never saw or remembered the movie again—only the lit up face.

I laughed and turned my head in his direction.

"You have a great laugh," he said. "Half the fun is trying to make you laugh."

December 17

It was dark, but I smelled morning time. Someone was touching my face.

My forehead, then my nose, my neck. I opened my eyes when he reached the freckle below my boobs. Once in a while Cress spoke to it, telling the birthmark how much he loved it or how hot it was. "It looks like you drew it with a Sharpie," he'd say.

We'd be leaving Santa Barbara in a few hours to spend the holidays at his parents' with Tallulah and Henry. My dad, brother, Accountant, and Cress' brother and wife would also be there.

"Did you sleep?" He pinched my nose.

"Yes, so good. Did you?" I stretched my arms and tapped on the wall behind me.

"I did." His white dress shirt was unbuttoned, and his brown hair was in my favorite style: un-styled after a shower, but before work, almost-dry pieces extending here and there. His entire head begged for a hand to touch it.

"Coffee?" I climbed over him and picked up my hotel robe from the bench in front of the bed. He nodded toward the bedroom door.

"Yeah, and a bucket of ice 'cause you're a dork."

"Thank you." I kissed his head.

Outside: no clouds, crispy air, serene ocean. Same as Pismo. I loved the cooler air more than the warm. Oil rigs dotted the horizon. I stood by the fireplace in the living room and noticed three boxes, wide and narrow, like the ones that held huge flat-screen TVs.

"Cress, where did these come from?" They stood four-feet-tall, at least, wrapped in butcher paper.

He walked out of the bathroom, wiping off shaving cream with a towel.

I set down my coffee and stuck a finger into the fold on top of the first one. An *E*, an *S*, then a *Q*. I tore the paper down to the floor.

It was a framed picture of Virna Lisi—posing as if she were shaving her face, with one finger touching her eye—on the cover of an *Esquire* magazine from 1965.

"Oh my god."

"You told me once you loved the picture, after you saw the one I have of Sinatra. And when I visited you in Pismo, I saw yours."

I had the same picture at home, *tinier*, torn from an old book my photographer uncle had given me: *Fifty Years of Esquire Covers.*

"Cress." All I could think was *do not cry.*

He walked over to me. I ripped open the second package. A Milton Greene portrait of Marilyn Monroe from the "Black Sitting." One knee bent, the other leg in the air, her body spread out as if lying on a balance beam. Fishnets with a back seam wound up her legs. The third: Gloria Swanson, taken by Edward Steichen in 1924. The third was my favorite photograph of all time.

"For your house."

"I don't have it yet." I wiped the last of his shaving cream off of his neck.

"You will." I put my hand on his lips.

"Thank you, thank you, thank you."

I kneeled in front of my gifts.

"Before you get lost in those, come here." I stood up to him gazing down as if he were looking at me from under the rim of a fedora.

"I'm in love with you, you realize that, right?" His face, the way he smelled, where we stood. I nodded. He didn't say "it" and I definitely couldn't say it. I hugged his waist with my head down and eyes shut tight against his chest. His voice vibrated into cheek,

"I wanted to make sure you knew what it was, what it felt like, when it happened."

Christmas that year was a Patsy Cline song: exquisite, meaningful, inspiring, emotional.

Transportive.

December 31, 2009

"Jesus."

Cress and I pulled up in front of what looked like a slanted off ramp. Below us was Blacks Beach, next to us were edges of cliffs and further down below the house, or north, was Torrey Pines. In front of us a heath of oceanfront and at least three, maybe four acres. We could see the ocean only because the Wallace Cunningham designed museum had enough glass to peer through. Croix lived in a fucking museum.

We were spending New Year's with St. Croix in La Jolla, where she would meet Cress for the first time. For the last three years she lived in Europe, wrote, and wore black leather and taffeta haut couture dresses while smoking at Le Georges in Paris. While wearing those dresses, she dated counts. Croix and her latest count purchased the Razor Residence (museum, residence, whatever) last year: a steel, concrete and—needless to say—glass structure occupying 11,000 square feet of jeweled cliffs. It belonged in an *Iron Man* movie. Maybe it was in an *Iron Man* movie, I wouldn't know.

"Dearheart! You look so gorgeous, and so happy." She greeted us as Cress opened up the back of the Range Rover. The 180-degree panoramic views of Southern Californian ocean lit up the entire structure and driveway, almost blinding you with white.

"Thank you. You look incredible," I told her. We hugged long enough for a flock of gulls to fly over the house. She did look incredible; her vibe: St. Tropez/Jackie O./dash of La Jolla socialite. Metallic and buttercup yellow Pucci dress. Sally Hershberger extended, styled, and flaxen-colored hair. Rings and bangles bought on Bond Street in London and Via Condotti in Rome. She floated towards Cress with arms open. Not *wide*, but a distance that made it clear,

Maybe by Monday you'll get full width.

3 p.m.

St. Croix dragged me to bottles of wine and sparkling waters in the living room, which spanned both indoors and out.

"Baby, what the hell has happened to you?" She bubbled as she asked.

"I don't hate the latest B!"

"I see that." She glanced at the Count and Cress smoking cigars on chaises by the infinity pool. If you could call it that; the extraterrestrialized hole filled with olive/silver/blue water didn't look like a "pool" at all.

"Your pool looks like Pac-Man," I told her.

Croix surveyed Cress. "Cute. Handsome, actually. And I won't know till after the weekend but I'm hoping not a dork, and not a fucknut. Again, won't know till after the weekend. You surprise me, Jan."

"He's kind of a dork."

"Not surprised, and I bet you let him come to you, right?"

"I guess I did." Surprised at my own answer.

I never thought about it. In fact I hadn't thought about what Childless Brad Pitt warned me of years ago.

"Told you."

"I still don't like the theory; are we 16? Please. So the Count pursued you?"

"Of course. He saw me on the Norway count's yacht in Capri and within two days I was on *his* yacht in Capri."

"From?"

"Hungary. He's the Hungary count."

We walked toward one of the glass doors from the living room. My long, blow-dried, ombré light brown/blonde hair blew in the breeze like an enlivened palm tree. A cliff jutted out, their only neighbor to the right. Croix's stories (Capri? Yacht? Counts?!) were dreamy and extraordinary, but she still maintained her Santa Barbara starving (but never vodka thirsty) student charm. We both did. We were humbled and blessed. *I promise.* Two adjectives I would never have predicted to implant into my life.

"Doesn't matter how old they are, Jan, they're hunters. And think of it this way, he found you, you didn't find him. Worlds away from Fat Fuck."

"Short."

"Right, Short Fat Fuck."

"The craziest part is, the other part of that theory, the "You only want what you can't have" bullshit, I don't have that. It's almost the opposite. I wanted him even more when I realized he wanted me back."

"You're growin' up girl. My baby's all growed up." She pulled me in and kissed my head.

A couple of hours before we rang in 2010, Croix and Cress ventured out onto the top floor of the "deck." The non-deck was also the roof.

"You're not my first interrogation," Cress said jokingly.

"You've known January six months?"

Croix probably thinks he's a dork for saying "interrogation."

"Dating for nine, 10, known her for a year or more."

"Job? Family? Everyday bullshit?"

He laughed a true laugh, which was really an exhale of air from his nose combined with a smile. "Agent, two kids, an ex-wife."

"Agent? An insurance agent?"

Cress smiled, holding his scotch and peered left to Mission Beach and San Diego.

They chatted and laughed a few more minutes. St. Croix put a hand on his shoulder before *St. Tropez/Jackie O./dash of La Jolla socialite. Metallic and buttercup yellow Pucci dress. Sally Hershberger extended, styled, and flaxen-colored hair. Rings and bangles bought on Bond Street in London and Via Condotti in Rome* whisked away.

"Be whatever she needs you to be. She'll take care of you if you let her, but be there for her. You're lucky. I promise you, you are."

"I intend to." They faced each other and Cress let go of the glass railing.

"Don't fuck it up. All she has ever sought in life is love."

January 12, 2010

North by Northwest, Cool Hand Luke, Casablanca, On the Waterfront, The Bicycle Thief, and *From Here to Eternity.* This set

296

of tall, artfully framed film posters kept watch over us in his home theater. Cress kissed me, paused, his mouth against mine. We kissed again. I loved, loved, loved his kiss pause kiss.

"Ughh. I want Bacara. I want room service. I want Alicia Keyes and John

Legend on the iPod in our room, Anthony Hamilton, too. I want popcorn."

"I can do popcorn," he inhaled my neck when he pulled me into him from my seat

on the couch.

"I liked you in Santa Barbara. I want you there, in the black bikini. I want this ass in Santa Barbara." I stood up to find a DVD while Cress checked emails.

"Oh my god, you have *Weekend at Bernie's*."

"Must be my kids'."

"Right. We're watching it."

"Wasn't the house insane? I love that house." I sighed. "I think they filmed it in South Carol ... ."

He stood up.

"Let's go, Bernie."

Upstairs we hugged in the doorway to his bedroom.

"It's always doorways with you, isn't it?" He asked, his face touching my forehead.

"Santa Barbara, the trip to Croix's, my gifts—did I ever thank you?"

He moved my hands to behind my back.

"Thank me now." Our lips met, but we didn't kiss, his mouth teasing mine and brushing my lips before he took everything I had.

"Now I'm going to fuck the shit out of you."

"Oh my god, *you* are a dork," I said, pushing him away. He reined me back in.

He laughed. "I cannot believe you like that movie."

297

February

I didn't like to fuck anyone I liked or respected. Jack, whom I loved with the enormity of a Manson disciple, was a touchstone for fucking. Sex, in any position: from behind, on my knees, oral, blow jobs, even missionary—became a menagerie of us in my head that I squinted through for days after. As much as getting bibulous was a hobby and goddamn right I honored, cherished, and upheld, sex with Jack was a sober activity amplified because of that very reason.

One night when we so fluently transitioned into the 69 position, I blacked out into a rapturous state, a nitrate film reel explosion under and on my unconscious. The combination of his brilliance in bed and the torment I grasped and depended on, was as annihilatory as any of my addictions. Ketel One had nothing on Short Fat Fuck.

With B9 and B11, sex was a chore and something I frowned at as I daydreamed of hooking up with Jack later in the night. With B11, I avoided sex successfully. B9 kissed like the devil. We had sex at least 20 times, and I remembered very little—except for a 30-second flashback of kitchen floor sex. Oh, and his 30th birthday. Jack fucked me through a stealthy and generous (however convoluted and evil) education. I didn't put any effort into, nor did I care about sex, until I met Jack and fucked him for four years. From then on, I traced confidence with my fingertips, touching, holding or clawing at his back like a hungry and lost falcon.

Volcanically, Cress altered the mold. He was handed those gifts without knowing where they originated: the facts stayed hidden under my skin, and in my fingers and toes. Now, for the first time in *my life*; sex evolved into lovemaking. An unfamiliar concept to me. And the transition didn't take long. I realized almost instantly *this* was not just sex. Teasing, pleasure, length of time, and perseverance taught me Cress was a maniacal genius, attentive and playful, but not cloying and romantic-y.

With his sexy smile hovering over me, I became more confident and uninhibited. The freshness allowed us to laugh and play. He was confident—but more important, he was confident about us and where he wanted us to go. There were no difficult-to-interpret poker game tells. He laid his ideas and opinions out for me to observe and made the choice for me. I moved into new states: the states of not being a dumbass, wasteful, or heedless. Not a *lunatic*. The serious moments became more significant. He made love by loving me. Not by using me, keeping his eyes peeled for a fire escape exit, or formulating a plan for my amputation. Quaking and breathing against my back, his skintight hold assured me the last year together changed him as much as it did me.

He was hilarious and gave me shit when necessary. He could be serious and stubborn too: serious when it came to Stanford football and stubborn when it came to cooking a steak.

"January, we grill a steak, we don't cook it."

"January, I only use hardwood charcoal."

"January, it's supposed to be pink on the inside. That's called *medium*."

He was a busy guy. He gave me space, and I reciprocated; the ease was why I liked him and how I stayed at ease around him. I liked him more because of it, and because he always came back. Cress helped in editing the adjectives and reconstructing me into the noun I'd wanted to be since 2004. Days and nights with Cress were lambent: 24-hour vacations I didn't want to end.

They scared me, too.

April 4, 2010

It wasn't all about sex, or Cress, or a book.

2010 was also about a house.

We drove east from Beverly Hills with a lady from Sotheby's wearing an eye patch. The house I birthday candle wished for was back in Los Feliz on Vermont Avenue, not between Finley and Franklin, but a quarter mile north, closer to Griffith Park and the Greek Theatre. In the part of the "T" I only dreamt of living. On quiet LA mornings, I used to walk up the angled streets with the familiar tree roots erupting from sidewalks and imagined my life in those homes. Each was a movie: *Double Indemnity*, *Sunset Boulevard*, or *LA Confidential*. An old dream, at least 10 years unfulfilled: to live where Hillhurst and Vermont intersected, where I peeped in windows from afar with Bette Davis' eyes. Greta Garbo's, too. The cross street? Aberdeen. The house? Magnificent.

April 30

"It's done, we closed." Eight months earlier, *Anti-Fat* sold to Simon and Schuster and was doing well while in negotiations for its film rights. Two months ago, I sold two more novels—*Thirty Blonde* and *Soulcrusher*—as well as a book of short stories I wrote last year, including one titled *Thank You for Killing me, Ted Bundy*. What came out of my head scared but fascinated me. Adjusting to my 30s meant accepting who I was and how my talent found its way into *Microsoft Word*. I didn't know life happened that way. I expected I'd always hate myself. Be alone. Stuck in between Phase 1 and 2.

I took pictures off of walls and emptied drawers while Ben and my lawyers did what they did best.

"I heard." He called from the car. "Congrats hooligan. Fuck Pismo. Now get down here. I wanted you back in LA by halftime."

It's about time Phase 2.

If you want a happy ending,
that depends, of course,
on where you stop your story.

— Orson Welles

May 2010

Pismo Beach

"So, what's Art Decoration?"

I was leaving in 48 hours, and VF came to help clean and organize. "Art Deco? Well, you'll know when you come down and see the house, but it's a style of home decor, pre-war, 'characterized by precise and boldly delineated geometric shapes and strong colors in architecture and objects.' That last part was what the decorator told me. I guess I've always loved it, it's so chic and gorgeous. I love everything about it, not just the house part. Jewelry, art, clothing."

"I can't believe you have a decorator. *Designer*. Right? Oh my god, five years ago we were waking up on the floor in your little, white *apartment*. It's crazy, J."

"There was no way I could create a whole house around it on my own. Not that the whole place is going to look like a black-and-white movie starring Myrna Loy. Do you know how many furniture stores there are in LA? I don't have to suffer in traffic to get it done."

"Myrna Loy? Wait, 'pre-war?' Ok, I have no idea what that means. But I do remember some of your necklaces and stuff, from how you described it. What are you doing with those?" Vanity Fair pointed to the petite-framed art prints I collected over the years.

"You saw the three Cress gave me. I guess the old ones will go into storage."

"Seriously? Why not get rid of them? Like an omen, in a ceremony."

"Burn 'em?" I asked her.

"Ok, maybe that's a no on the ceremony idea. Let's not do fire." V laughed. She ran down the driveway and placed them on the curb with a bunch of other stuff piled under a flimsy "FREE" sign.

We couldn't think of another way to do a "ceremony," other than fire.

It had been seven months since the urges to launch a grenade into Jack's house, or car, left me. Leaps, successes, and distractions made wrongs, un-wrong. Self-improvement and quality (and expensive) mental health treatment wouldn't erase the obsessed, manipulated lunatic I was five years ago. But today, my life stripped off some of the noir overgarments I wore. The lesson? If you are bipolar, depressed, and require medication, it's helpful if you are pornographically rich.

One thought ran through my head: Did I go through something so ferocious over a boy I never "dated?" Never sat next to while we drove to the beach or to his parents' house while changing the station on the radio and laughing? Never stood next to, holding his hand as he bought us movie tickets? *I wanted to die* over an extended sexual encounter? I didn't have to understand, but I still wondered.

We walked back upstairs. The Princess Packers from the local student-run moving company wrapped glass-and-gold pitchers with tiny matching martini glasses I never drank from again. Three tanned and toned sorority sisters, with peach-plump boobs, who waitressed at Applebee's Friday through Sunday. They stood around my apartment in their pristine states: Heavenly skinned and formed from those darn supermodel scientists. Princesses one through three treated my possessions with care and believed they were as beautiful as I did. A tranquility washed over me.

"Do you think he'll like it?" Instead of packing we took a final once-over of my view. I strained to count the people walking on the Pismo pier. It still looked like a caterpillar.

She frowned, like she wanted the envelope.

"He's going to love it. You're going to win a girlfriend award or something."

"After everything, just being him, what he did, for me. It took me a while to figure out what I should get him."

After V and I gossiped for a decent 10 minutes about good 'ole Intern 5 getting fired from the magazine for failing drastically as a features writer, Vanity Fair lifted her lemonade glass to her lips. "He's single again."

One second later: heart inverted, breath stopped, breath then made a small outburst, neck tingled.

Ice. Vodka. Club soda. Limes.

"I saw it on a friend's Facebook page. It didn't end well."

"Huh. That's weird." I couldn't believe it. SFF. Why was she bringing this up now?

I thought for a minute then stated the obvious, "I mean, kind of odd timing, right?"

We walked downstairs under the sun and into the shade of the moving truck. I walked up the angled ramp where my boxes assembly-lined back to Los Feliz.

Why did she tell me? Maybe she knew, I knew, she had to.

"I'm proud of you, January." She always said January cutesy, like a baby, then long and drawn out. Maybe to lessen the fact she was actually saying my name, which she rarely did.

"What, proud. Proud of what?" We went back inside with cleaning supplies.

"I didn't think you were going to make it. I didn't think you were going to make it, definitely not this far. I honestly thought you'd never get over him."

Ha, I knew she had doubts.

"But I see the progress you've made with Dr. D. I'm so happy. I'm happy for you."

I miss St. Croix. I miss VF already.

"Don't call him."

"Who?"

"You know who."

May 5, 2010, the next day

805-817-9091.

Holy crap.

The last text I received from him, the last time we communicated, was in '09:

Jack: *I feel bad u mistake this for love. i swear i wont send nemore*

Now ...

Jack: How are you, Sweetheart

Me: Hi, I'm well. I moved back to LA actually.

Jack: to LA? u serious? You meet a guy down there

Me: I did.

Jack: That's great sweetie. Can we grab dinner before you go?

Two minutes later

Jack: I'm happy for you sweetie. Everyone loves the book. I've read some. Good for you. And I get it, if you're mad still. I wasn't such a nice guy back then. I've changed. Hairtrix and her kid, made me grow up and be a better man.

Me: You were fine, no worries.

I didn't have the luxury or emotionally stunted gene allowing me to deconstruct what he said and how his thoughts pertained to me. For once I wasn't a swirl of *So they're broken up for good / is this my chance / can we have sex now?*

I was empowered.

Jack: When will you be up again?
Me: Few months maybe? Rain check on dinner?
Jack: Absolutely.

The next day
Jack: Sure you can't do dinner?
I laughed to myself. I didn't answer.
Jack: Let's hang out one last time before you leave.
Me: Let me see how today goes.
Jack: ok, if not cruise by before you take off.
Me: I'll try for sure.

While double checking drawers and cabinets and booking the carpet cleaning, I found it painful and regrettable I couldn't say *yes* to him—my favorite response (and most dangerous one) to Jack. I could count on two fingers how many times I said no to him. I wouldn't dare make it a point to see him one last time. It wasn't an option. I didn't need what I once sought. As a unit, and separately, we had grown up and developed. Deep down I wasn't convinced he *had* developed in the last two years. If he had, he wouldn't have texted. His claim of a newfound maturity was another lie, yet he still wanted to play that old, tired game. He might have guilt, he might have wonder, but I had my future. Without the damage and baggage. Me, not him.

Cress. My boy and his arms wrapped me in beauty and love and joy. I felt sick with these two people side-by-side in the atmosphere, again. One requited, one unrequited. Jack smiled and squeezed my heart for so long: choking, using, and brutally shattering it. It was a game to him as I committed myself to reside within his boundaries because no other boundaries seemed worthy of my time. I was scared to have a real conversation, scared to be without him, scared to be with him, scared I'd never lay my head next to his, scared to not have what we had, but most of all terrified of absolute truth before I was ready to know it. I dreaded this truth for all of those years I wanted him. Jack wanted a beheaded version of me.

I was guilty of the choking, using, and shattering as well. I blamed myself for Jack and Pismo and my disruptions. I thought back to when I wanted him dead. Hairtrix dead. His brain dead, friends dead. Thunderstruck by fist shakes, tirades, and a memorial of drinks, I found solace in his death. I never got over anything; I survived.

I wanted to reject him, but the kernel he chased gave me energy to go one more mile chasing *him*. Through painstaking undertakings, I sketched myself into his sociopathy, developed first by my paranoid expectations from nothing more than a pinprick of total fantasy. A *fling*. Sociopath, psychopath, or serial murderer of hearts, I still loved him. I hated him, too. He loved me in his own way. With time passed, I didn't want to commit at least a half dozen serious felonies when I thought of him.

May 15

Jack: Here is how I look now, after losing 40 pounds.

For a few seconds I studied his smile and neck stretched above his friends, a neon beer sign behind them—it was always neon. A group of guys approaching Friday night with full wallets and hope: an image he never texted before. This was the picture I attached to his contact in my phone.

An hour later, he texted a picture of his cock.

Here we go.

"Dick pics" was the title of his sense of humor. I accepted him and all the wicked, unmalleable shit running through his head from the first minute I laid eyes on the back of him on a barstool. Years after the barstool, I didn't have to absorb his antics, laugh at or with them, or pretend they turned me on. He wouldn't know how I cared for someone else so differently and so miraculously, I didn't want what I once required. He'd never comprehend what had happened to me, with him, or with Cress. Jack wouldn't be offended, or couldn't be, by the deletion; by the split. My life was separated now: two chapters, two novels divided, each with its own conclusion—or upcoming conclusion. I humored his humor. We became friends (not again, but for the first time) with a safe and worthy 170 miles between.

Mrs. Z told me once, "Don't let anyone get too close."

I think her statement could've saved me. Would have saved me back then. But it didn't seem like a motto my DNA would allow.

SFF was no longer SFF. He was Jack. The boy who changed everything: my sex life, my taste in music, my clothes, my need for flavored lube, and my need to be trashato Thursday through Sunday. And then my need to be sober. I dreamt of the every day things for him. Smiling at work, hugs from his mom, a genuine conversation with a girlfriend. Peace.

While sailing away on shallow river rapids of ice cold Ketel One, he could cum on my face, reject every cell of me, claim another love, and use me for years, but during that period of my life, he was my comforter of bedrock constructed on a vespertine alliance.

June 5, 2010
Los Angeles

Cress and I drove home from the Getty, after I bribed him with a blow job to check out the Pollock and Steichen exhibits.

"If I hadn't left the magazine and moved back, I probably wouldn't be here right now."

"Right?" Our hands met on top of the piano-wood and leather center console.

"Selling a book doesn't exactly scream Pismo Beach, does it?"

"No, it doesn't." I laughed and brought his hand to my mouth. *Anti-Fat* was doing well, readership was growing across the board—in print and on Amazon and iTunes.

"I would've tracked you down in that ridiculous bar you love. What was it? The Trailer?"

I died laughing, "No!"

"Ramshackle?"

"Oh my god, the Shack."

"Ah yes, the Shack."

"I liked the view."

"You don't remember the view."

"Sure I do: There is no view." We laughed. He took my hand and bit it.

"It soothed me, I was comfortable there. Is that weird?"

"Soothed you? The vodka soothed you."

Measureless hook ups spilling out; me on a sloppy path to a surfer's condo or a rich guy's palatial house on the cliffs. I grew up there, again, and for a few fragments in time, I had the B (Bs) the job, and the friends I wanted. I also had nothing at all. The Shack. I'd still go there if I lived in Pismo. To write or drink Too Tan's Virgin Bloody Marys.

He reached for his Blackberry. Mr. Esquire: magical, sexy, handsome, cool, successful. He was all of those because he *did* reach. Perfectly behaved boys, and the various fairytales they inhabited, didn't exist. The truth was an acquired taste.

July 15
Journal entry

I'm learning an LA relationship has criteria. Concerts at the Greek and Hollywood Bowl, dinners at every restaurant between Santa Monica and West Hollywood. We went to the Farmers' Market last weekend and CR cringed when I bought kale. He bought candy. Driving on Wilshire that night, I spied on him from the corner of my eye, STILL captivated by all of his movements and sounds. We are so busy. His life, the circle around him, is intimidating. I guess

*I'm a part of that too now. It's unreal I get to do this stuff with him.
ok, my groupie mentality with him and my new life needs to chill. I
deserve this! VF said about Millionaire, "I wouldn't leave him alone
last night." I get it. I've never wanted someone as much as I want
him and he wants me in the same voracity! Even touching his arm
as he brushes his teeth in the morning. I'd eat glass to be near him.*

July 20

"Come here."

I found him checking emails and drinking water after his run. In
a truly alone, 16-year-old-esque, Saturday spare half hour I led him
into the garage and we made out in the backseat of the Range Rover.
Not undignified, but exhilarating as he threw an umbrella and tissue
box out of the way and pushed up the center console. We laughed
and kissed so hard a tear ran down my cheek.

Tallulah and Henry were at their mom's this weekend. Each week
I watched him be a dad, so beautiful and loving, he turned me on.
Cress' kids were always on my mind, especially now since we were
taking our first mini road trip together in a few days. I'd been through
what they were going through and what I needed to be for them:
not annoying and not their parent. They accepted me after a few
meetings (I insisted we meet in groups and with some of their friends
so they weren't overwhelmed). Cress planned a pool day for the first
time we met, but talked to them before, a few times. I cried in worry
and fear their little souls would be eaten up by this, by me being in
Cress' life, and in theirs—if not today, in 20 years. I didn't want to dis-
rupt those beautiful faces I saw on Cress' phone in Vegas and again
in his hallway before we made love for the first time.

I didn't have to worry, because they weren't me. They were stron-
ger and wiser than I was at their age. They'd never be hot, broken
messes—a credit to their mom and dad.

Lately Tallulah used me as a sounding board, or friend, when her
parents wouldn't do. Henry showed off his art any chance he had,
explaining to me in detail how he developed each stroke or line. They
didn't roll their eyes when they saw me. They sang out, "January

first!"—intrigued my name was a month on a calendar. They were the kids you'd see at a party who didn't react to an adult doing something crazy or saying something moronic. They'd empathize or smile, and act grown up in a situation where I would've thrown a fit, or yelled out, *"Oh my god! What are you doing? Mommy, I'm scared!"*

I cooked and baked for them, took them to art galleries, and shopped with them at H&M. Tallulah and I were obsessed. I flipped through the kids' clothes while they played dress up and hauled out as much as my hands could carry for all four of us. Again, so unlike me as a kid. I didn't know there was such a thing before I met the Reiter family—a childhood generated by (and padded with) love and respect, fun, and fairness.

Those were Cress' kids in a nutshell: adorable, affectionate, and well adjusted. I loved kids I could look to, and roll my eyes with.

July 25, 2010

"They love you." He looked over at me in bed in his adorably chic glasses. I wrote, and he watched *Sports Center*. The four of us spent the last two days in San Diego with Cress' parents.

"I adore them. Do you know how much I love watching you with them, taking care of them?" I set my laptop aside. When I got within an inch of his face, his breathing changed.

"You are so sexy as a dad." My hands pushed against the head-board. "Patient, loving, funny, firm."

"Firm."

"Yes, firm. You are so beautiful." I snuggled into him.

"Want me to take care of you?" He wrapped an arm around my neck and made the "mind blowing" gesture, flicking his hand from the side of his head with an explosion sound. I moved to get off of him before he snatched me back.

August 5, 2010

"Kale's in the fridge, goofball." Cress sat next to me on the bed, his arms in a push-up position over my shoulders and head, dressed in gray, wool/silk Brioni.

"No." I sat up a little and nuzzled my face into his chest. *Bulgari.*

Dressed in one of his James Perse shirts, I stood up on the bed. He pulled me closer.

The attraction to him, to everything about him, boiled so rapidly—like the lingerie lidocaine sensation from Agent Provocateur—sometimes only sex quelled it.

"If you want to get out of here alive, you cannot look the way you do right now," I assured him as I straightened his tie.

Oh my god, I loved that tie. Not wide or thin, just Cress/*Esquire*/stylish. I lost minutes in my day thinking about that tie, and his hand when he undid the top button, pulling the tie loose, and the way his skin smelled underneath.

"I was thinking the same thing." He lifted me up and wrapped me around him.

"You're going to smell like me in your meetings!"

"Exactly."

Five minutes later I heard his car engine, and rolled over on my side. Before I went home, I blended kale, ice, almond milk, banana, kiwi, celery, pineapple, spinach, and apple. I drank it straight out of the blender while I cleaned his kitchen, then closet. That newly realized tranquility from the Princess Packers day had yet to wash away. Now I smelled like him. Anything I wanted I had with Cress. Jack in complete reverse. However, what Jack and Cress did have in common was my need for time to stand still.

August 7

Work wore him out, so I left him alone and played *Mario Kart* with Henry until we heard, "J, T, H!" from his office. During these times, with the four of us under one roof, I felt safest. The Reiters were my Xanax.

"You're coming with us." In bed, while he was lying on his back with his head in my lap, I noticed new stubble on his face and a relaxation in his eyes of cotton root bark.

I still can't believe you bought him a trip to Italy for cooking classes, with his kids.

You're going to get an award or something. I missed VF.

"Where?" I knew what he meant. His hand reached up and pinched my cheek. I fought his generosity and urged him to go just with his kids.

So this is how this goes.

August 10

For the last 10 years I failed, at the one thing I did well. Writing was the perfect occupation for someone like me: worrier, analytical, curious, sloshed, and a slut. I couldn't *tell* a good story out loud, I only *wrote* one well. I had to write. My imagination had been vivid since I could walk. Every word I'd ever read ran through my very own internal projector like a movie reel. After meeting a person, I conceived story arcs they'd never know about. I never had writer's block—a concept (myth) made up by lazy wannabes. There wasn't enough writable paper in my car; or enough antiquated mini-tapes for my old-school, but reliable recorder; or enough pens, legal pads, or suede-bound notebooks in my purses. Bouquets of black, sometimes green, pens sat on tables in most of the rooms in my new house.

Before, writing stories wasn't an occupation because I made no money doing it. With the exception of freelance and my salary at the magazine, I wrote because I had to. If I documented whatever I wanted for the day, drew a picture with words, deleted the pain and boredom, then someone in the world might have the same exact thought and feel less alone. I wrote every day, until I didn't. The easiest thing and the hardest thing to do in the world, was writing. Writing saved me, every time. When I deserted my work a couple of years ago, I jotted a sentence here or there, but the hell I plunged into could've been prevented if I'd kept writing.

My salvation is to let all this roll over me,
to write, write and write some more

The office, my "writing room," in my house, was sick. Insane. The *entire* house spellbound me with swan-like arches and hexagons.

Sit:

Ottomans. Long, square couches (more mid-century). Yellow, leather, curved chairs with black piping.

Look:

Mirrors. And more mirrors. Pictures and art. Instead of stacks of books, I stacked frames. Marilyn, Frank, Jean, Tallulah, Myrna, Bacall, and vintage film posters. My favorite photographers went on every wall—even above the toilets.

Live:

There were more mirrors, but not for looking. A mirrored vanity in one room, a mirrored dresser and bedside table in another. The remainder of the house filled out with tray ceilings, black-and-white wallpapers, tufted chaises, stark white bathrooms, and pops of orange, Prussian blues, browns, and silvers. Most of it transported me into my own movie set from the 1920s, '30s and '40s, but with contemporary touches. Once a month I woke up believing my house was only a dream.

Reservations about moving into a house with multiple rooms challenged me to enjoy the design process one fabric sample and idea at a time. The room I chose for writing presided over the pool and the luscious, but rat-attracting, bougainvillea. It checked off each box on the "typical office" checklist: laptop, back up laptops, files of notes, notebooks/diaries, dozens of reams of paper, a monitor wide enough to hold several pages on the screen in their actual size, printer, and flash drives. I amassed enough pencils, highlighters, magic markers, felt-tip pens, roller ball pens, and Sharpies to fill a dump truck. There was a simple, shiny white desk for Cress and his kids, but I didn't work at a desk. My desk was really an extended kitchen counter, but an inch or two higher and encompassing three fourths of the room. I could stand and work if I wanted to. Stand and edit. Stand and type. Stand and dig through files. Stand and wait for something to spit out of the printer. *Sitting is the shittiest part about being a writer. So is bending over.*

The other requirements for my house, besides a one-mile island in my kitchen, were a gym and a water closet. A toilet next to a shower was unholy.

The water closet. The tall rectangle was closed off from everything else in my black-and-white tiled bathroom with the modern, half-a-Tyrannosaurus-Rex-egg-shaped-bathtub. The WC represented everything and the most important "thing." I never gave up. If I stopped writing and worked at Wells Fargo, I guaranteed myself failure. I promised myself, if I could do anything different, to not be a writer, or have a new personality, I would do anything to attain it. Flex that first superhero power. Instead of being "unique" or the "I've never met anyone like her" girl, I'd blend into my barstool instead of falling off. No one would care, remember, or be hurt by me. Denegations from agents, boys, fathers, women, friends, stray kittens, wind, flat tires, and my bathroom scale would happen, but would never be on my radar. Yep, a toilet *not* next to a shower did all of that.

The last year or two elevated me to palmier times, and the lost and crazy failure in me dried up a bit. Although, the hating what I wrote part would never go away. I had a little superhero in me after all.

Life decanted into a champagne flute. As I watched the fizz settle, loyal anxieties boomeranged.

I am not jealous
of what came before me.
Come with a hundred men in your hair,
Come with a thousand men between
your breasts and your feet,
...Bring them all to where I am waiting for you.

— Pablo Neruda

September 24, 2010

I stepped out of the marble shower and dabbed my face with a tissue. Hanging next to me was the framed picture of Sinatra shaving, covering the entire wall, his cheek as big as my body. While grabbing the edge of the sink, my old enemies—doom and fear—slipped their hands under my tricep, jerking me down, and not gently. Anxieties I thought evaporated, moisturized my clean skin, smelling of lavender and mint. Doom lay deeper, clogging my insides with plaque. *It's the Neapolitan thing again. And toast. Again with the toast. Is this it? A stroke?*

"January, get in here." I walked around the corner. He sat in bed, his iPad in his lap. I wanted to run over to him, so freaking adorable in his pajama bottoms and glasses.

"What's up?" I asked.

"Look at thi—" He looked up. "What's wrong? You look weird." *Fear.*

"I'm fine." I fidgeted and crossed my arms.

"January."

"Cress, I don't want to … I'm embarrassed. I'm just tired. It's too … ." I blabbered into my hand. "I'm sorry."

He carefully moved to the foot of the bed, where I stood. "Don't be sorry, tell me what's going on."

"It's … it's the book, it's you. Moving back."

He pulled me toward him.

"I'm ok. I'll be fine."

"You're ok and you're fine? I'd say you aren't either. Come here." He pulled me closer. "You're having doubts about moving?"

"Yes, and I'm going to mess up: your life, mine. I'm scared of you. I'm scared of me, what I'll do. I'm terrified. I don't deserve any of this. And I love being with you." I clutched my robe.

"Listen. January. Don't be scared of me." I drew back, but he held on. "Listen.

Absolutely you deserve all of this. You're scared, and I get that. This is new for you. I get that, too. Change is always, well, it's change. But all of this is a part of you now. It's yours because it was meant for you."

"Why do you want me? Why are you here?" *Ugh.*

"Why? Because I am in love with you." He gently shook my hips in that way that was supposed to relax me.

"No." I shook my head. I pulled away again and his hands went below my waist.

"Yes. I am, come here. You're sweet, kind, sexy, generous, funny."

My robe fell open. I wanted to remind Cress of something else. Sex. *Yes, sex would end this.* "No."

"Don't say no. You give money to every homeless guy we see. You give the valet guys our leftovers from Spago. You have 10-minute conversations with the weird, drooling, stuttering girl who bags your groceries at Whole Foods. You won't let my housekeeper keep house. You're so beautiful sometimes I can't believe it. I think about you in the car, in meetings, at parties when you're not there, and when you are. The way you look at me." He hugged my legs. "January, we fit. I don't know how else to say it. We fit together. What we have in common, what we don't, it works, and I know this is lame, but I have never felt about anyone, the way I am feeling now, about you, right here."

"Jack. I was such a … I feel like I ruined something with him, in me, he didn't want me. I don't want to—"

"Jan. He has nothing to do with this, us, your work, your life now. We both have exes. But he isn't here. They aren't here."

Technically he's not even an ex. Just a murder/suicide lasting four years.

"I don't know if I'm better now, if I can be better for you. I want to, but I don't know if I'm even capable." *Where was this coming from?*

I touched his hair as he lowered his head near the opening of my robe. His head was so soft against my skin where the freckle was. I tried to breathe away the tears. I slowed down and sped up at the same time.

"Cress, if you don't … I can't be here. I can't do this if we feel differently about what *this* is. What this will be."

He raised his aristocratic face.

"Stop. Stop. Put all of that out of your head. I'm here. You're here. You belong here. Tallulah and Henry are here. I'm not going anywhere, they're not going anywhere. Neither are you. I want you here, and I think—I hope—you want that, too. We are way past the point of having a discussion about this."

My robe opened again. He never took his eyes off of mine.

"I'm … unlovable. I rubbed my forehead. "It's too much for me."

"What is too much? Me? January, breathe. Tell me whatever it is you think you need to say." I stood frozen in between his legs as he slipped his hands under my robe, holding me above my thighs.

"I realized something; I like you. You are the only man I've ever met who I actually like. Who I respect. I am so in love—Oh my god. I will ruin this; I will fail. I'm not good enough for you, and Tallulah and Henry. I'm doomed … and I have these horrible feelings … a horrible feeling."

"No, no you won't. You aren't. Come here." I pulled back. "You won't fail; I won't let you. I know the pressure, the fear. I understand it. You're talented, and you're not only good enough for us, you are *better* than me. And as for how I feel about *this*, January, there has not been one day since I met you that I haven't thought about you. I saw you. I asked you out. I want you. All of the time. I would not be here talking about this if I didn't feel the same way. I may be a prick, but it goes away when I come home, when I know I'm going to see you in a half hour. I can't wait for you, to touch you, kiss you, smile at you, see you with my kids. And after all of that, at the end of the day, I get to go to bed with you, sleep with you next to me, wake up with you. You belong here. January, you are LA, but LA is not you."

———

Cress held me under the sheets until he felt my body relax.

Car alarms skimmed the panes of glass, and night lights hummed near the baseboards. I thought about mischievous/loving Tallulah and funny/sometimes serious Henry down the hall, asleep in their rooms. Pintsized versions of their mom and dad. The panic ceased, exchanged for a rapid, warm thirst moving from my brain to my throat, then to my chest. The same looked-forward-to feeling on Christmas morning, or in any time or place I wanted to be. The sinuous, internal hiss arrived quickly and left just as fast, lasting a second, or two, at most. Cress let me go and moved over to his side of the bed.

"I need to tell you one more thing—and this is important." He began to sing,

"I can see the sunset in your eyes,
brown and gray, blue da de da
… baby I love your way, everyday.
Wanna tell you I love your way.
Wanna be with you night and day."

"Oh my god." Red faced, I closed my eyes and breathed in. "What did you want to tell me earlier?" Still in my robe, I turned over and faced him.

"Tell you?"

"You wanted to show me something."

"Ah yes," he smiled. "I have indisputable proof that you are not and never could be *unlovable.*"

He picked up his iPad and scrolled the screen with his finger. It lit up.

India and olive greens. Loch Ness monster-looking mountains dipped in and out of Tiffany blue water. Some islands hemmed with mangroves, others outlined with tusk-colored shores and tie-dyed currents. Bamboo on sand and bures above water.

He pointed, "See that?"

Fiji.

October 2010

The dread broke away, but a golden, defanged sadness remained for SFF. For Jack. B10 used to say Jack was my scratching post. Like a cat.

"Your tone changes when you get a text from him." B10 told me.

When Jack called or texted every six months, Cress left the room. He never complained, confronted, or asked. Cress might not have understood our communication, but the check-ins (*from* Jack) proved my satisfaction with the places I went after Pismo. He didn't think of Cress' viewpoint. Sociopaths didn't acknowledge boyfriends or husbands in their quest to touch base and catch up. I could easily never be rid of him.

I watched my new movie montage over and over, pressing the rewind and pause buttons during the bits of progress in each frame.

I recognized, worked, fixed, reshaped, rewrote, took pills, and smiled at my boyfriend. After the 20 seconds, I was as complete and prepared as the girl getting her makeover or assembling her zombie invasion survival kit. Transformation set to a Q-Tip song.

I remembered something St. Croix told me in front of her Pac-Man pool:

"When you're feeling overwhelmed or anxious, trust and rely on Cress. He isn't your dad or SFF. Respect the fact he is someone else entirely. Different mindset, set of morals, different blood in his veins. You can trust him, J." She laughed. "Only you would meet 'the one' in Vegas."

TMZ offices, October 17, 2010, 7 a.m.

Boy Reporter: "We have January Estlin and Cress Reiter leaving the Greek."

Harvey: "Oh yeah … right."

Boy Reporter continued, "She wrote *Anti-Fat* and … ."

Harvey: "Uh, they're making it into a movie, I think. It takes place in LA, right?"

Girl Reporter 1: "Oh my god, I love her. It's insane, have you read it?"

"It's so good," Girl Reporter 2 agreed.

Girl Reporter 1: "I swear, she is describing my life. It's hilarious. But deep, too."

"Anyway," Boy Reporter continued, "They're coming out of the Greek and our guy asks, 'What's your favorite bar in LA?' I guess her book has a lot of boozin' in it, and he's kind of this straight-edge, professional, serious agent type."

Harvey asked. "Who is?"

Boy Reporter: "Cress Reiter."

Harvey: "Oh yeah, ok. His agency merged with CAA a couple of months back. He's a partner, I think."

Boy Reporter: "So he asks, 'If you could be drinking in any bar right now, which bar would it be?' She looks up, smiles, and says 'Daddy's'."

"What did he say?" Harvey asked.

Boy Reporter: "He smiled and put his arm around her. Didn't say anything."

Harvey: "Oh, She bought it."

Girl Reporter 1: "Yeah, saved it from developers, actually—the guys who wanted to build the Hard Rock, It's the book's main character's favorite bar."

Girl Reporter 2: "Yeah, and I heard she doesn't even drink."

"So he bought Daddy's?" Harvey asked.

Boy Reporter: "No, she bought Daddy's. Or maybe they bought it together."

Au domoni iko

October 22, 2010

"Estlin, what are those things? You brought five pairs." We stood at the bow of the boat as we docked. On a 70-foot white-sailed schooner, Cress made fun of my Dramamine wristbands.

"Would you rather me wear these or spend our entire trip throwing up over the side of the boat? I get sick riding in the front seat of a car." I raised my hands. The islands towered behind me, the green bumps greeting us from of the water,

Like the curves of your body when you're on your side, Cress observed the night before in bed.

"Got it," he replied.

We sailed to four or five islands, the bands an essential for our 10-day trip. Fiji expected two things: sunscreen and us. There was nothing else.

We invaded schools of barracuda while snorkeling in Savusavu Bay and took pictures with fingers pointed at the spinner dolphins. We went mountain biking, hiking, and kayaking. On the beach afterward, we ate picnics the resort packed for us. He liked the outdoorsy/

sports stuff, and I obliged. When I found out old plantations remained on some of the islands, a driver took us on a tour.

The other 85 percent of the trip went something like this,

Wake up and laugh hysterically realizing where we were. Sex. Dive/swim from bure. Breakfast. Lagoon. Lunch (fish). Waterfall. Sex. Beach. Nap in bure. Sex. Dinner (fish!). Sex (not kidding!).

I wonder if we have too much sex.

Of course Cress Reiter's Ralph Lauren resort-wear ad in *Esquire* traveled to Fiji. Runway chic. Ecru linen pant, white or blue shirt at night, his board shorts in the day: I could've eaten him alive, his 40ish chest toned just the right amount for me. His back was a work of art. To appreciate it fully, mirrored ceilings would have to be involved. In the mild heat and trade winds, I wore Pucci (and Top Shop and H&M) dresses, long and short and in every color of Fiji's skies, orchids, and the Koro Sea. I interspersed days and nights with saris I bought from Fijian women with fat, caramel babies on their hips. I also wore white, and again, canvas wedges belonging on a yacht.

"Who taught you to dress like this?" I asked while getting ready for dinner.

"No?" He pointed at himself with both hands.

"Oh no, I love it, *Esquire*" I slapped his rear end as we walked from our bure to the sets of piers connecting us to the resort and other bungalows.

"Your kids would love it here." I pushed him ahead and took a picture of his back, the fantail and umbrella palm trees in front of him swaying in the mild and fragrant air. He looked like he stepped off of a yacht, too. The water around us defined Fiji, resting unobtrusive, and translucent. Up close, the colors didn't fade and their sweetened voices softened:

Come here, I'm warm and safe.
Swim in me. Make love in me.
Change your life in me.

"Are you ok now?" I caught up with him a few feet ahead of me. After dinner we watched fire walkers, and he communicated with brown-eyed peripheral peeks of how many seconds he would wait after returning to our bungalow before he touched me. We didn't sit glued to one another, or in front of each other like in a Lamaze class. *Ick*. We sat side-by-side, our pinkies or legs unintentionally brushing against each other. I loved the six inches of grass or sand between us.

"I am. What do you mean?" I snapped the wind and sky, framing tops of trees in top or bottom corners, off center. My shoulder under his arm, I inhaled Cress and molasses.

"The shower night." His hands met my waist when he purred the words into my neck.

"Ah, yes, the old pickup truck breakdown. Don't you just love crackpot me?"

"You said you didn't deserve this, me." I peeled myself away and walked ahead to take more pictures.

"I'm better now. How could I not be better?" *Look at where we are. Where I am. With you.*

"Fiji will do that to you." The tranquillized day ended over the mountains.

I took its picture.

He stood beside me, not touching me, and spoke.

"When I saw you in Vegas, there was no way I wanted only one thing from you. I wanted everything, and I wanted it from the beginning. Remember, I told you this was going to be a fine tuned piece of machinery. Indestructible. It is, Jan. Croix said we balance each other out. She said he couldn't handle you. Everything I absolutely love about you, your hooliganess and goofballness. He couldn't handle it."

I turned to him. I saved my response for back in the bure.

"What he ran from, I love." He had the Laker game face, but tanned.

As I clicked my camera, I ran through a film roll in my mind: Cress kicking the back of my chair at the restaurant in Las Vegas, the Laker game, giving me a piggyback ride in his house.

Cress—I'm ok because of you.

We arrived at one of the lounges for an after-dinner drink and live music.

"Bula! Mr. and Mrs. Reiter, right this way."

"See, that? That takes some getting used to."

No, we weren't married, but the resort assumed otherwise. I *loved* that they assumed otherwise.

We relaxed on the sofa in the bure. Back from the beach, our warm skins smelled of coconut and tasted of salt. On the table behind him, an orchid framed his face. No boats or kayaks today; the only activity was taking the few steps to the shore.

"Hot tub," I stood up to put on a different bikini. He set down his Kava. Like a good girl, I drank water extracted from green coconuts by Arieta, an indulgent and mothering native who took care of us and our bure.

"Are you crazy? Stop putting on clothes," he ordered. I already had the bottoms on. He threw the top piece on the floor and picked me up. I went sideways.

I crawled on top to his outstretched arms, and our mouths met cinematically, like our bodies and attitudes. The bed smelled of us postbeach, more Cress than me. He disagreed: "It smells like you." He buried his face in my neck and the front of my chest. I relaxed over him and we rotated.

"Cress."

"Yes?" We laughed hard into each other's mouths. A rougher, bronzed Cress with hair I couldn't abandon, glided over me.

"Cress."

"January."

Keep it simple. "Ok, don't laugh, but I want to know, what you're thinking about. Like, right now."

He pushed his arms up over me.

Omg I love when he does his push-up over me.

"Honestly, at this moment?" I brought his hands above my head and nodded.

"You're such a dork. Let's see. Your skin. How warm it feels. Those tiny yellow threads in the blue of your eyes. Right this second I'm thinking I want to stop talking."

"Oh my god, you're the dork," I teased him. He brushed a line over my eyes.

"I'm trying not to think past Fiji. Or beyond now." His voice lowered as he lay down.

The water underneath rippled and he arranged my body where he wanted. We came together deeply for a long time, up and down, and in a labyrinth. I sunk into him to an intense depth. He cupped my breasts. I covered his hands with mine, and pushed harder.

I fell down on him to differences: unprecedented faces, sounds, vibes, textures. Our eyes met, and nothing happened. Everything happened.

I sat up, then Cress sat up. (The movie position, ha!) A masterful kiss and his hands taking over my face told time. Hugging me, touching my back, my hair, then my back again. I stayed where I was when his face came into my neck, my hands in his hair like two combs. I moaned, my legs wrapped around him, meeting behind his back when he let out a soft breath. *Oh my god.* He kissed and licked my neck and breasts, urging my body to come closer by my shoulders, holding me on top of him. My legs bent, bridging the last of the gap between us.

He pulled his head back. "January."

"Cress, don't stop … ." The words barely escaped my mouth, sweeping by his face, straight back to the headboard. I couldn't *not* let something come out, and as soon as I did he followed with his subdued, elegant gasp, bringing my head to his.

I smoothed back his hair, damp from the heat and his sweat. "What's wrong, do you want to stop?"

A tiny headshake I almost didn't see.

"I love you."

Holy fuck.

The changing of the world wasn't sex with a guy in Fiji. Like a wedding or a baby being born (I had no idea of either: I assumed) the words held a lifetime of fear, joy, and lust. Explosive and rattling, they contained their own spectrum of time: years before and years after. Hearing him say what he wanted to say in Fiji melded into a quiesced eternity. Cress wasn't an agent, a dad, a brother—he was the man who told me he loved me. The delicate, eloquent words. I held his unshaved, tanned, serious Laker game face. I felt him (in my soul) echoing the three words, again and again, without speaking. We kissed, and then I pulled back.

"I love you, too." With a slit of a smile, all he had to do was hold me. I couldn't stop from crying a little in front of the human being I loved more than anything, anyone else. I figured he understood. For once I didn't feel weakness or fear—fears of impending emptiness, abandonment, and deafening failure. I would live with this passion on my shoulders because Cress would do anything to protect me, from me. He knew without me saying out loud, these were seminal experiences. In a way, they were for him too. We *fit* on the imperfect evenness bridging us. For once, I wanted no closure.

His eyes opened, and he said sleepily, "Estlin, I never asked what you were thinking."

I faced him.

"Um, that you just told me you love me." I inched toward him under the white sheets no longer flawlessly folded and creased by Arieta. "Now I'm thinking about how much I want to fuck you, again."

He laughed, the deep and throaty chuckle only heard from under bed sheets. Fijian bed sheets, this time. I reached over, brought his laughter into mine, and into the profoundest kiss of the day. The sweet stickiness of the air and my meek breaths (saying very un-meek things) into his mouth, were the two elements holding us together. Tight. When my hands held his face to mine, I wondered if we looked like how I imagined. From the outside. *Perfect.*

Fiji: It was her fault. Confirmation of our love was totally her fault. I'd always refer to our last night in Fiji as *Fiji*, like a person—a priest, a chaperone, or not a person at all—a mantled memento. Just that night: the one when he told me he loved me for the first time. *Fiji.*

The thatched ceiling and wide open doors exhaled and Cress slept.

I slid out of bed. The air surrounding me shifted.

He buried his nose deeper in the pillows. I stepped outside and onto the deck above the ocean.

It's always about the ocean.

Cress is right in there. In our bed.

I pictured the dormant volcanoes, footings of solid lava, and how warm the water would be.

Come here, I'm warm and safe.
Swim in me. Make love in me.
Change your life in me.

I'm ok because of you.

In two seconds, he changed the world.
I took off my robe and jumped.

It is a wise father that knows his own child.

— William Shakespeare

2011

*A*t my worst, he was at his best.

My dad. At his worst, I was at my best. Half-cocked, he had impulsive instances of tricky wonderfulness and wisdom. Then *whoosh*. A subterranean venom arrived for 10 minutes, 30 minutes, or overnight. Memories weren't long when this happened, but the unseen stings and scars embedded in me a walloping fear of men and a hunger for bedlam to slice my life into 30 pieces of moist birthday cake.

Flipping and ripping around a room like a pissed-off rabid red bat, cussing, demonically drinking, and—finally—apologizing, my dad disintegrated me with one gruff breath and paid three car payments with the next. I didn't condemn him for what he was given and what he chose. I chose wrong for so many years and applauded my choices. My dad was a part of me I couldn't duplicate—not in real life or outside of myself, anyway.

I remembered a futile Saturday night in 2005. Christopher Columbusing failed to find Jack, and I spent 8 to 10 p.m. dialing his number 80 times and pacing around my dad's living room. The mantled rifle did its best impression of an emperor: imposing and maniacal. *Stupid fucking gun.* My dad nodded as I cried and unraveled a temper tantrum in front of the warm fire.

Why doesn't he love me?

How am I going to survive this?

Why this guy?

Why Pismo?

As he watched *Law & Order*, he said casually about Short Fat Fuck: "Maybe he'll be the best friend you ever had."

It didn't change the fact that I'd never ridden in his car.

Goodbye, my almost lover
Goodbye, my hopeless dream.

— A Fine Frenzy

Love at first sight? I absolutely believe in it.

— Leonardo DiCaprio

Unrequited love, unconditional love: It's the same exact thing in a girl's world. In my world.

Jack was me. Jack was training wheels.

A propensity to lie, manipulate, cheat, and torment: I was guilty. Liberties, vodka, timing, fate, work, mental illness, torture, misery, and desire: One of these circumstances, or a mix, possessed and led me to Jack's door. Whether recent or years old, an artery connected us, connecting a piece of our hearts.

What finally drove me away into someone else's world was Jack himself. I loved him for his no's, our encounters, and the pieces of broken heart I earned. He never demanded anything from me; only I demanded during the 1,400-plus days I seized him (as best I could).

No meant try harder.

I don't want anyone else.

331

Hope and hopelessness were my Jack bookends. He would whip me up, let me go, and every year, month, and after every yes/no yes/no yes/no I said, "I won't ever see him again, we won't ever have sex. This is it." I was wrong every time—until I wasn't in the nasty little house of hysteria I erected. The bookends had their own bookends. Jack symbolized love, an experience of love, an experience of love's catastrophic messes and time wasters. But the experience was mine to possess.

"I've passed up a lot of great women. Sorry, Sweetie."

During those ill-fated drunk years, how could I not have grown? Jack tutored me on how to grow up. His forces led me to certain places: Dr. D's for instance. I zoned in on nurturing myself and coping correctly, rather than living my life with a cocktail straw trapped under my tongue. My 30s arrived the fastest of any other period in my life for a reason: The goodness wanted out.

———

I still cried for Jack. The lesions faded from the kamikaze ligatures that once strangled me. But once a year for 20 seconds, something swept through the back of my eyes. The artery pulsed. I smelled and saw his hair, face, and penis: which produced so much ruckus, and so much fun. My love for him, the current kind—not the unrequited kind—followed a hollow bend. I saw his face one more time, then, a vanishing. If my annual 20-second pulsation wasn't the consequence of him somersaulting over my soul, then I knew absolutely nothing about everything.

Would Cress have been possible without Jack? I didn't know, but *with* Jack, Cress was guaranteed. Jack wasn't a disgusting experience anymore, or an everlasting, evil, prick. He was a lesson learned "the hard way." Forever linked to me by the artery.

Short Fat Fuck/SFF/Jack wasn't an unrequited "spark."

Sparks weren't real, not in my world.

There wouldn't be a spark between Cress and me.

We were the whole goddamn fire.

———

The B's

Where are they now?

B1: Played football in college and married a cousin of St. Croix's. Moved to Fresno.

B2: Married, had two kids with names I hate and works at a job I also find unattractive:

manager at Busch Gardens or Wet 'n Wild. I can't remember which.

B3: After spending four months in rehab for the robbery (Remember—he's a possible DuPont, which equals no meaningful punishment) his penis is now on display at LACMA in their permanent collection.

B4: Ended up producing two little TV shows called *Breaking Bad* and *The Big Bang Theory*. Moved to Bel Air. And Malibu.

B5: I'm still friends with Ben Harper Drummer and Capitol Exec. Not sure about all of those one-night stands, though.

B6: Owner sold the Shack and bought a casino and brothel in Primm, Nevada.

B7: Grew out (or out grew?) the mohawk. Hasn't been seen since.

B8: Stopped fucking/dating his cousin and moved to Costa Rica to study the travel patterns of turtles and surf. Six months later, Stalker Cousin moved to Costa Rica.

B9: Had two long-term relationships, one of which was a live-in situation. In between those and after the last one, he texted me, asking to "meet up for a drink."

Me: You must be single.
He chuckles. It's a text, but I know he's chuckling as he types.
B9: How'd you know. Meet at Bankhead?

(Cress and I were going to Santa Barbara in a few weeks: I didn't respond.)

B10: Still dead.

B11: He and his knit sweater won the Pulitzer for breaking news reporting. He moved to New York and met a nice girl who wasn't bipolar, didn't cry in Chinese restaurants or desert him at bars.

(B12) Jack: He closed the record store and opened a skateboarding (skateboard?) shop. He's probably not quite the "best friend I ever had," but he will always be extraordinary.

(B13) Cress: Still a dork and still loves me. In 2012 we bought a cliffside plot of land in Pismo from Millionaire.

Crazy, right?

Thank you Thank you Thank you

- Anyone who is reading this, and read *Unrequited*.
- Matt Bett
- Naomi Shibles
- Jen Anthony
- Ken and Kathy Smith
- Daniel Heron
- Duane Heron
- Christie Bartkowski
- Tracie Stricklin
- Ryan Miller
- Rena Doud
- Elizabeth Howard and everyone at Lola Red
- Mark Adam
- Bruce McClanahan
- Jack White and Third Man Records
- Alex BBQ
- Bill's Place
- Ralph and Duane's
- McCarthy's Irish Pub
- Dolphin Bay Resort and Spa, and Lido Restaurant
- Los Feliz and Los Angeles, California
- Cities of Pismo Beach, Arroyo Grande, Santa Maria, Avila Beach, San Luis Obispo, and Paso Robles, California
- Richard Abate, the most amazing literary agent in the world, although he doesn't represent me, he is kind, and a true gentleman.
- A special thank you to all of the Jacks (and Cress') in the world. Without you, there would be no story to tell.
- Belvedere Vodka
- Ketel One vodka
- Limes
- Club soda
- b.w.
- r.

A Dictionary For Drink, Drank

or Drunk

I n case you were wondering what all those strange words and phrases were, popping up around the "drunk" scenes, here's a recap / answer key. Synonyms were used as verbs, adjectives, and quite possibly, nouns.

1. Bashed
2. Barrellhouse drunk
3. Bar-tuned
4. Befuddlement (ed)
5. Bendering
6. Betty Forded
7. Boris Yeltsined
8. Charlie Sheened
9. Creamulated
10. Daxxled
11. Dot cottoned
12. Drunk as 40 Billy Goats
13. Footloosed
14. Fur On His/Her Tongue
15. Gold-Headed
16. Graveled
17. Gut-Fucked
18. Had The Uglies
19. High As An Oregon Pine
20. Imbibed
21. Inabstinent
22. Legless
23. Lighting Myself Up Like A Firefly (Lit Up Like)
24. Lushingtons (The) = Drunks
25. Merle Haggard
26. Moulin Rouge (ed)
27. Muzzied (Muzzy)
28. Navy Sailor Drunk
29. Paralytic
30. Phalanxed
31. Puckered
32. Rat legged
33. Red-in-the-face
34. Red-in-the-nose
35. Scumbled
36. Sloppy Tonk
37. Slurried
38. Snakebitten
39. Snockered
40. Spiflicated
41. Swacked
42. Tee-lit
43. Tile Counting (Counting Tiles)
44. Tippled
45. Trashato
46. (Riding The) Vodka Trail (or riding any [insert liquor here] trail)
47. Vulcanized
48. Watering Your Tonsils
49. Well-Heeled
50. Wild Turkeyed (again you can use any booze for this)
51. Zambonied

Get more information about *Unrequited* and
Christy Heron's upcoming
writing projects
unrequitedthebook@yahoo.com
unrequitedthebook.blogspot.com
facebook.com/unrequitedthebook
twitter: @sheisunrequited
plus.google.com/+Christyheron_unrequited
pinterest.com/losfelizchristy

Purchase *Unrequited*

Amazon.com / iTunes / In print at www.createspace.com// 4645419 et's be honest. Some of this shit happened. However, all of *Unrequited* is fictionalized. Most of the story is entirely the work of the author's imagination. The traits of those who have inspired characters in this novel have been altered to protect identities.

Some names and identifying details have been changed to protect the privacy of individuals. This is a work of fiction. Names, characters, businesses, places, events and incidents are either the products of the author's imagination or used in a fictitious manner.

Unrequited, One Girl, Thirteen Boyfriends, and Vodka.
Written by Christy Heron
Published by Waverly Blonde Books and Easiest/Hardest Publishing
Copyright 2013-2014 / TXu 1-890-979
All rights reserved
Edited by Ryan Miller
Cover by Lola Red Design Group
ISBN: 978-0-578-13756-8

Credits for quotes, song lyrics, and poetry

1. "Monster," by Lady Gaga; Written by Dresti, Nick/Khayat, Nadir/Germanotta, and Stefani.
2. "Diamonds," by Rihanna; Written by Sia Furler, Benny Blanco, and StarGate.
3. "Mr. Brightside," by The Killers; Written by Brandon Flowers, Ronnie Vannucci Jr., Dave Brent Keuning, and Mark August Stoermer.
4. "Sweet Dreams," by Beyonce; Written by Wayne Wilkins, Beyonce G. Knowles, James Scheffer, and Richard Preston Butler, Jr.
5. "Ain't No Fun (If Your Homies Can't Have None)," by Snoop Dogg; Written by Calvin Broadus, Jr., and Andre Young, Ricardo Brown, Nathaniel Hale, and Warren Griffin.
6. "Love Interruption;" Written by Jack White.
7. "Try a Little Tenderness," by Otis Redding; Written by Reg Connelly, Jimmy Campbell, and Harry M. Woods.
8. "I Want You to Want me," by Cheap Trick; Written by Rick Nielsen.
9. "Blue Christmas;" Written by Billy Hayes and Jay Johnson.
10. "Love the Way You Lie," by Eminem; Written by Marshall Mathers, Alexander Grant, and Holly Hafermann.
11. "Brass in Pocket," by The Pretenders; Written by Christine Ellen Hynde, and James Honeyman-Scott.
12. "Jar of Hearts," by Christina Perri; Written by Christina Perri, Drew Lawrence, and Barrett Yeretsian.
13. "Sex on Fire," by Kings of Leon; Written by Anthony Caleb Followill, Matthew Followill, Jared Followill, and Ivan Followill.
14. Excerpt from *Fear and Loathing in Las Vegas* written by Hunter S. Thompson.
15. "Love Lockdown," by Kanye West; Written by Kanye West, Jeff Bhasker, Laneah Menzies, Malik Yusef (El Shabbaz), and Esthero.

16. "Give It to Me," By Timbaland; Written by Timothy Clayton, James David Washington, James Harmon, Dhanjan Amarpreet, Dwayne Carter, Amarpreet Dhanjan, Nate Hills, Nelly Furtado, Justin Timberlake, Shakira Isabel, Mebarak Ripoll, and Timothy Mosley.
17. *Gone With the Wind*, novel written by Margaret Mitchell, screenplay by Sidney Howard, Oliver H.P. Garrett, Ben Hecht, Jo Swerling, and John Van Druten.
18. Seinfeld quote taken from the episode, "The Gymnast;" Written by Alec Berg and Jeff Schaffer.
19. "Always;" Written by Pablo Neruda.
20. "Baby I Love Your Way," by Peter Frampton; Written by Ronnie van Zant, Paul John Weller, Allen Collins, and Peter Kenneth Frampton.
21. The term "Anti-Seducer" is taken from the book, *The Art of Seduction* written by Robert Greene.
22. *Pretty in Pink*; Written by John Hughes.
23. "Almost Lover," by A Fine Frenzy; Written by Alison Sudol.
24. "Maps," by the Yeah Yeah Yeahs; Written by Brian Chase, Nicholas Joseph Zinner, and Karen Lee Orzolek.
25. "You Belong to Me," by Patsy Cline; Written by Redd Steward, Pee Wee King, and Chilton Price.
26. "My salvation is to let all this roll over me, to write, write, and write some more" is a quote from L. Ron Hubbard.
27. Many of the unusual words/synonyms used for "drunk" or a variation of "drunk" came from the book *Drunk—The Definitive Drinker's Dictionary*, written by Paul Dickson, illustrations by Brian Rea.
28. William Shakespeare quote taken from *"The Merchant of Venice."*

www.ingramcontent.com/pod-product-compliance
Lightning Source LLC
Chambersburg PA
CBHW061927170626
46813CB00006B/2321